GAIJIN
AMERICAN PRISONER OF WAR
a graphic novel by Matt Faulkner

𝒟ISNEY · HYPERION
LOS ANGELES   NEW YORK

First Hardcover Edition, April 2014
First Paperback Edition, October 2019
10 9 8 7 6 5 4 3 2 1
FAC-029191-19242
Printed in Malaysia

This book is set in Prater Sans One/Monotype
Designed by Tanya Ross-Hughes
Library of Congress Control Number for Hardcover Edition: 2013029795

ISBN 978-1-368-05416-4

Visit www.DisneyBooks.com

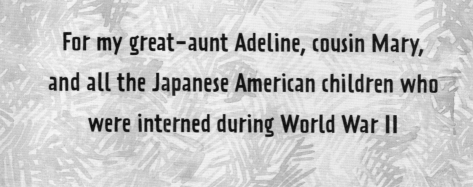

For my great-aunt Adeline, cousin Mary,
and all the Japanese American children who
were interned during World War II

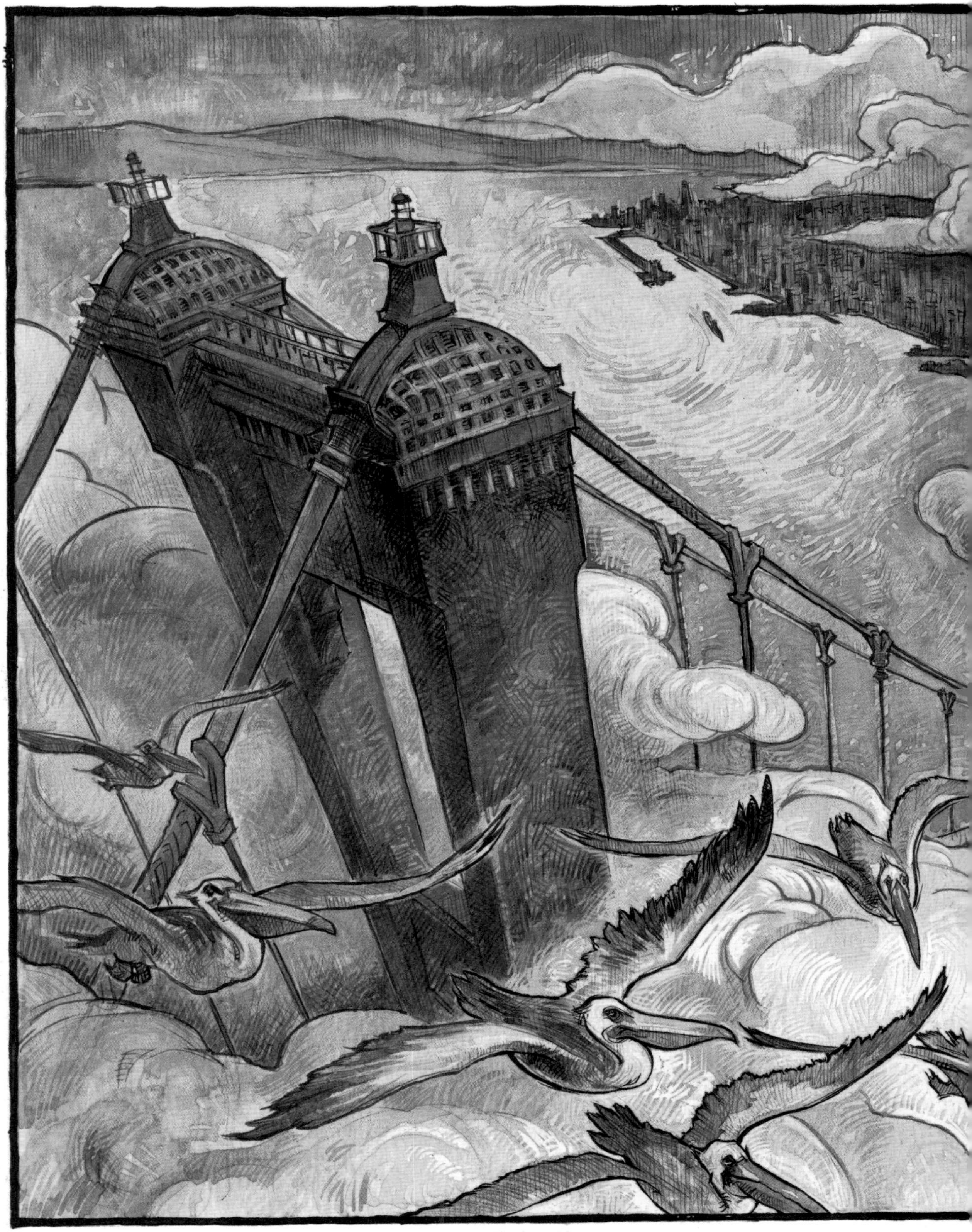

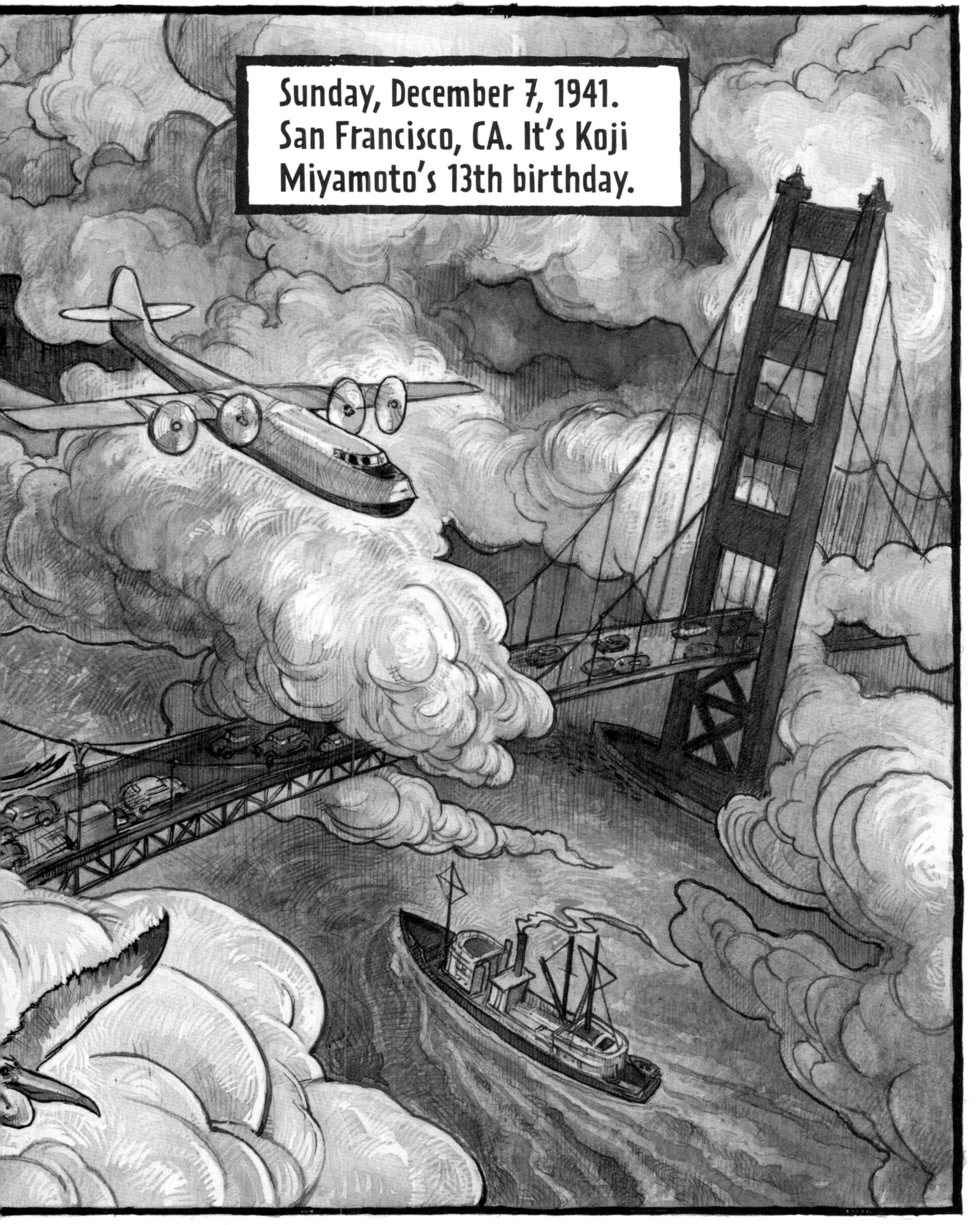
Sunday, December 7, 1941. San Francisco, CA. It's Koji Miyamoto's 13th birthday.

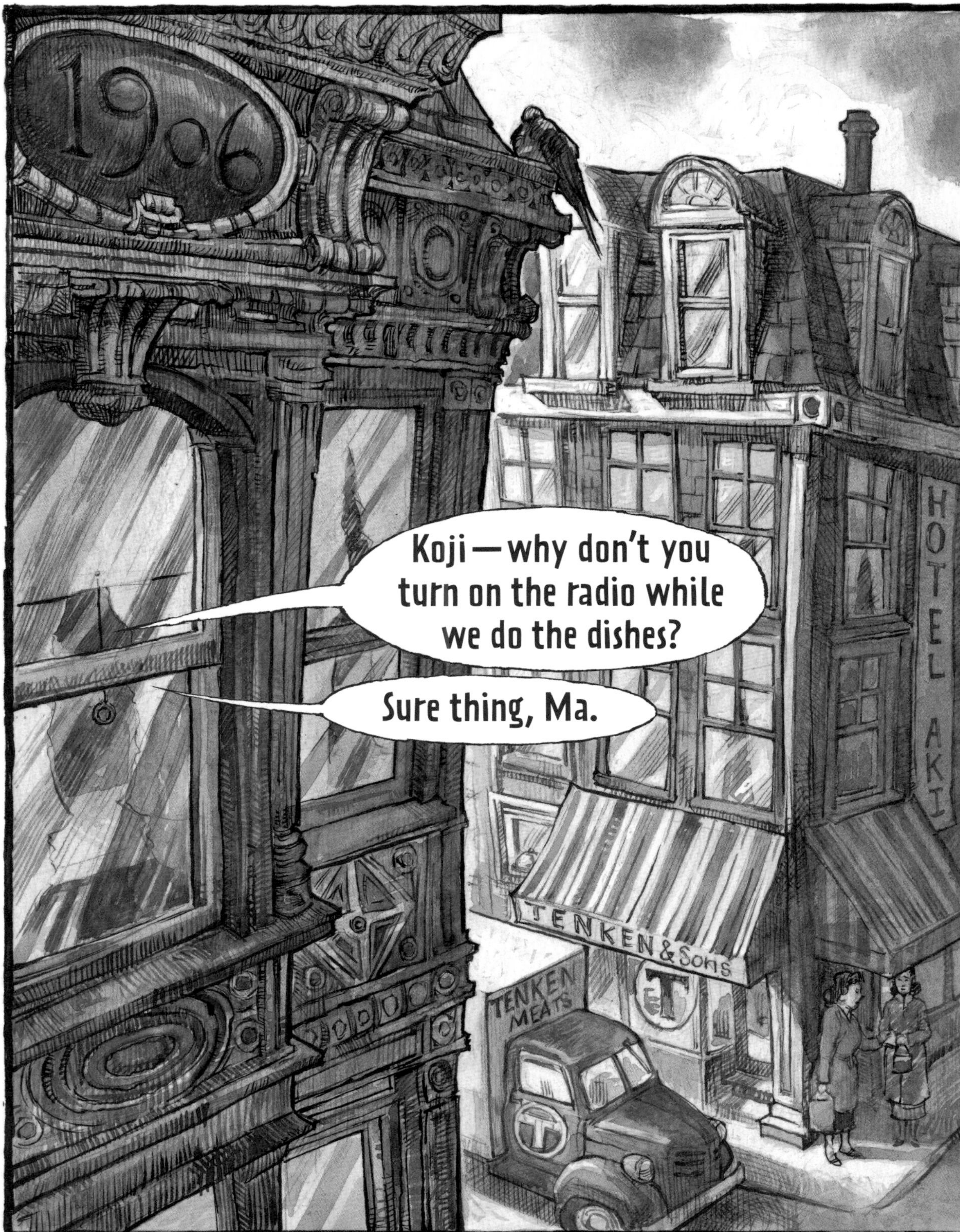
1906
Koji—why don't you turn on the radio while we do the dishes?
Sure thing, Ma.
HOTEL AKI
TENKEN & SONS
TENKEN MEATS
T

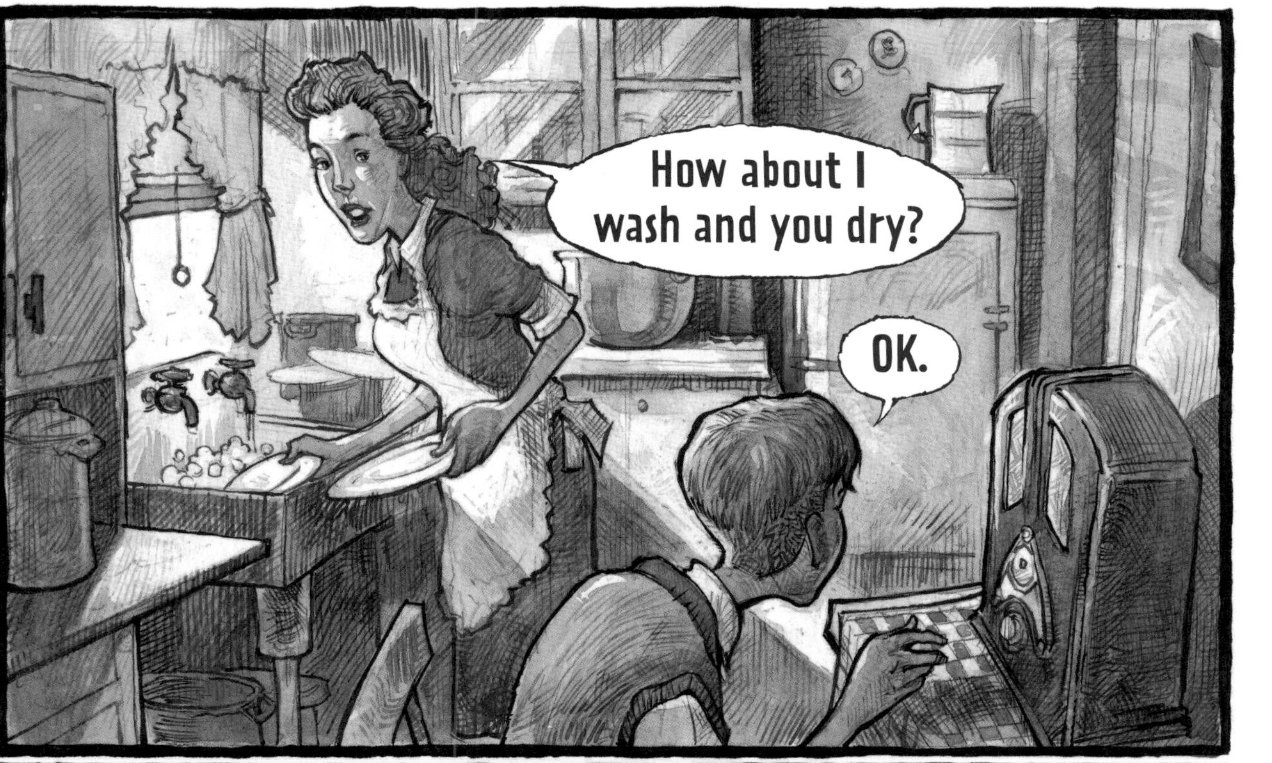
How about I wash and you dry?
OK.

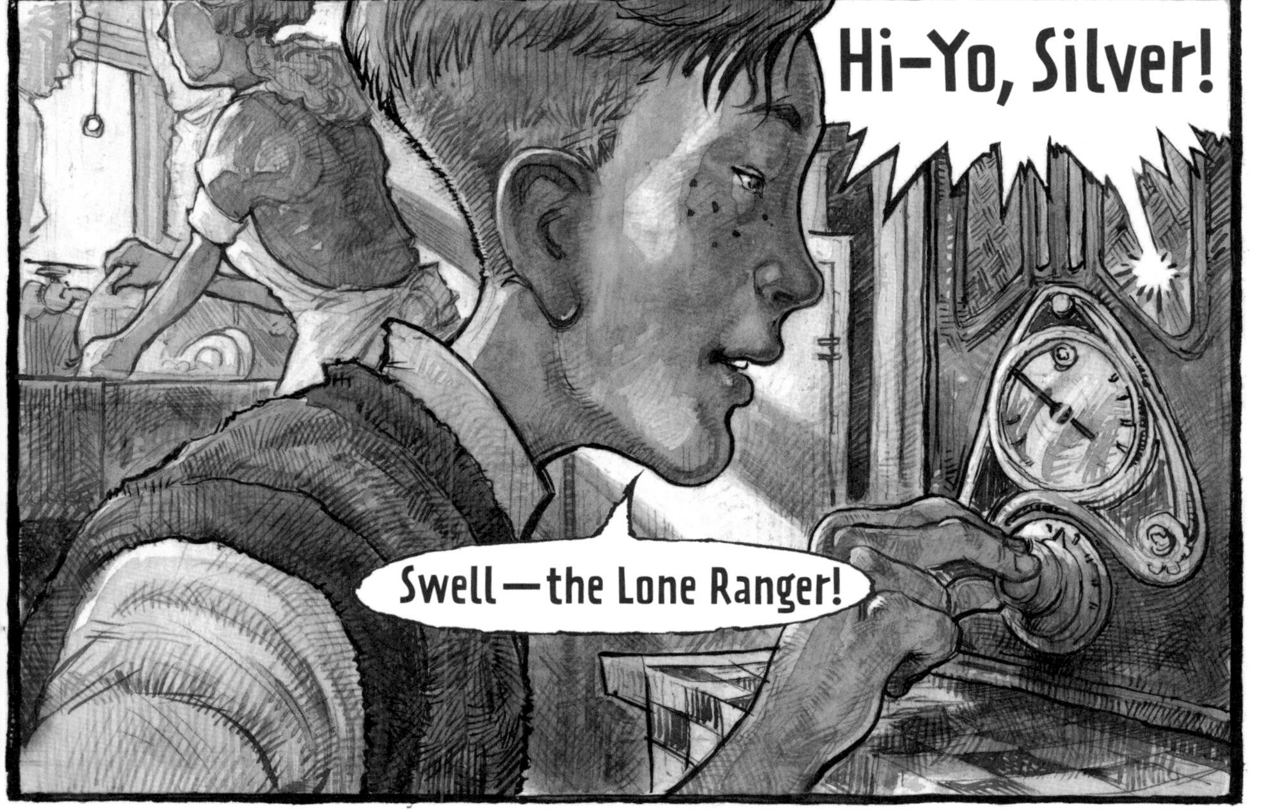
Hi-Yo, Silver!
Swell—the Lone Ranger!

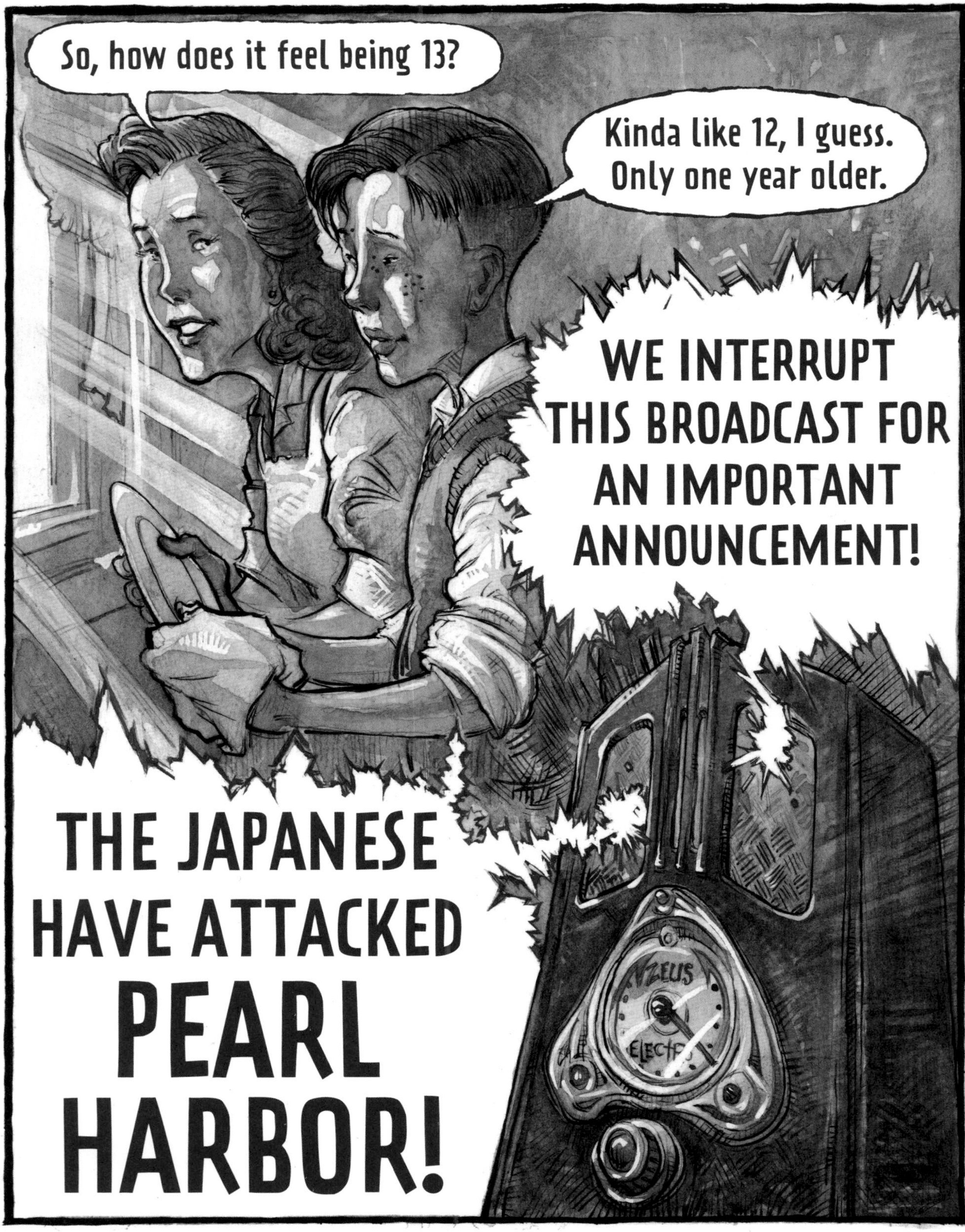
So, how does it feel being 13?
Kinda like 12, I guess. Only one year older.
WE INTERRUPT THIS BROADCAST FOR AN IMPORTANT ANNOUNCEMENT!
THE JAPANESE HAVE ATTACKED PEARL HARBOR!

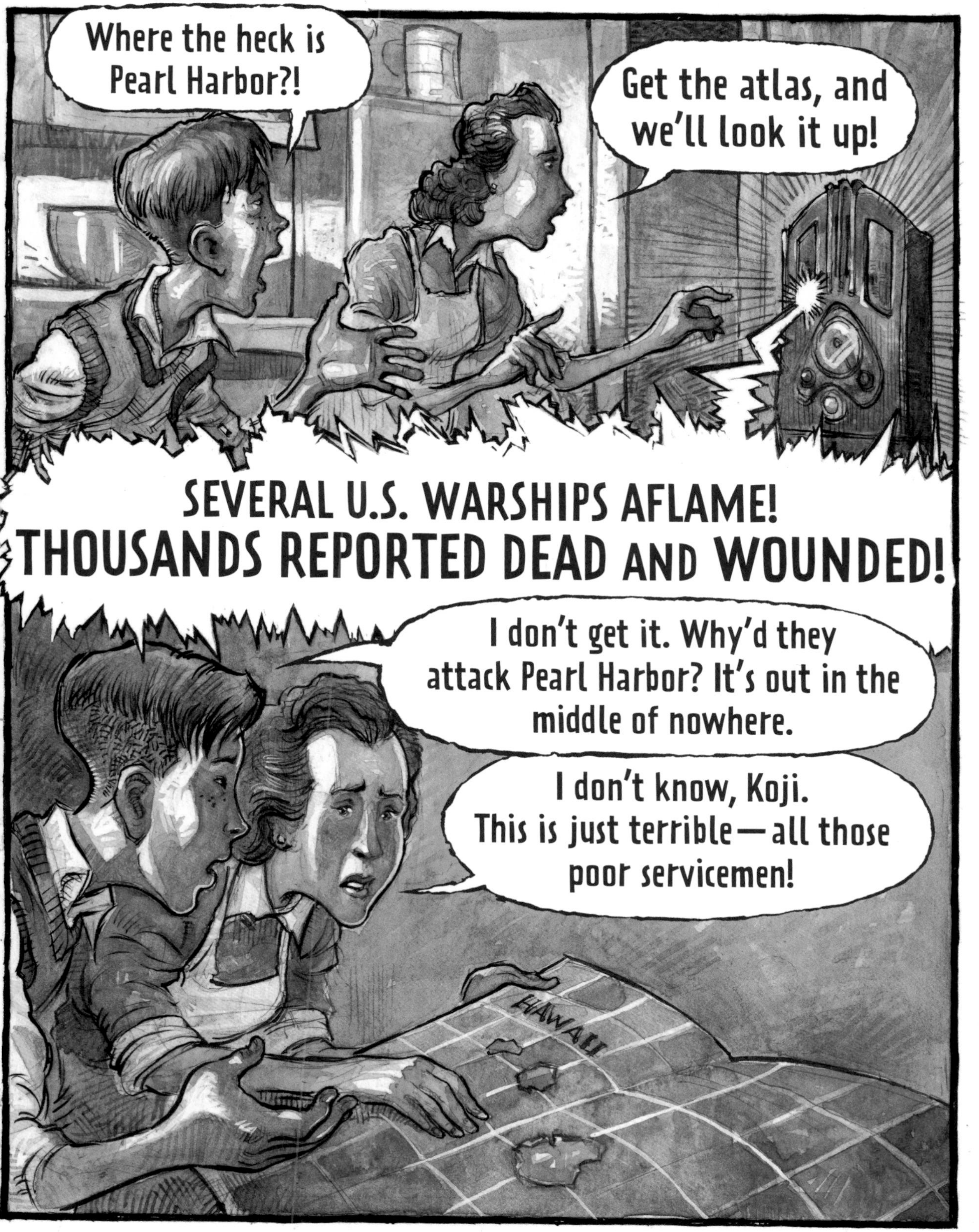
Where the heck is Pearl Harbor?!
Get the atlas, and we'll look it up!
SEVERAL U.S. WARSHIPS AFLAME!
THOUSANDS REPORTED DEAD AND WOUNDED!
I don't get it. Why'd they attack Pearl Harbor? It's out in the middle of nowhere.
I don't know, Koji. This is just terrible—all those poor servicemen!
HAWAII

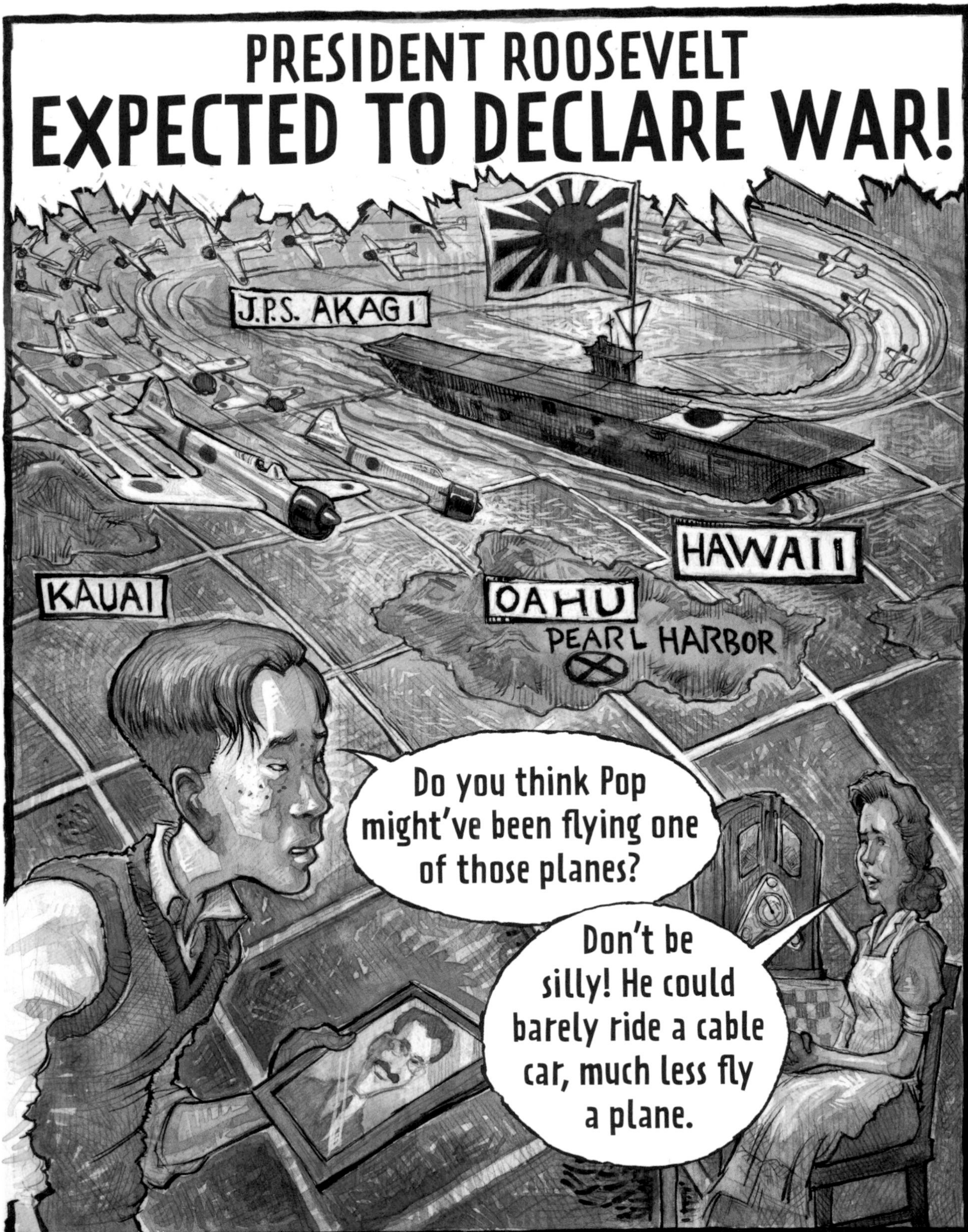
PRESIDENT ROOSEVELT
EXPECTED TO DECLARE WAR!
J.P.S. AKAGI
HAWAII
KAUAI
OAHU
PEARL HARBOR
Do you think Pop might've been flying one of those planes?
Don't be silly! He could barely ride a cable car, much less fly a plane.

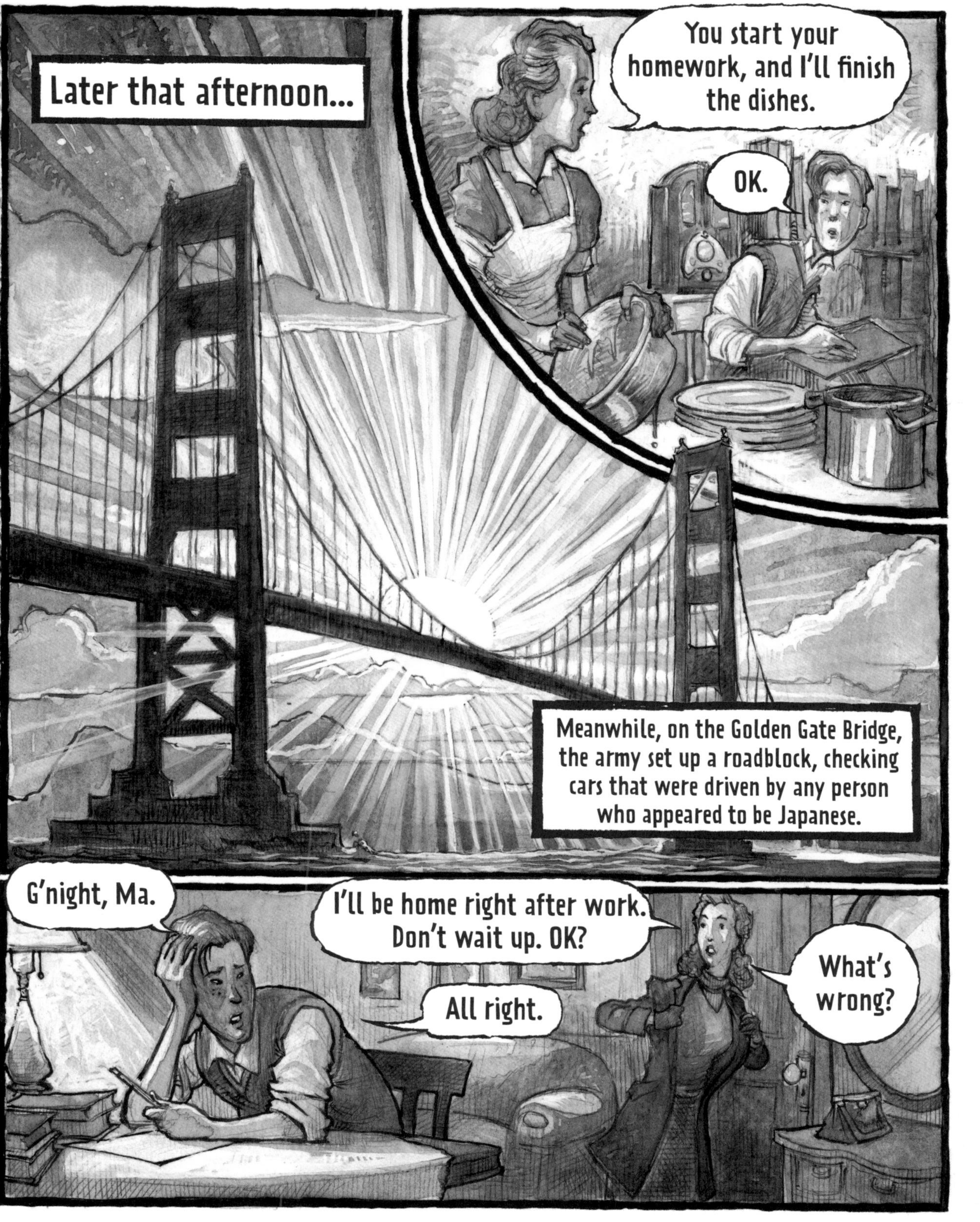
Later that afternoon...
You start your homework, and I'll finish the dishes.
OK.
Meanwhile, on the Golden Gate Bridge, the army set up a roadblock, checking cars that were driven by any person who appeared to be Japanese.
G'night, Ma.
I'll be home right after work. Don't wait up. OK?
All right.
What's wrong?

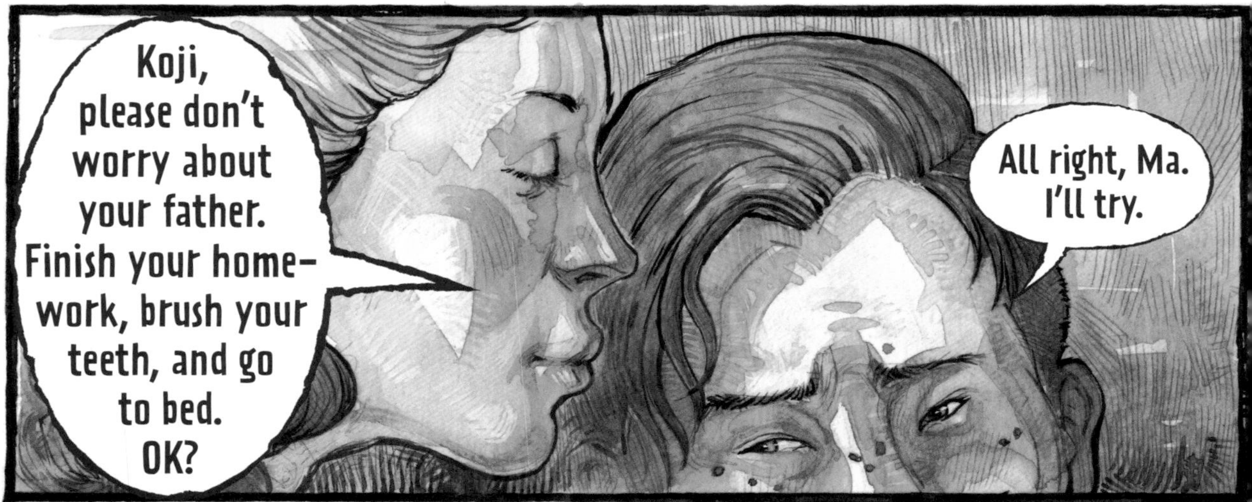
Koji, please don't worry about your father. Finish your home-work, brush your teeth, and go to bed. OK?
All right, Ma. I'll try.

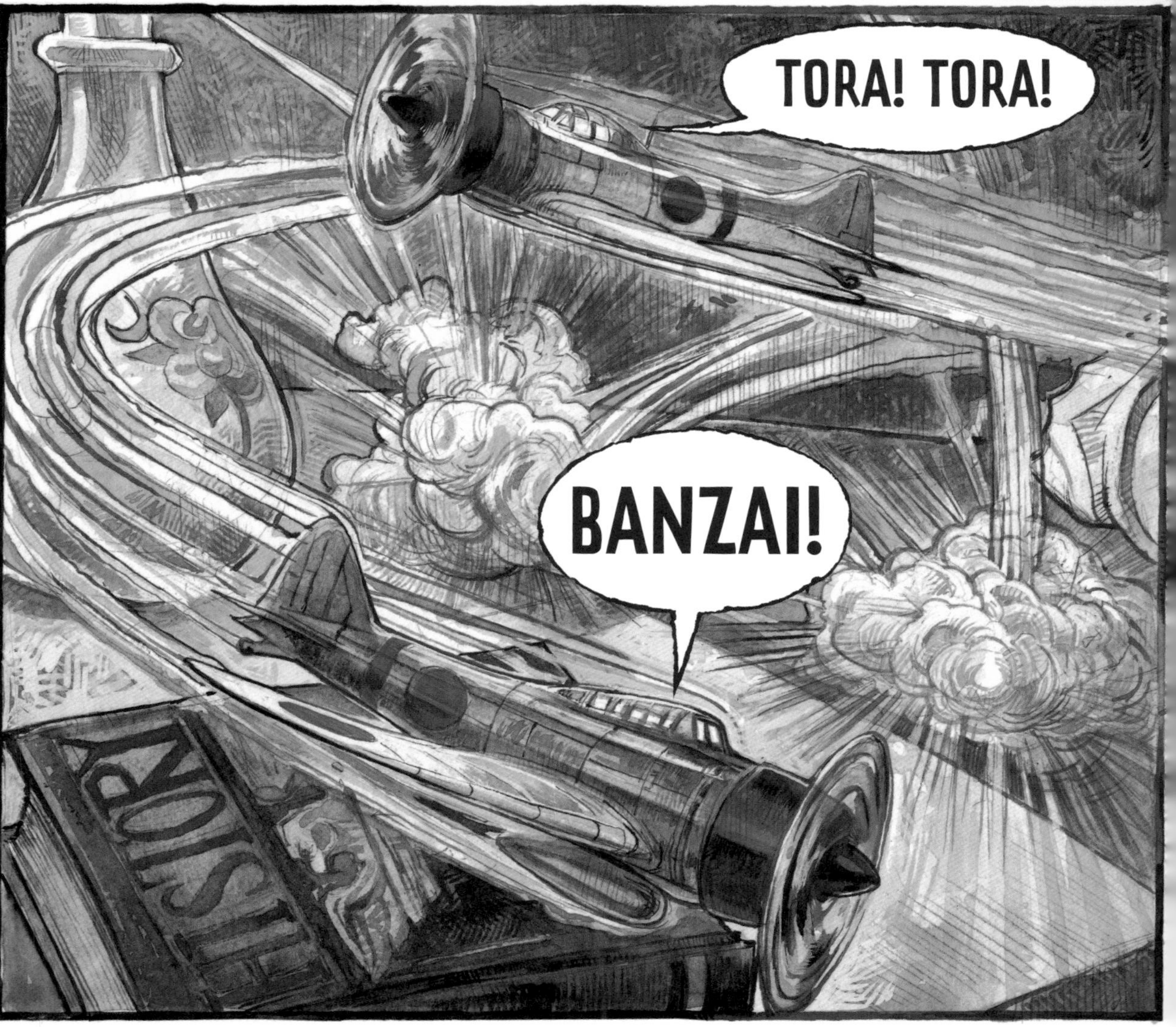
TORA! TORA!
BANZAI!

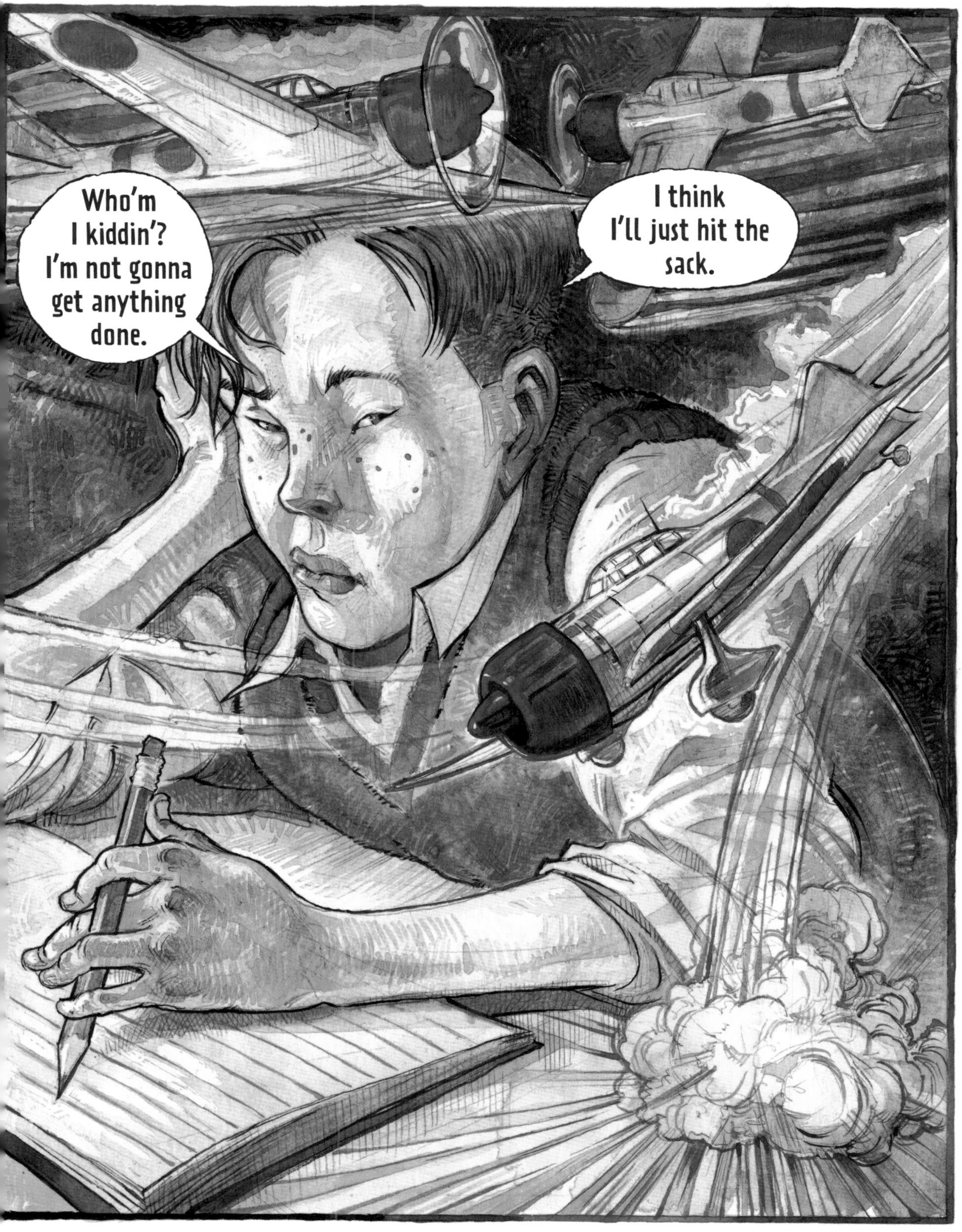
Who'm I kiddin'? I'm not gonna get anything done.
I think I'll just hit the sack.

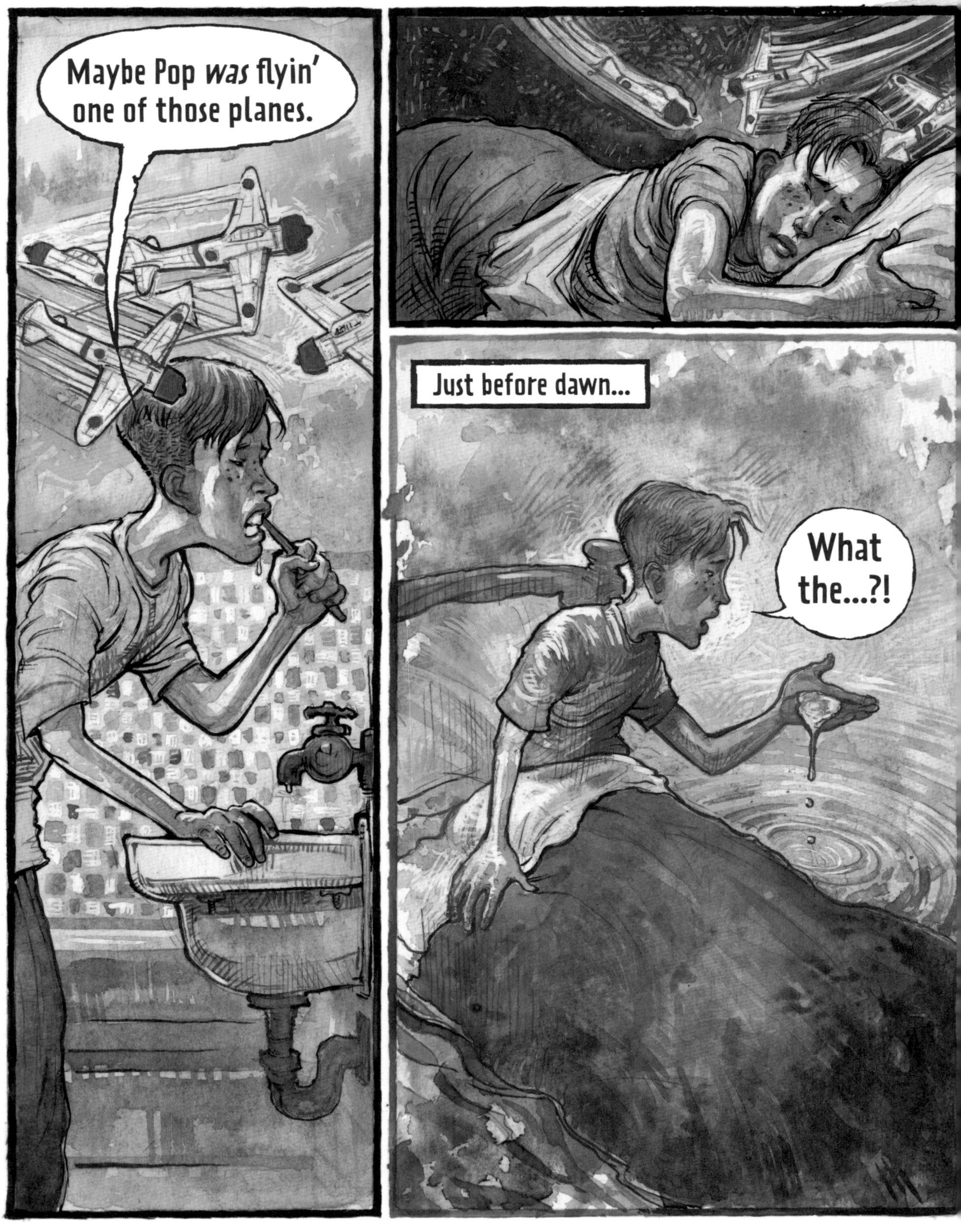
Maybe Pop *was* flyin' one of those planes.
Just before dawn...
What the...?!

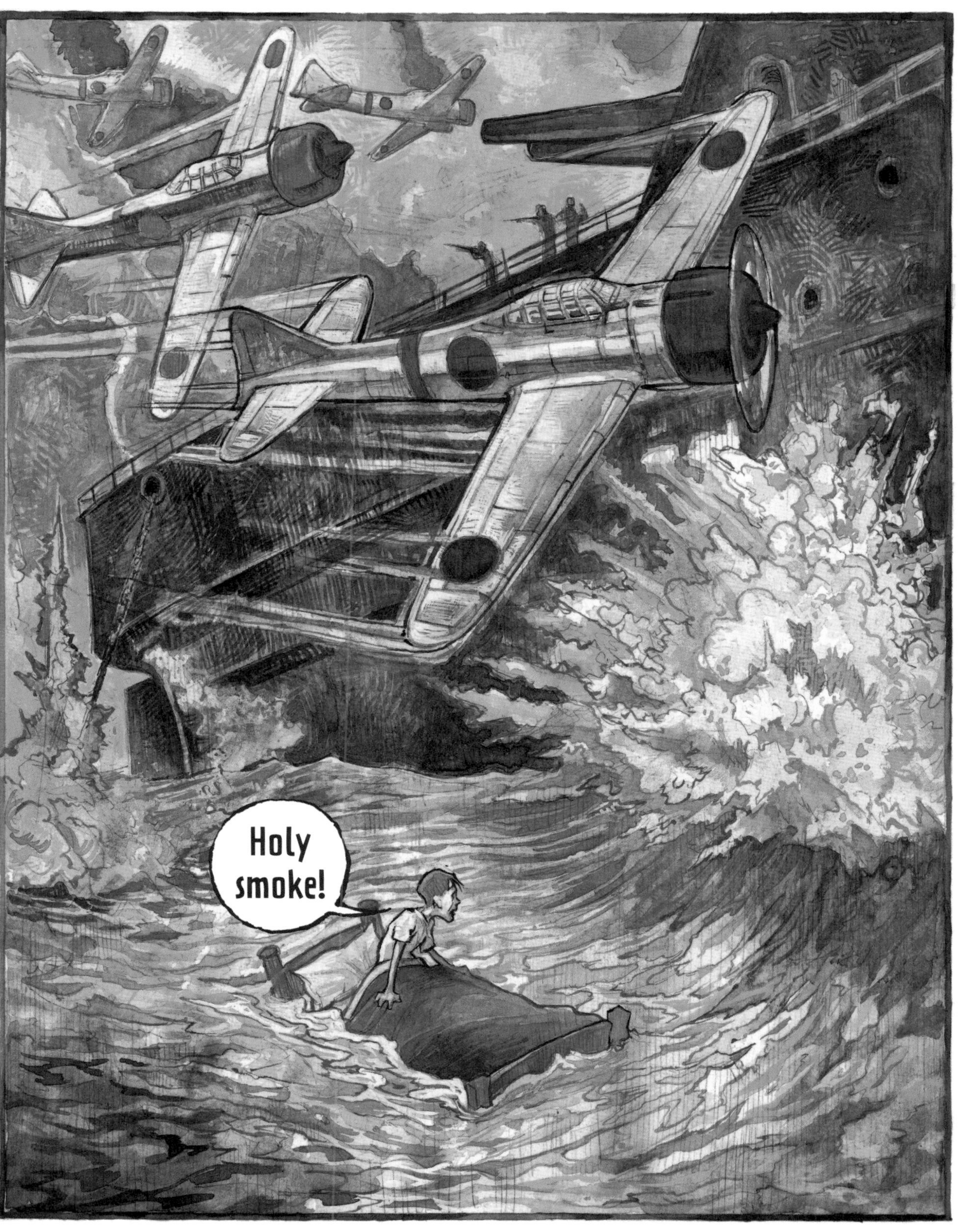
Holy smoke!

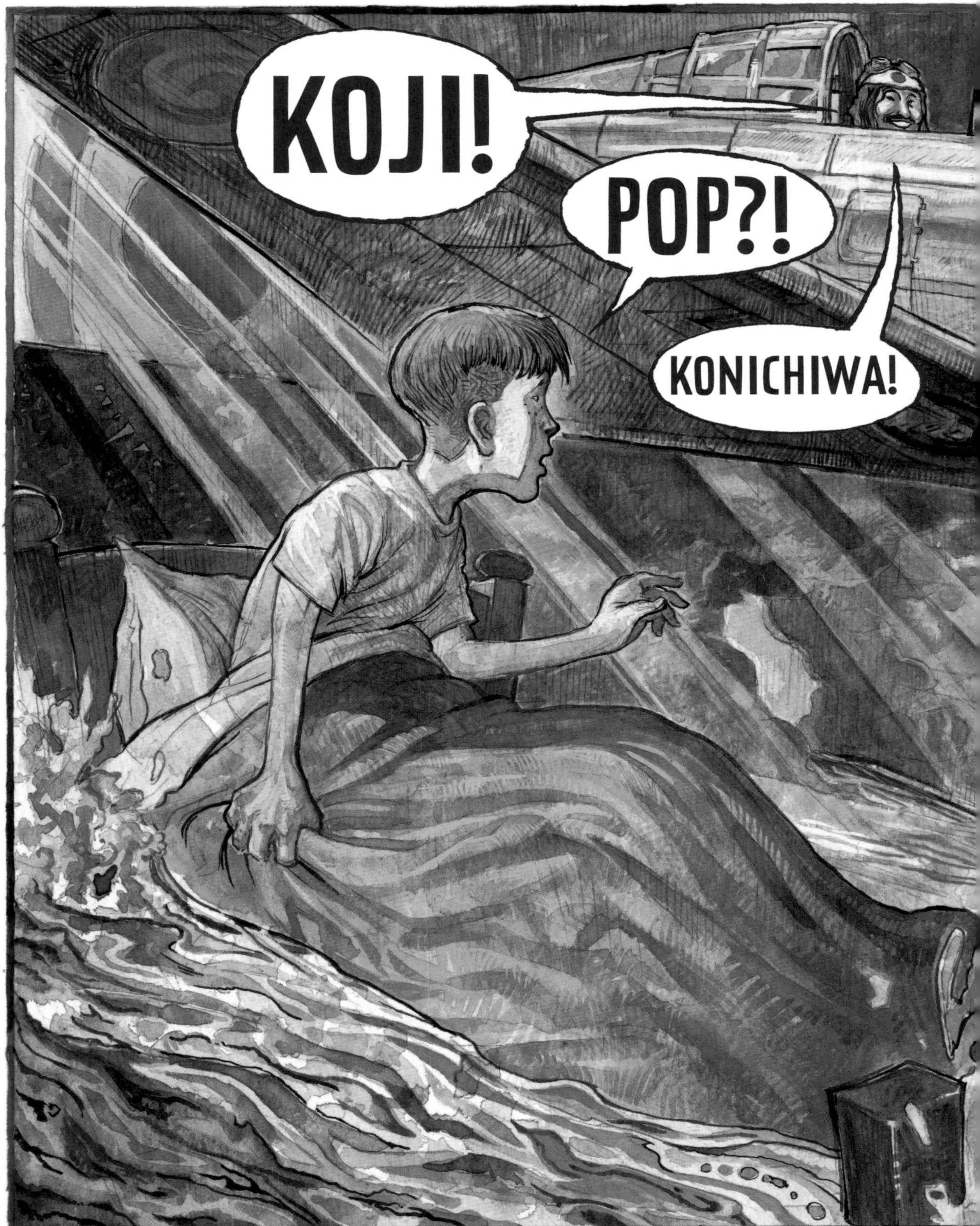
KOJI!
POP?!
KONICHIWA!

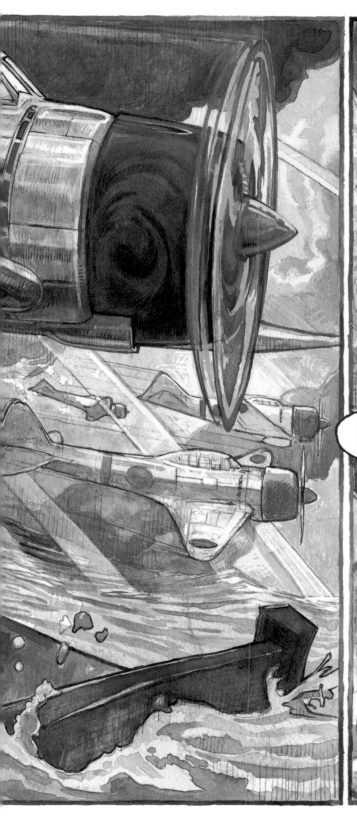

See you later, alligator!

Pop! Wait! Come back!

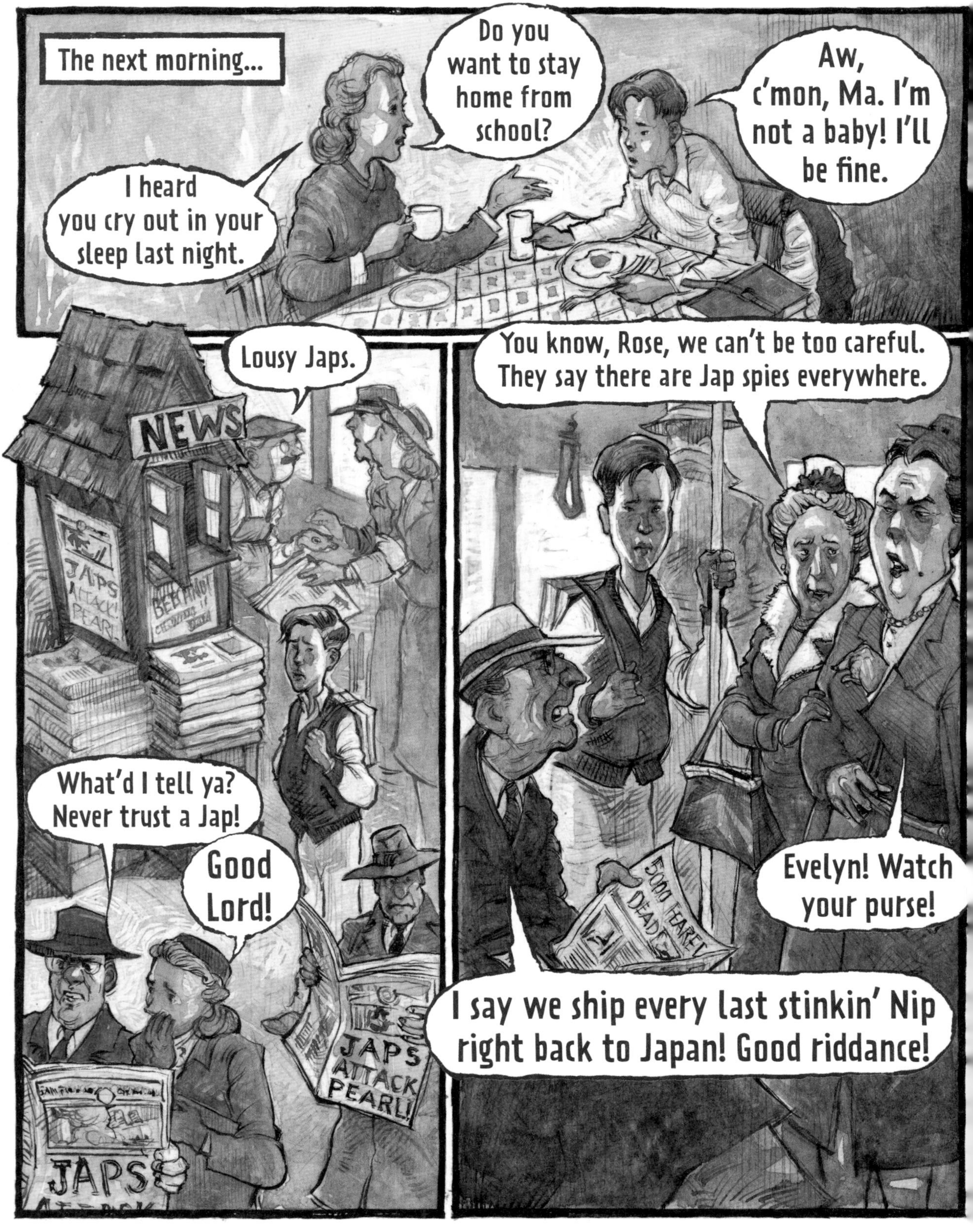
The next morning...
I heard you cry out in your sleep last night.
Do you want to stay home from school?
Aw, c'mon, Ma. I'm not a baby! I'll be fine.
NEWS
Lousy Japs.
JAPS ATTACK! PEARL
What'd I tell ya? Never trust a Jap!
Good Lord!
JAPS ATTACK PEARL!
JAPS
You know, Rose, we can't be too careful. They say there are Jap spies everywhere.
Evelyn! Watch your purse!
I say we ship every last stinkin' Nip right back to Japan! Good riddance!

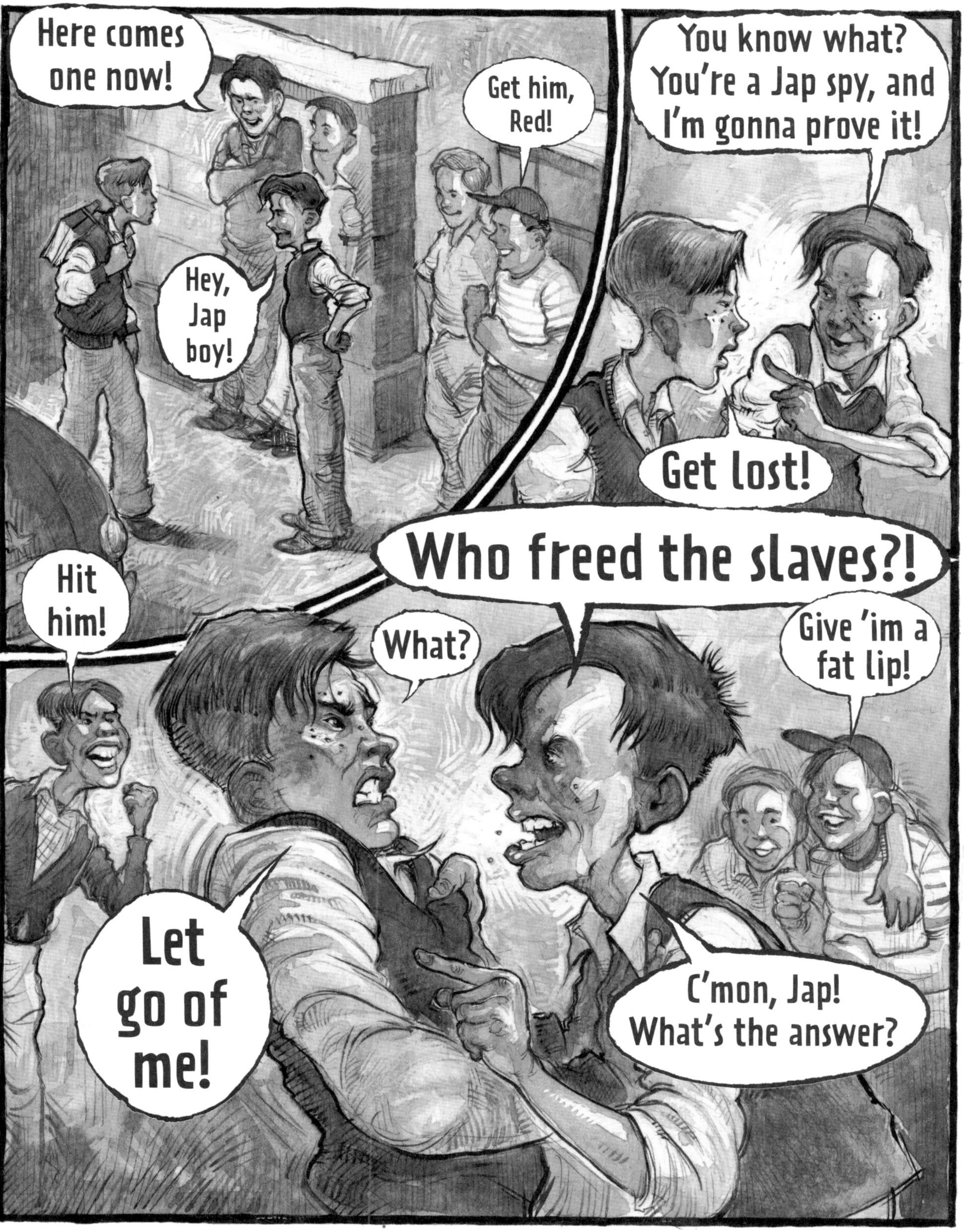
Here comes one now!
Get him, Red!
Hey, Jap boy!
You know what? You're a Jap spy, and I'm gonna prove it!
Get lost!
Who freed the slaves?!
Hit him!
What?
Give 'im a fat lip!
Let go of me!
C'mon, Jap! What's the answer?

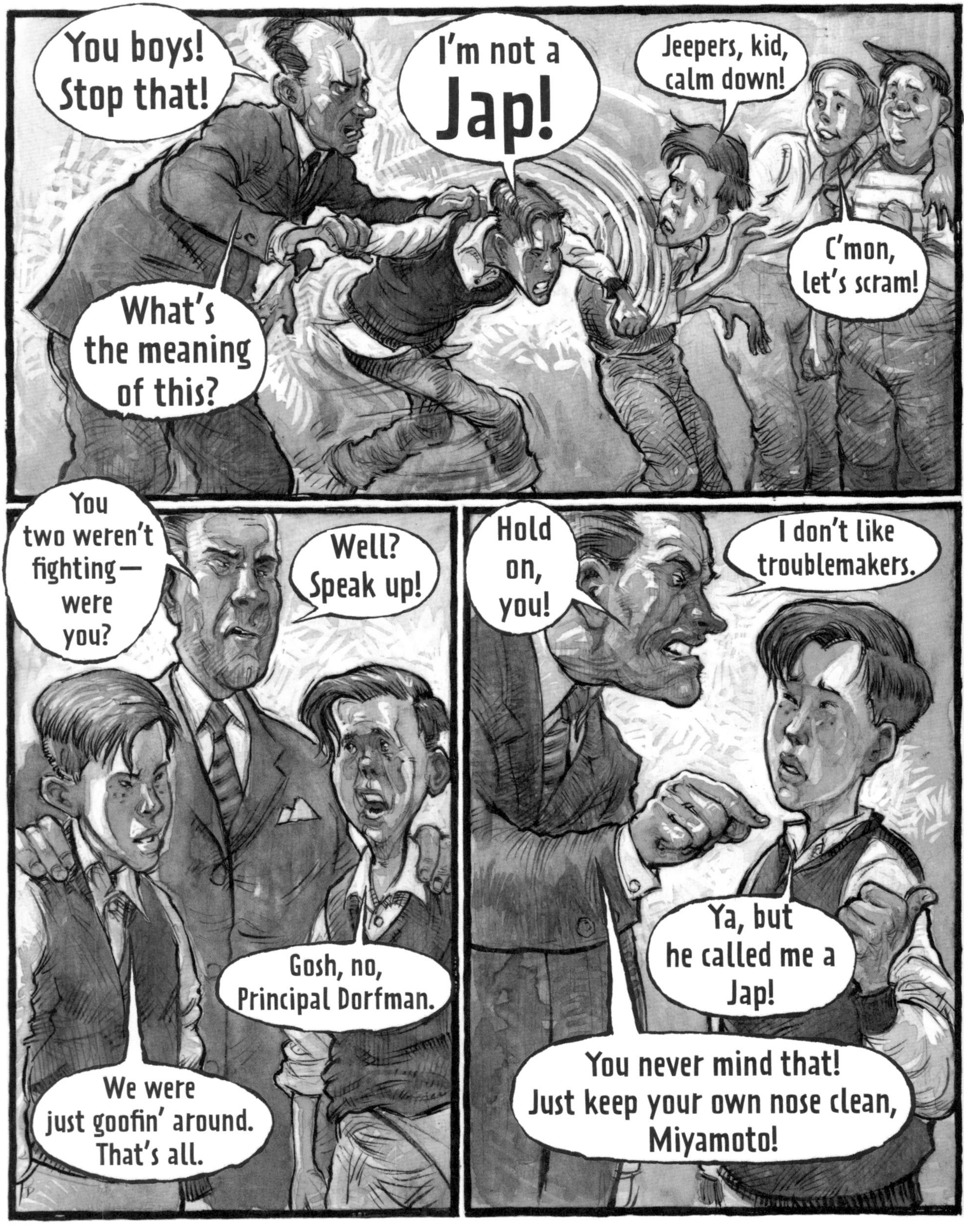
You boys! Stop that!
What's the meaning of this?
I'm not a Jap!
Jeepers, kid, calm down!
C'mon, let's scram!
You two weren't fighting— were you?
Well? Speak up!
Gosh, no, Principal Dorfman.
We were just goofin' around. That's all.
Hold on, you!
I don't like troublemakers.
Ya, but he called me a Jap!
You never mind that! Just keep your own nose clean, Miyamoto!

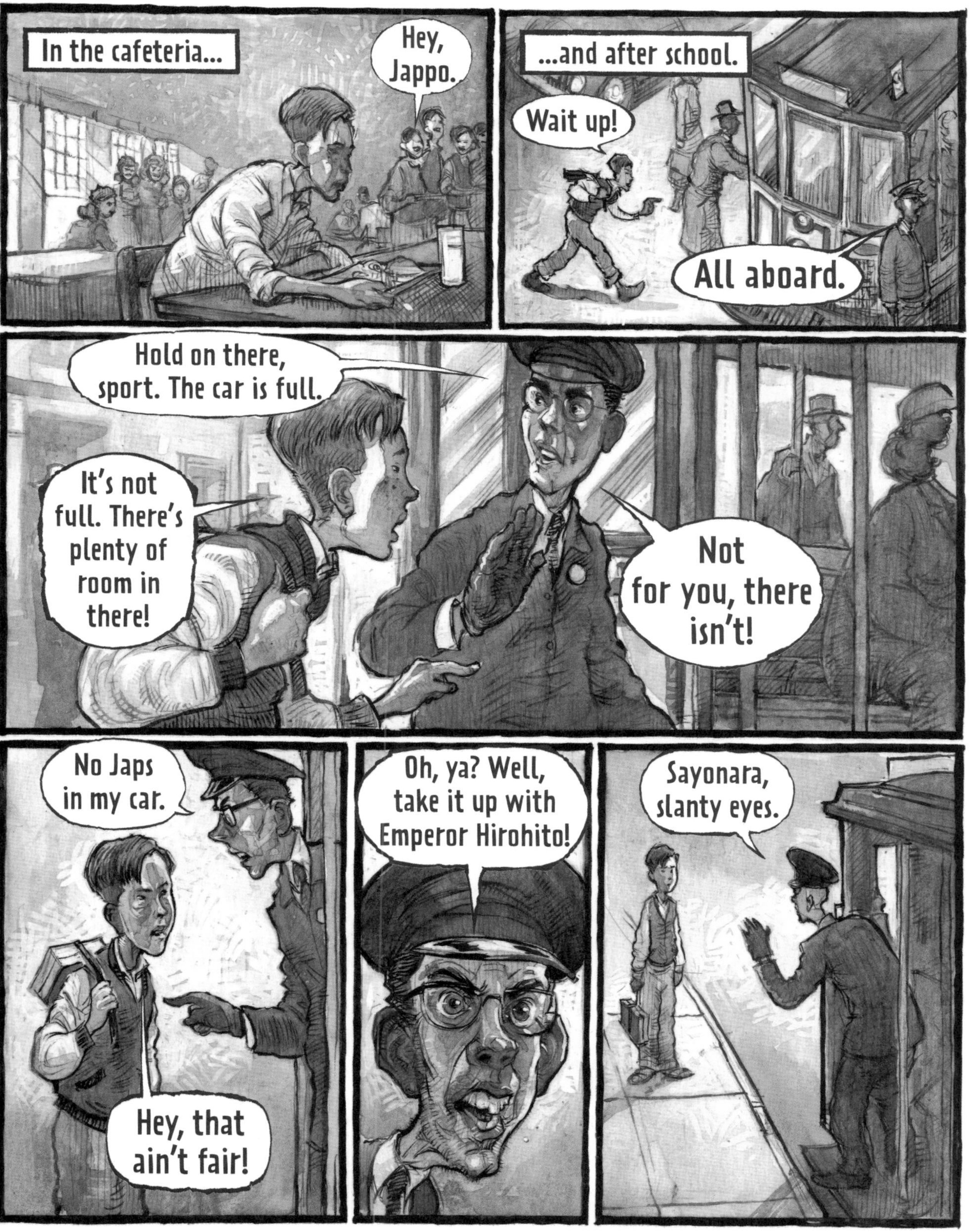
In the cafeteria...
Hey, Jappo.
...and after school.
Wait up!
All aboard.
Hold on there, sport. The car is full.
It's not full. There's plenty of room in there!
Not for you, there isn't!
No Japs in my car.
Hey, that ain't fair!
Oh, ya? Well, take it up with Emperor Hirohito!
Sayonara, slanty eyes.

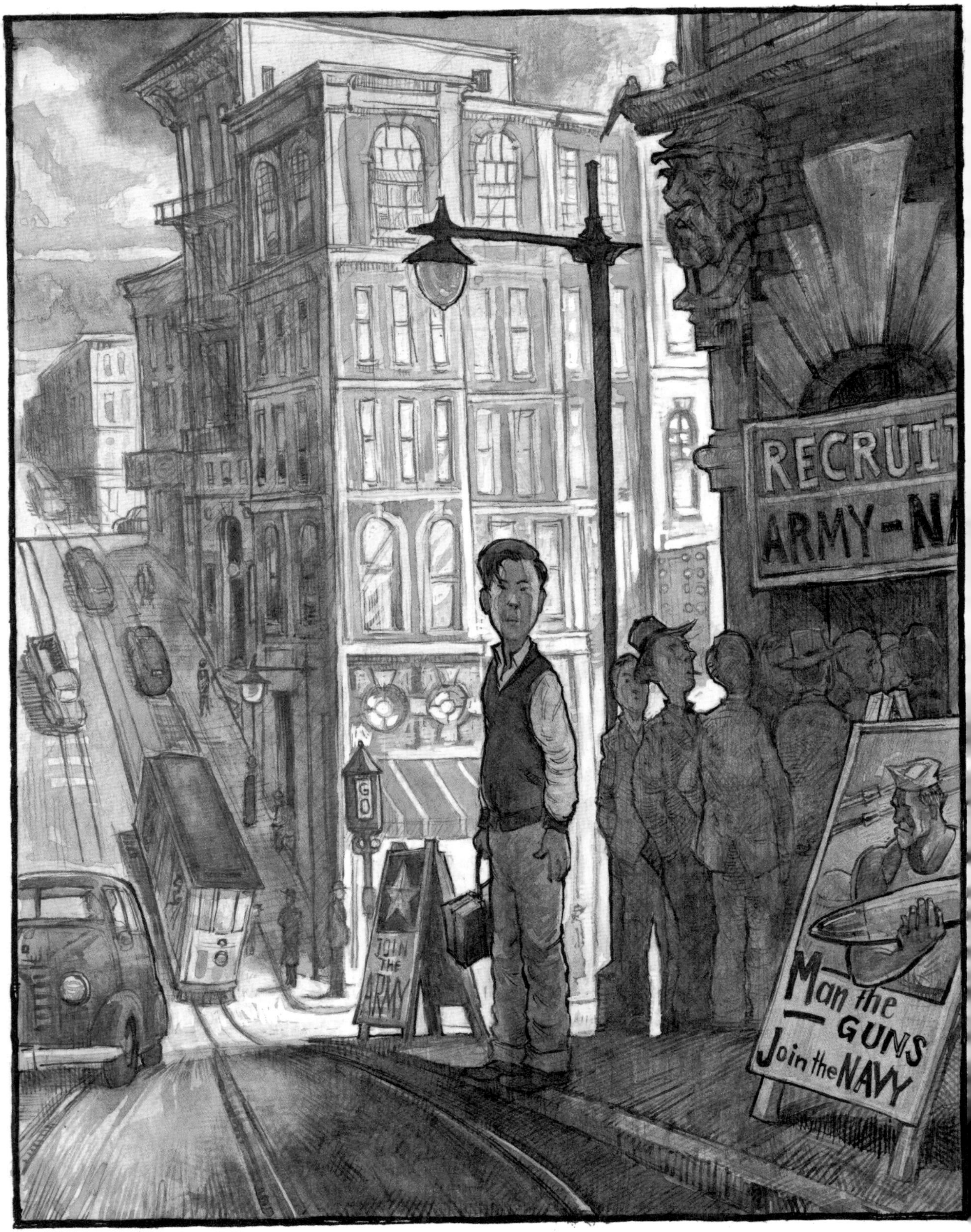
RECRUIT
ARMY-NA
GO
JOIN the ARMY
Man the GUNS
Join the NAVY

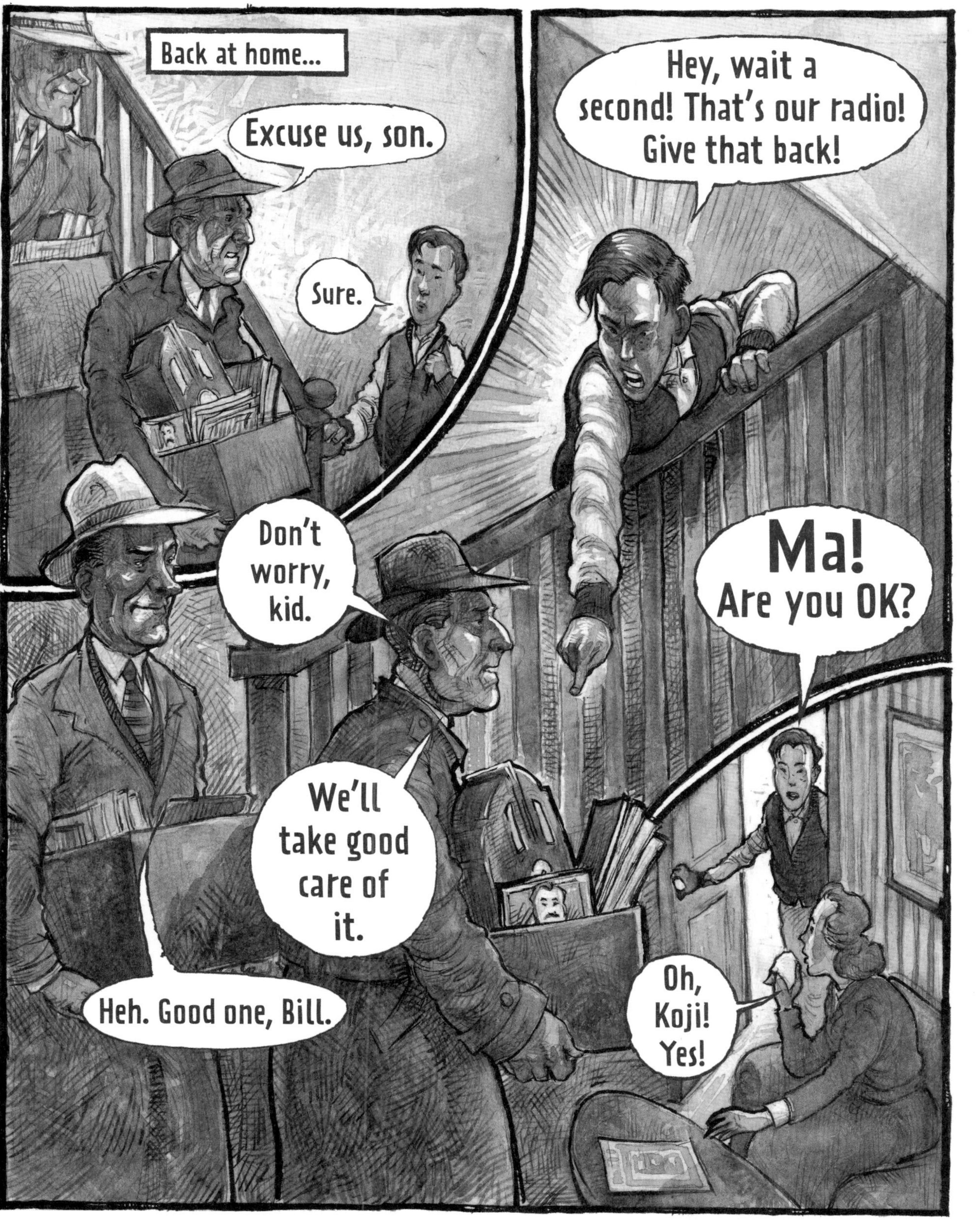
Back at home...
Excuse us, son.
Sure.
Hey, wait a second! That's our radio! Give that back!
Don't worry, kid.
We'll take good care of it.
Heh. Good one, Bill.
Ma! Are you OK?
Oh, Koji! Yes!

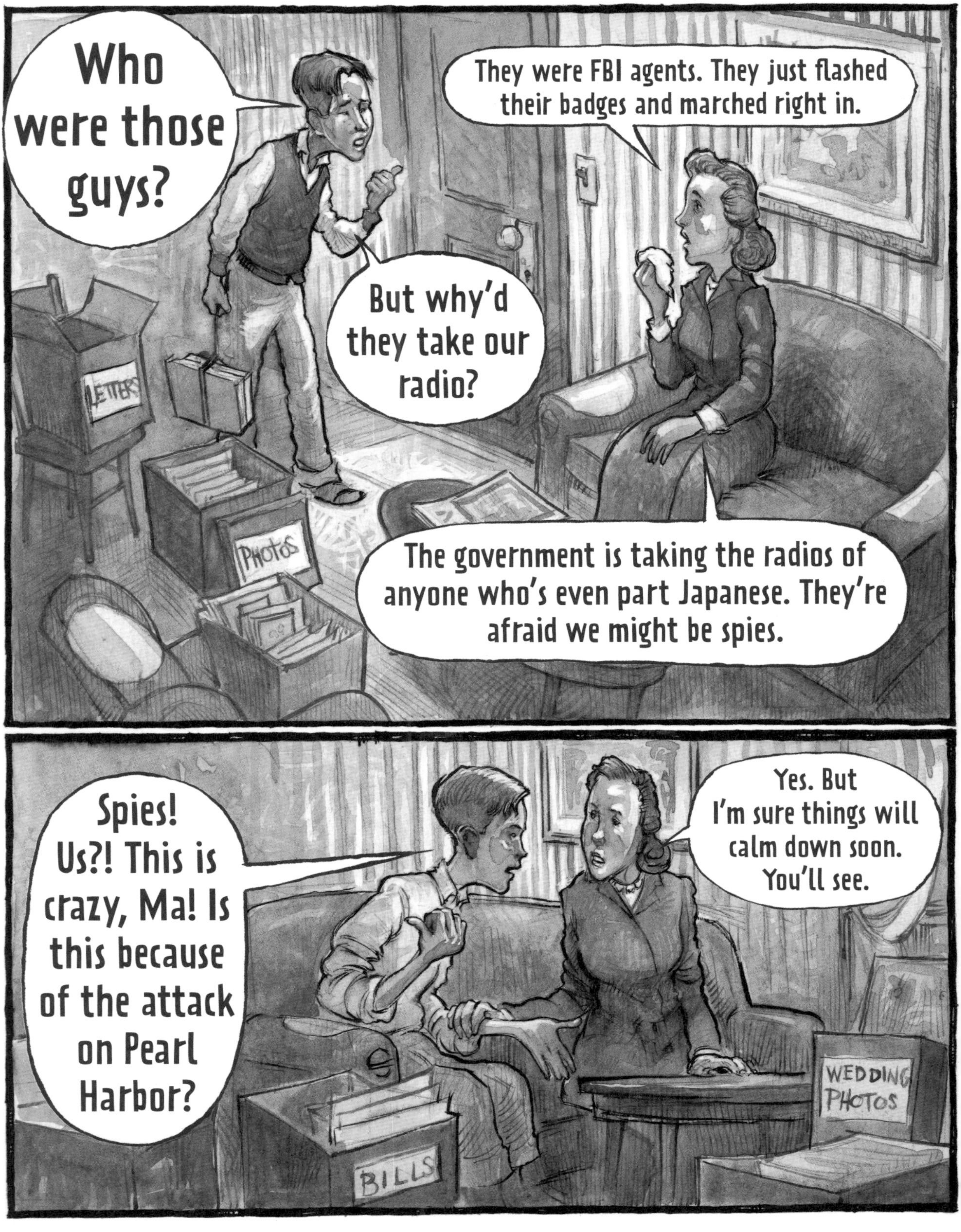
Who were those guys?
They were FBI agents. They just flashed their badges and marched right in.
But why'd they take our radio?
LETTERS
PHOTOS
The government is taking the radios of anyone who's even part Japanese. They're afraid we might be spies.
Spies! Us?! This is crazy, Ma! Is this because of the attack on Pearl Harbor?
Yes. But I'm sure things will calm down soon. You'll see.
BILLS
WEDDING PHOTOS

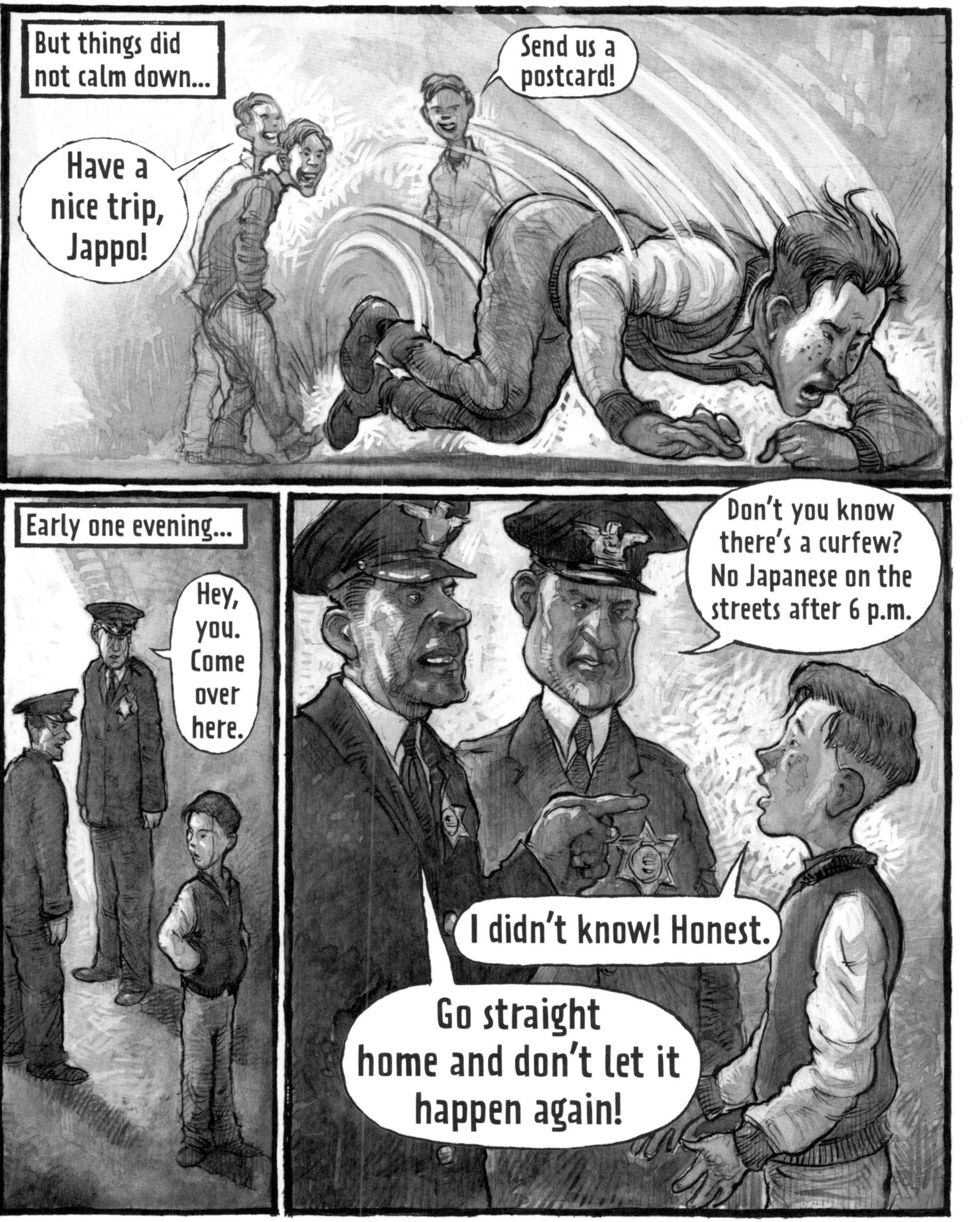

But things did not calm down...
Have a nice trip, Jappo!
Send us a postcard!
Early one evening...
Hey, you. Come over here.
Don't you know there's a curfew? No Japanese on the streets after 6 p.m.
I didn't know! Honest.
Go straight home and don't let it happen again!

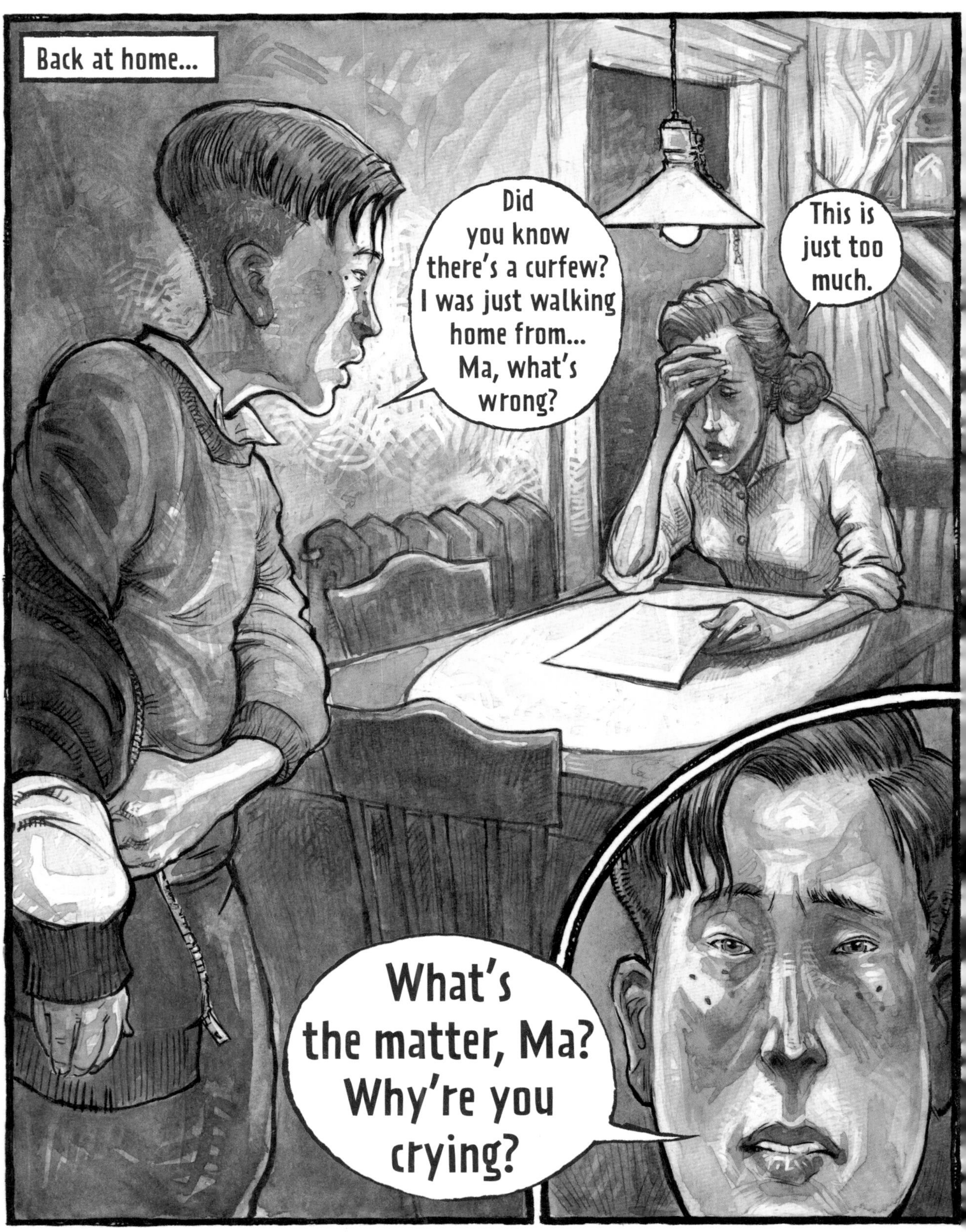
Back at home...
Did you know there's a curfew? I was just walking home from... Ma, what's wrong?
This is just too much.
What's the matter, Ma? Why're you crying?

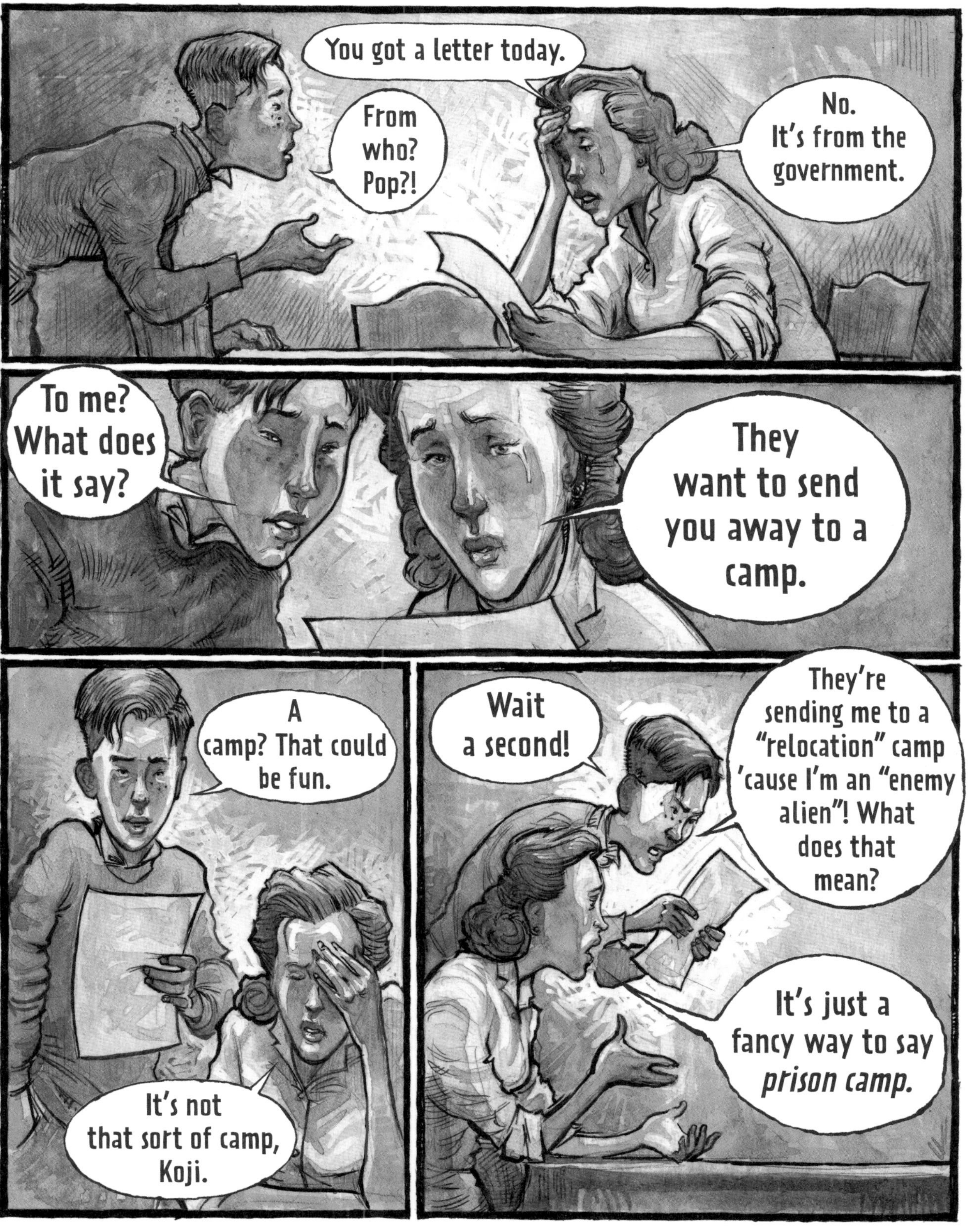
You got a letter today.
From who? Pop?!
No. It's from the government.
To me? What does it say?
They want to send you away to a camp.
A camp? That could be fun.
It's not that sort of camp, Koji.
Wait a second!
They're sending me to a "relocation" camp 'cause I'm an "enemy alien"! What does that mean?
It's just a fancy way to say *prison camp.*

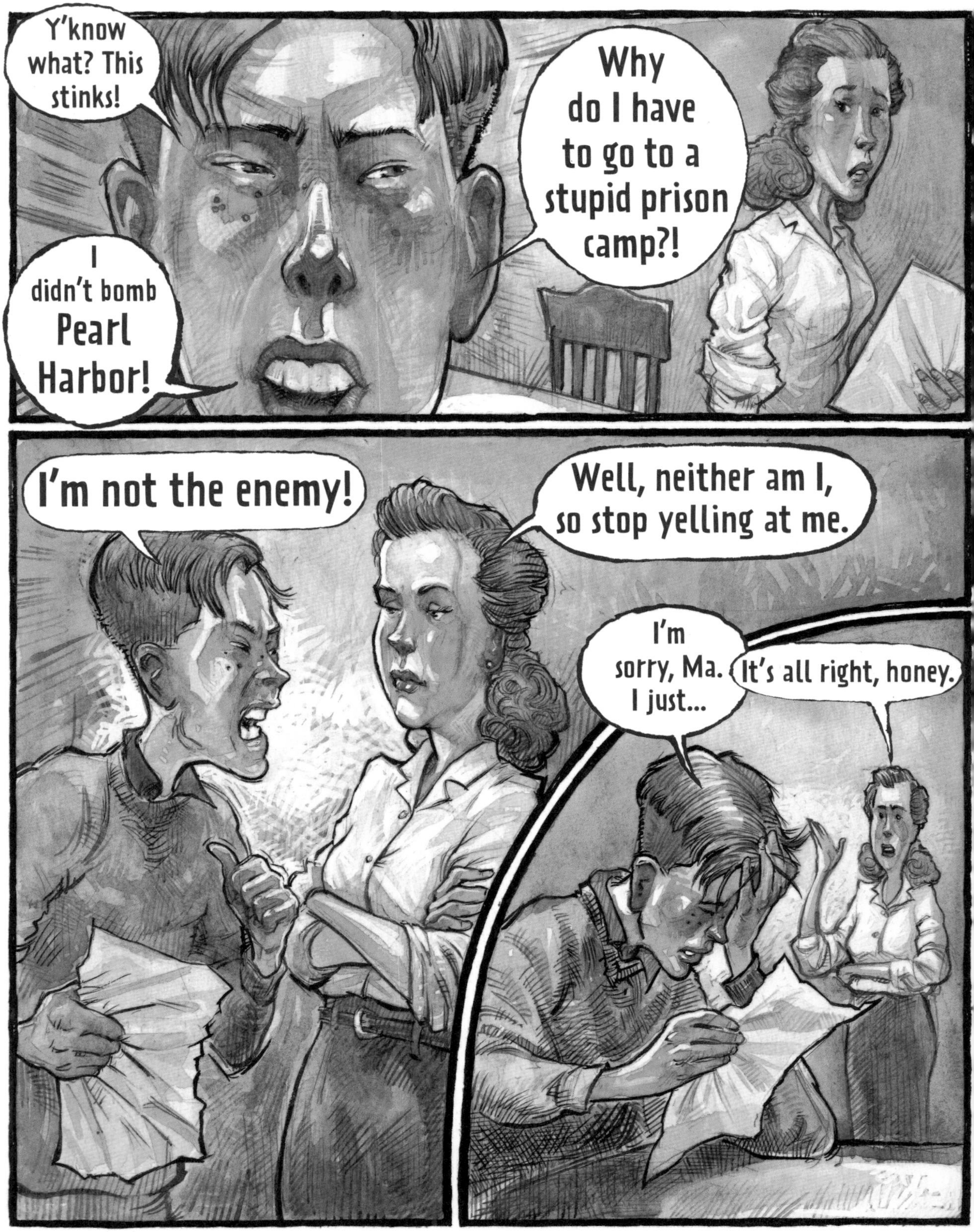
Y'know what? This stinks!
I didn't bomb Pearl Harbor!
Why do I have to go to a stupid prison camp?!
I'm not the enemy!
Well, neither am I, so stop yelling at me.
I'm sorry, Ma. I just...
It's all right, honey.

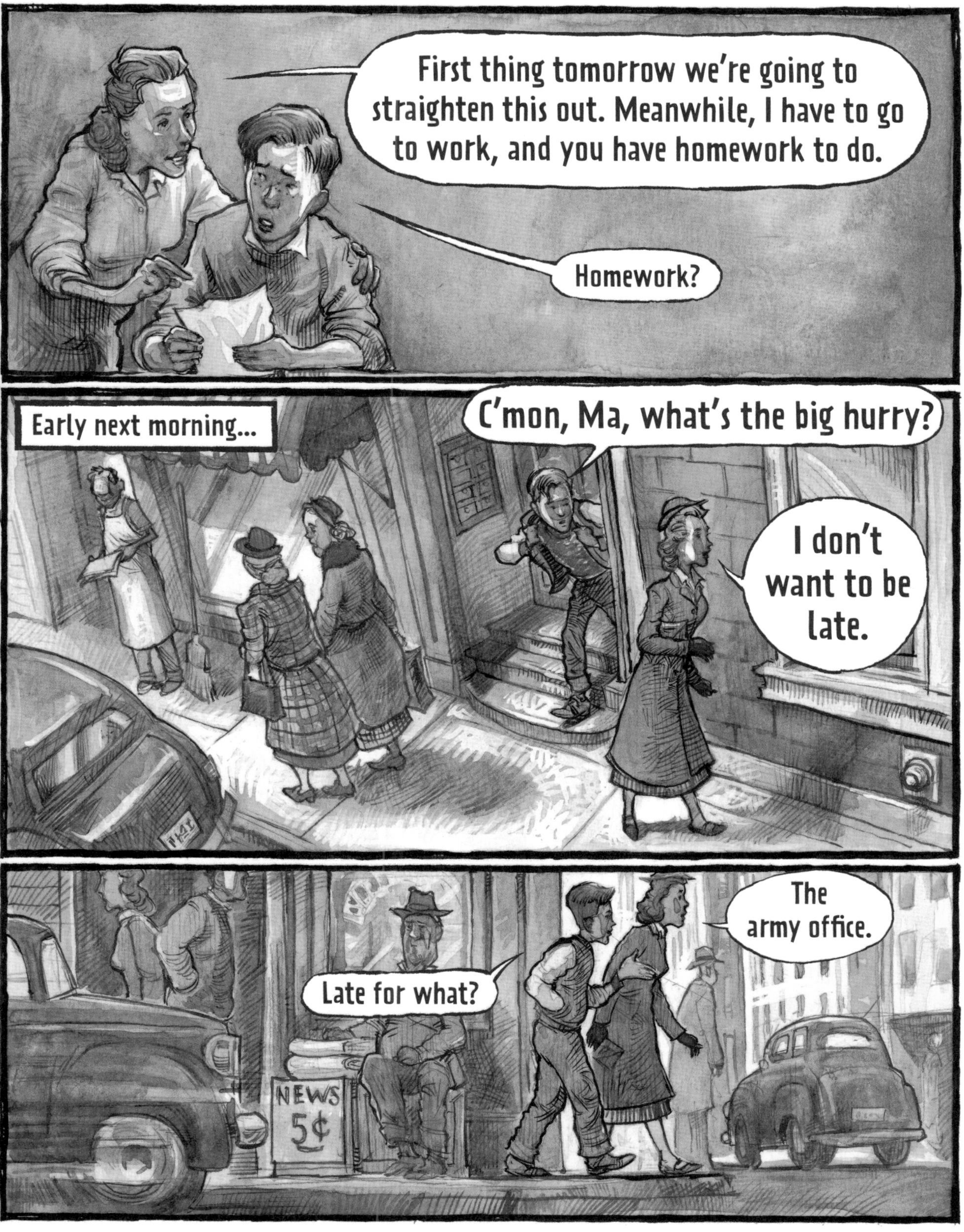
First thing tomorrow we're going to straighten this out. Meanwhile, I have to go to work, and you have homework to do.
Homework?
Early next morning...
C'mon, Ma, what's the big hurry?
I don't want to be late.
Late for what?
The army office.
NEWS 5¢

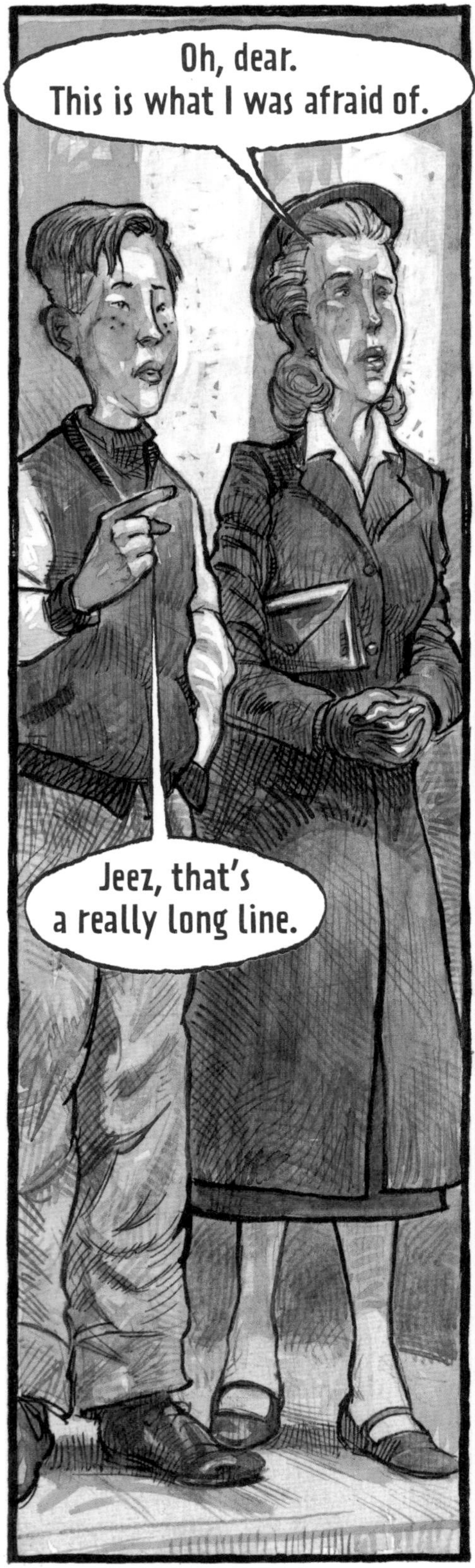
Oh, dear.
This is what I was afraid of.
Jeez, that's
a really long line.

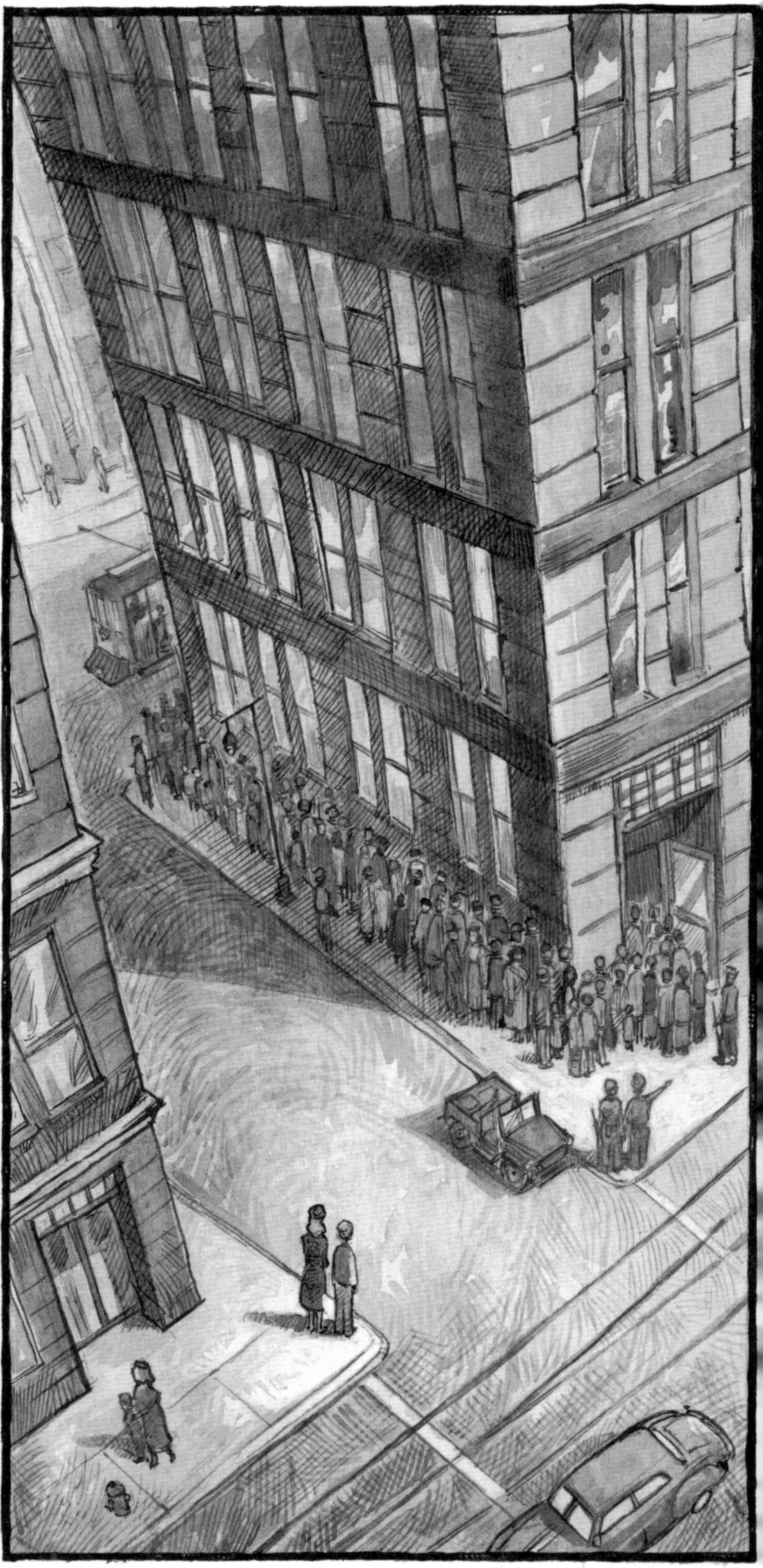

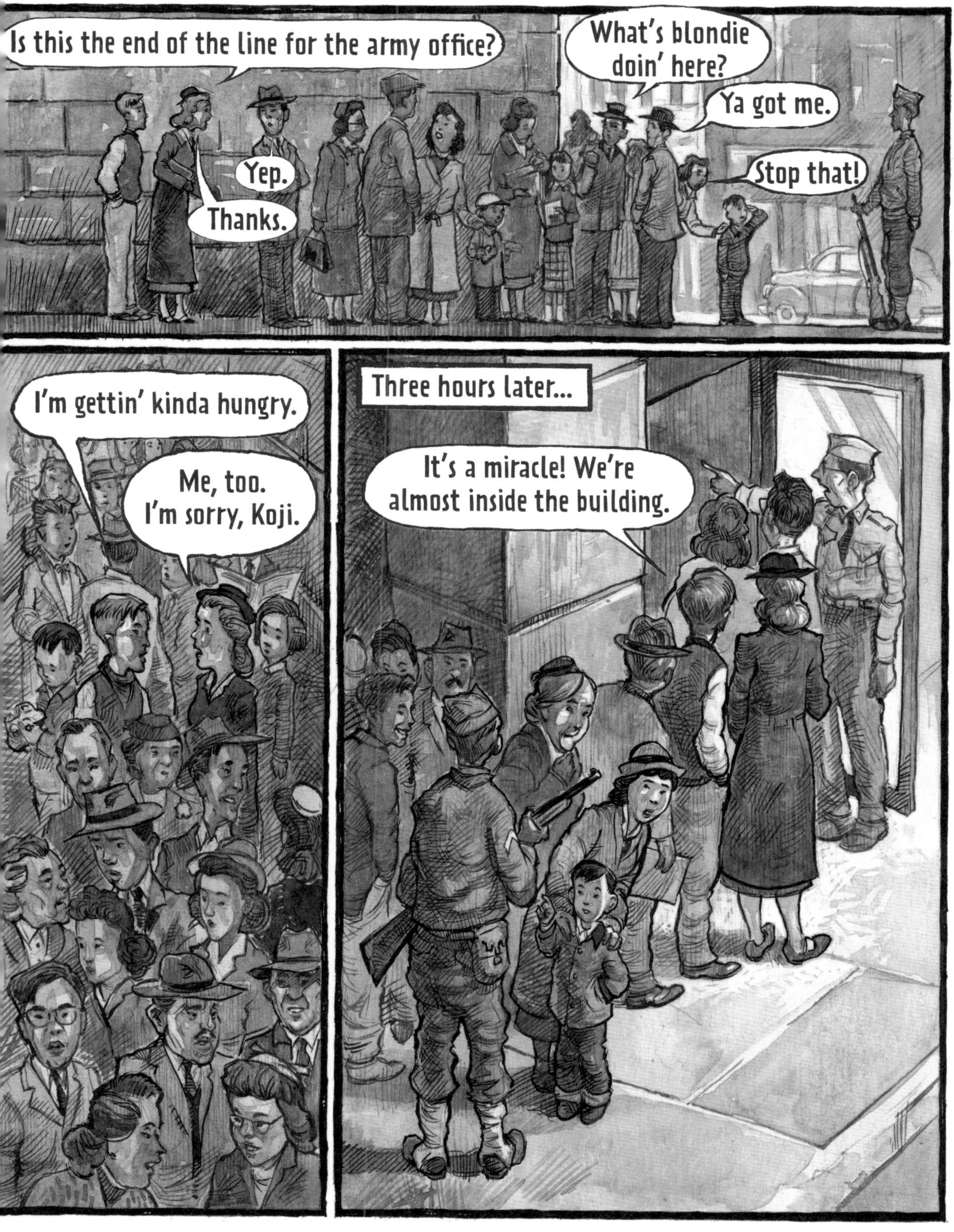
Is this the end of the line for the army office?
Yep.
Thanks.
What's blondie doin' here?
Ya got me.
Stop that!
I'm gettin' kinda hungry.
Me, too. I'm sorry, Koji.
Three hours later...
It's a miracle! We're almost inside the building.

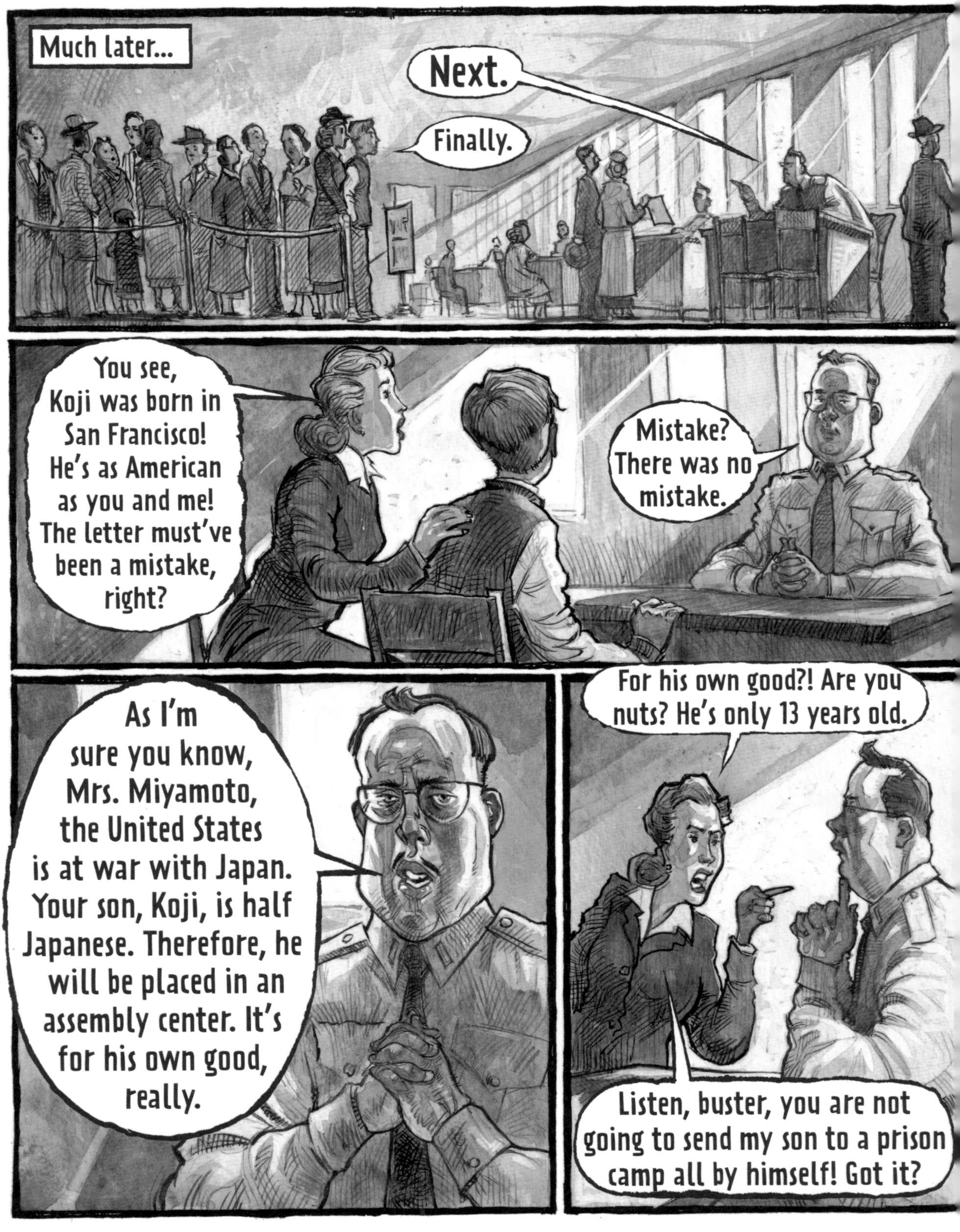
Much later...
Next.
Finally.
You see, Koji was born in San Francisco! He's as American as you and me! The letter must've been a mistake, right?
Mistake? There was no mistake.
As I'm sure you know, Mrs. Miyamoto, the United States is at war with Japan. Your son, Koji, is half Japanese. Therefore, he will be placed in an assembly center. It's for his own good, really.
For his own good?! Are you nuts? He's only 13 years old.
Listen, buster, you are not going to send my son to a prison camp all by himself! Got it?

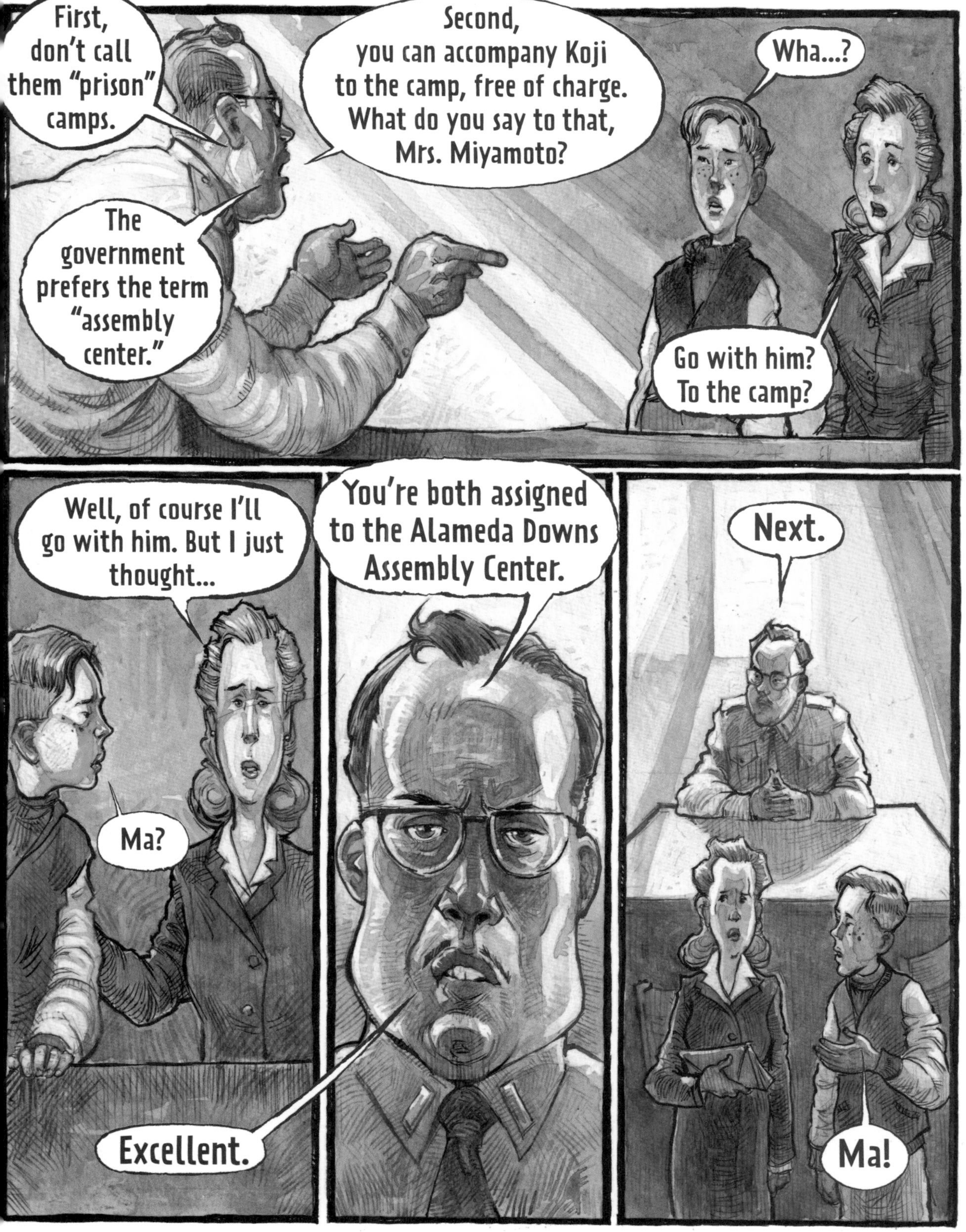
First, don't call them "prison" camps.
The government prefers the term "assembly center."
Second, you can accompany Koji to the camp, free of charge. What do you say to that, Mrs. Miyamoto?
Wha...?
Go with him? To the camp?
Well, of course I'll go with him. But I just thought...
Ma?
You're both assigned to the Alameda Downs Assembly Center.
Excellent.
Next.
Ma!

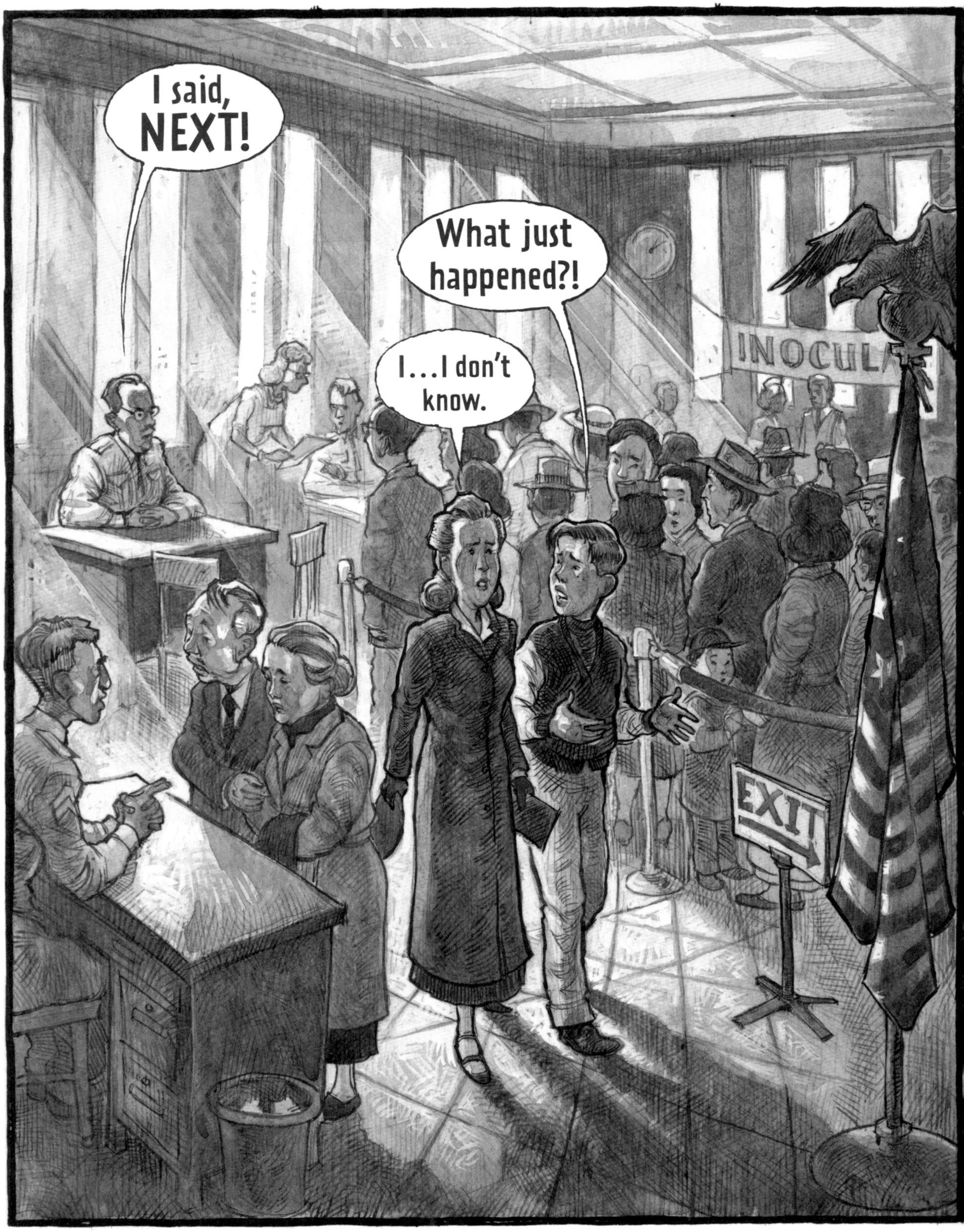
I said, NEXT!
What just happened?!
I...I don't know.
INOCULA
EXIT

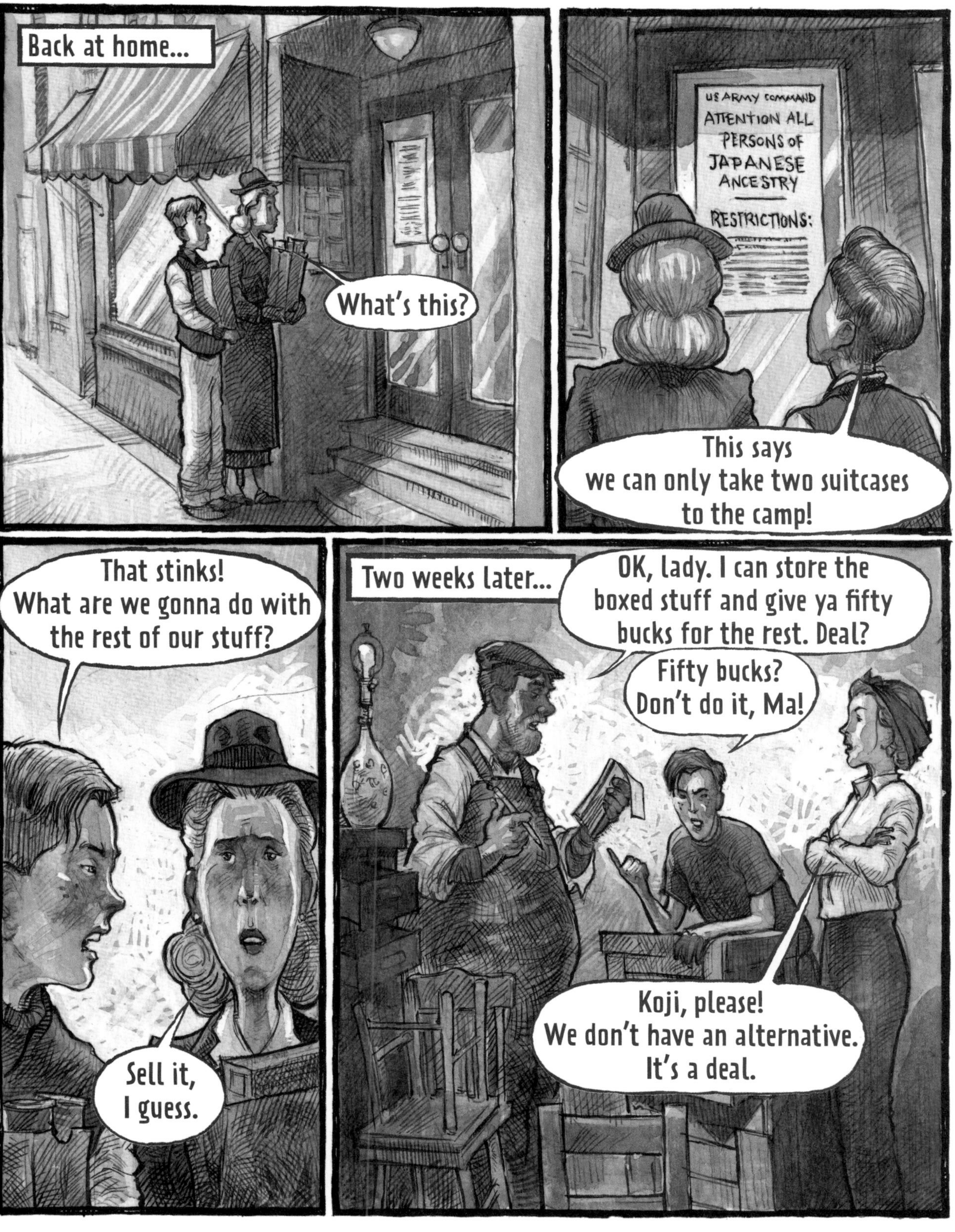

Back at home...
What's this?
US ARMY COMMAND
ATTENTION ALL PERSONS OF JAPANESE ANCESTRY
RESTRICTIONS:
This says we can only take two suitcases to the camp!
That stinks! What are we gonna do with the rest of our stuff?
Sell it, I guess.
Two weeks later...
OK, lady. I can store the boxed stuff and give ya fifty bucks for the rest. Deal?
Fifty bucks? Don't do it, Ma!
Koji, please! We don't have an alternative. It's a deal.

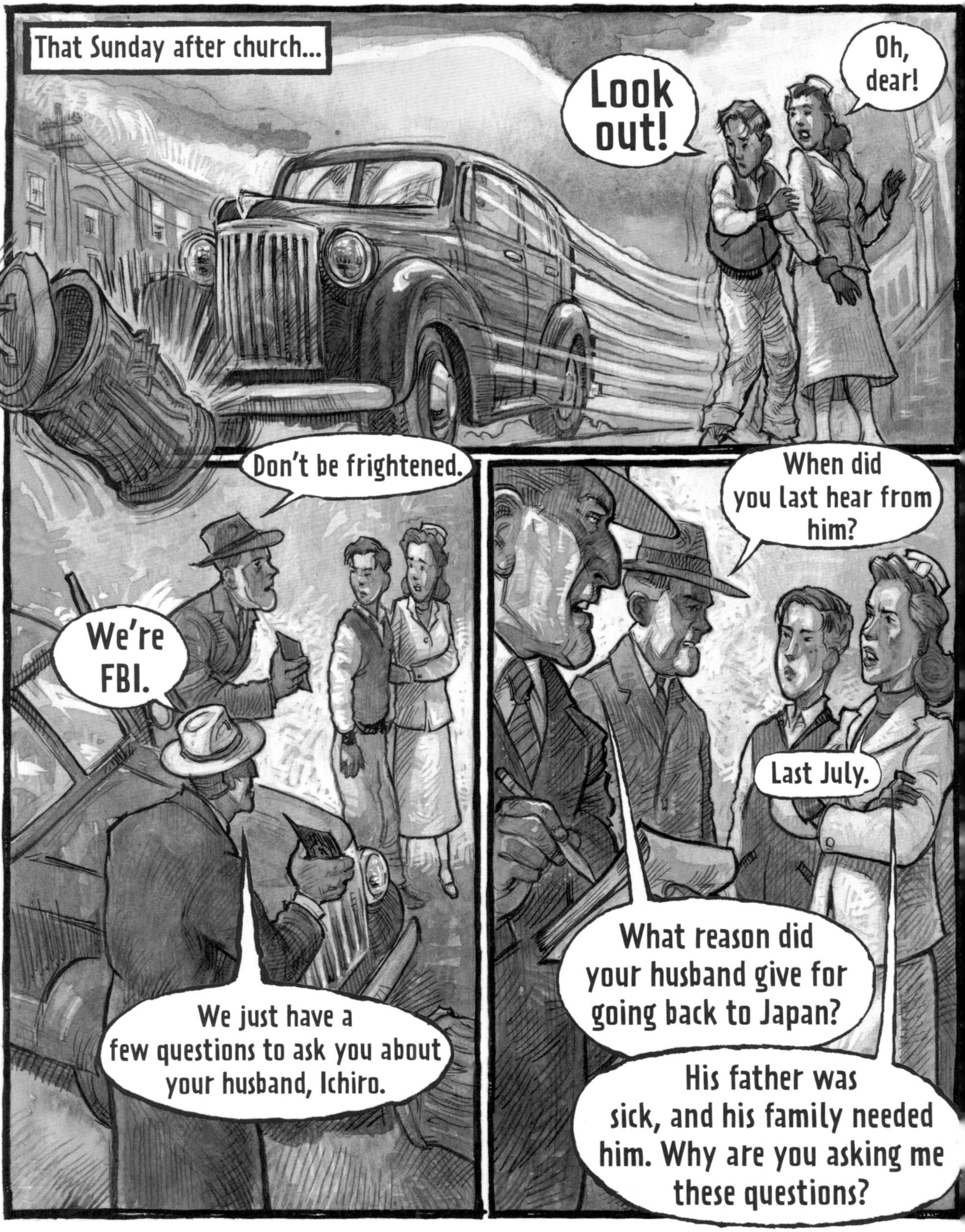
That Sunday after church...
Look out!
Oh, dear!
Don't be frightened.
We're FBI.
We just have a few questions to ask you about your husband, Ichiro.
When did you last hear from him?
Last July.
What reason did your husband give for going back to Japan?
His father was sick, and his family needed him. Why are you asking me these questions?

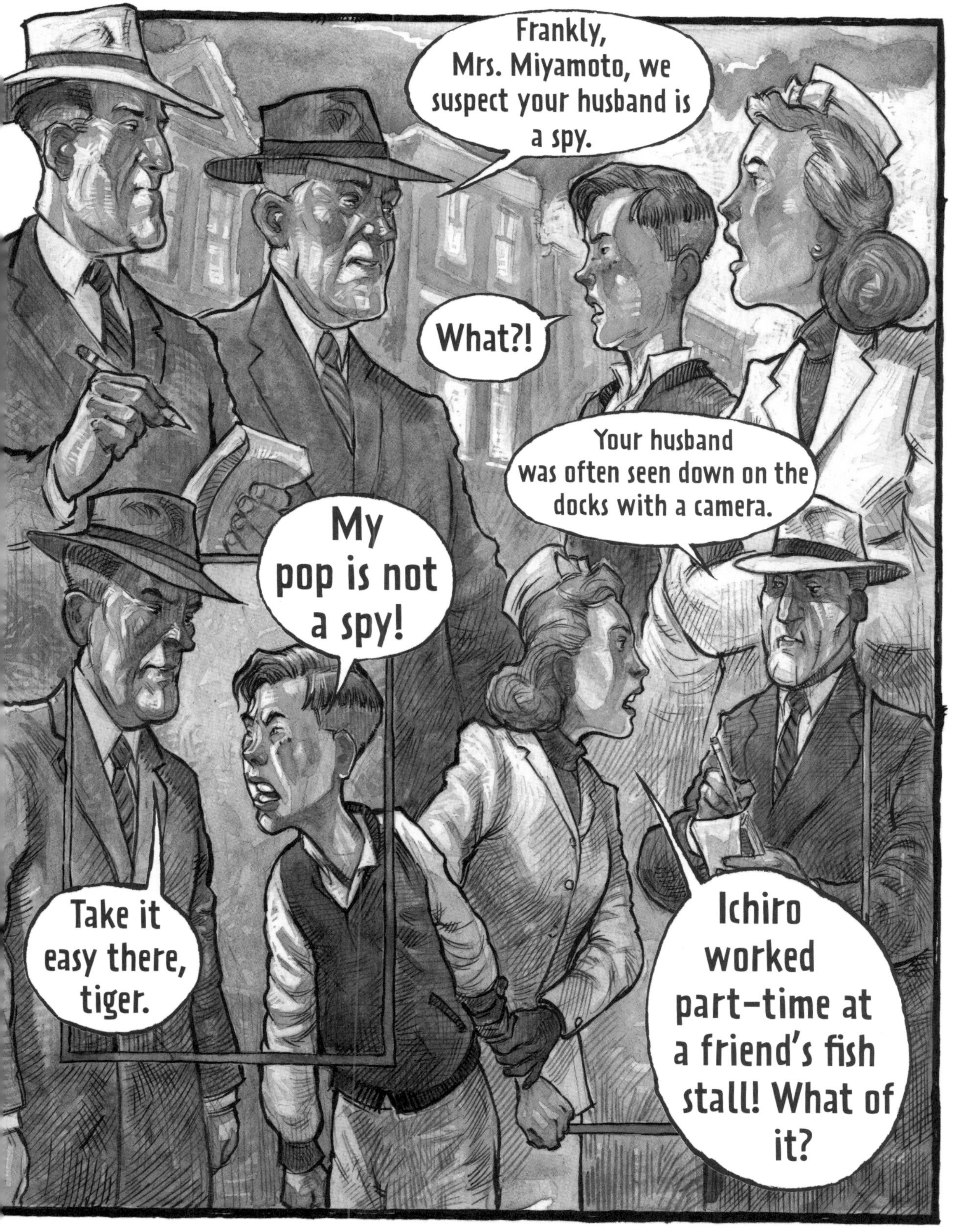
Frankly, Mrs. Miyamoto, we suspect your husband is a spy.
What?!
Your husband was often seen down on the docks with a camera.
My pop is not a spy!
Take it easy there, tiger.
Ichiro worked part-time at a friend's fish stall! What of it?

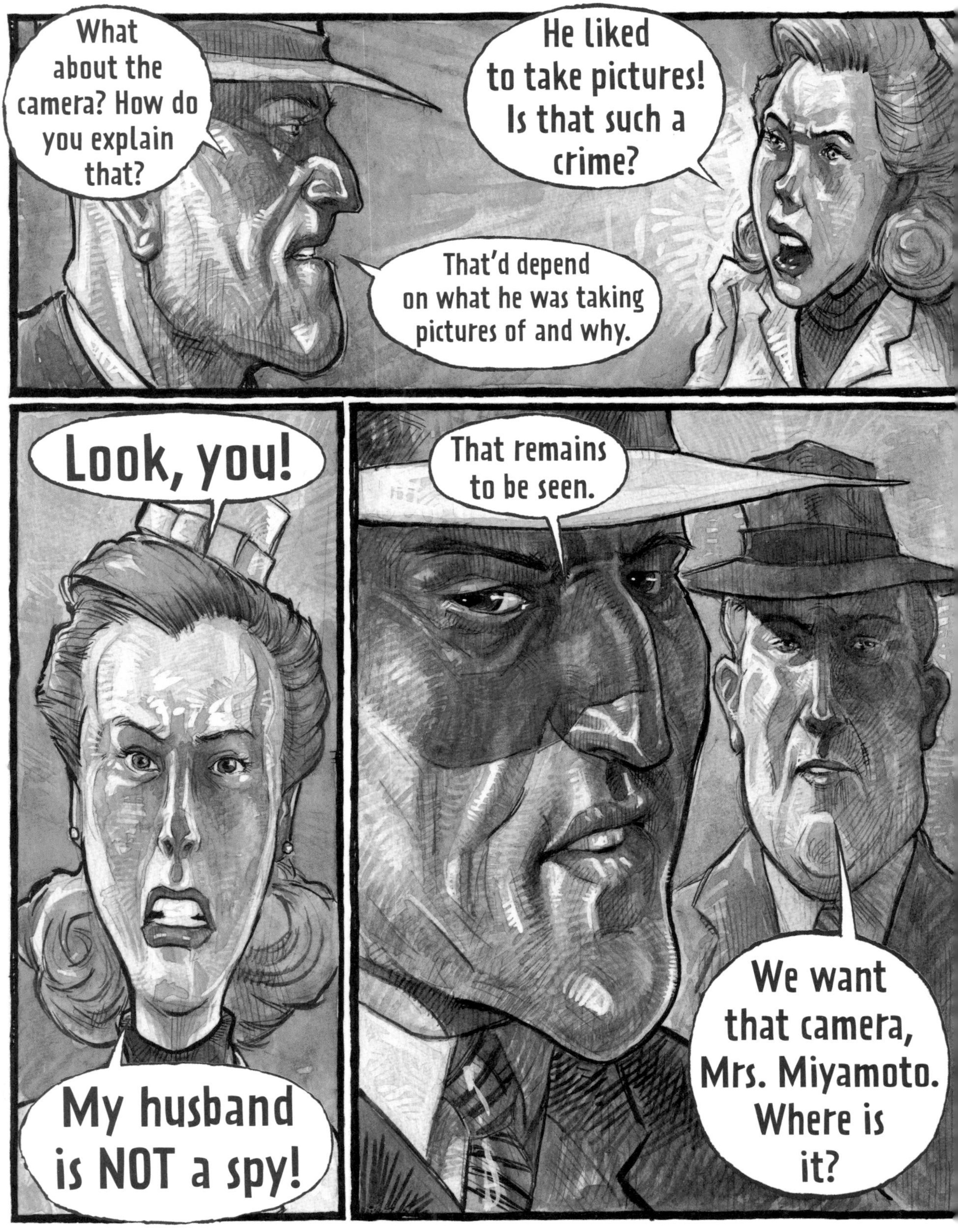

What about the camera? How do you explain that?
He liked to take pictures! Is that such a crime?
That'd depend on what he was taking pictures of and why.
Look, you!
My husband is NOT a spy!
That remains to be seen.
We want that camera, Mrs. Miyamoto. Where is it?

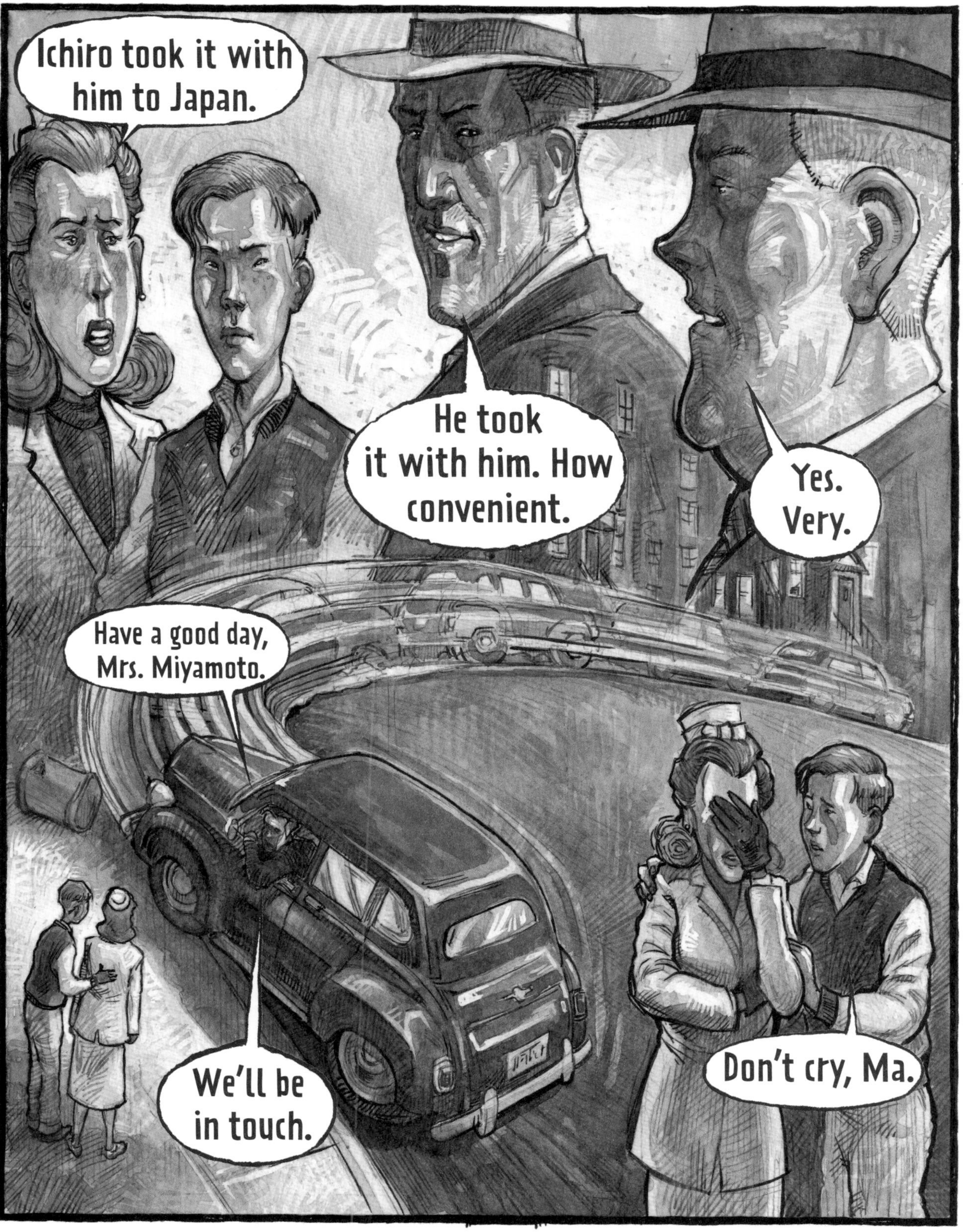
Ichiro took it with him to Japan.
He took it with him. How convenient.
Yes. Very.
Have a good day, Mrs. Miyamoto.
We'll be in touch.
Don't cry, Ma.

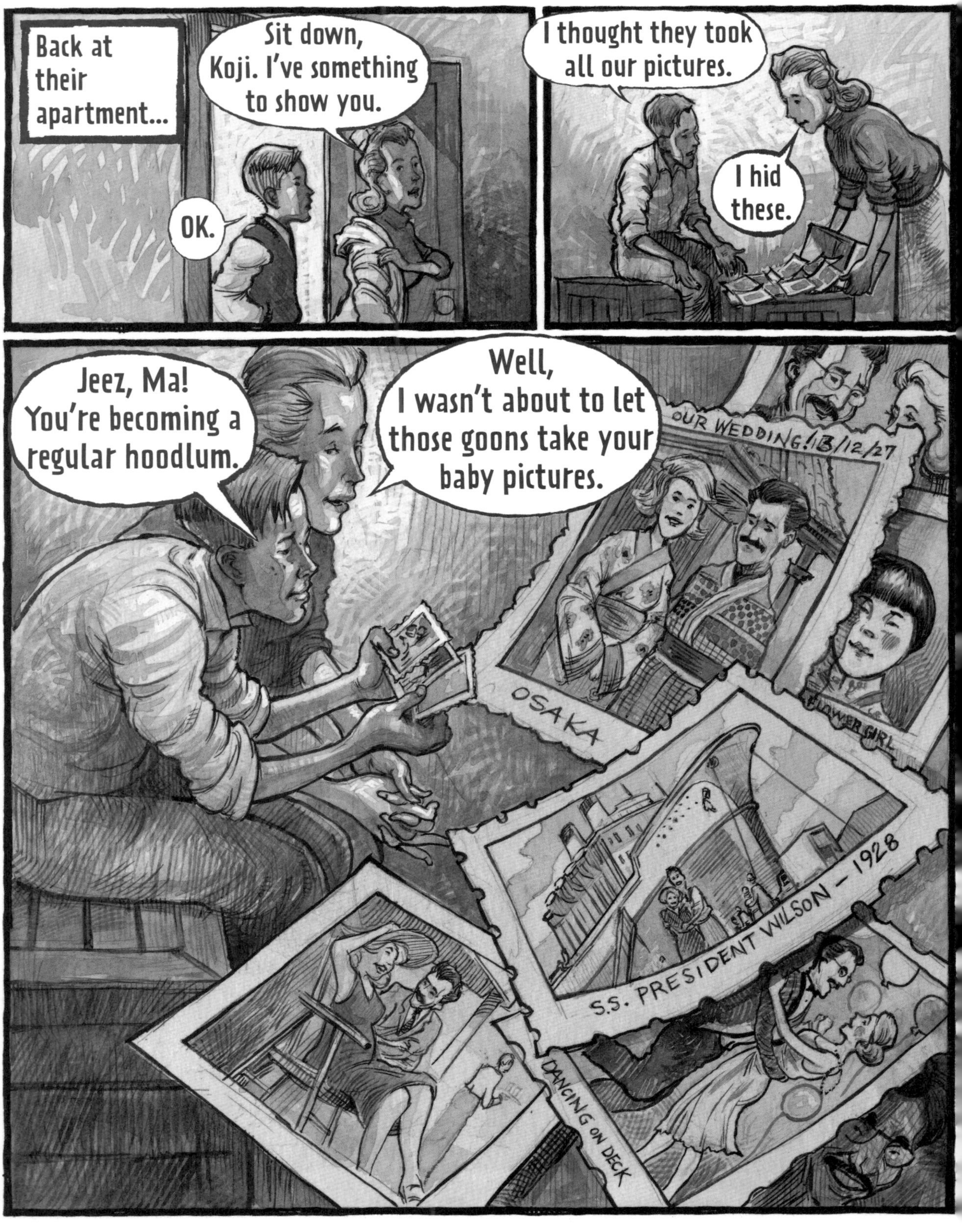
Back at their apartment...
Sit down, Koji. I've something to show you.
OK.
I thought they took all our pictures.
I hid these.
Jeez, Ma! You're becoming a regular hoodlum.
Well, I wasn't about to let those goons take your baby pictures.
OUR WEDDING! 13/12/27
OSAKA
FLOWER GIRL
S.S. PRESIDENT WILSON – 1928
DANCING ON DECK

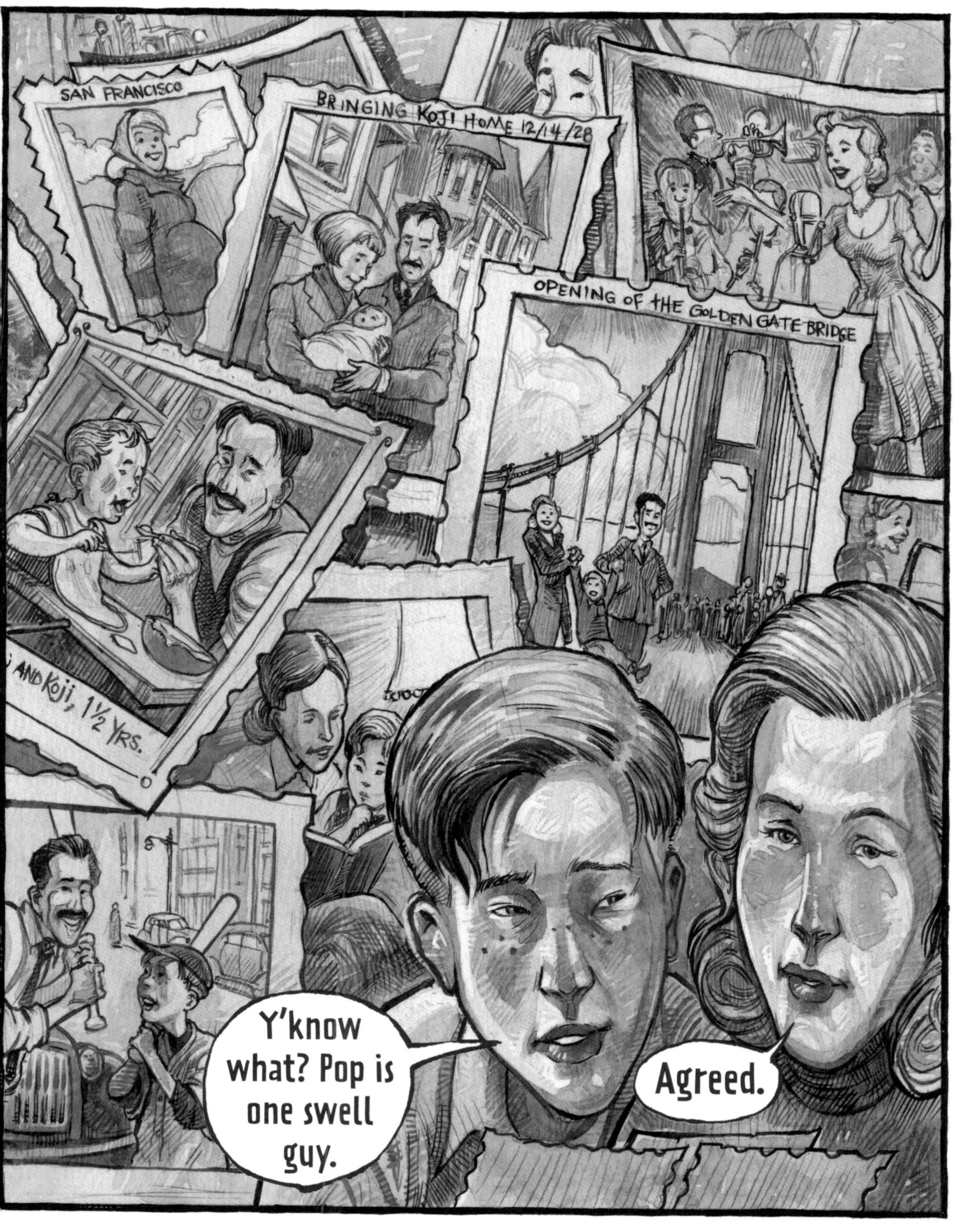
SAN FRANCISCO
BRINGING KOJI HOME 12/14/28
OPENING OF THE GOLDEN GATE BRIDGE
AND Koji, 1½ YRS.
Y'know what? Pop is one swell guy.
Agreed.

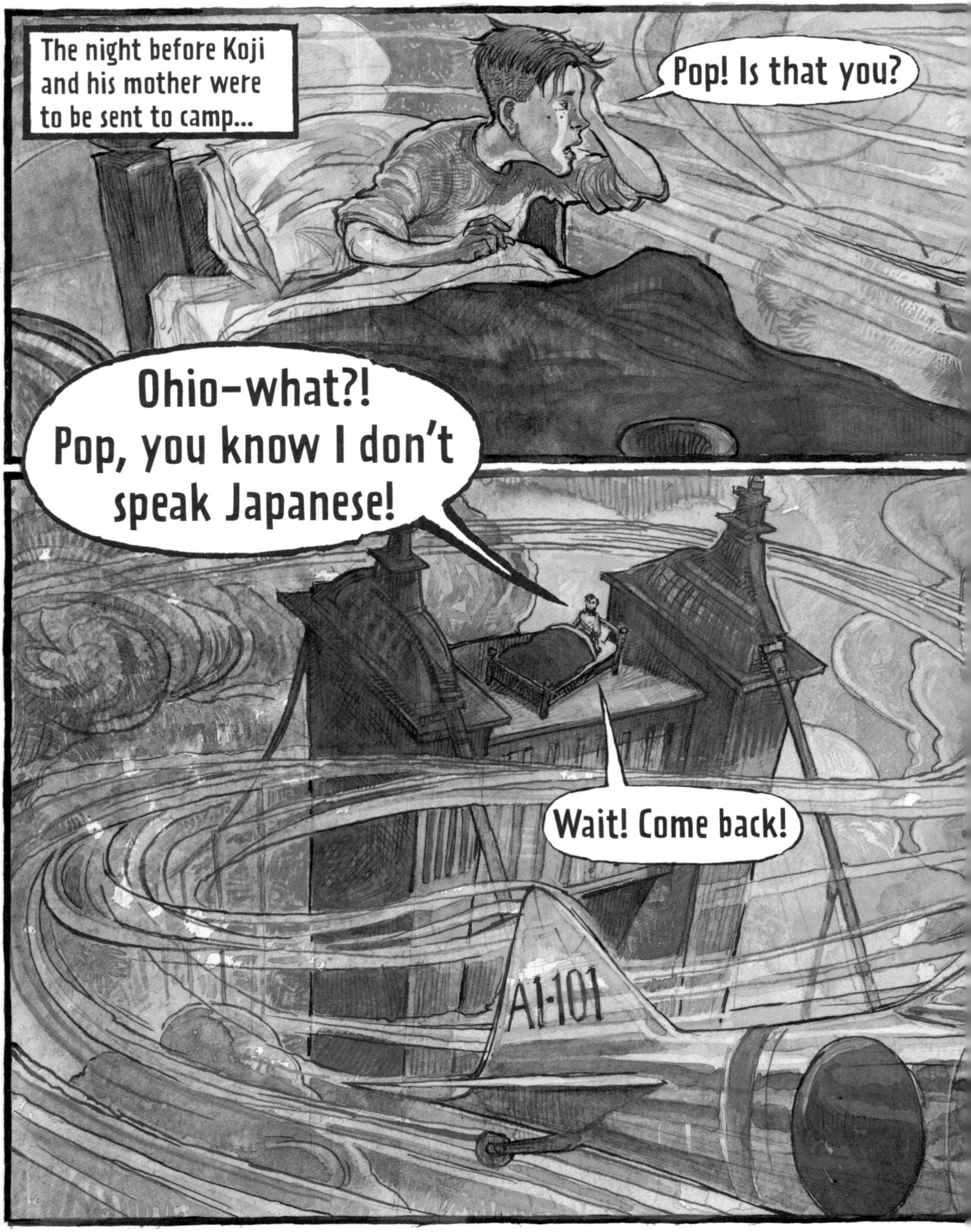
The night before Koji and his mother were to be sent to camp...
Pop! Is that you?
Ohio-what?! Pop, you know I don't speak Japanese!
Wait! Come back!
AI-101

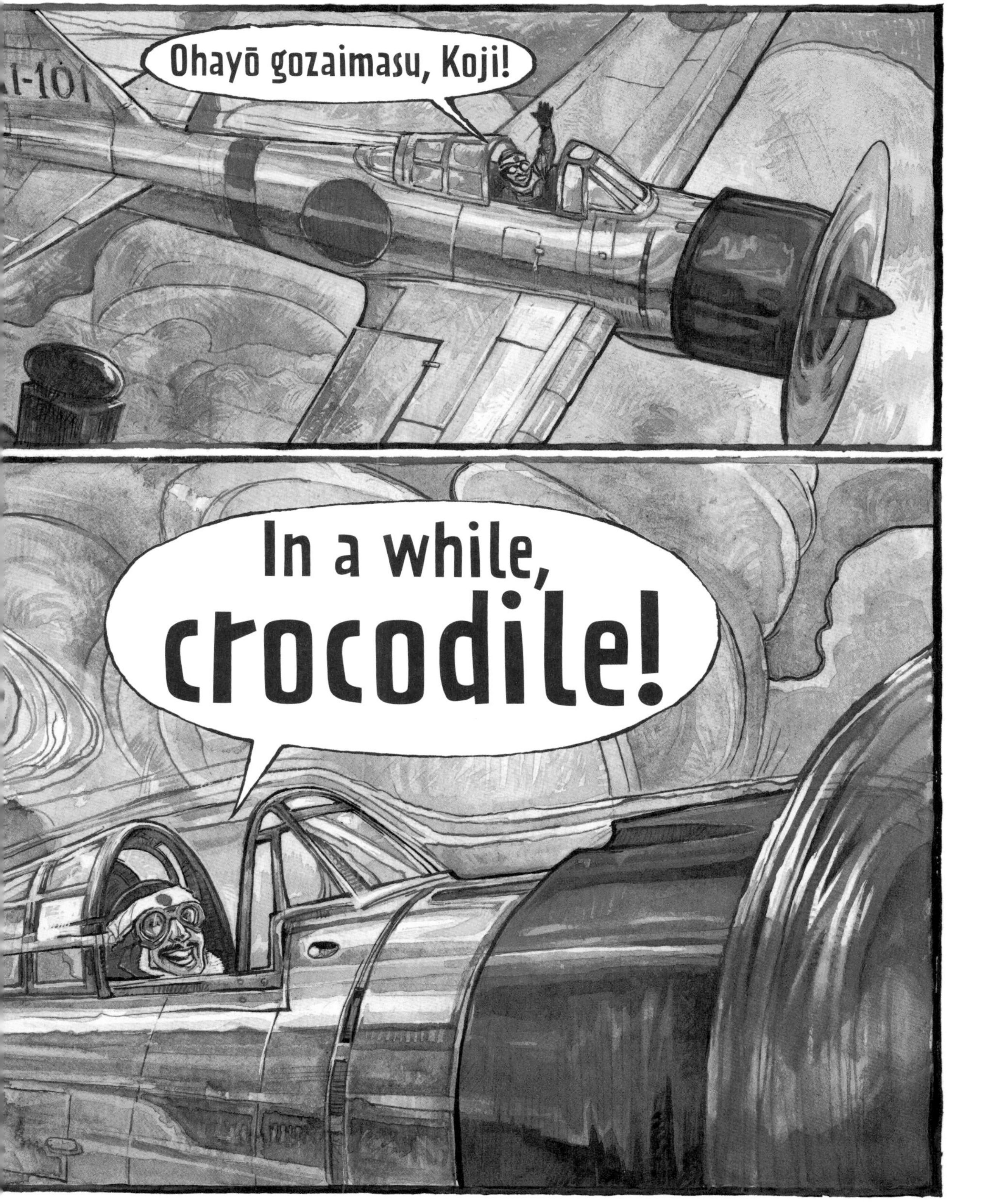
Ohayō gozaimasu, Koji!
In a while, crocodile!

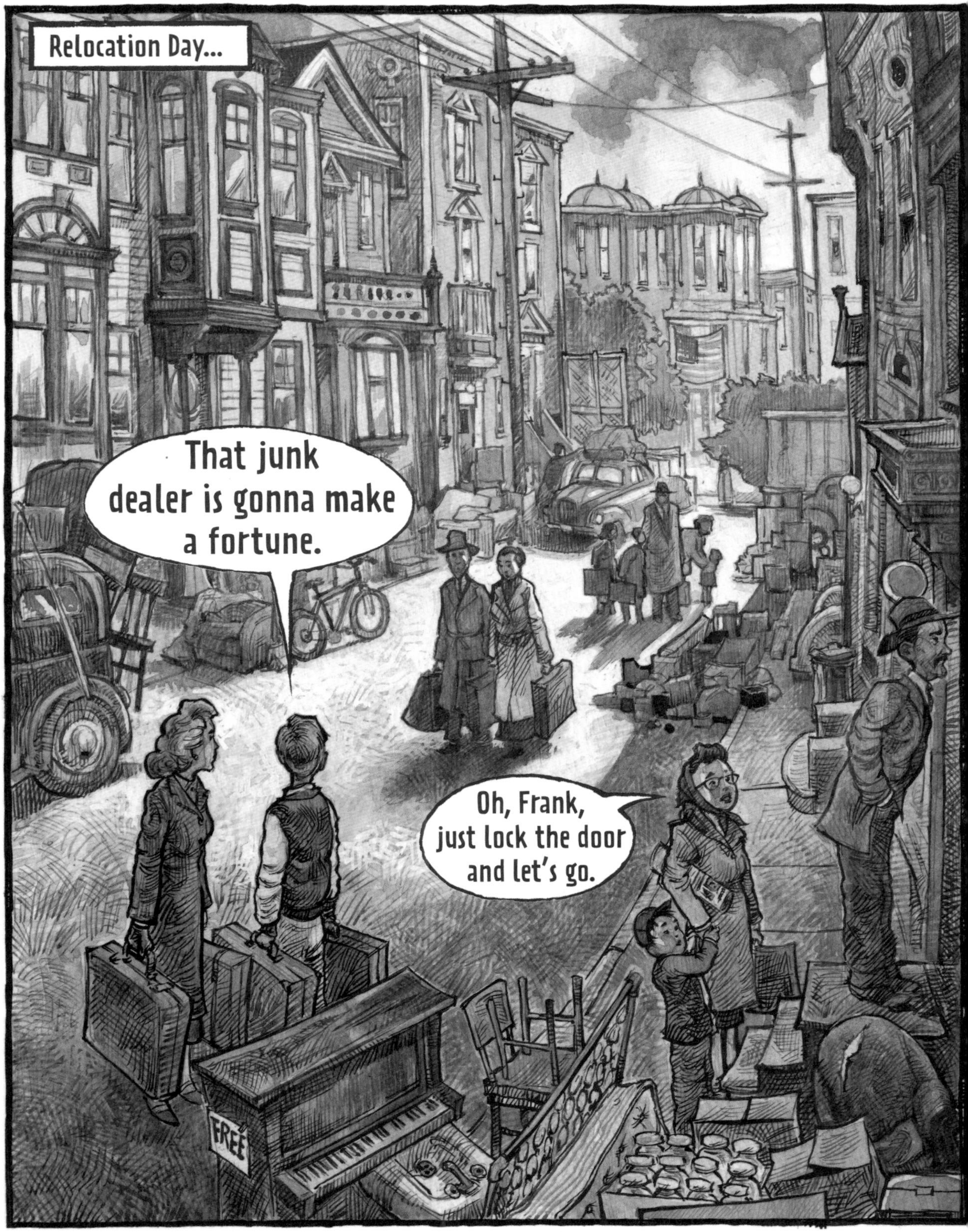
Relocation Day...
That junk dealer is gonna make a fortune.
Oh, Frank, just lock the door and let's go.
FREE

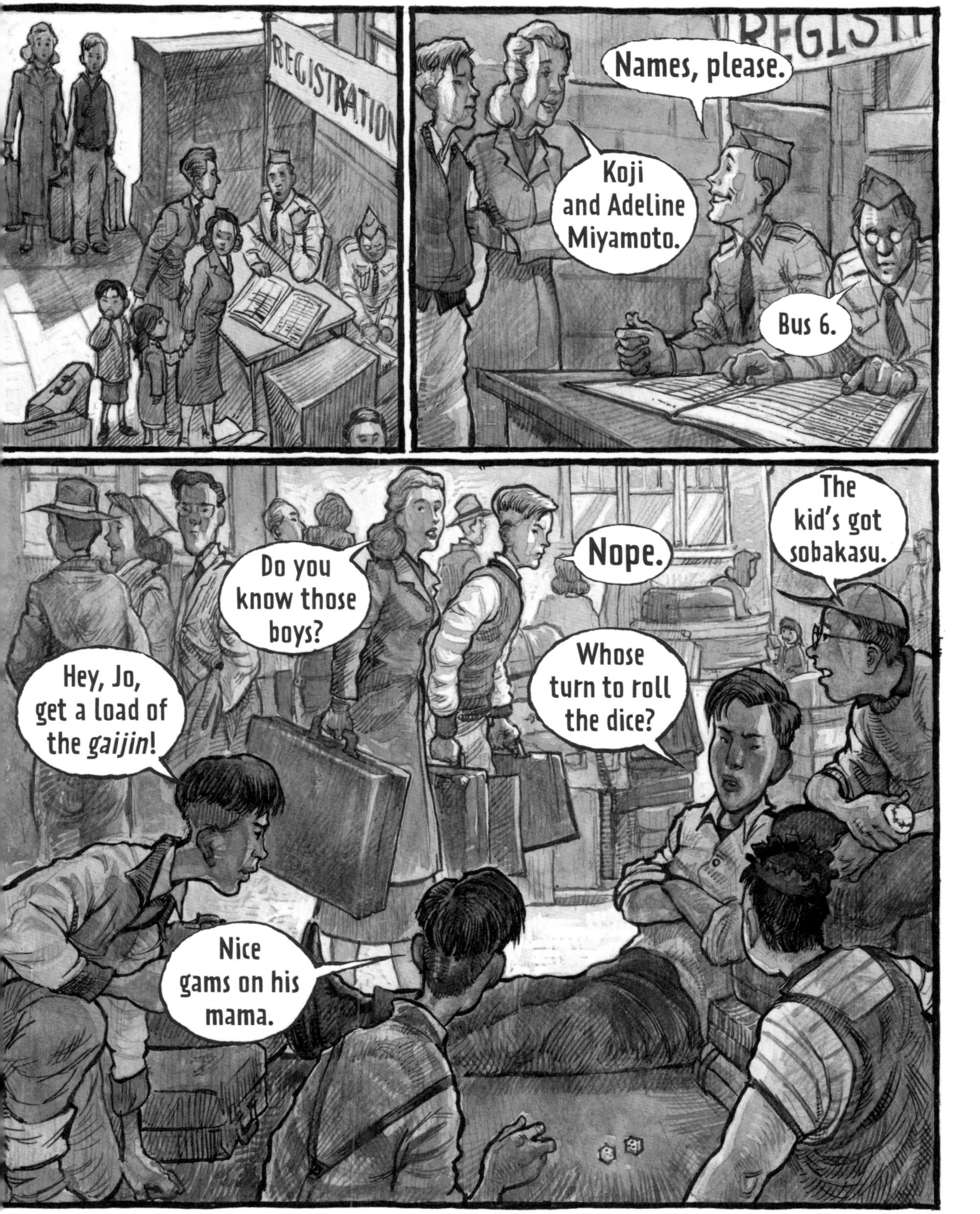
REGISTRATION
REGIST
Names, please.
Koji and Adeline Miyamoto.
Bus 6.
Do you know those boys?
Nope.
The kid's got sobakasu.
Whose turn to roll the dice?
Hey, Jo, get a load of the *gaijin*!
Nice gams on his mama.

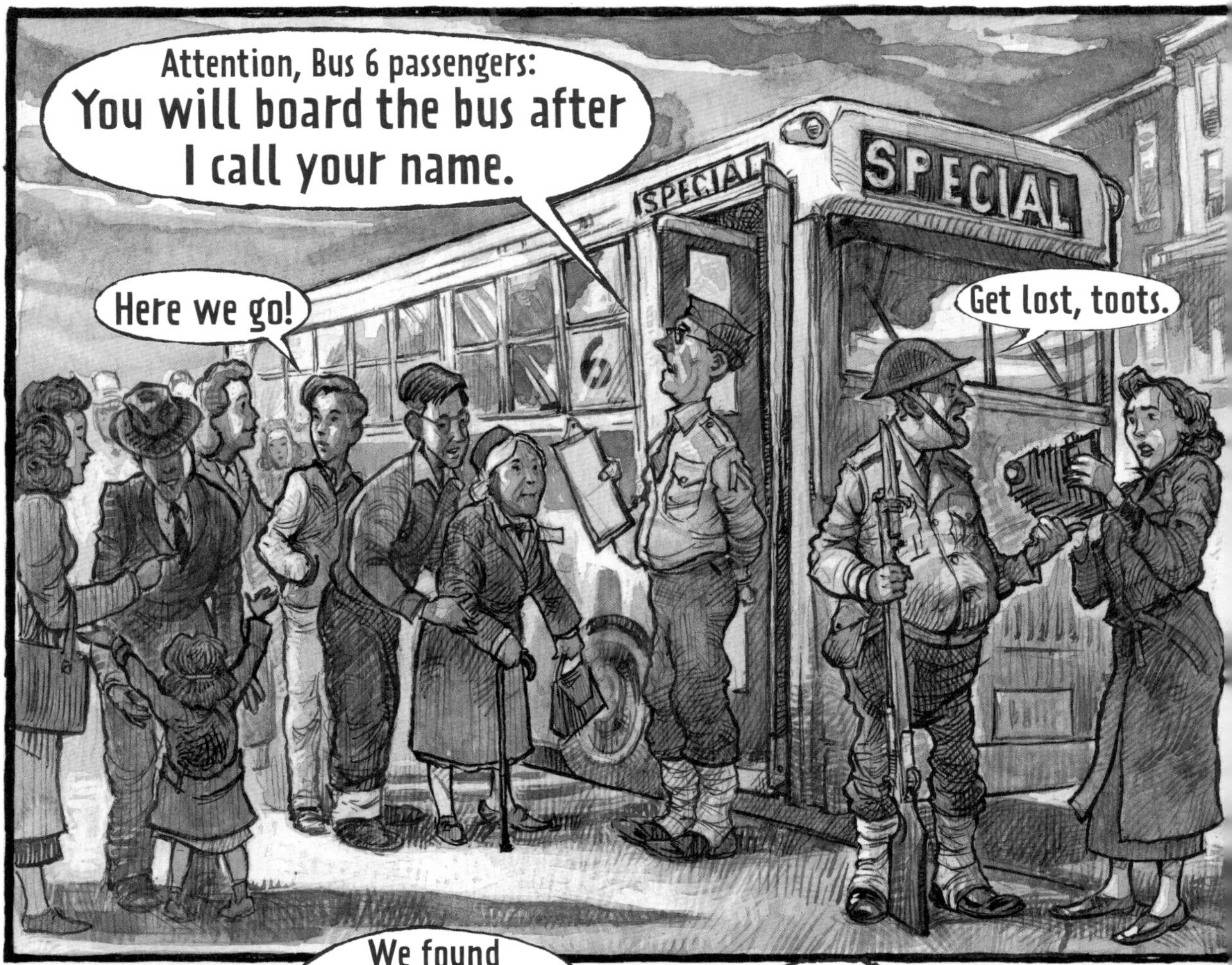
Attention, Bus 6 passengers: You will board the bus after I call your name.
SPECIAL
SPECIAL
Here we go!
Get lost, toots.

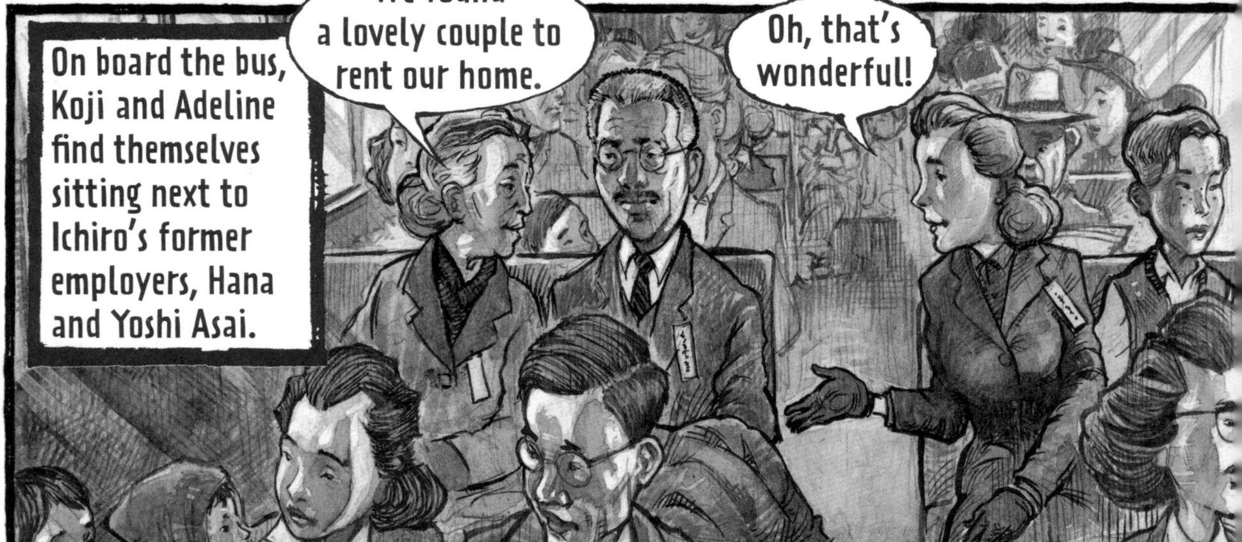
On board the bus, Koji and Adeline find themselves sitting next to Ichiro's former employers, Hana and Yoshi Asai.
We found a lovely couple to rent our home.
Oh, that's wonderful!

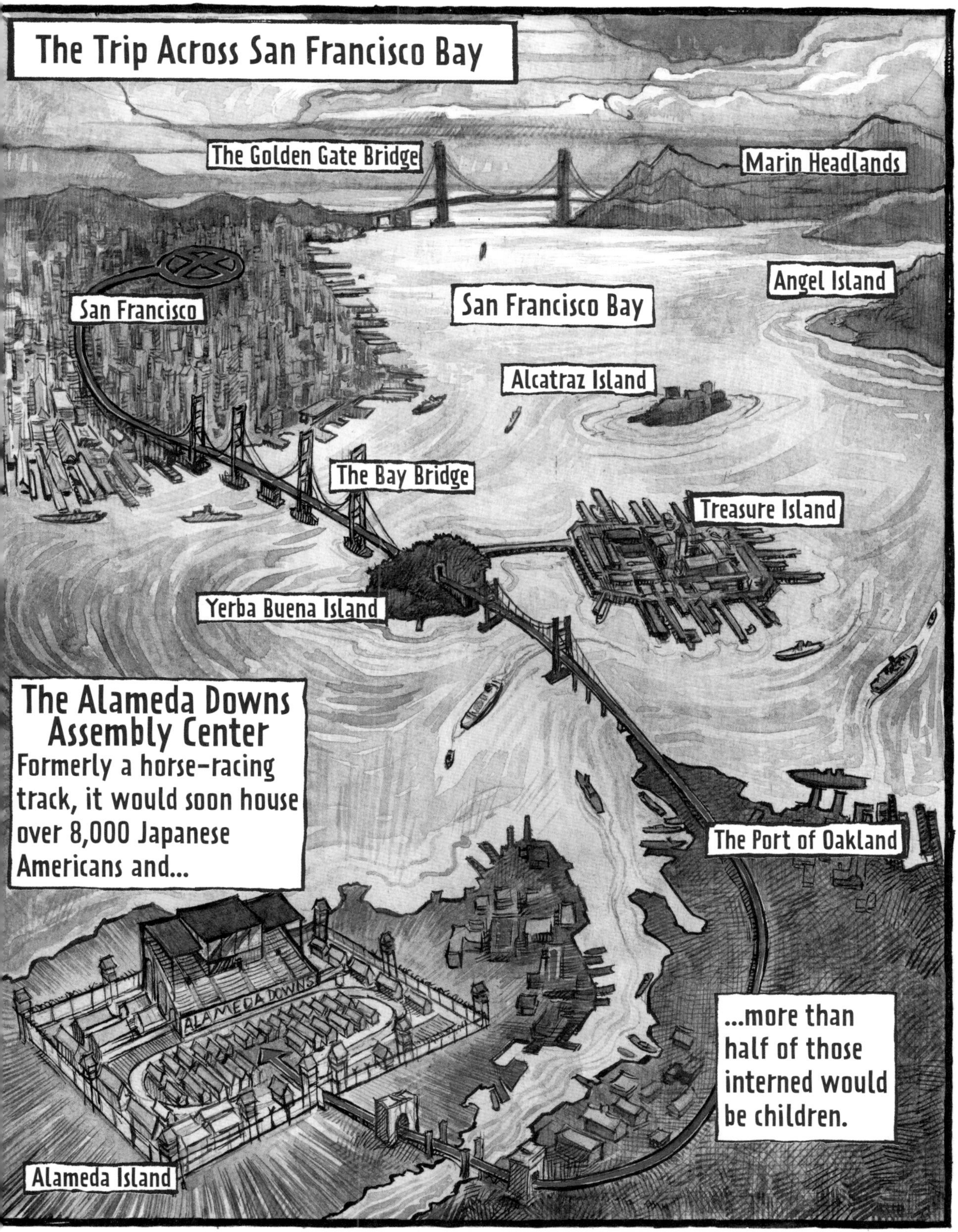
The Trip Across San Francisco Bay
The Golden Gate Bridge
Marin Headlands
Angel Island
San Francisco
San Francisco Bay
Alcatraz Island
The Bay Bridge
Treasure Island
Yerba Buena Island
The Alameda Downs Assembly Center
Formerly a horse-racing track, it would soon house over 8,000 Japanese Americans and...
The Port of Oakland
ALAMEDA DOWNS
...more than half of those interned would be children.
Alameda Island

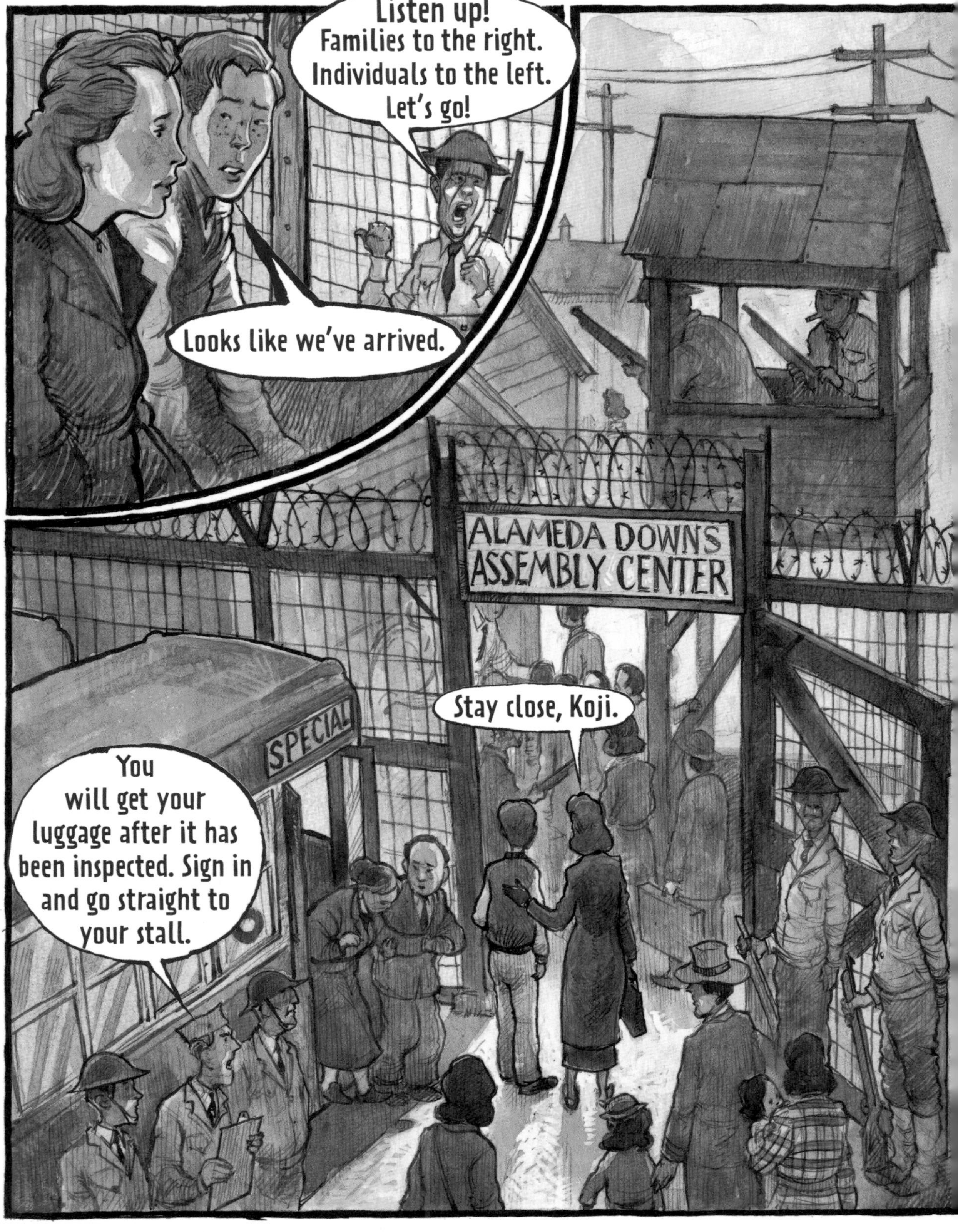
Listen up! Families to the right. Individuals to the left. Let's go!
Looks like we've arrived.
ALAMEDA DOWNS ASSEMBLY CENTER
SPECIAL
Stay close, Koji.
You will get your luggage after it has been inspected. Sign in and go straight to your stall.

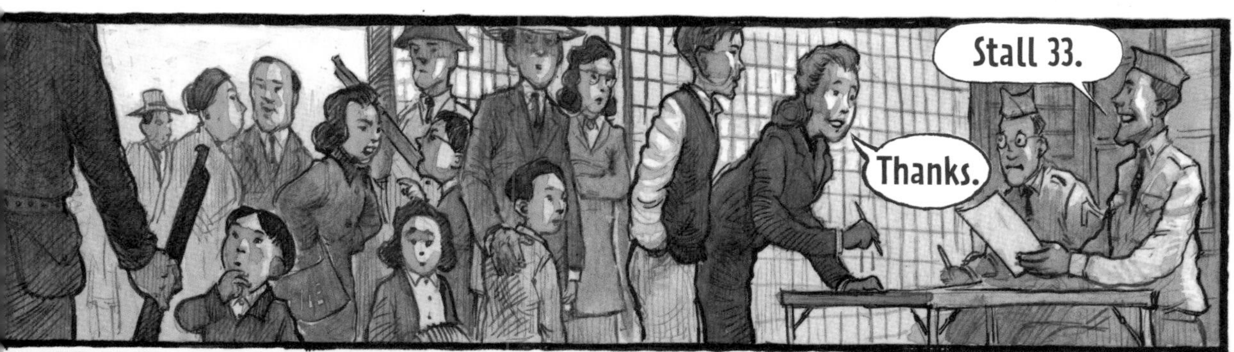
Stall 33.
Thanks.

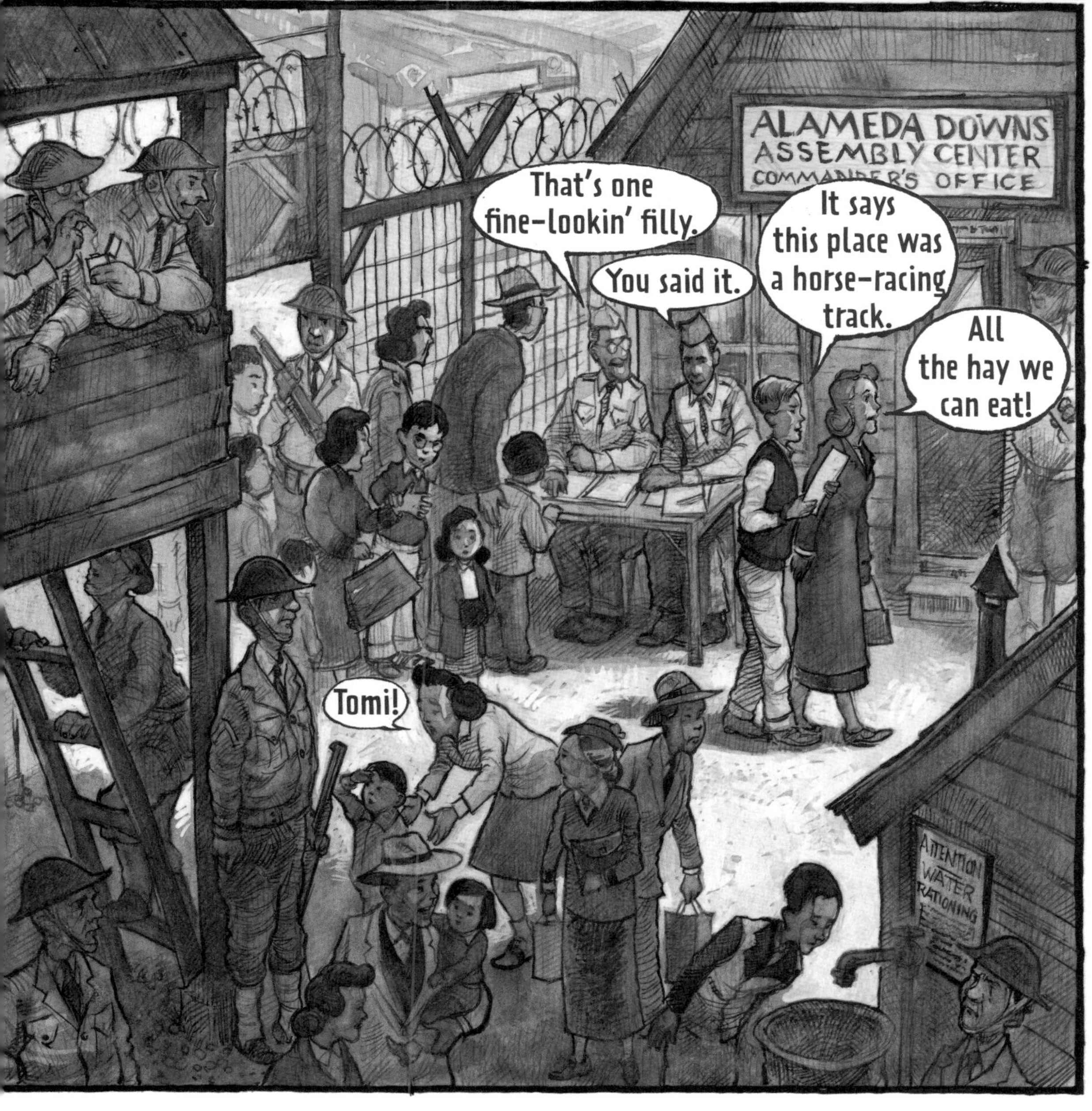
ALAMEDA DOWNS
ASSEMBLY CENTER
COMMANDER'S OFFICE
That's one fine-lookin' filly.
You said it.
It says this place was a horse-racing track.
All the hay we can eat!
Tomi!
ATTENTION WATER RATIONING

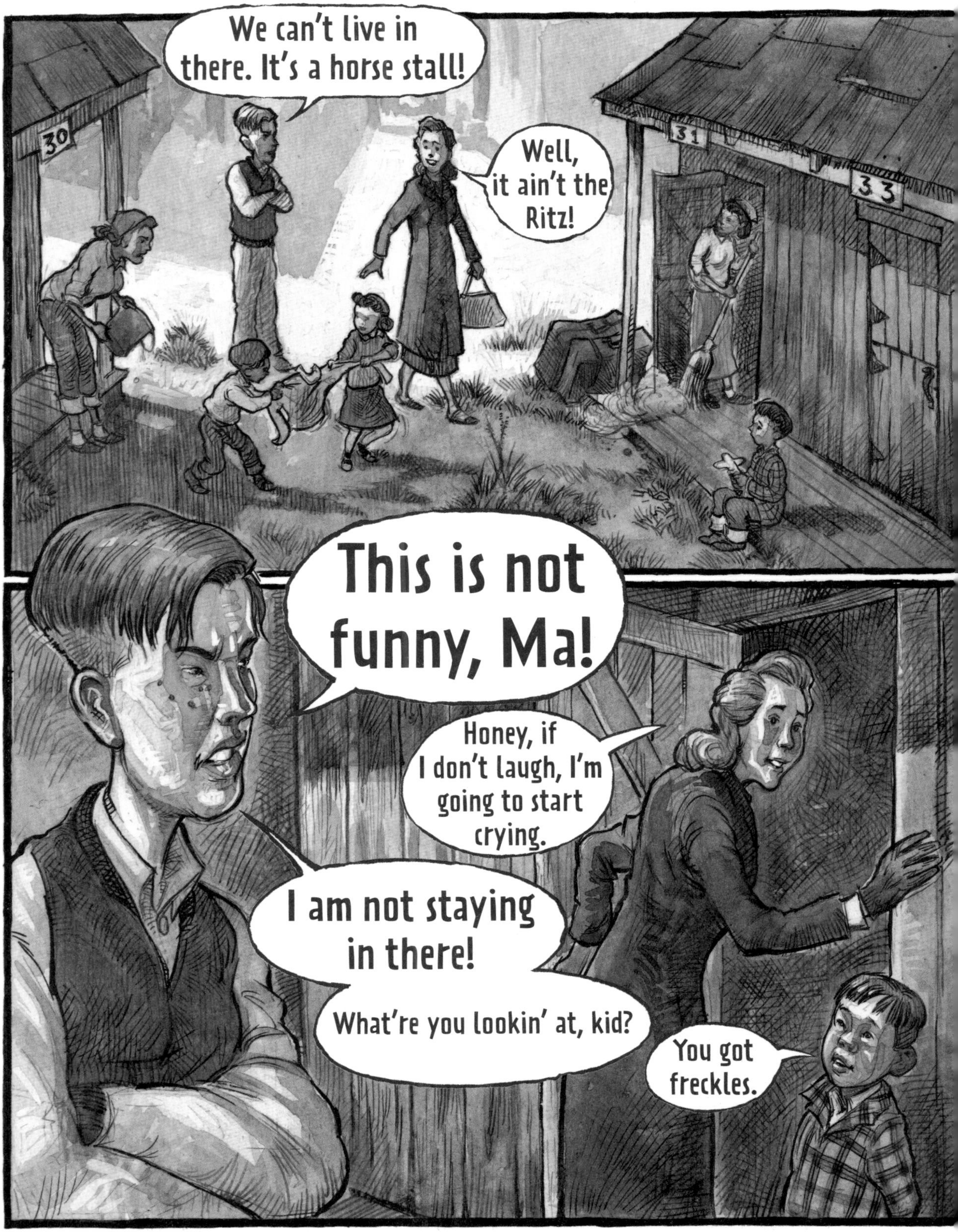
We can't live in there. It's a horse stall!
Well, it ain't the Ritz!
This is not funny, Ma!
Honey, if I don't laugh, I'm going to start crying.
I am not staying in there!
What're you lookin' at, kid?
You got freckles.

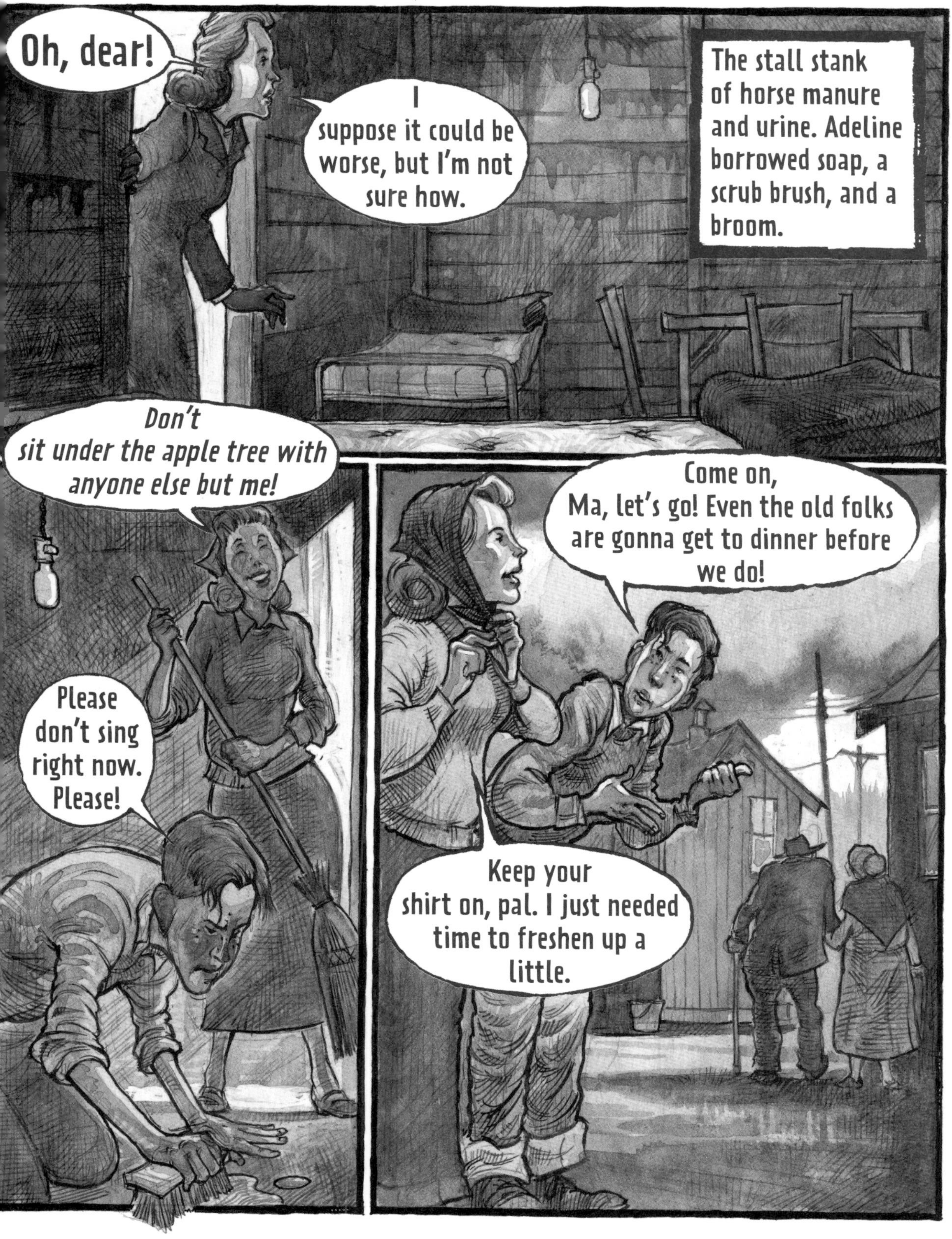
Oh, dear!
I suppose it could be worse, but I'm not sure how.
The stall stank of horse manure and urine. Adeline borrowed soap, a scrub brush, and a broom.
Don't sit under the apple tree with anyone else but me!
Please don't sing right now. Please!
Come on, Ma, let's go! Even the old folks are gonna get to dinner before we do!
Keep your shirt on, pal. I just needed time to freshen up a little.

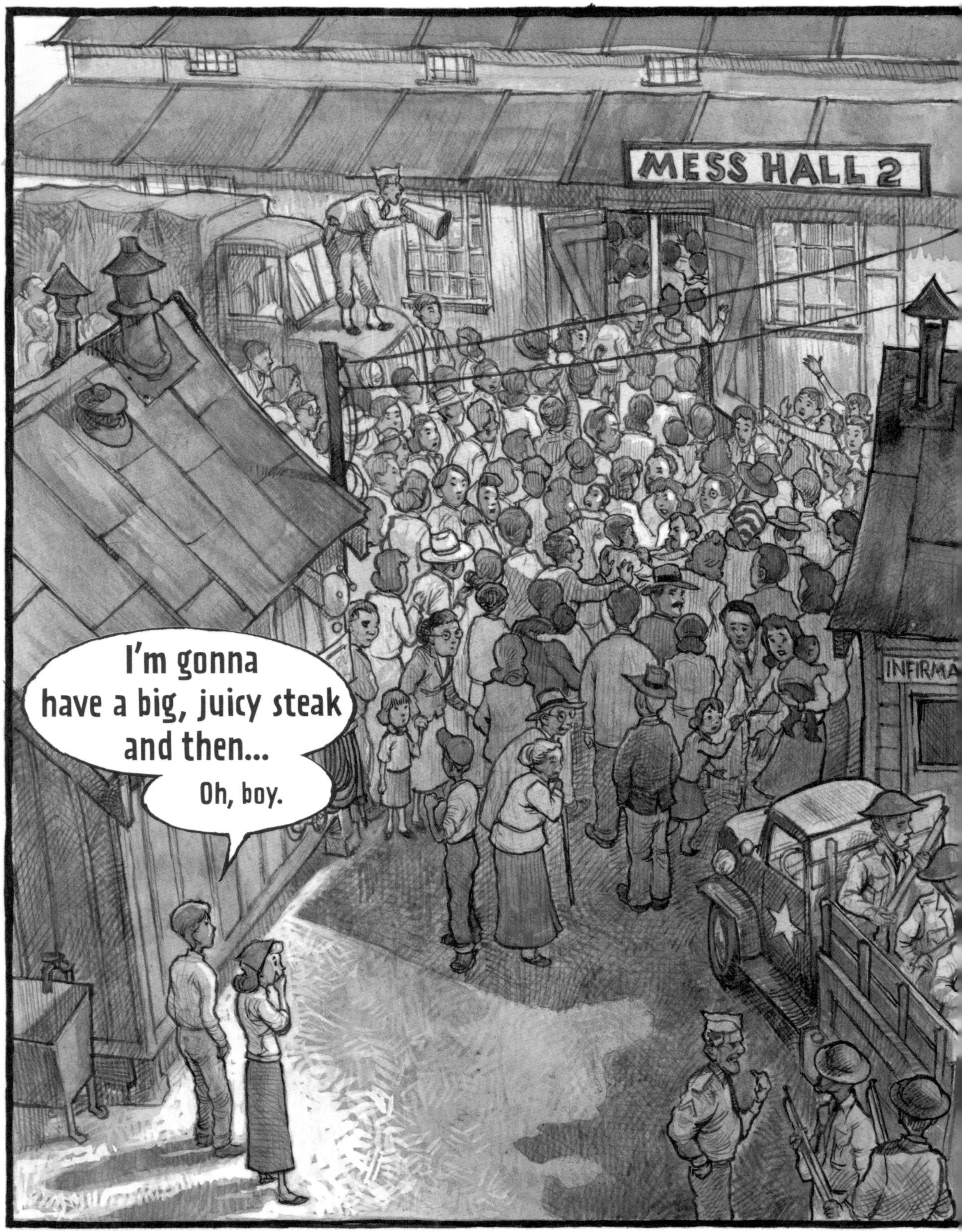
MESS HALL 2
INFIRMA
I'm gonna have a big, juicy steak and then...
Oh, boy.

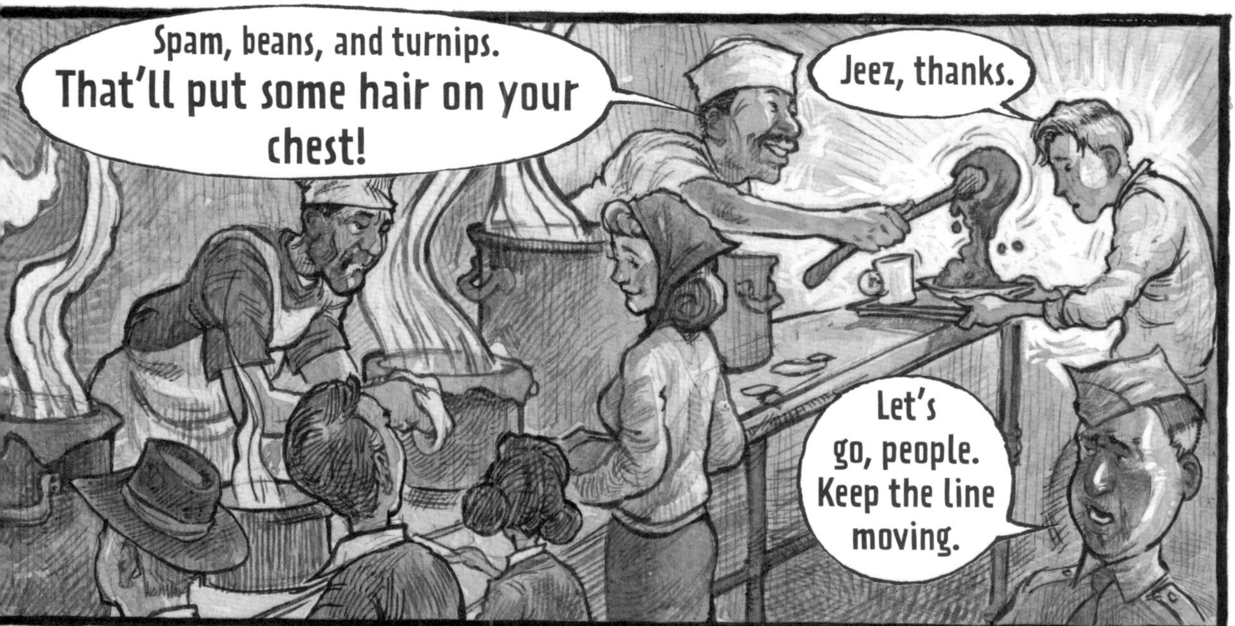
Spam, beans, and turnips. That'll put some hair on your chest!
Jeez, thanks.
Let's go, people. Keep the line moving.

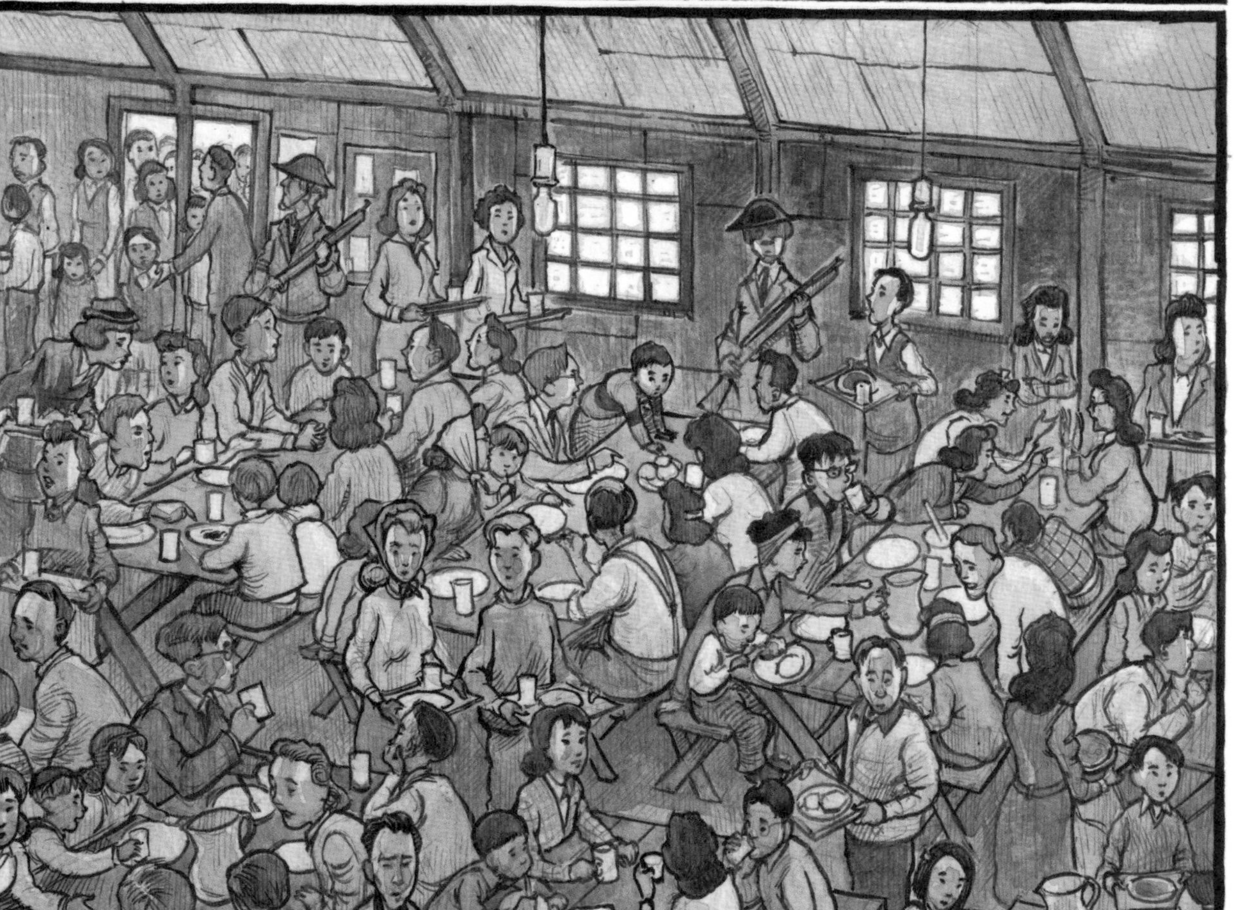

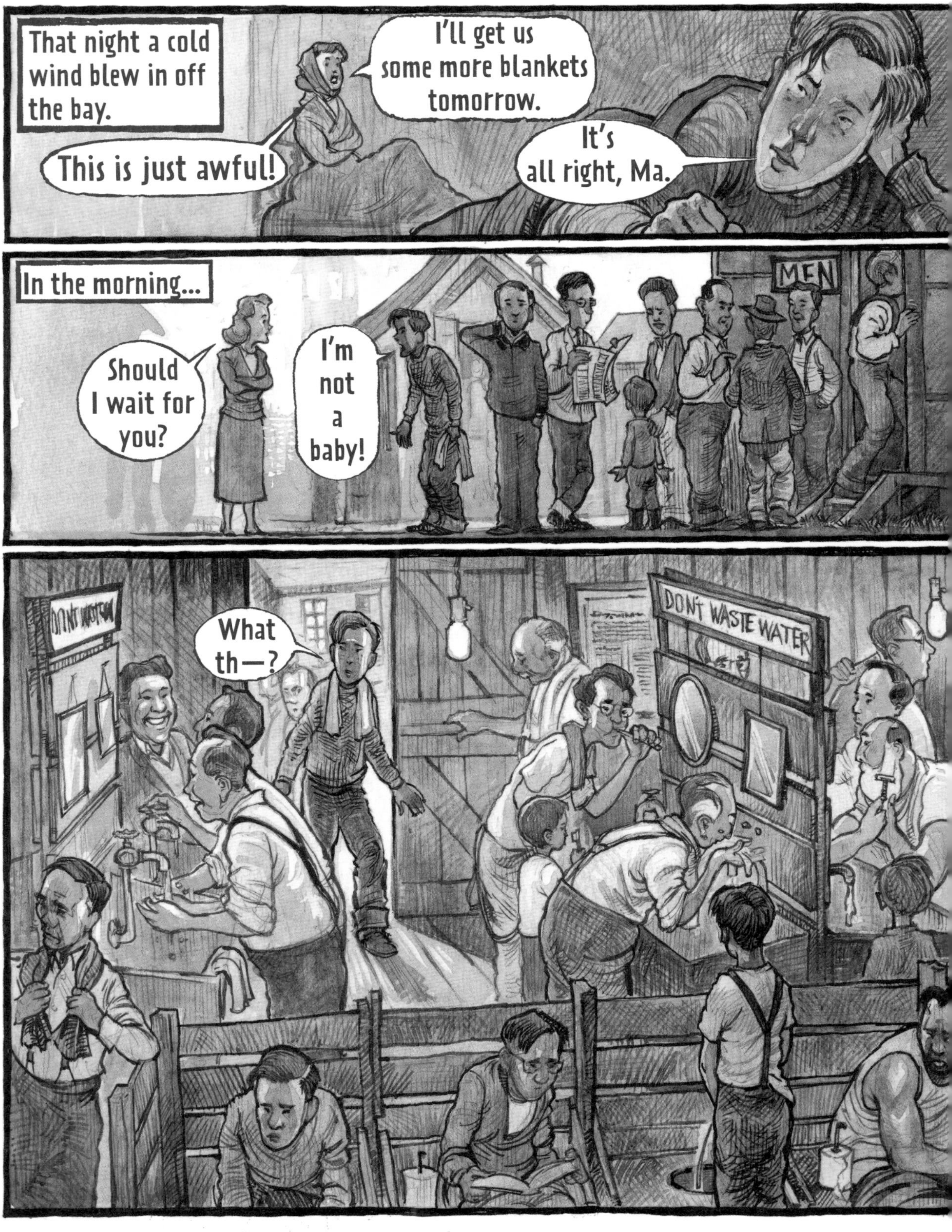
That night a cold wind blew in off the bay.
This is just awful!
I'll get us some more blankets tomorrow.
It's all right, Ma.
In the morning...
MEN
Should I wait for you?
I'm not a baby!
What th—?
DON'T WASTE WATER

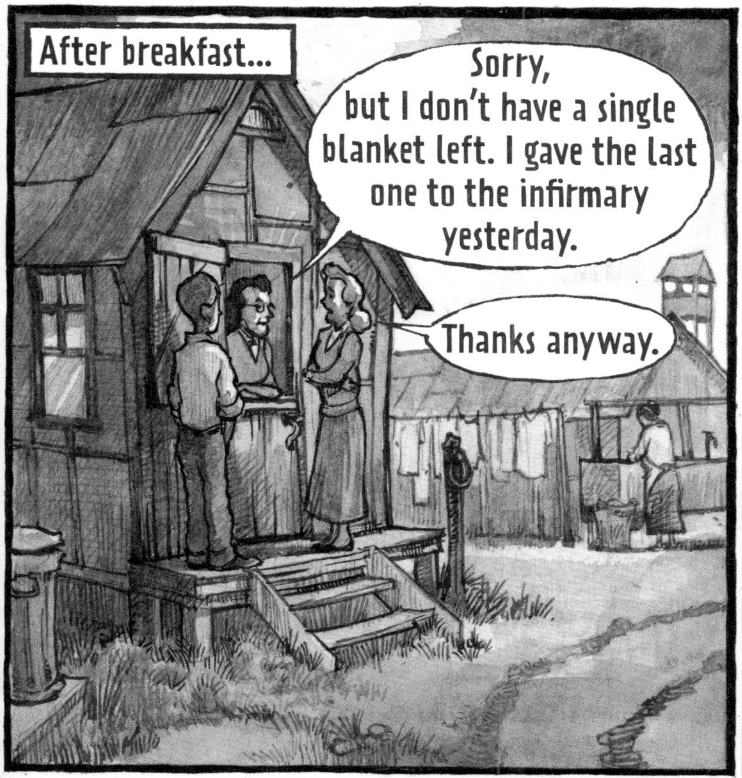
After breakfast...
Sorry, but I don't have a single blanket left. I gave the last one to the infirmary yesterday.
Thanks anyway.

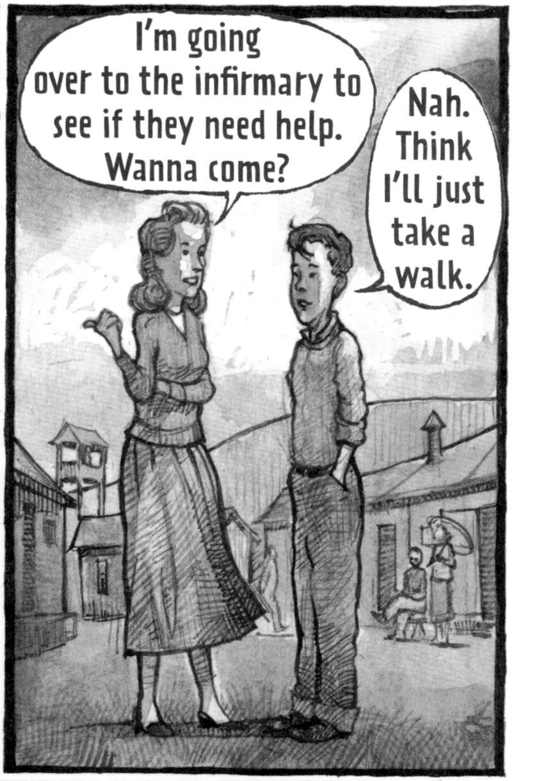
I'm going over to the infirmary to see if they need help. Wanna come?
Nah. Think I'll just take a walk.

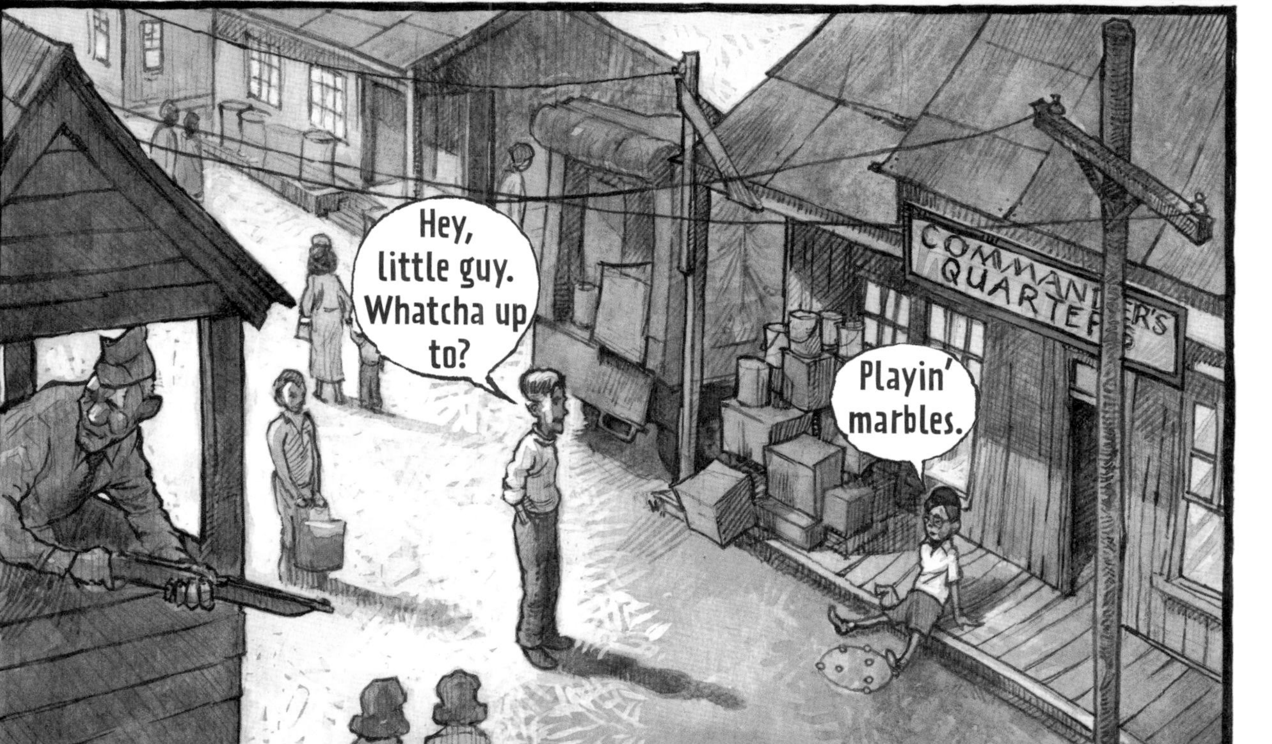
COMMANDER'S QUARTERS
Hey, little guy. Whatcha up to?
Playin' marbles.

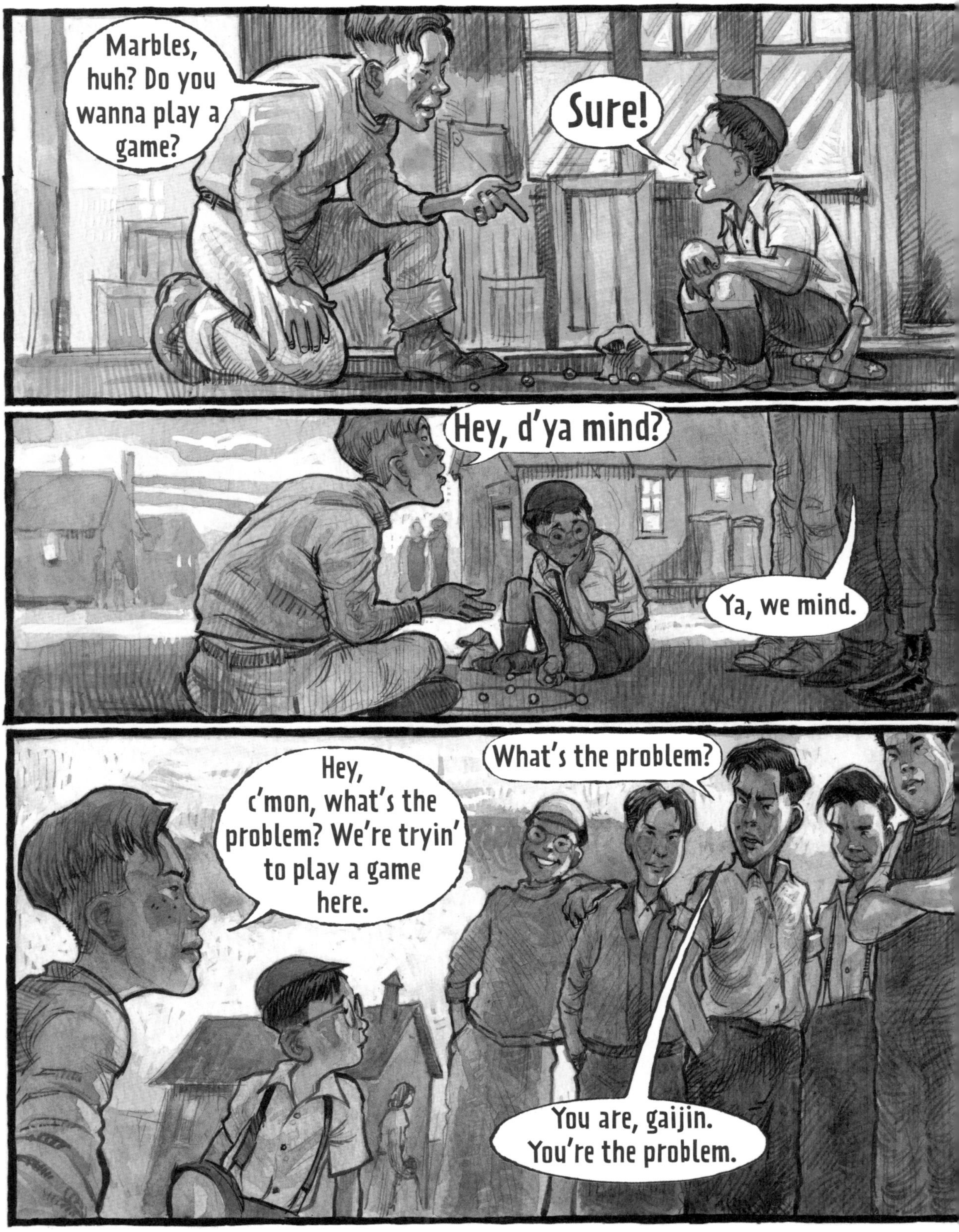
Marbles, huh? Do you wanna play a game?
Sure!
Hey, d'ya mind?
Ya, we mind.
Hey, c'mon, what's the problem? We're tryin' to play a game here.
What's the problem?
You are, gaijin. You're the problem.

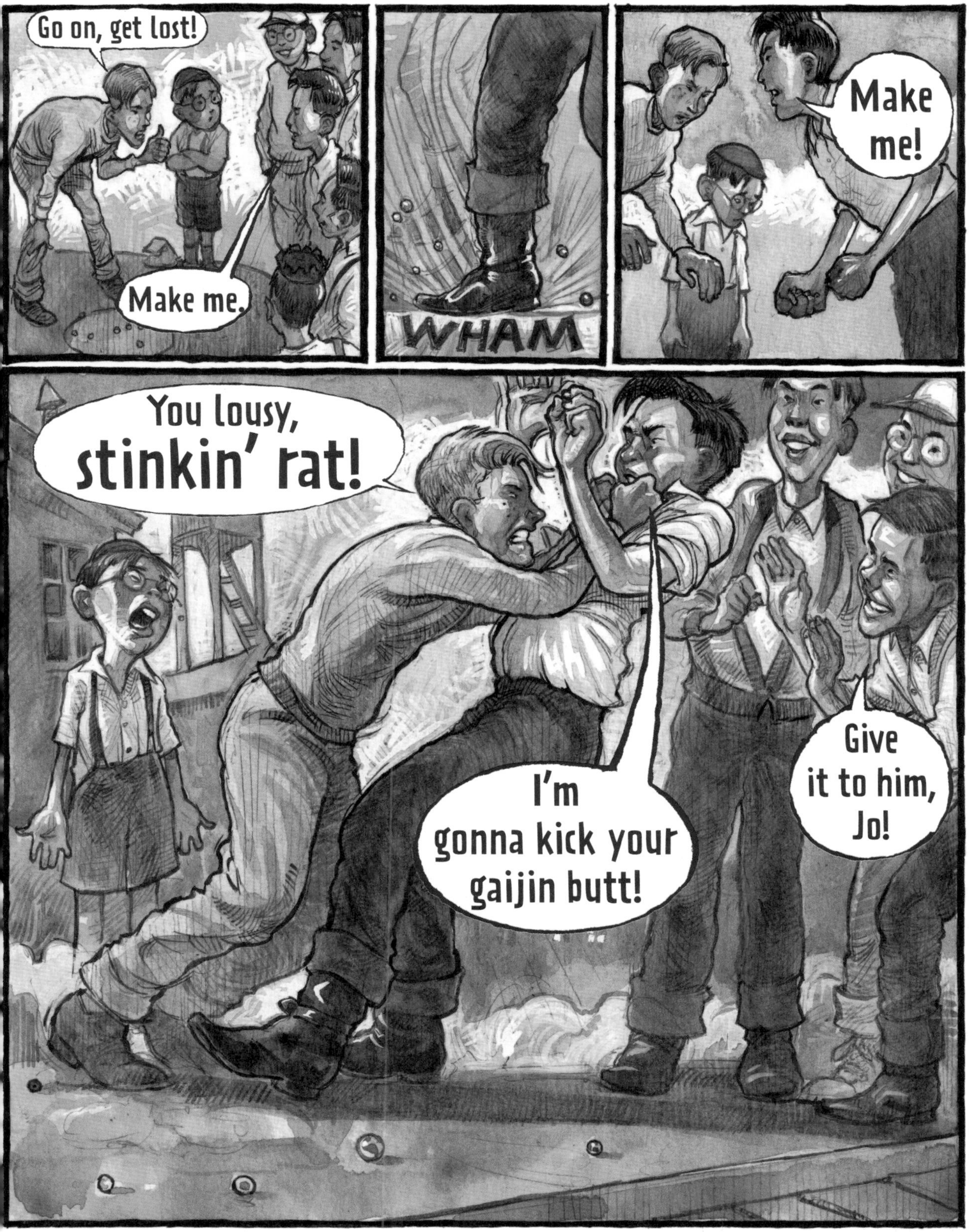
Go on, get lost!
Make me.
WHAM
Make me!
You lousy, stinkin' rat!
I'm gonna kick your gaijin butt!
Give it to him, Jo!

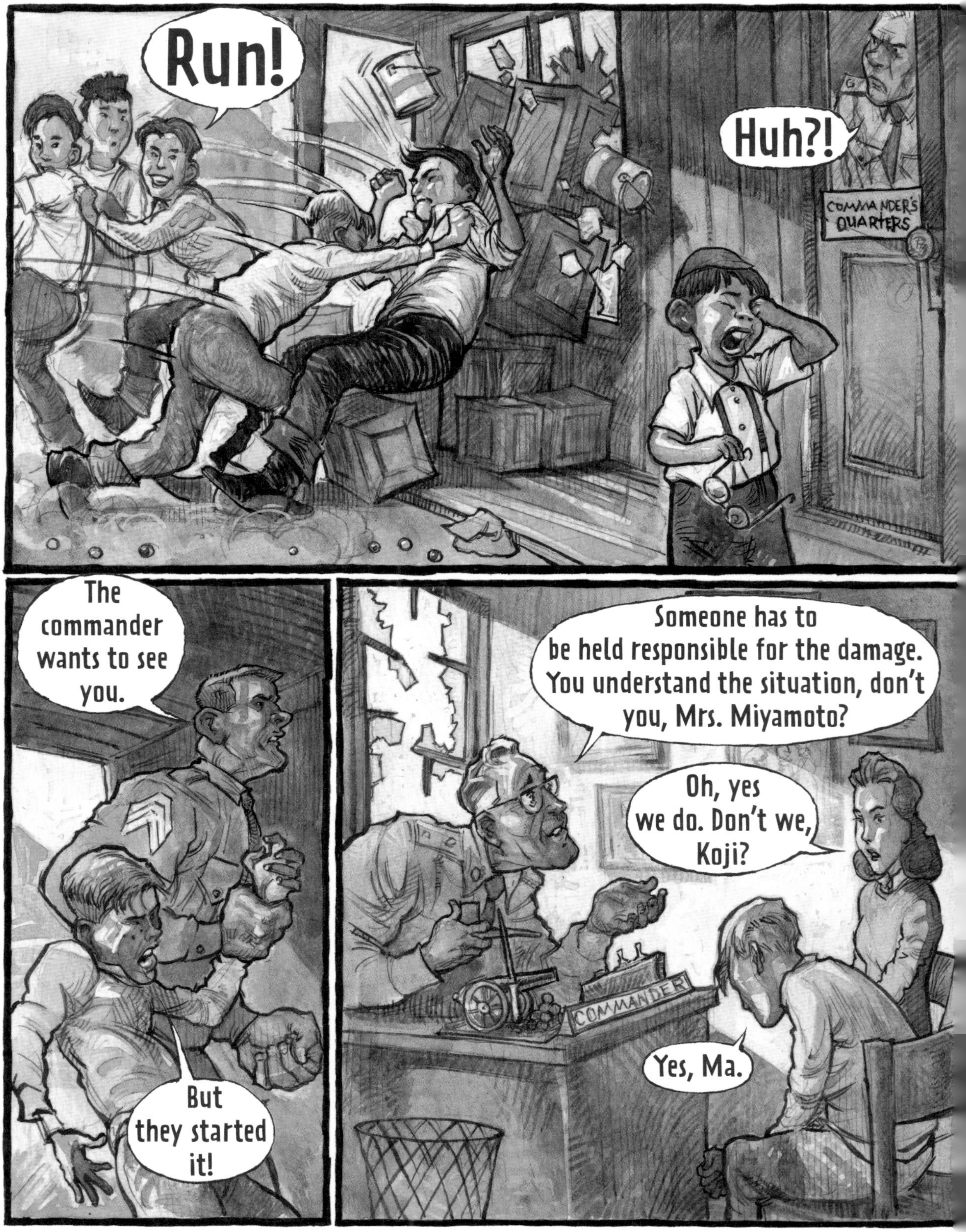
Run!
Huh?!
COMMANDER'S QUARTERS
The commander wants to see you.
But they started it!
Someone has to be held responsible for the damage. You understand the situation, don't you, Mrs. Miyamoto?
Oh, yes we do. Don't we, Koji?
COMMANDER
Yes, Ma.

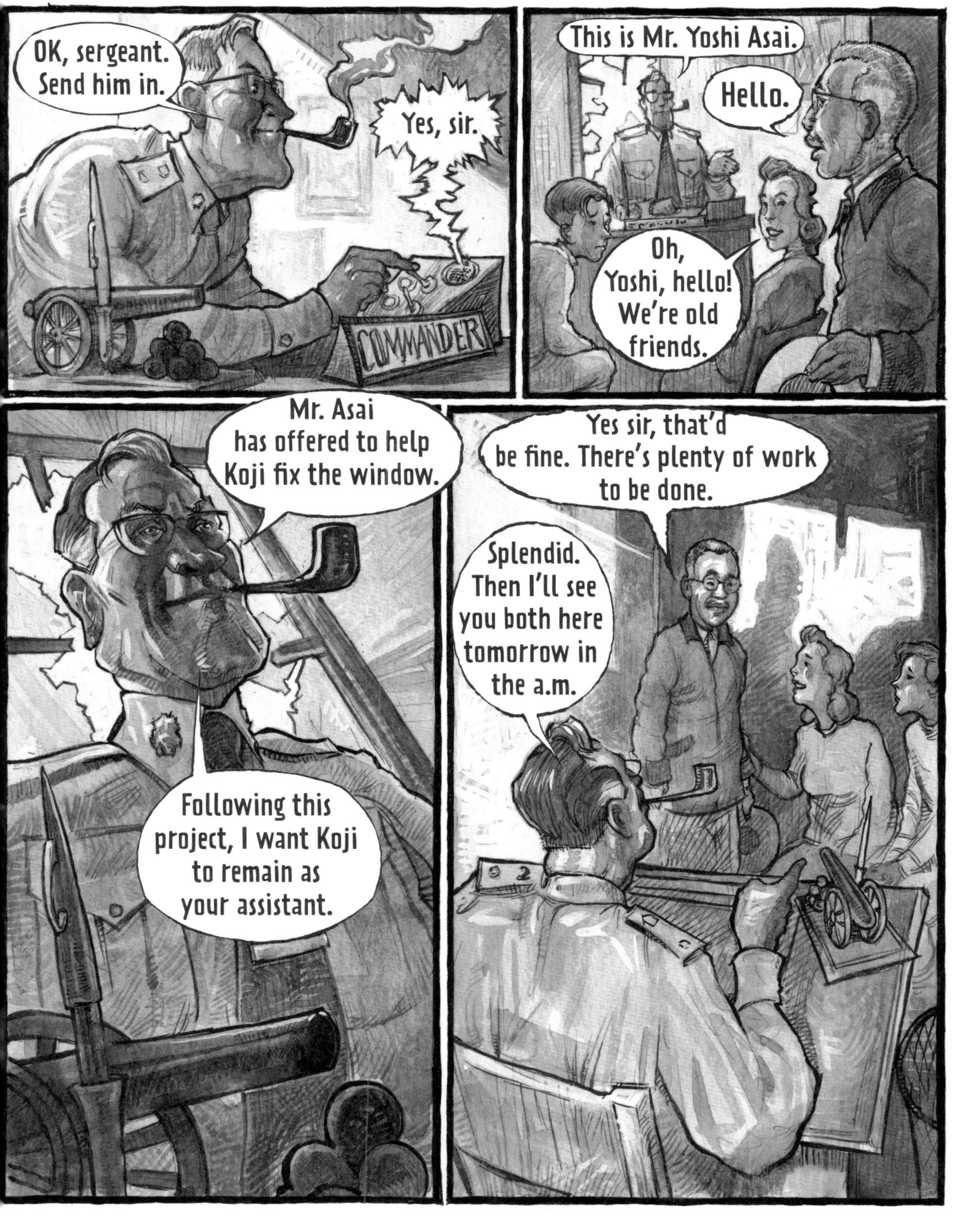

OK, sergeant. Send him in.
Yes, sir.
COMMANDER
This is Mr. Yoshi Asai.
Hello.
Oh, Yoshi, hello! We're old friends.
Mr. Asai has offered to help Koji fix the window.
Following this project, I want Koji to remain as your assistant.
Yes sir, that'd be fine. There's plenty of work to be done.
Splendid. Then I'll see you both here tomorrow in the a.m.

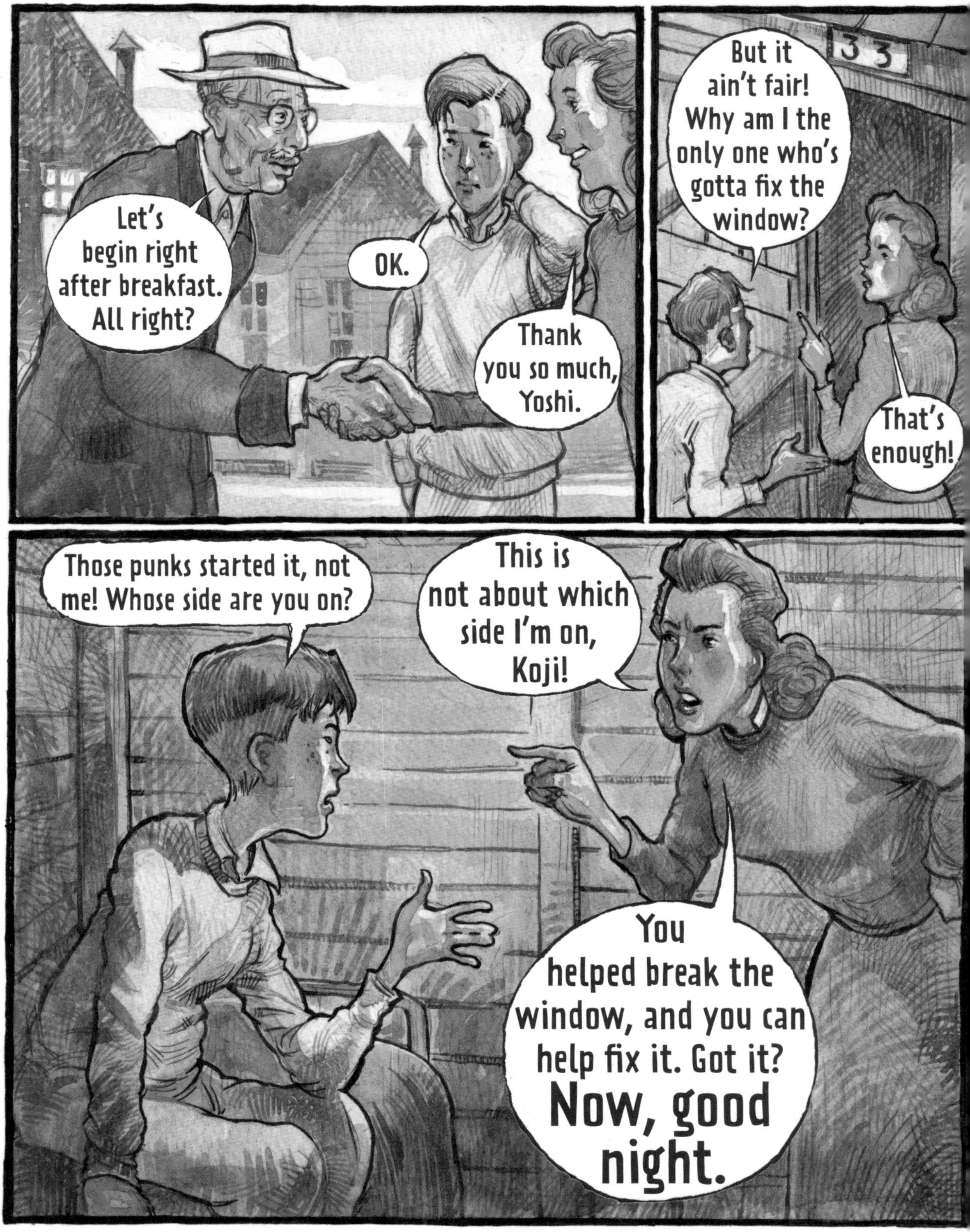
Let's begin right after breakfast. All right?
OK.
Thank you so much, Yoshi.
But it ain't fair! Why am I the only one who's gotta fix the window?
That's enough!
Those punks started it, not me! Whose side are you on?
This is not about which side I'm on, Koji!
You helped break the window, and you can help fix it. Got it?
Now, good night.

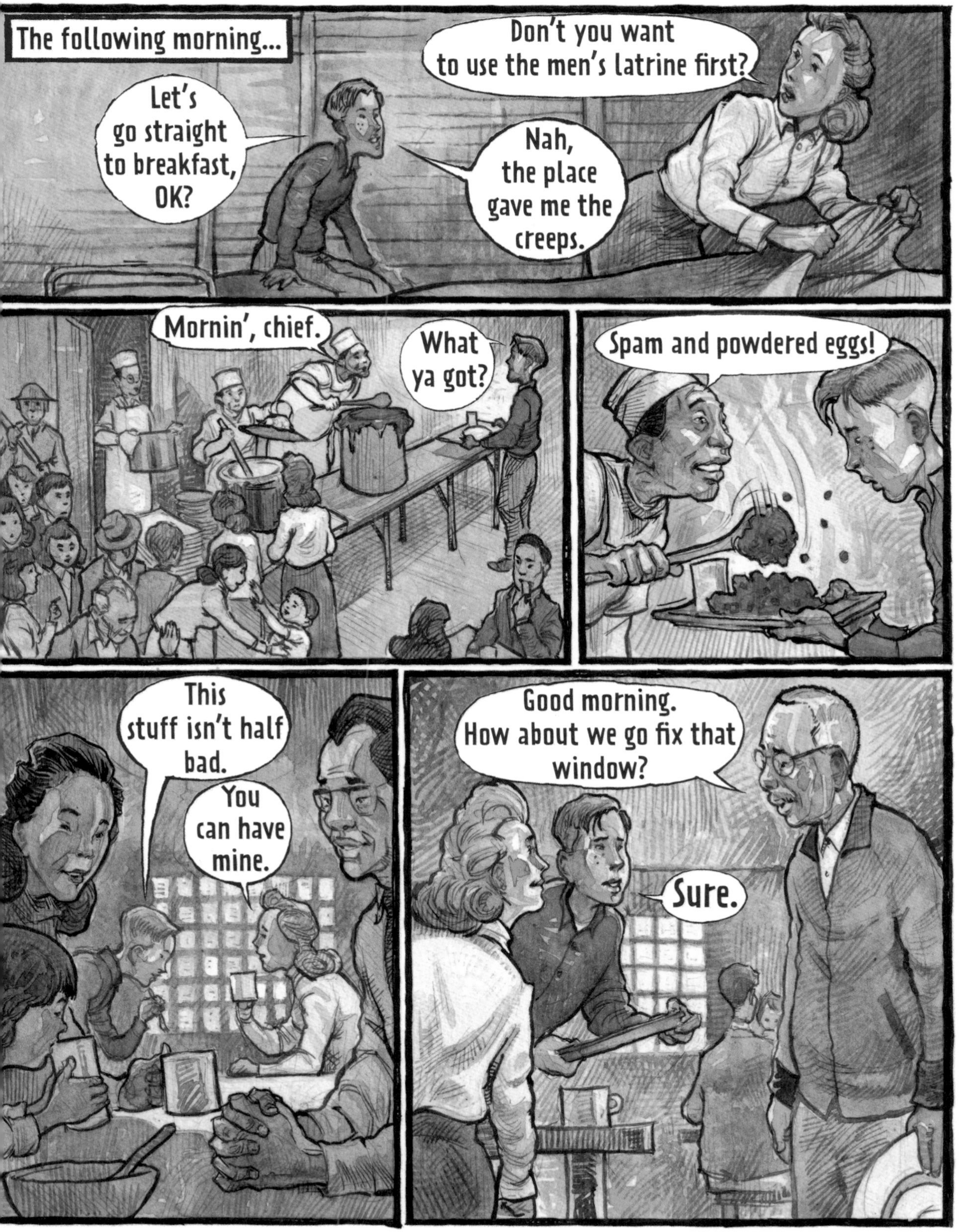
The following morning...
Let's go straight to breakfast, OK?
Don't you want to use the men's latrine first?
Nah, the place gave me the creeps.
Mornin', chief.
What ya got?
Spam and powdered eggs!
This stuff isn't half bad.
You can have mine.
Good morning. How about we go fix that window?
Sure.

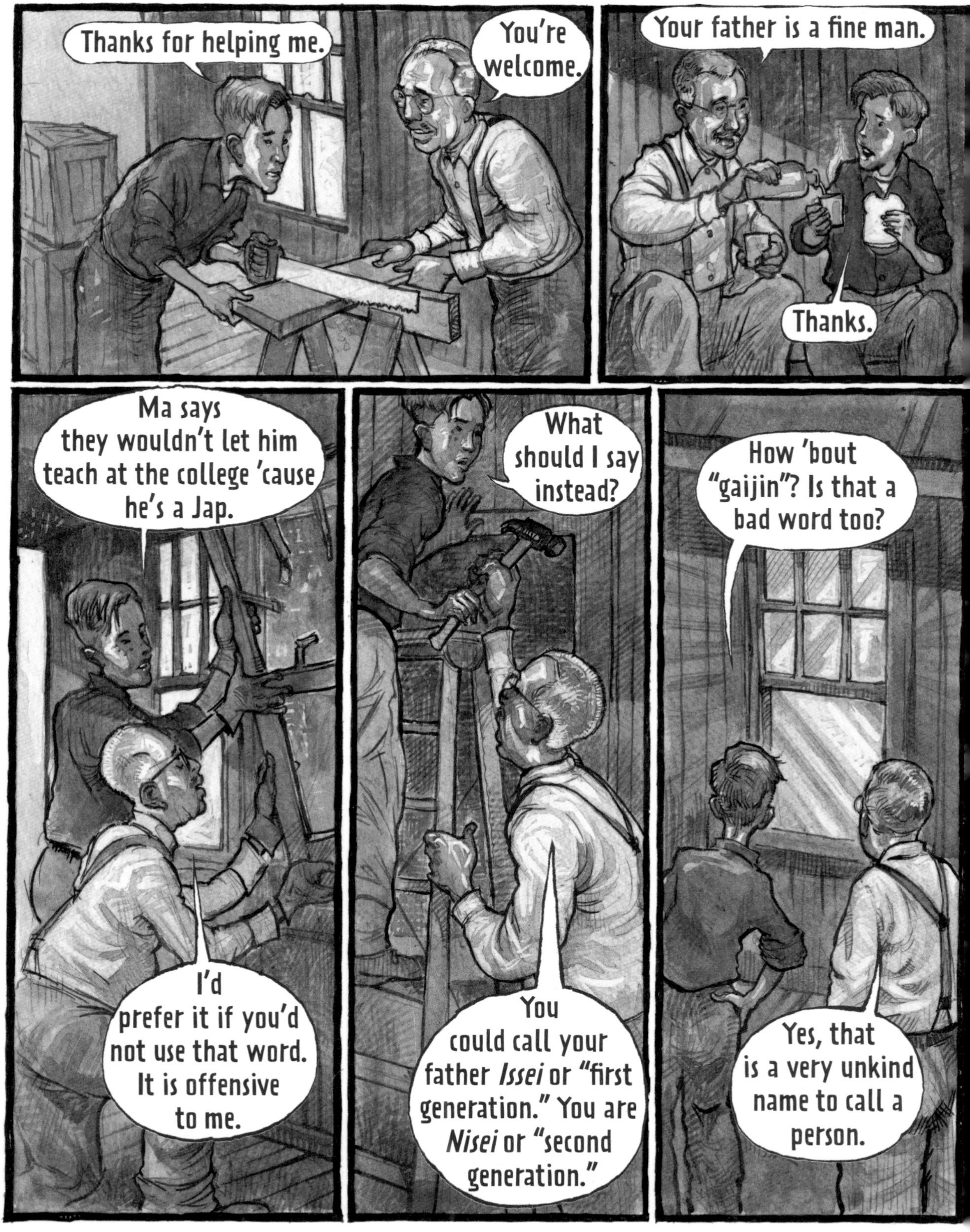

Thanks for helping me.
You're welcome.
Your father is a fine man.
Thanks.
Ma says they wouldn't let him teach at the college 'cause he's a Jap.
I'd prefer it if you'd not use that word. It is offensive to me.
What should I say instead?
You could call your father *Issei* or "first generation." You are *Nisei* or "second generation."
How 'bout "gaijin"? Is that a bad word too?
Yes, that is a very unkind name to call a person.

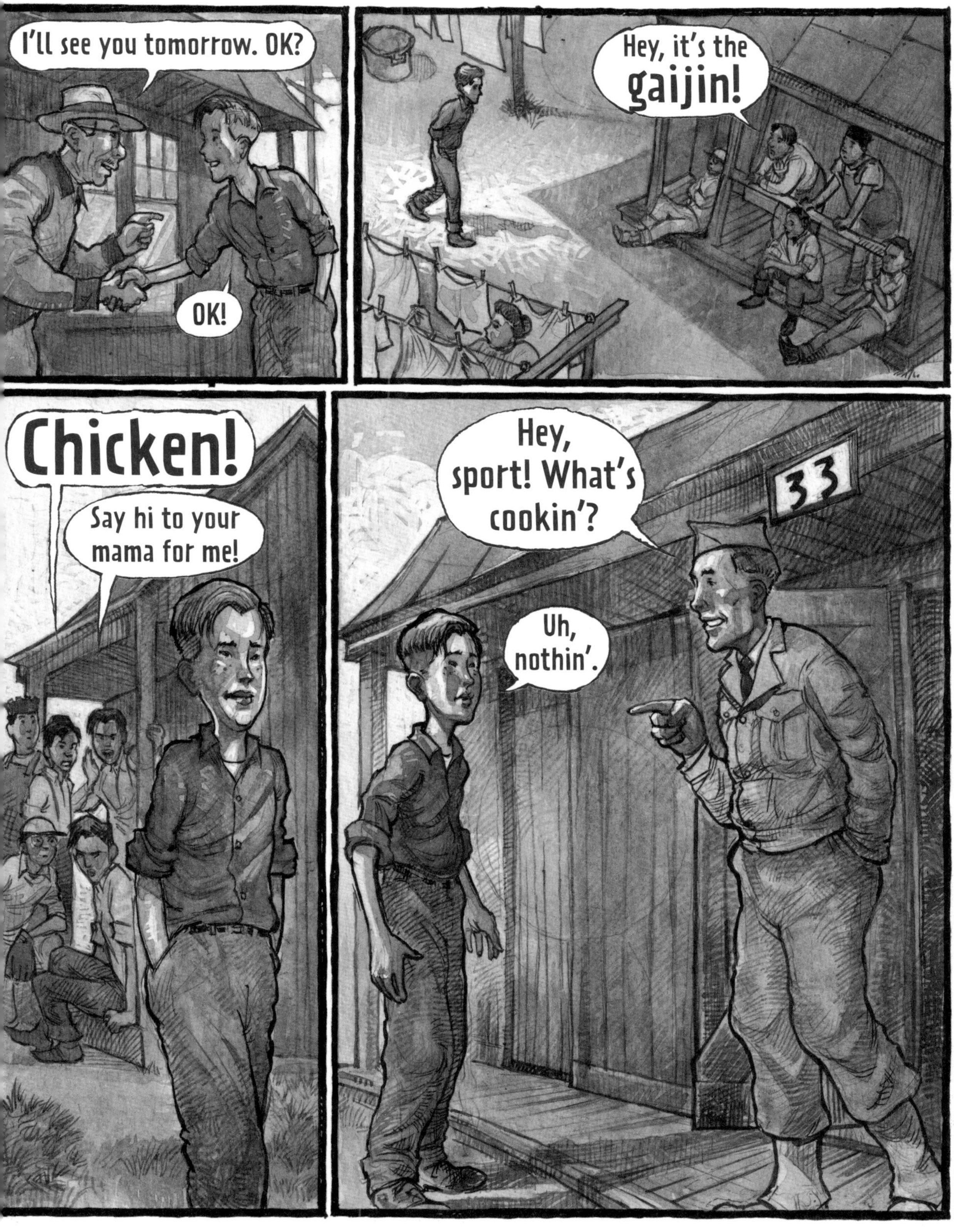
I'll see you tomorrow. OK?
OK!
Hey, it's the gaijin!
Chicken!
Say hi to your mama for me!
Hey, sport! What's cookin'?
33
Uh, nothin'.

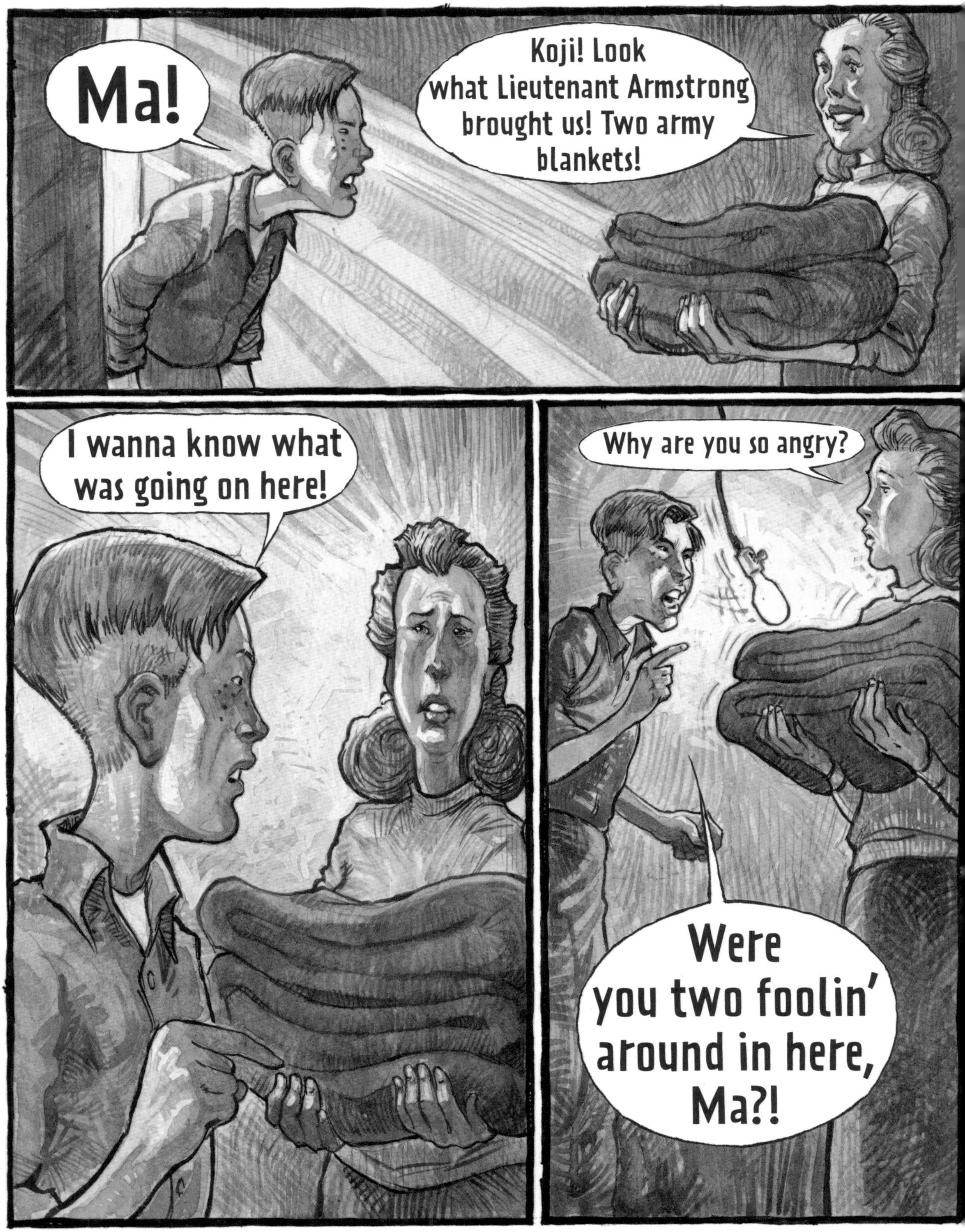
Ma!
Koji! Look what Lieutenant Armstrong brought us! Two army blankets!
I wanna know what was going on here!
Why are you so angry?
Were you two foolin' around in here, Ma?!

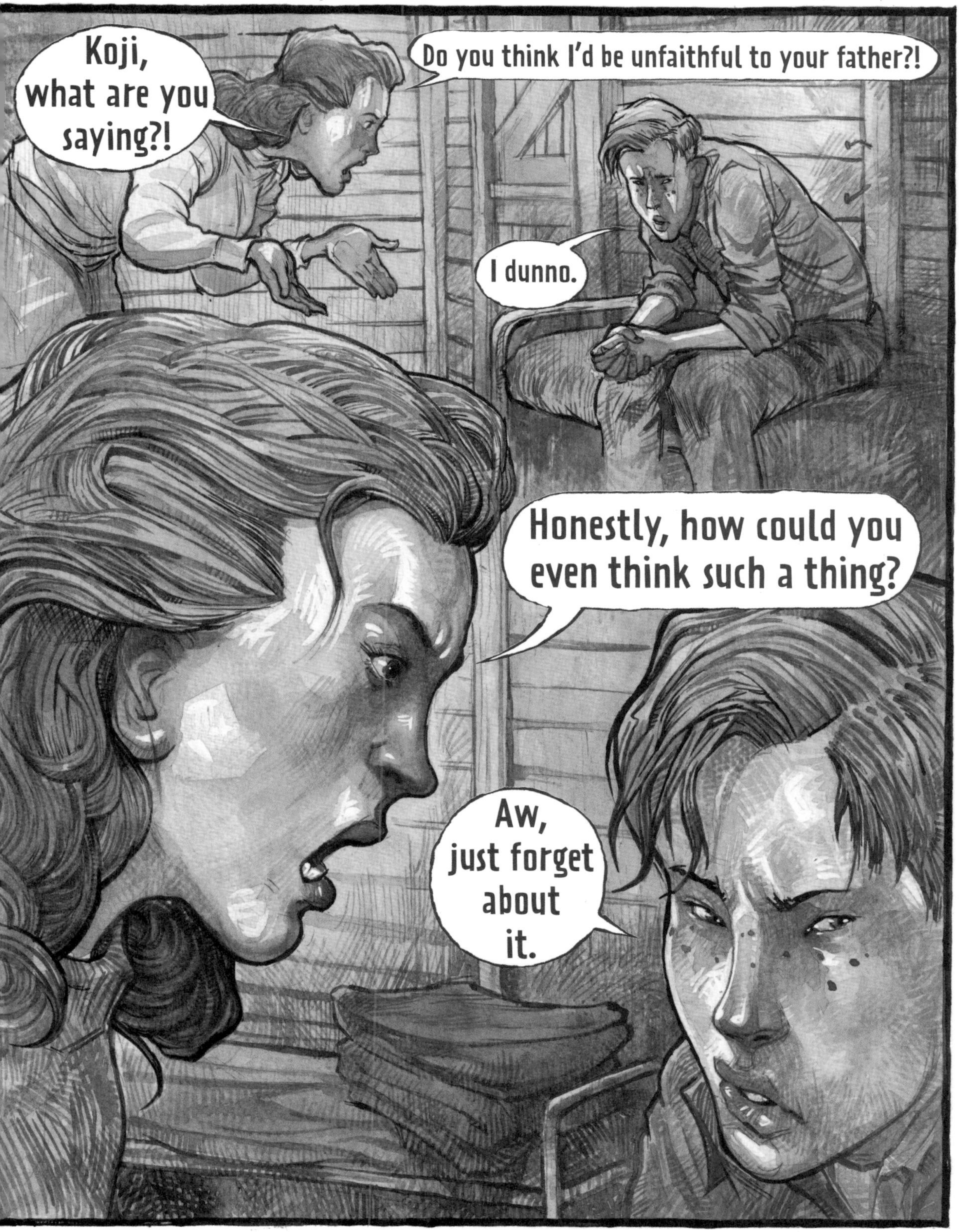
Koji, what are you saying?!
Do you think I'd be unfaithful to your father?!
I dunno.
Honestly, how could you even think such a thing?
Aw, just forget about it.

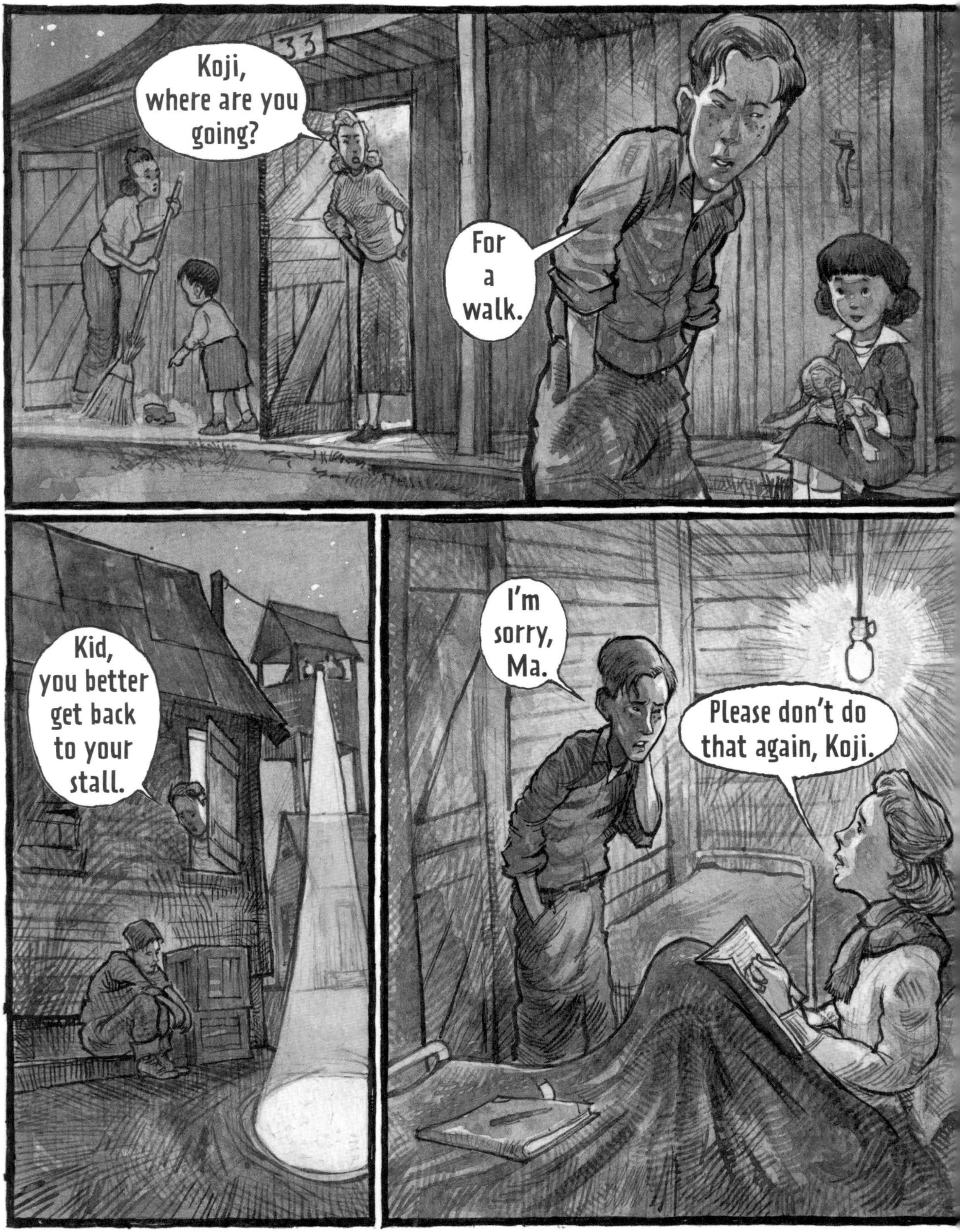
Koji, where are you going?
For a walk.
Kid, you better get back to your stall.
I'm sorry, Ma.
Please don't do that again, Koji.

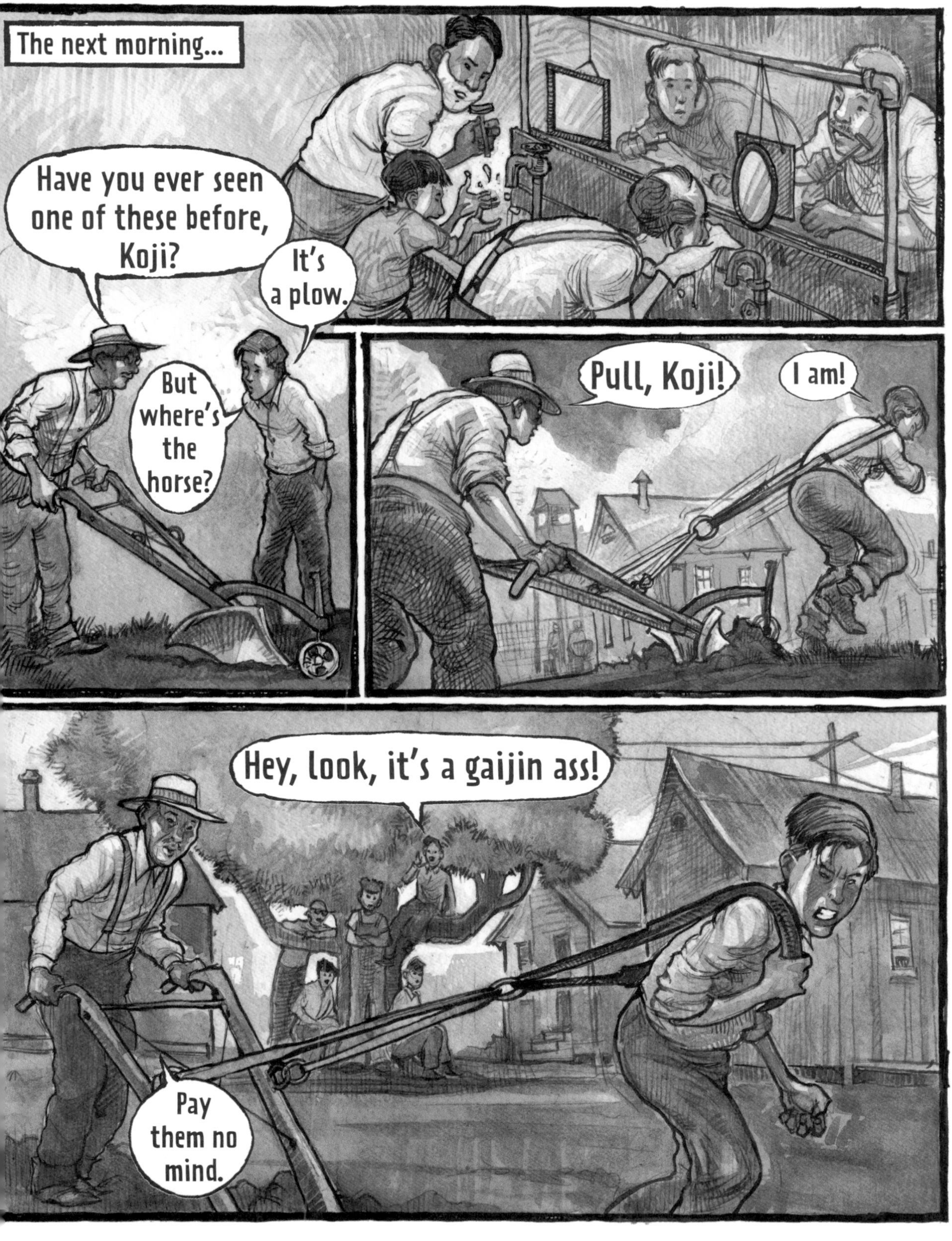
The next morning...
Have you ever seen one of these before, Koji?
It's a plow.
But where's the horse?
Pull, Koji!
I am!
Hey, look, it's a gaijin ass!
Pay them no mind.

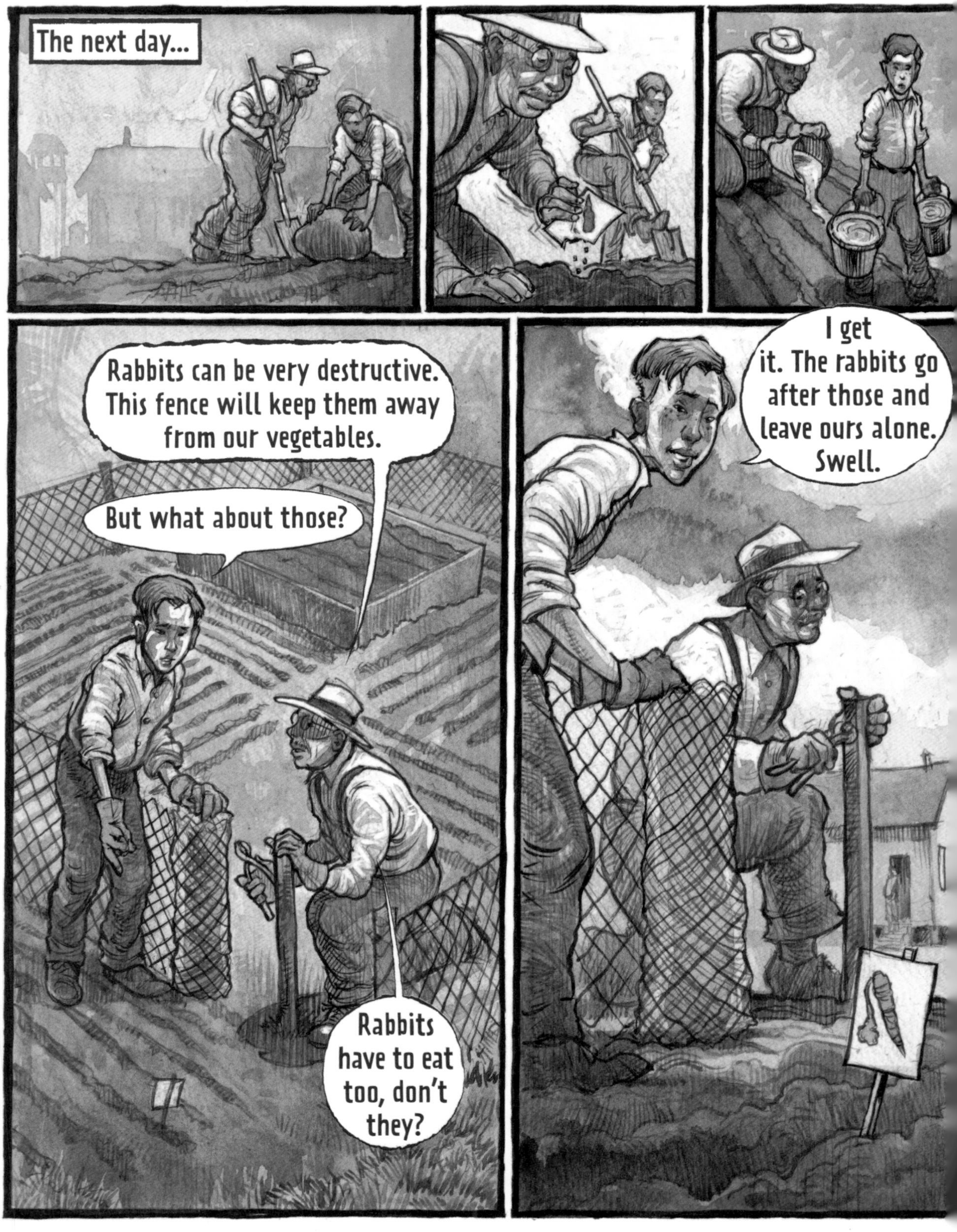
The next day...
Rabbits can be very destructive. This fence will keep them away from our vegetables.
But what about those?
Rabbits have to eat too, don't they?
I get it. The rabbits go after those and leave ours alone. Swell.

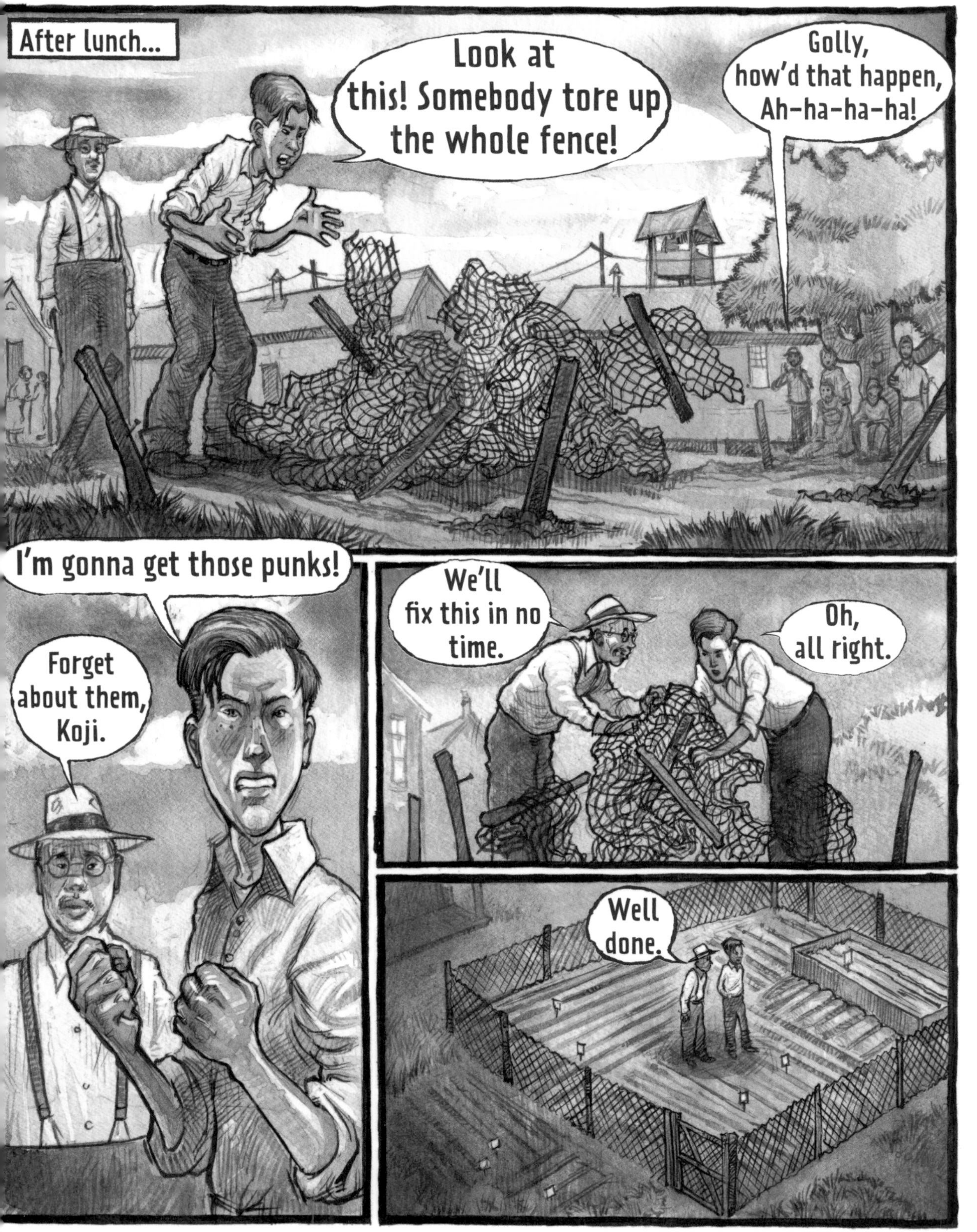
After lunch...
Look at this! Somebody tore up the whole fence!
Golly, how'd that happen, Ah-ha-ha-ha!
I'm gonna get those punks!
Forget about them, Koji.
We'll fix this in no time.
Oh, all right.
Well done.

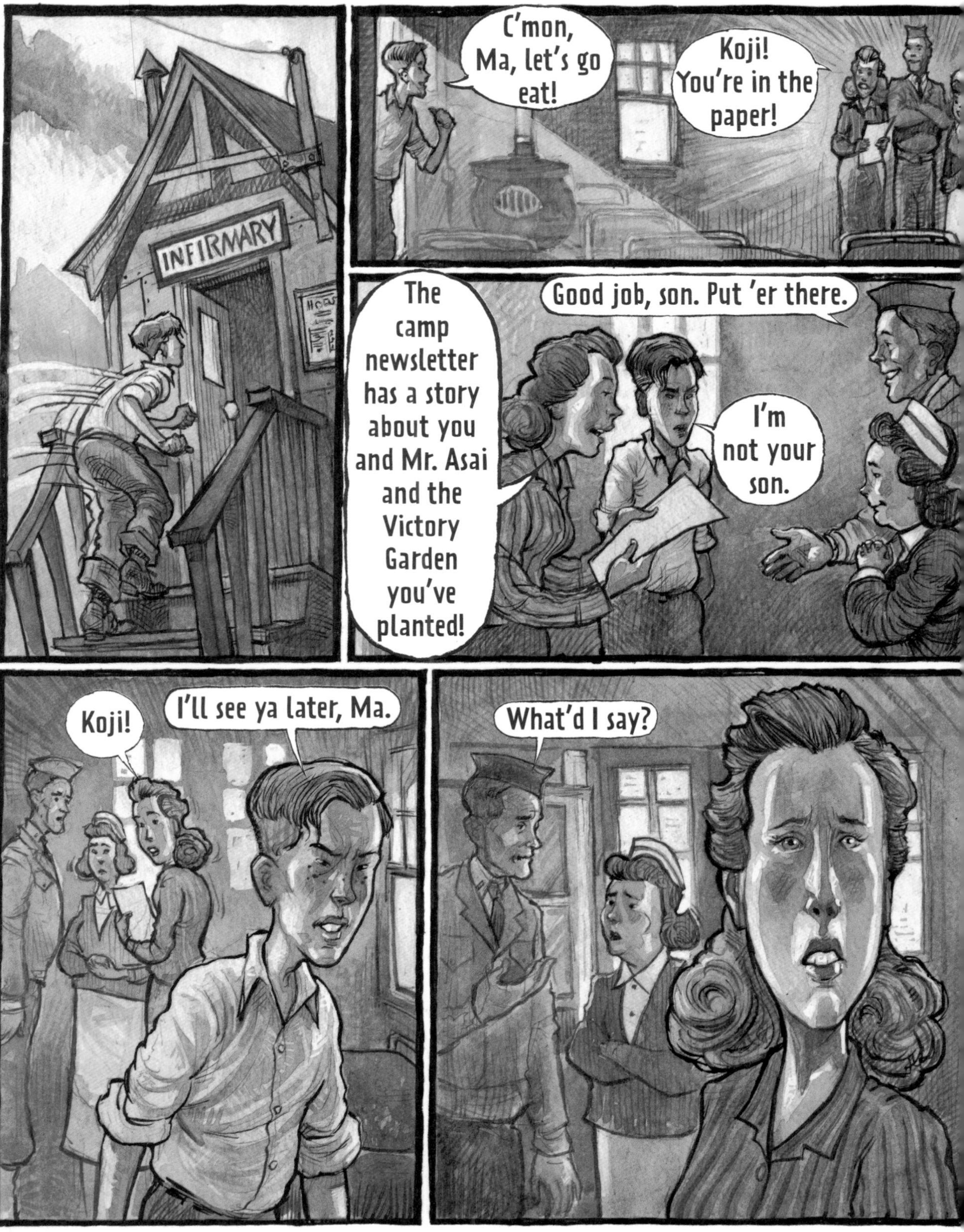
INFIRMARY
C'mon, Ma, let's go eat!
Koji! You're in the paper!
The camp newsletter has a story about you and Mr. Asai and the Victory Garden you've planted!
Good job, son. Put 'er there.
I'm not your son.
Koji!
I'll see ya later, Ma.
What'd I say?

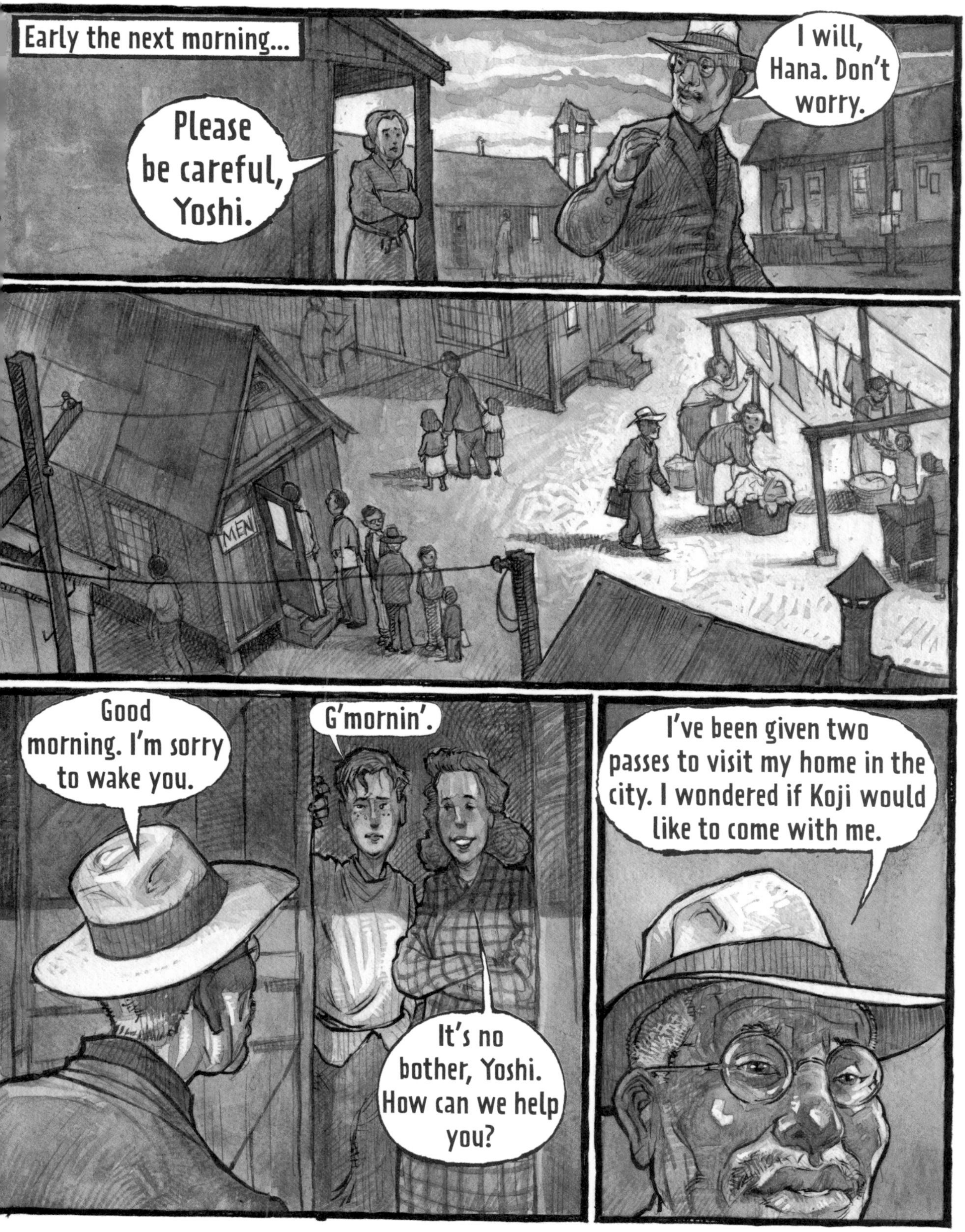

Early the next morning...
Please be careful, Yoshi.
I will, Hana. Don't worry.
MEN
Good morning. I'm sorry to wake you.
G'mornin'.
It's no bother, Yoshi. How can we help you?
I've been given two passes to visit my home in the city. I wondered if Koji would like to come with me.

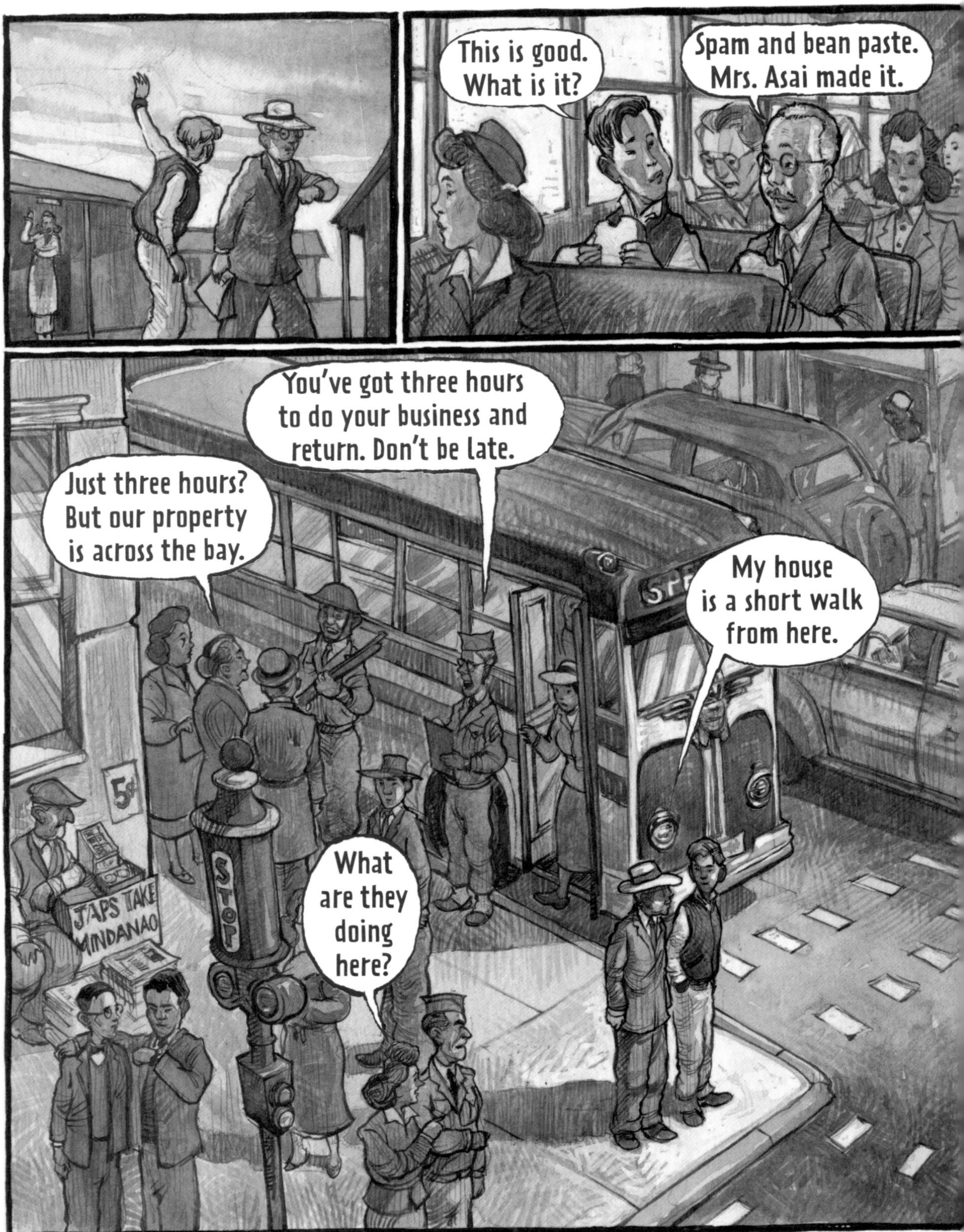

This is good. What is it?
Spam and bean paste. Mrs. Asai made it.
You've got three hours to do your business and return. Don't be late.
Just three hours? But our property is across the bay.
My house is a short walk from here.
What are they doing here?
5¢
JAPS TAKE MINDANAO
STOP

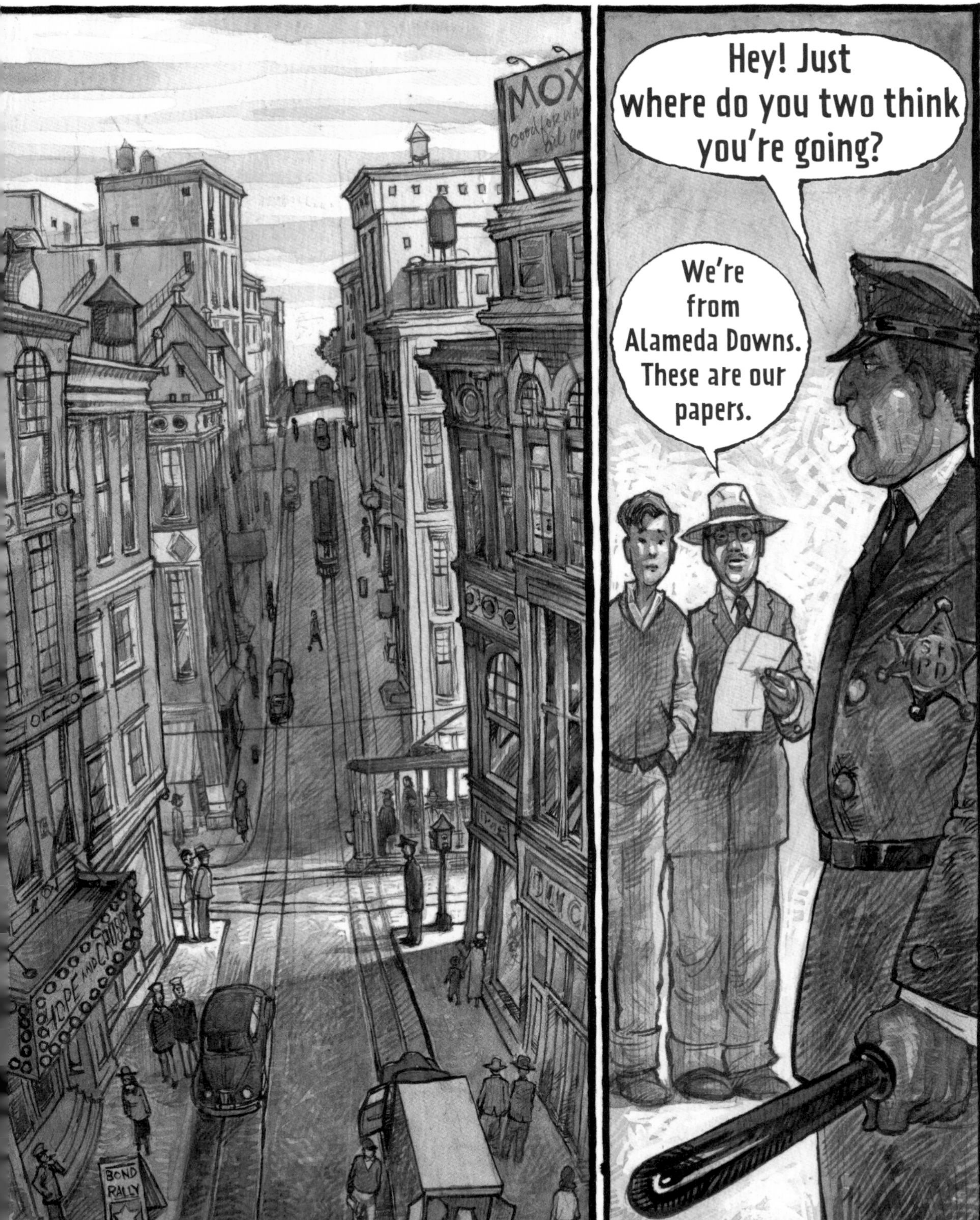
BOND RALLY
Hey! Just where do you two think you're going?
We're from Alameda Downs. These are our papers.

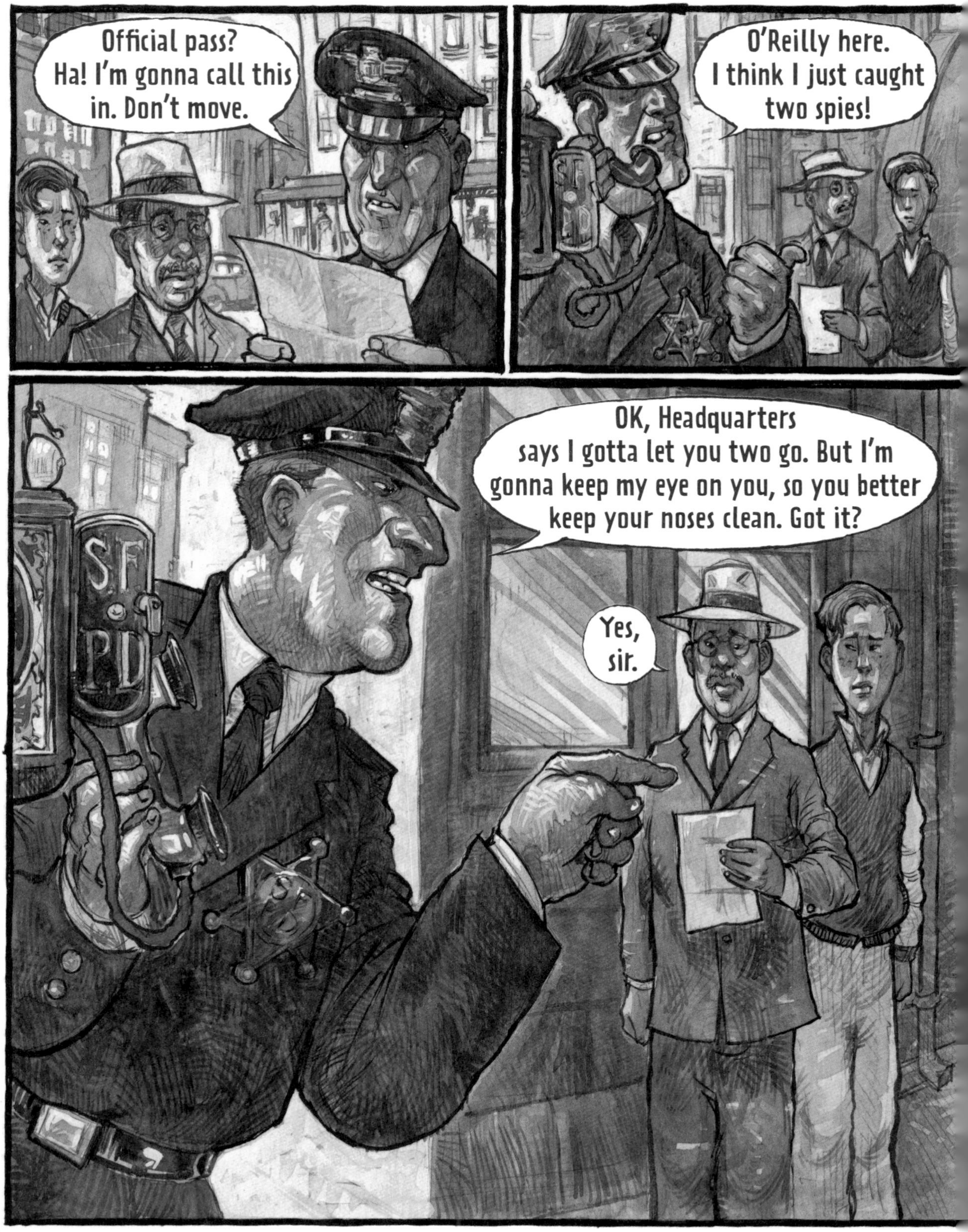
Official pass? Ha! I'm gonna call this in. Don't move.
O'Reilly here. I think I just caught two spies!
OK, Headquarters says I gotta let you two go. But I'm gonna keep my eye on you, so you better keep your noses clean. Got it?
Yes, sir.

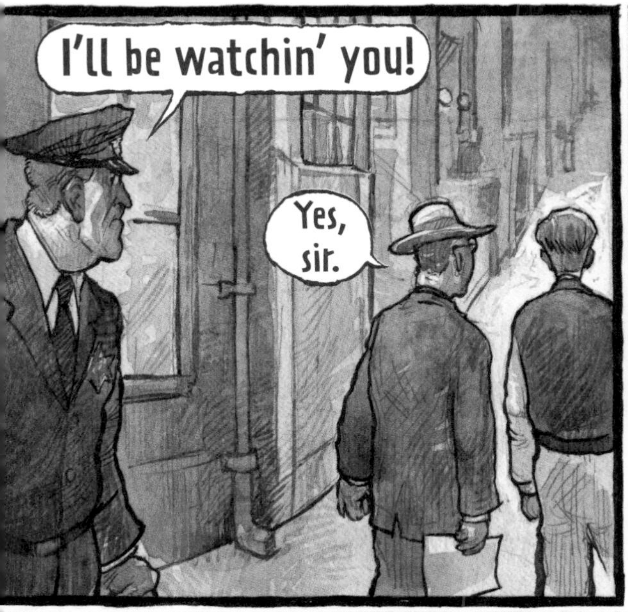
I'll be watchin' you!
Yes, sir.

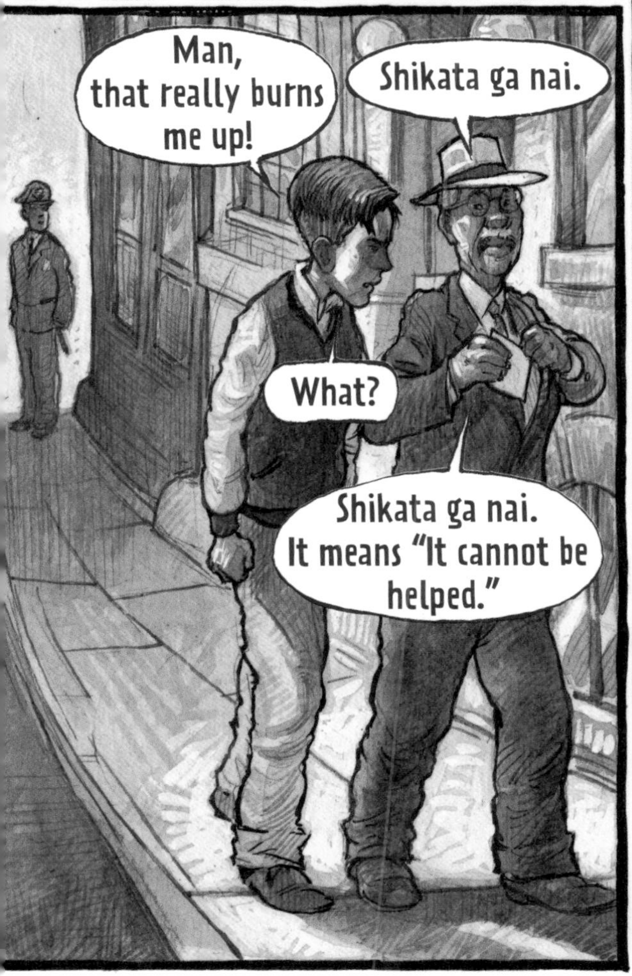
Man, that really burns me up!
Shikata ga nai.
What?
Shikata ga nai. It means "It cannot be helped."

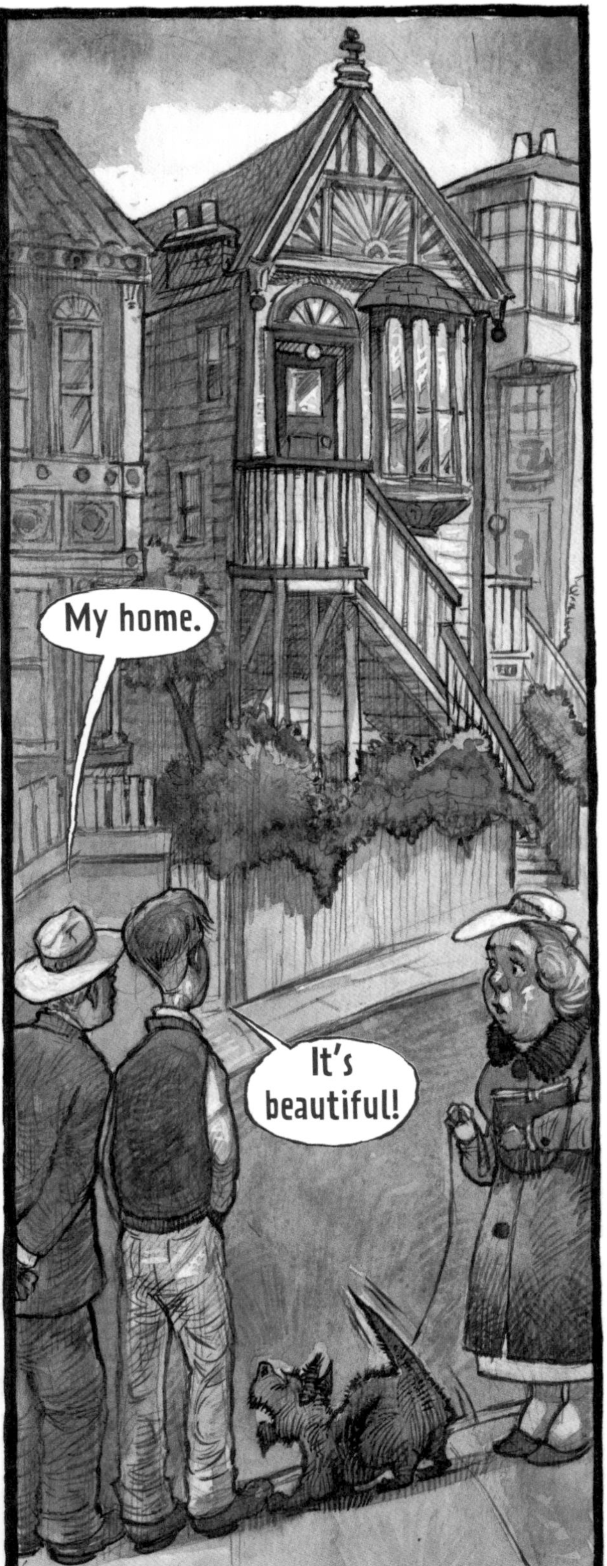
My home.
It's beautiful!

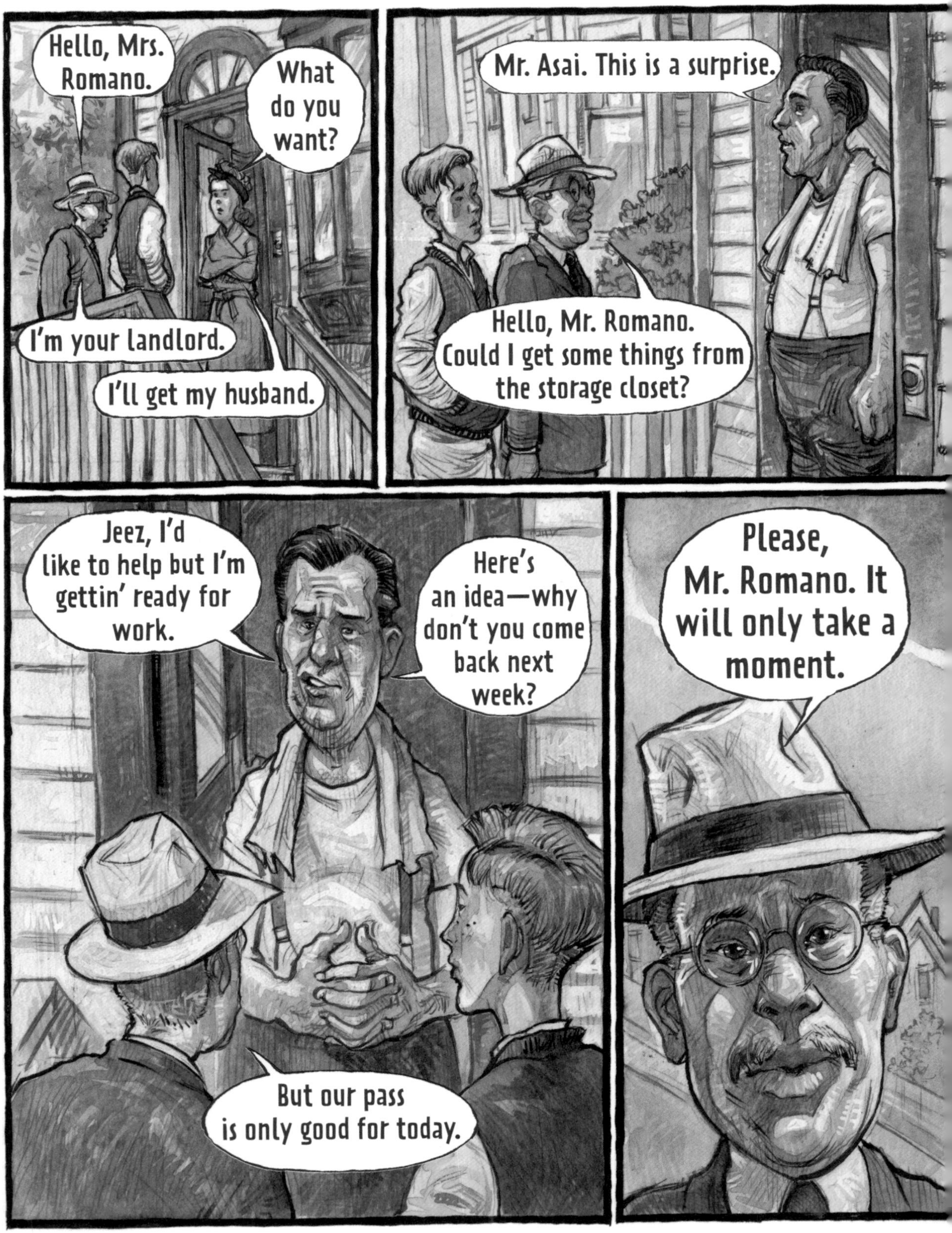
Hello, Mrs. Romano.
What do you want?
I'm your landlord.
I'll get my husband.
Mr. Asai. This is a surprise.
Hello, Mr. Romano. Could I get some things from the storage closet?
Jeez, I'd like to help but I'm gettin' ready for work.
Here's an idea—why don't you come back next week?
But our pass is only good for today.
Please, Mr. Romano. It will only take a moment.

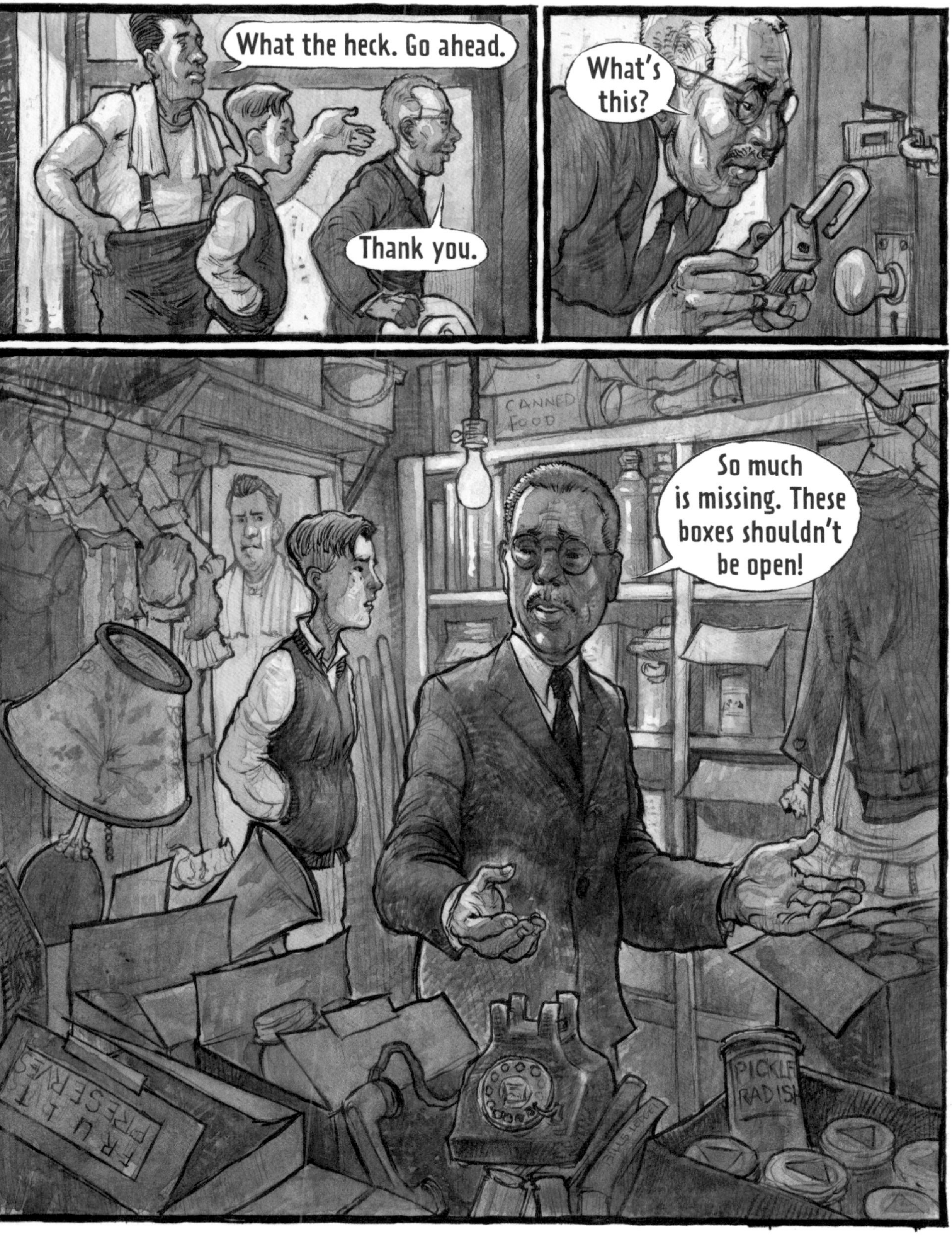
What the heck. Go ahead.
Thank you.
What's this?
CANNED FOOD
So much is missing. These boxes shouldn't be open!

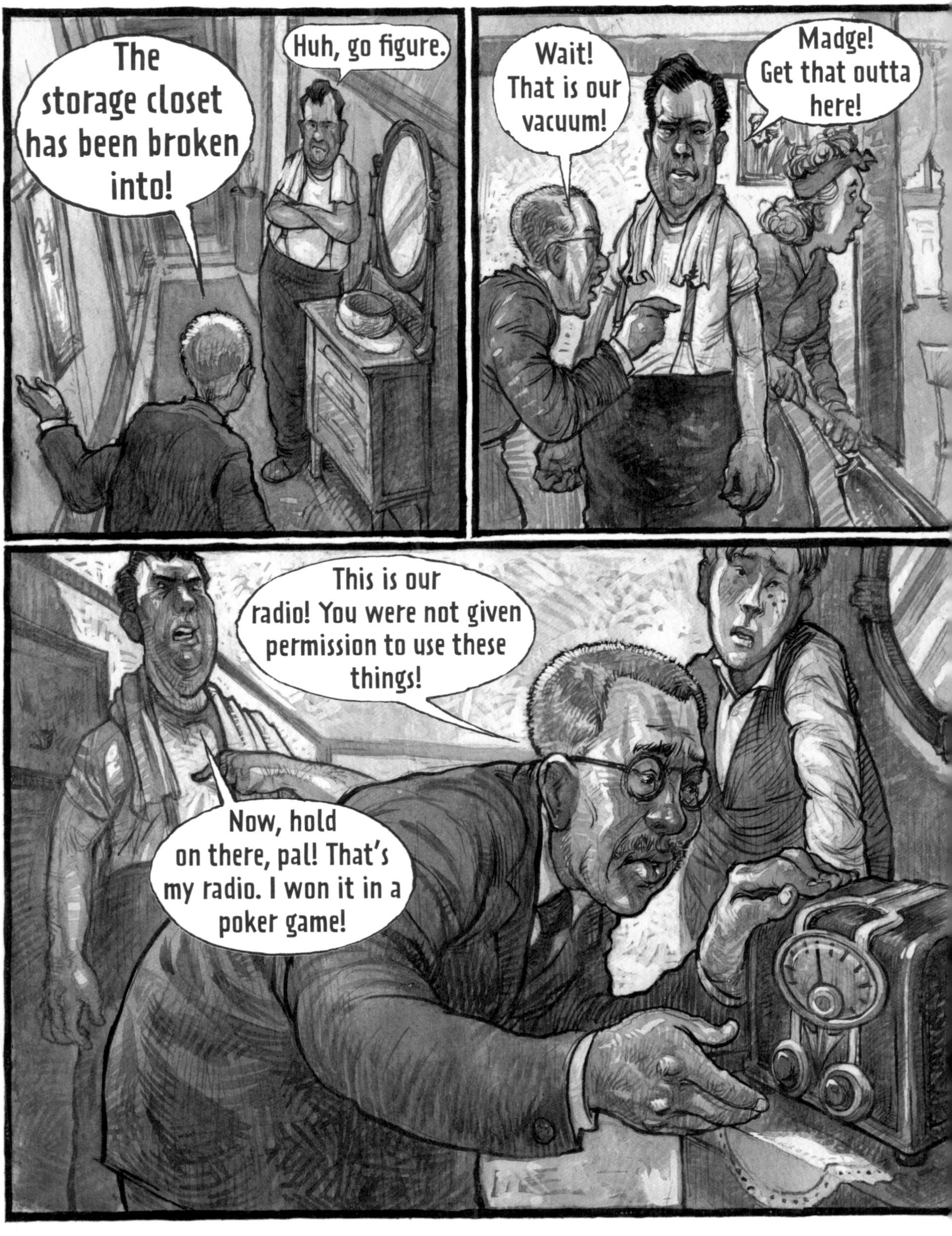
The storage closet has been broken into!
Huh, go figure.
Wait! That is our vacuum!
Madge! Get that outta here!
This is our radio! You were not given permission to use these things!
Now, hold on there, pal! That's my radio. I won it in a poker game!

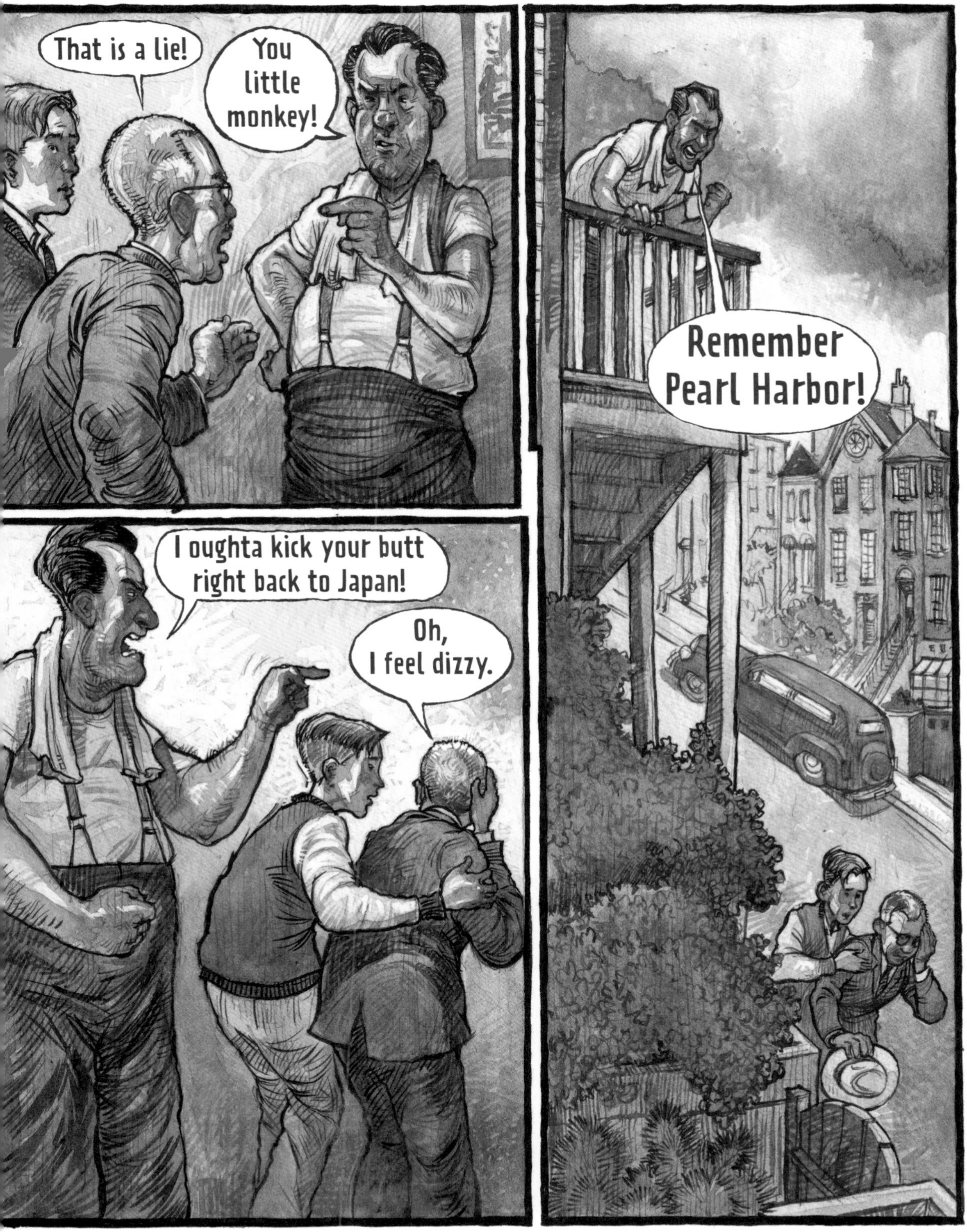
That is a lie!
You little monkey!
Remember Pearl Harbor!
I oughta kick your butt right back to Japan!
Oh, I feel dizzy.

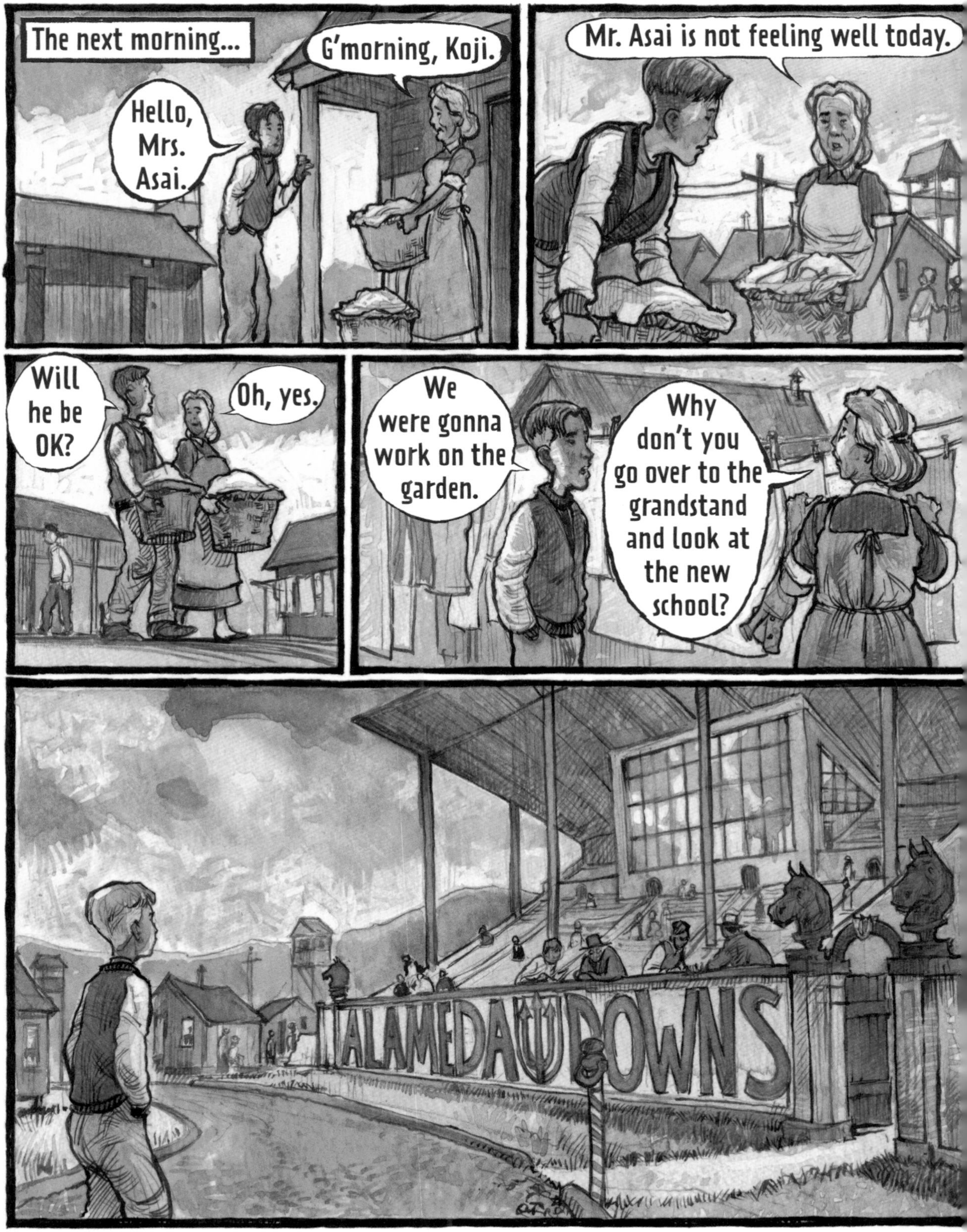
The next morning...
G'morning, Koji.
Hello, Mrs. Asai.
Mr. Asai is not feeling well today.
Will he be OK?
Oh, yes.
We were gonna work on the garden.
Why don't you go over to the grandstand and look at the new school?
ALAMEDA DOWNS

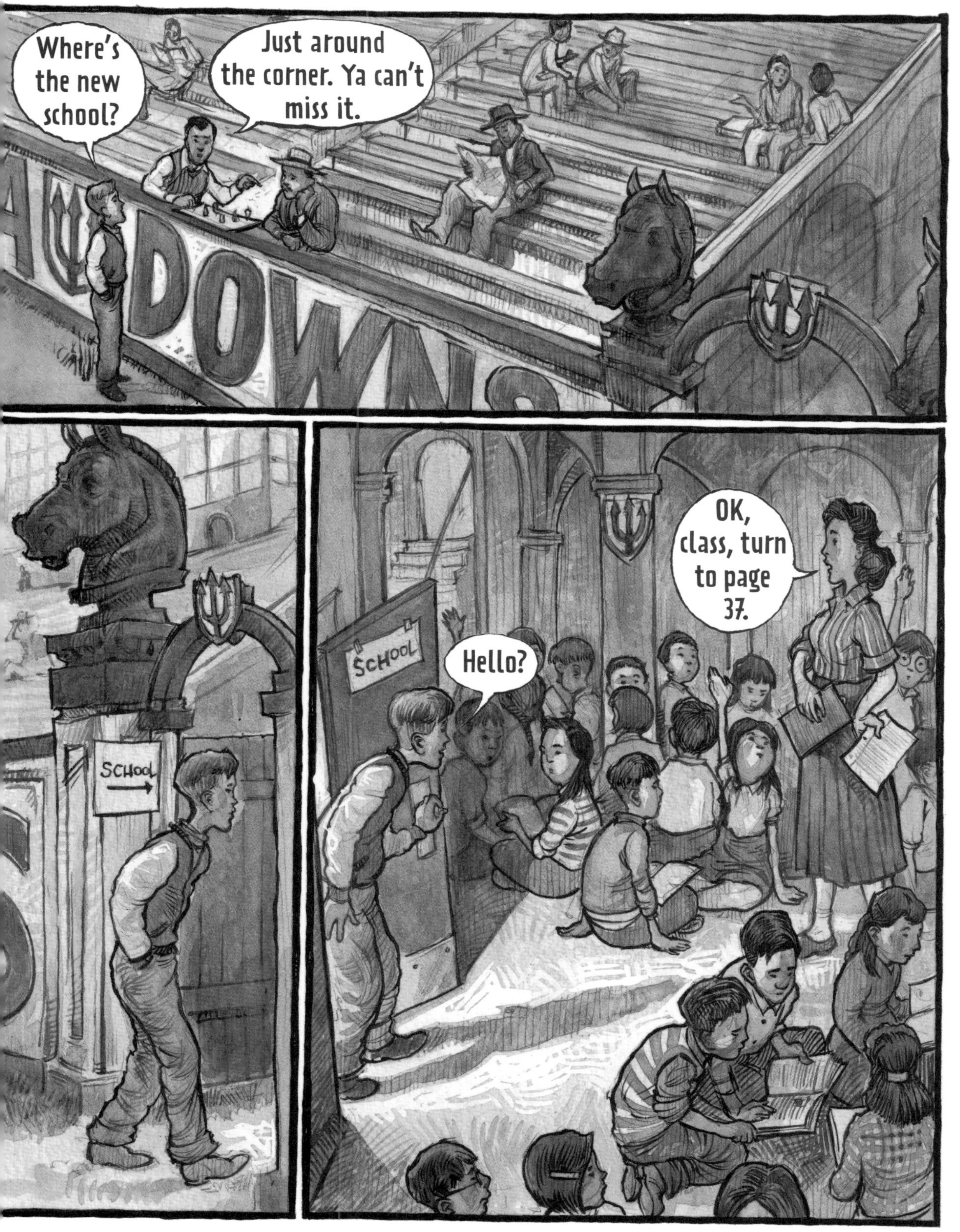
Where's the new school?
Just around the corner. Ya can't miss it.
SCHOOL
OK, class, turn to page 37.
Hello?
SCHOOL

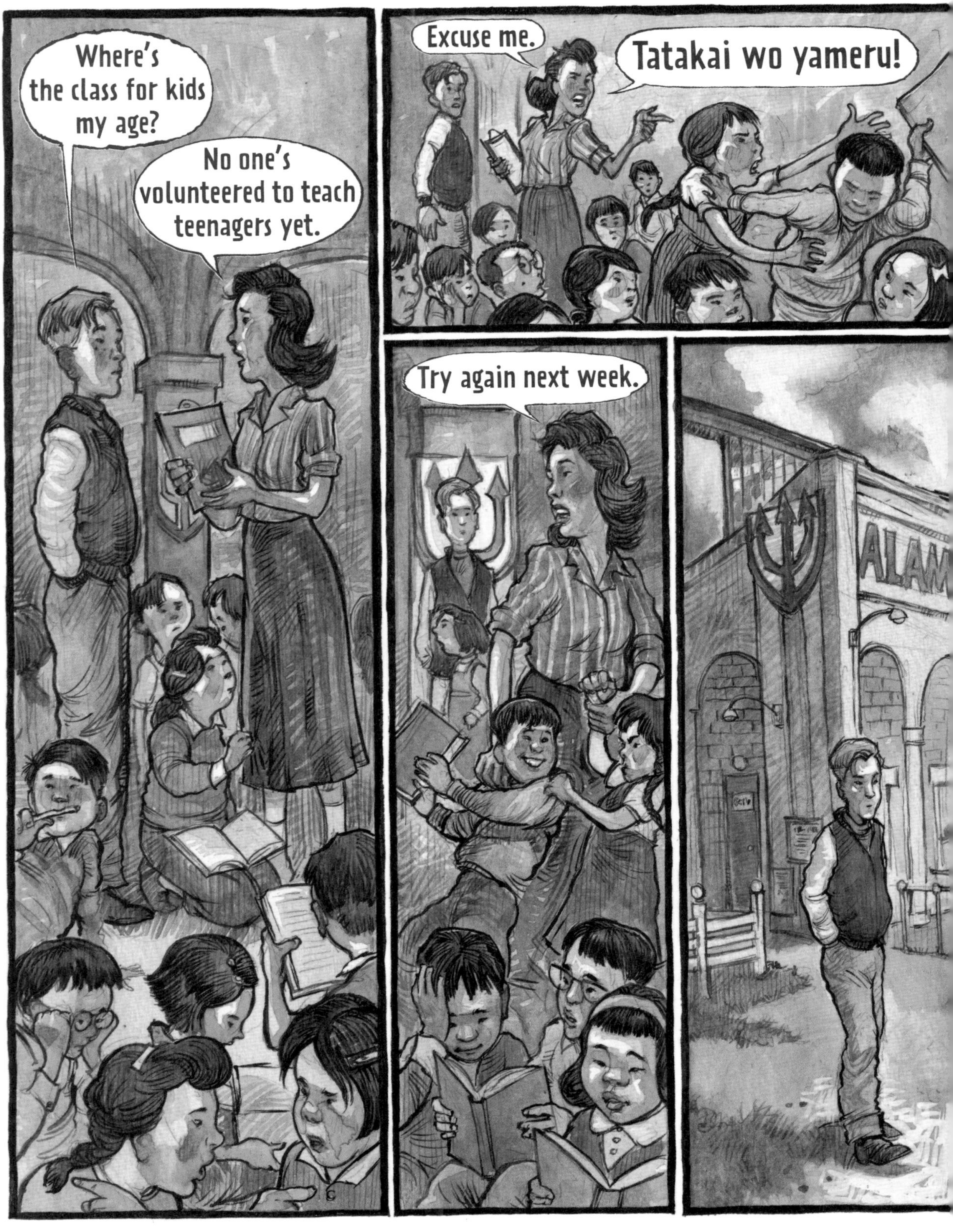
Where's the class for kids my age?
No one's volunteered to teach teenagers yet.
Excuse me.
Tatakai wo yameru!
Try again next week.
ALAM

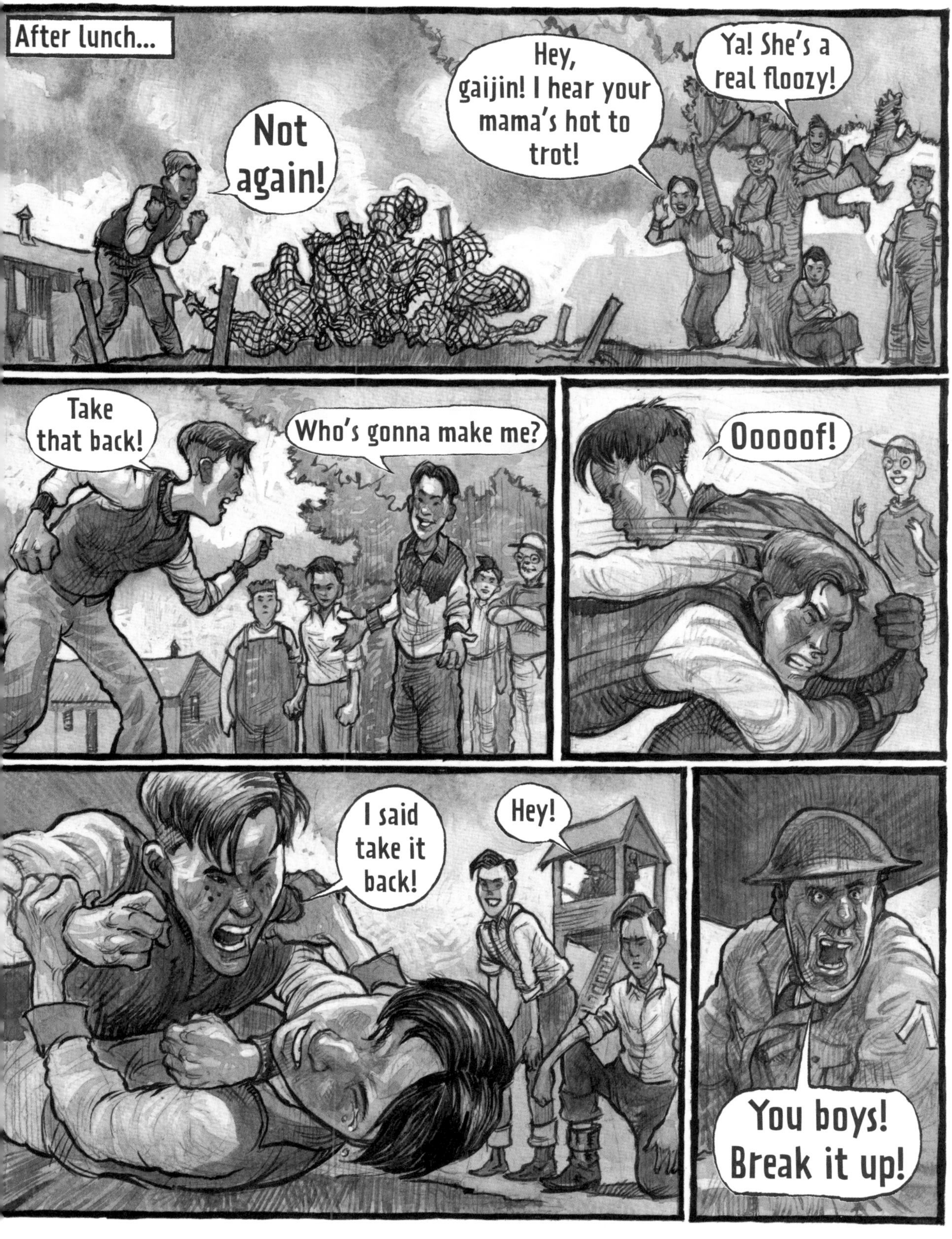
After lunch...
Not again!
Hey, gaijin! I hear your mama's hot to trot!
Ya! She's a real floozy!
Take that back!
Who's gonna make me?
Oooooof!
I said take it back!
Hey!
You boys! Break it up!

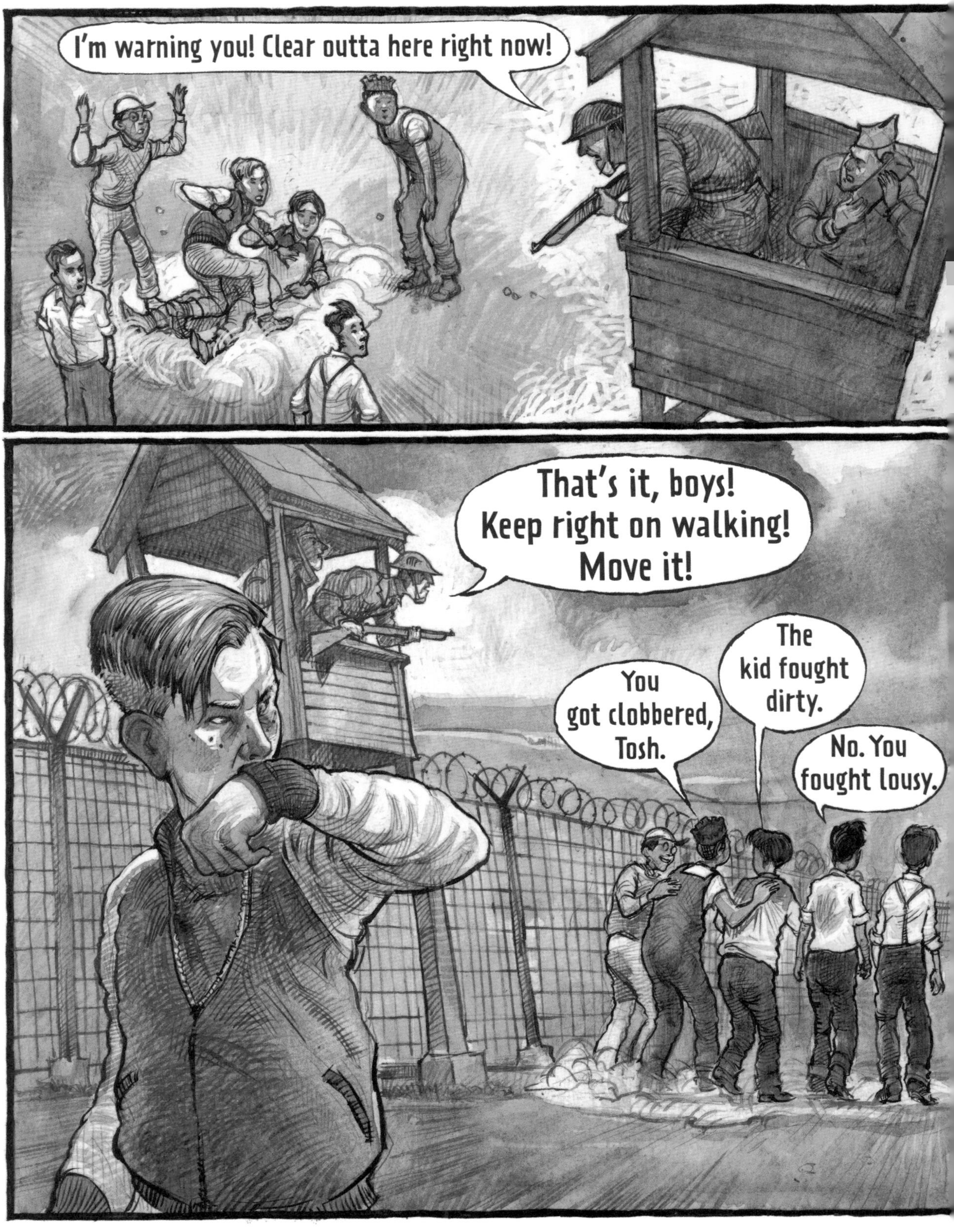
I'm warning you! Clear outta here right now!
That's it, boys! Keep right on walking! Move it!
You got clobbered, Tosh.
The kid fought dirty.
No. You fought lousy.

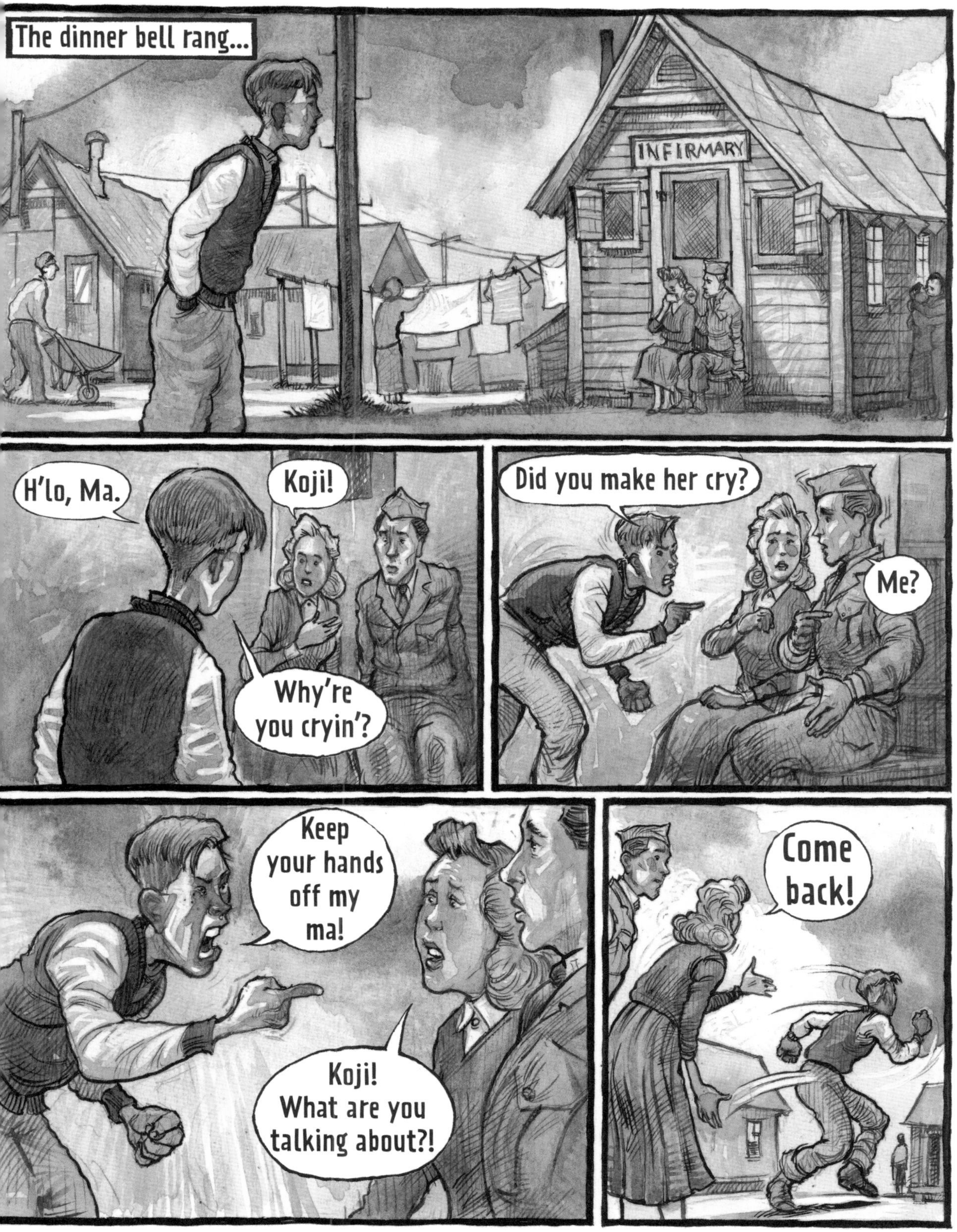
The dinner bell rang...
INFIRMARY
H'lo, Ma.
Koji!
Why're you cryin'?
Did you make her cry?
Me?
Keep your hands off my ma!
Koji! What are you talking about?!
Come back!

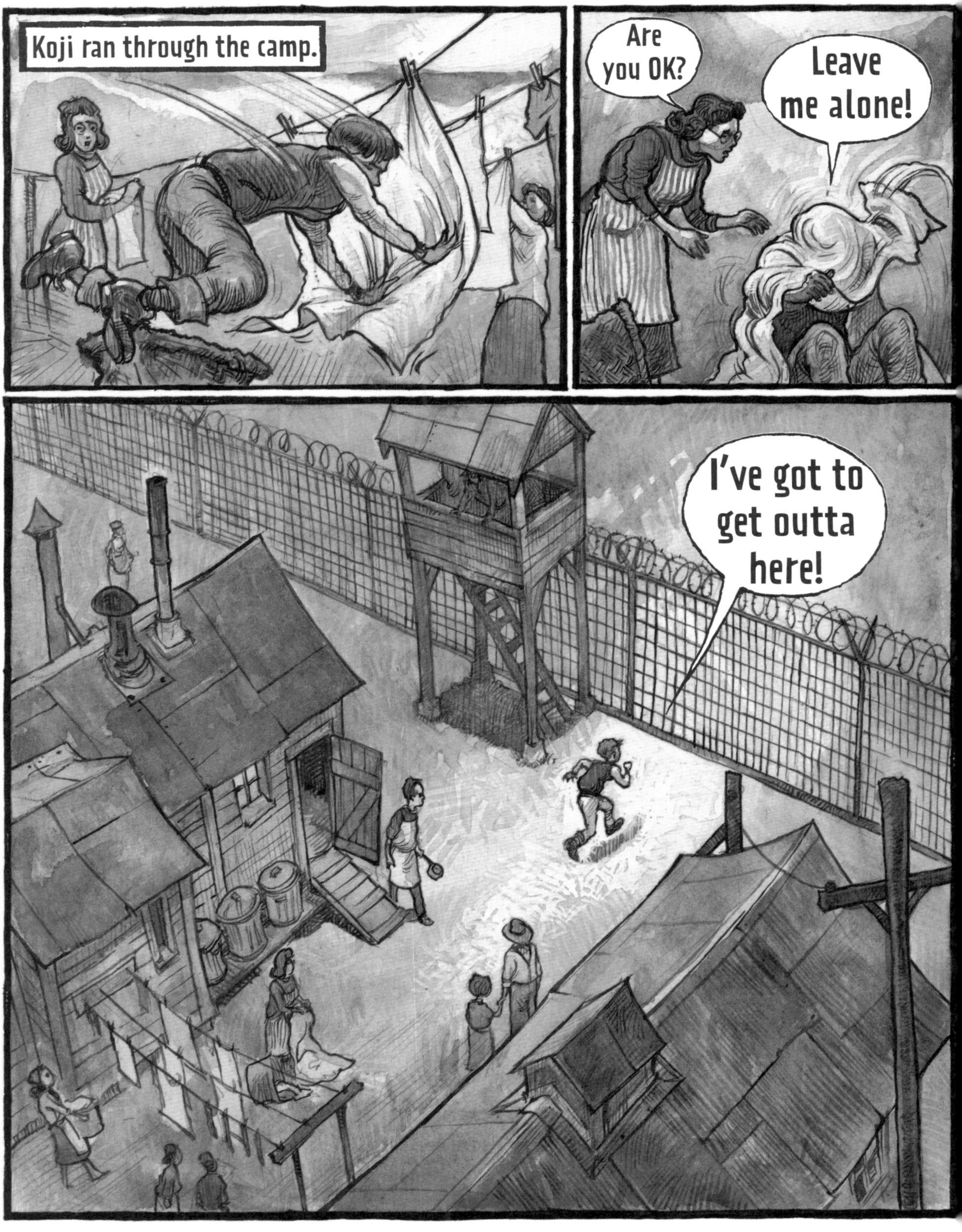
Koji ran through the camp.
Are you OK?
Leave me alone!
I've got to get outta here!

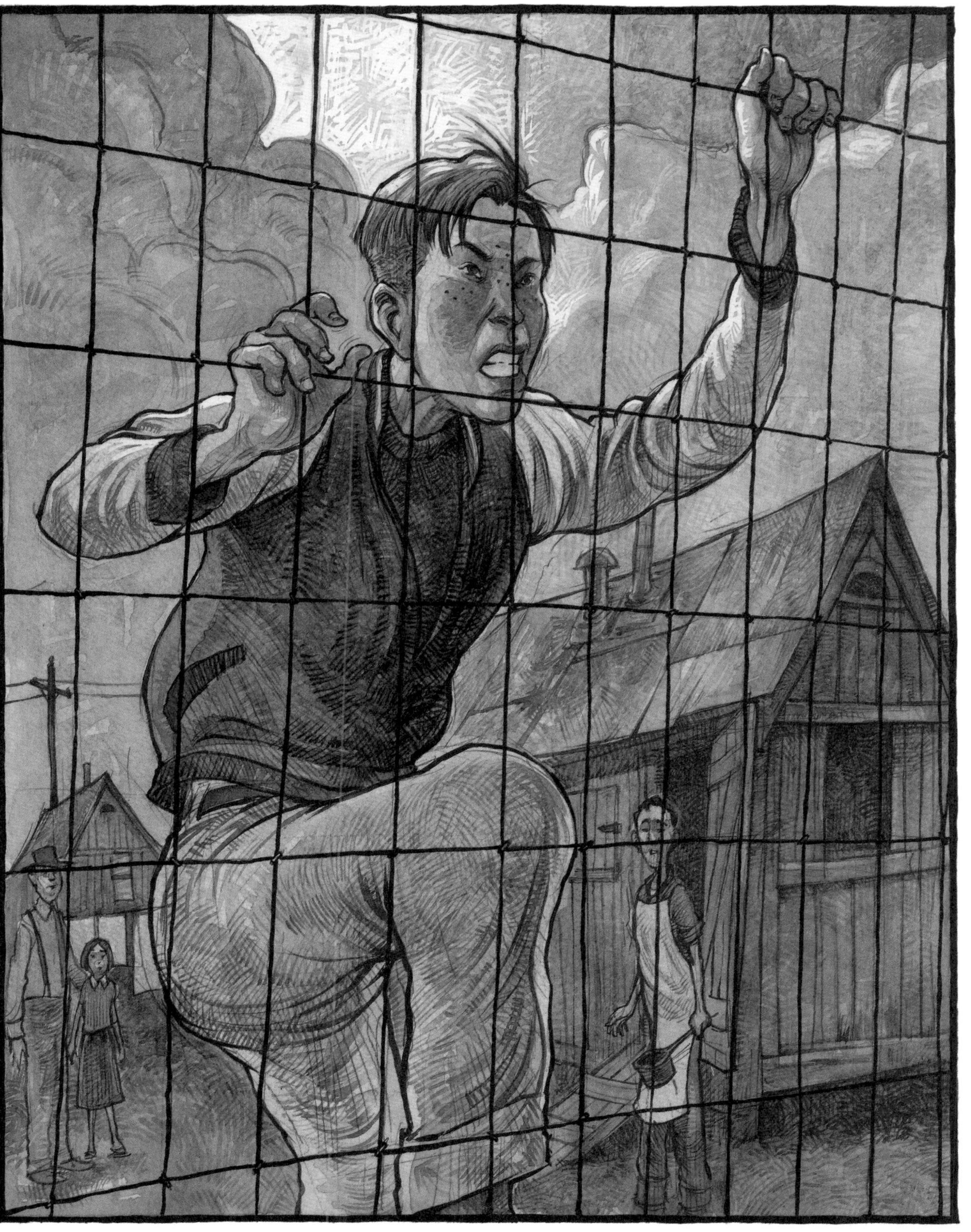

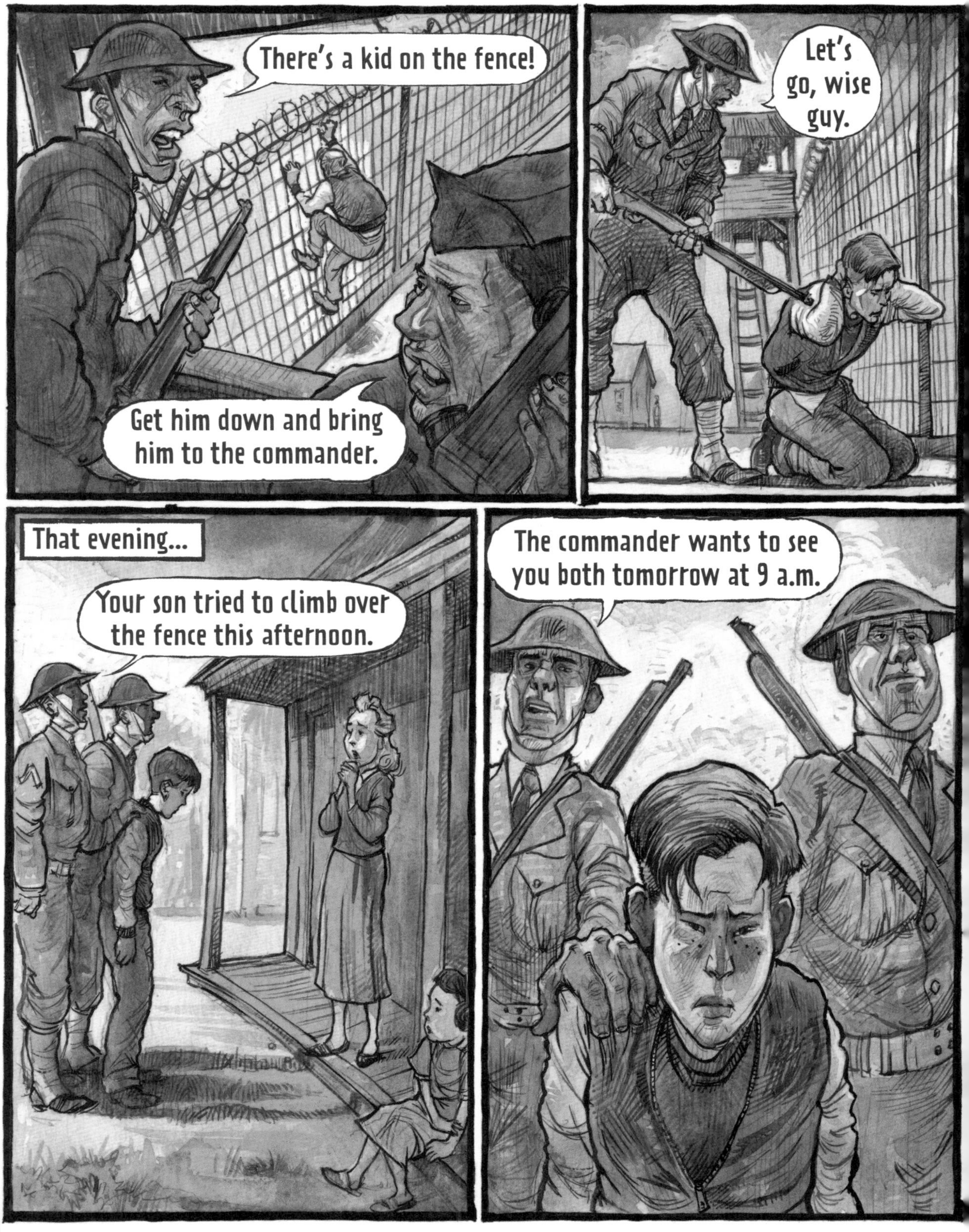
There's a kid on the fence!
Get him down and bring him to the commander.
Let's go, wise guy.
That evening...
Your son tried to climb over the fence this afternoon.
The commander wants to see you both tomorrow at 9 a.m.

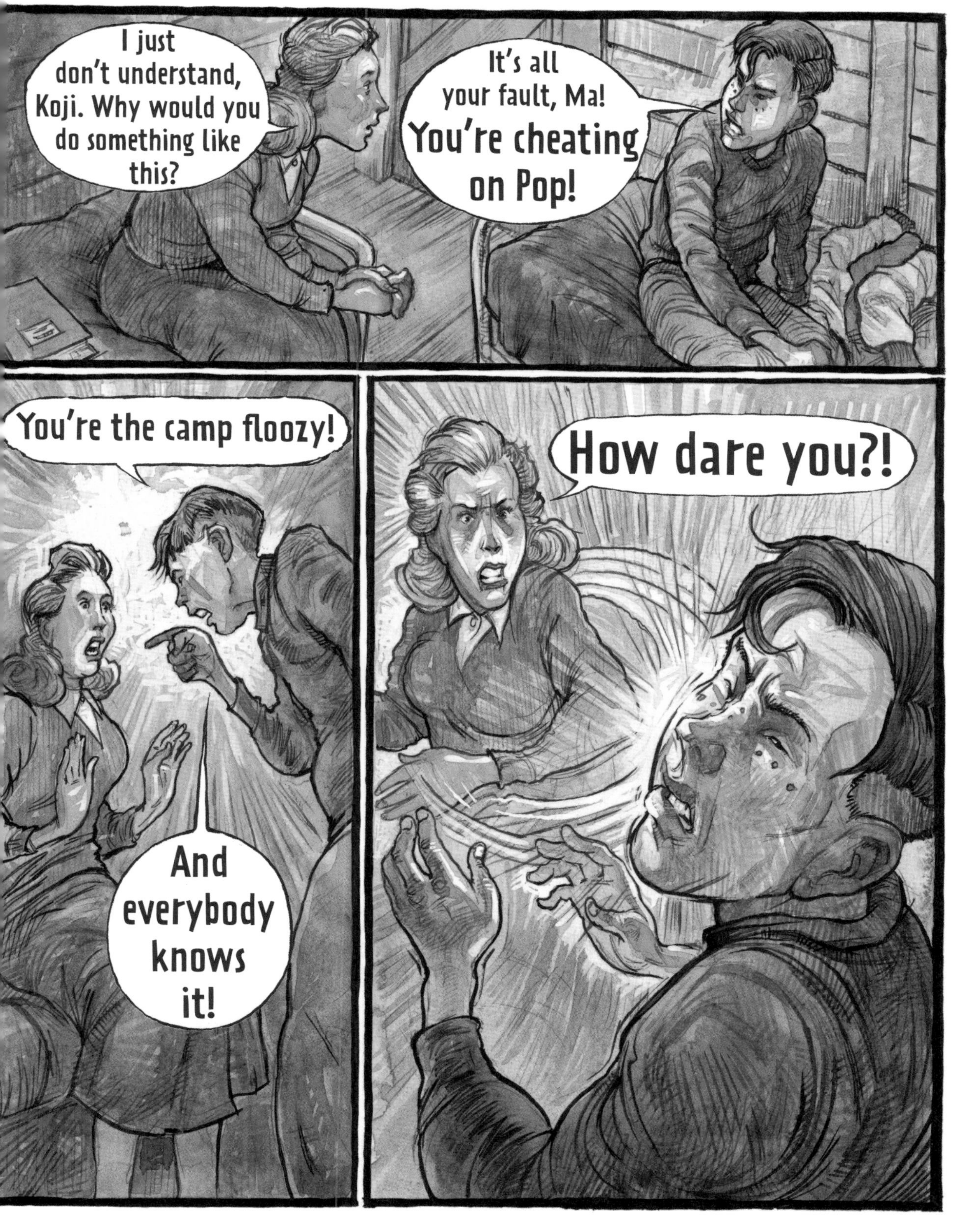
I just don't understand, Koji. Why would you do something like this?
It's all your fault, Ma! You're cheating on Pop!
You're the camp floozy!
And everybody knows it!
How dare you?!

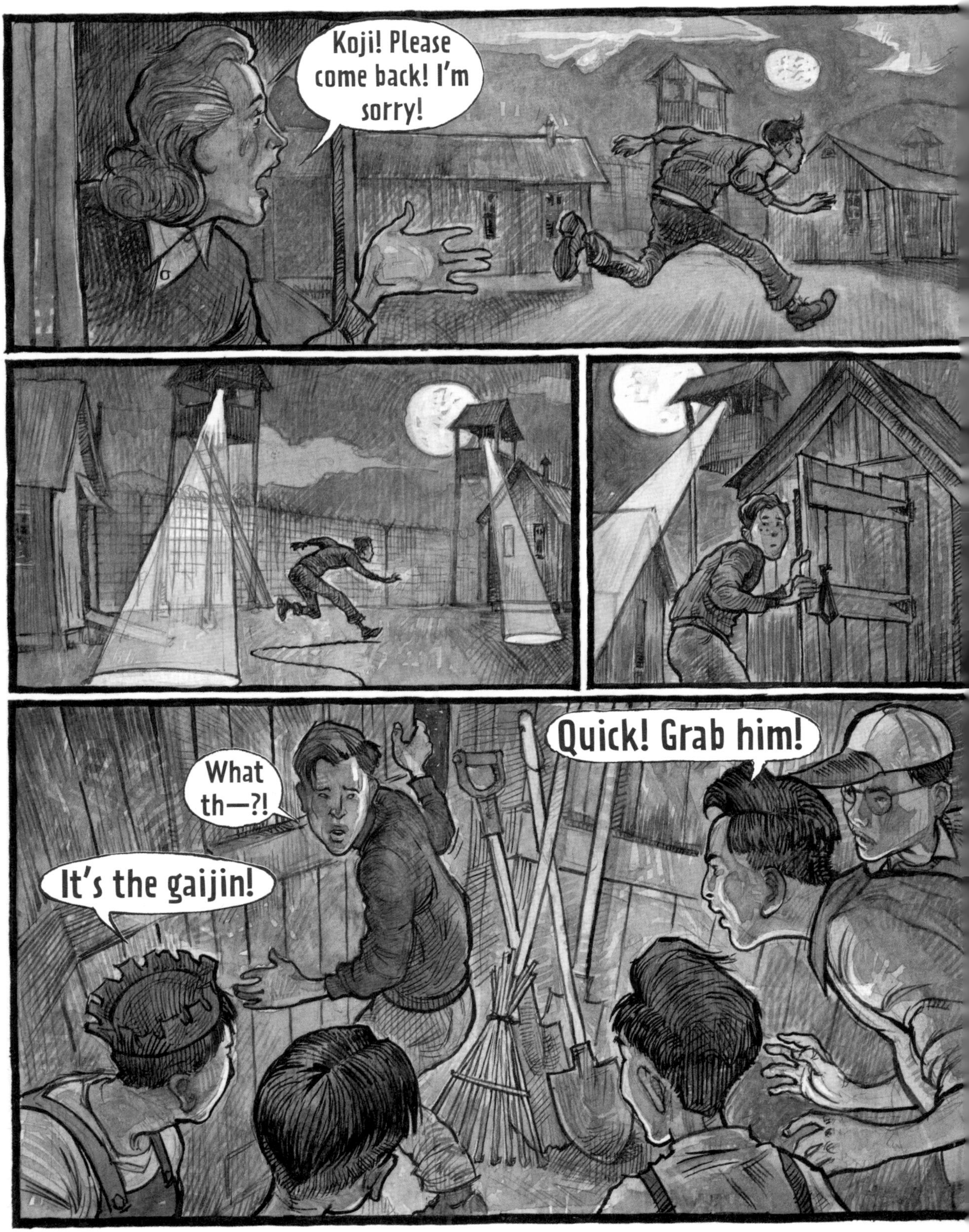
Koji! Please come back! I'm sorry!
What th—?!
Quick! Grab him!
It's the gaijin!

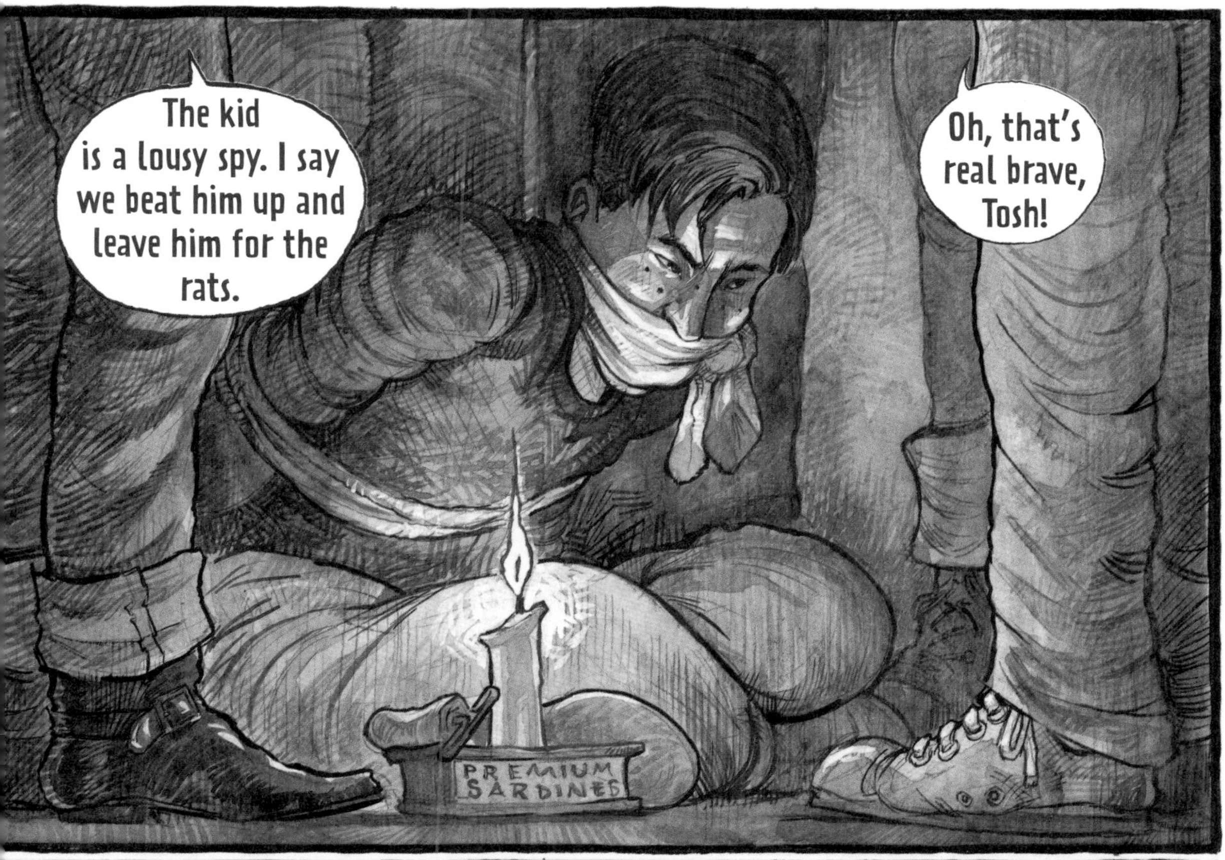
The kid is a lousy spy. I say we beat him up and leave him for the rats.
Oh, that's real brave, Tosh!
PREMIUM SARDINES

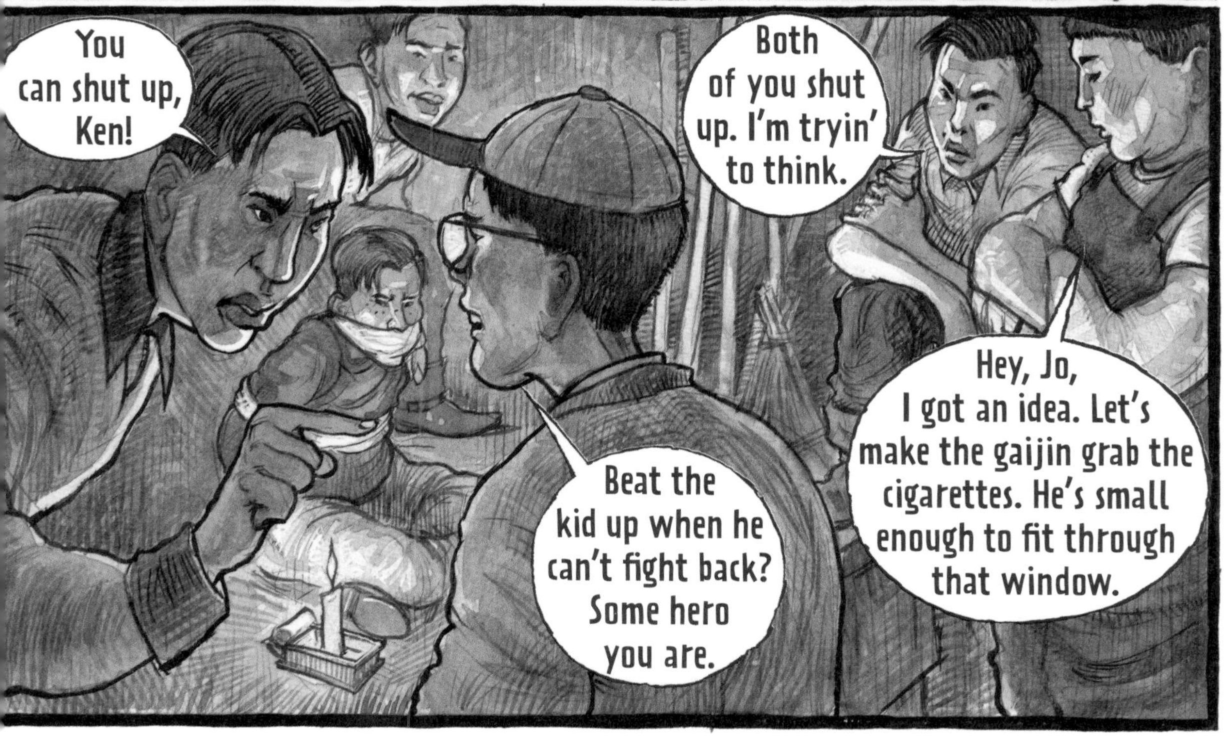
You can shut up, Ken!
Both of you shut up. I'm tryin' to think.
Beat the kid up when he can't fight back? Some hero you are.
Hey, Jo, I got an idea. Let's make the gaijin grab the cigarettes. He's small enough to fit through that window.

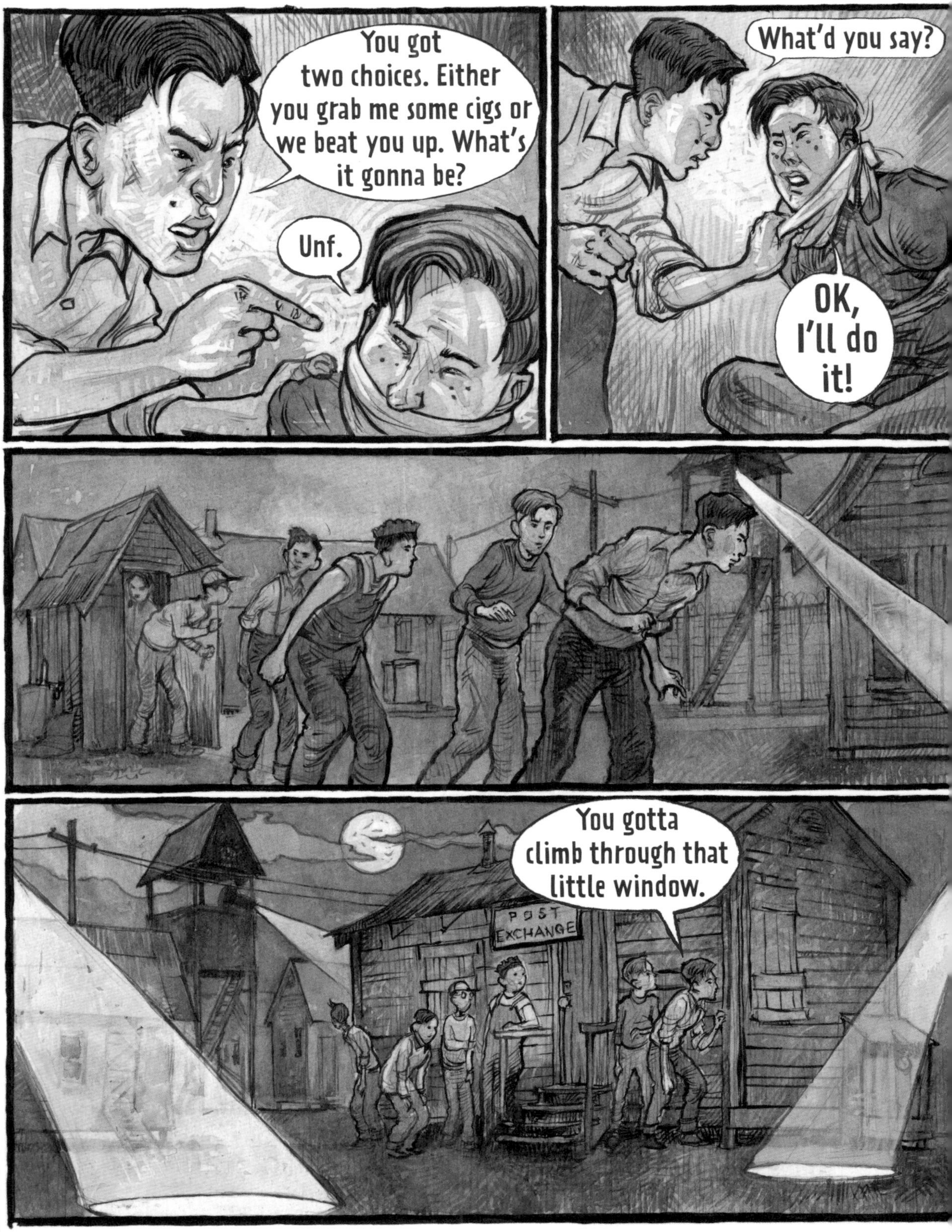
You got two choices. Either you grab me some cigs or we beat you up. What's it gonna be?
Unf.
What'd you say?
OK, I'll do it!
POST EXCHANGE
You gotta climb through that little window.

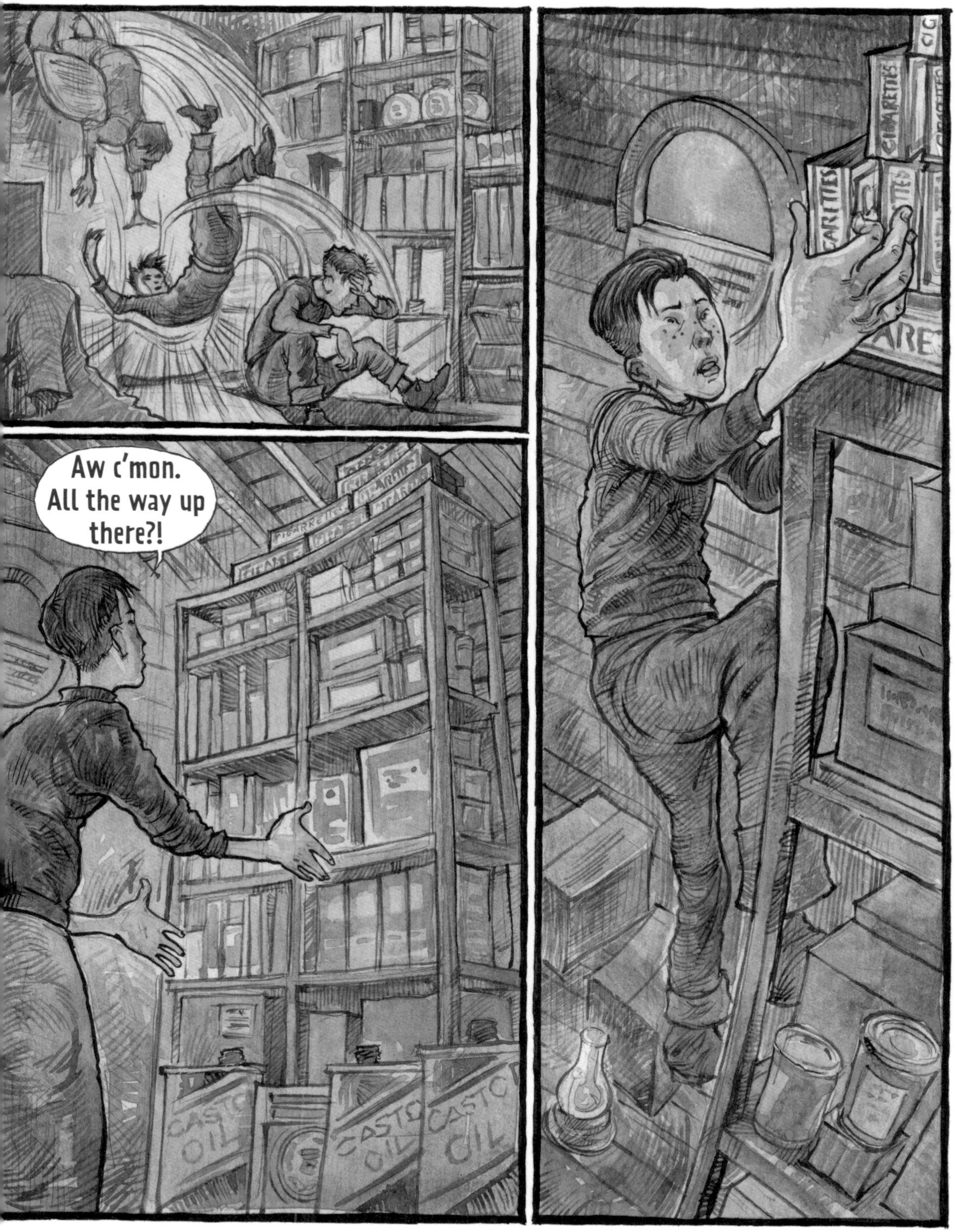
Aw c'mon. All the way up there?!

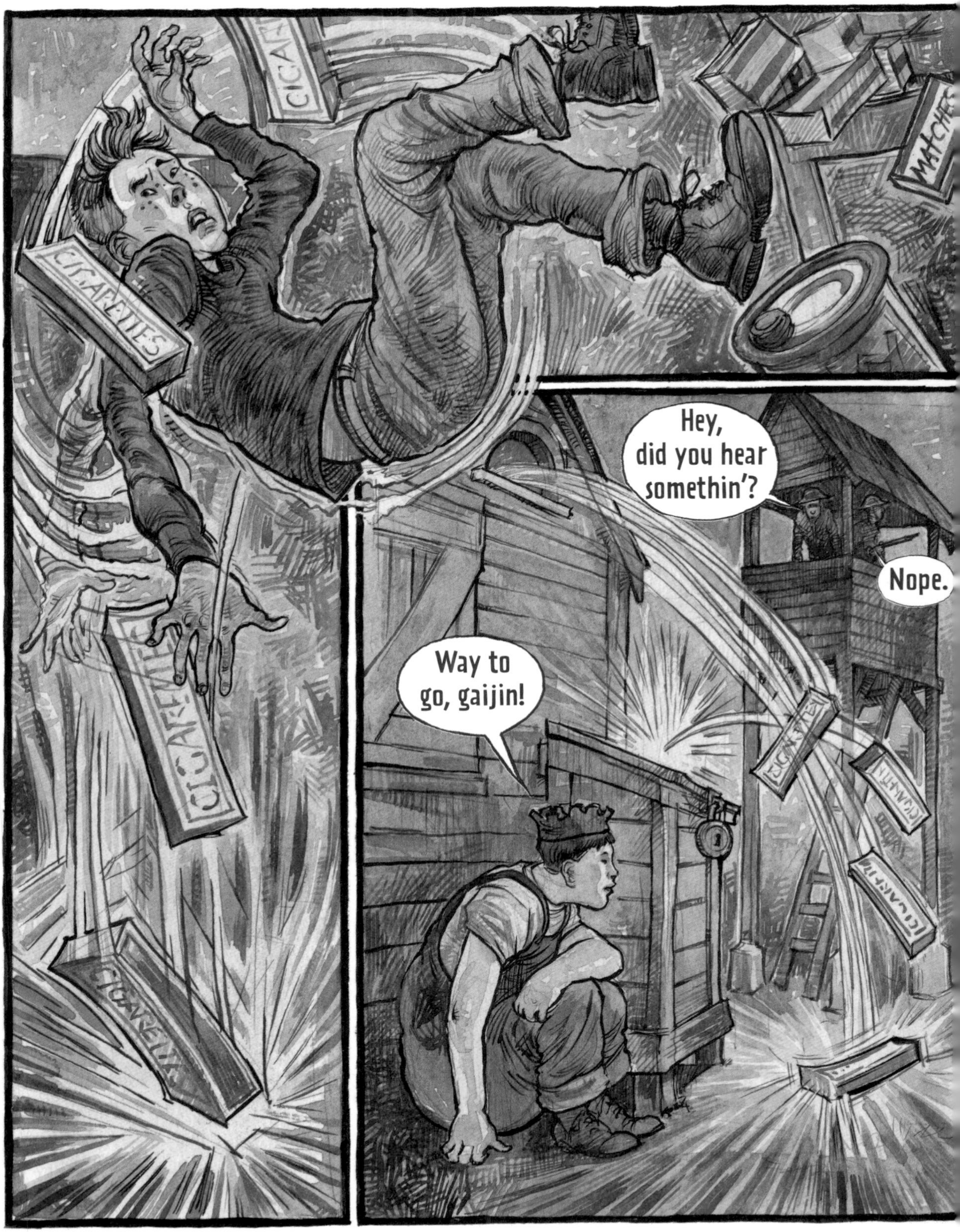
Hey, did you hear somethin'?
Nope.
Way to go, gaijin!

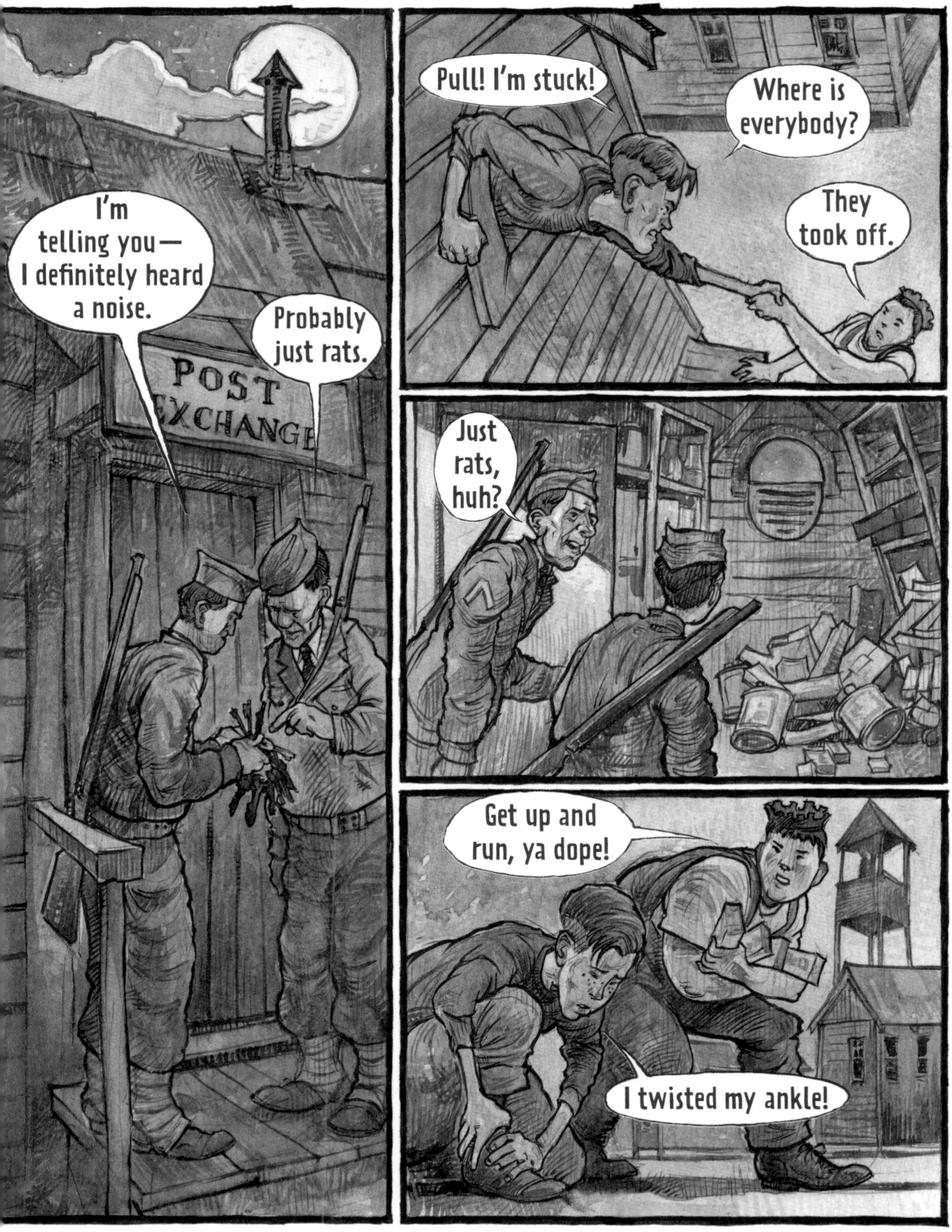

POST EXCHANGE
I'm telling you— I definitely heard a noise.
Probably just rats.
Pull! I'm stuck!
Where is everybody?
They took off.
Just rats, huh?
Get up and run, ya dope!
I twisted my ankle!

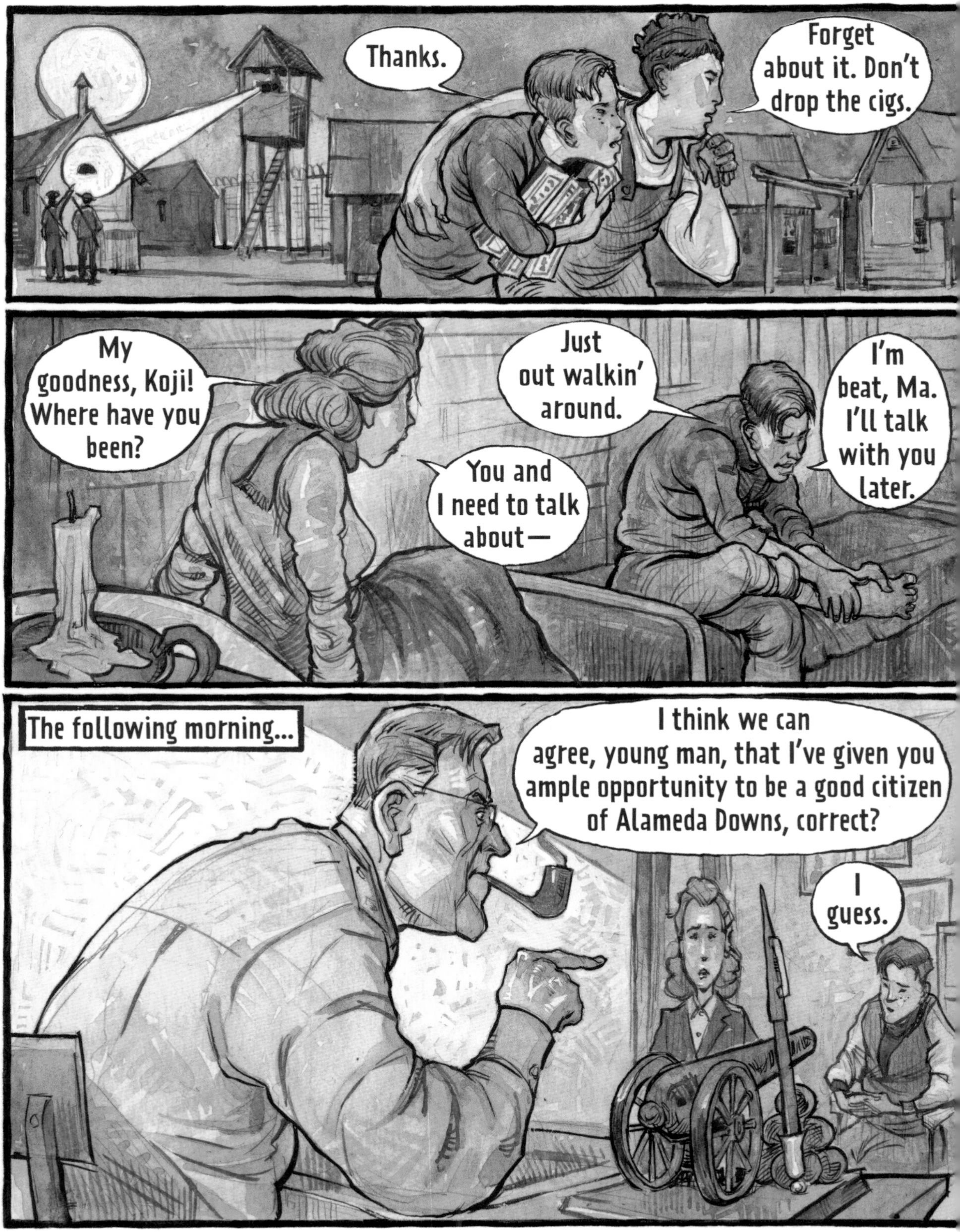
Thanks.
Forget about it. Don't drop the cigs.
My goodness, Koji! Where have you been?
Just out walkin' around.
You and I need to talk about—
I'm beat, Ma. I'll talk with you later.
The following morning...
I think we can agree, young man, that I've given you ample opportunity to be a good citizen of Alameda Downs, correct?
I guess.

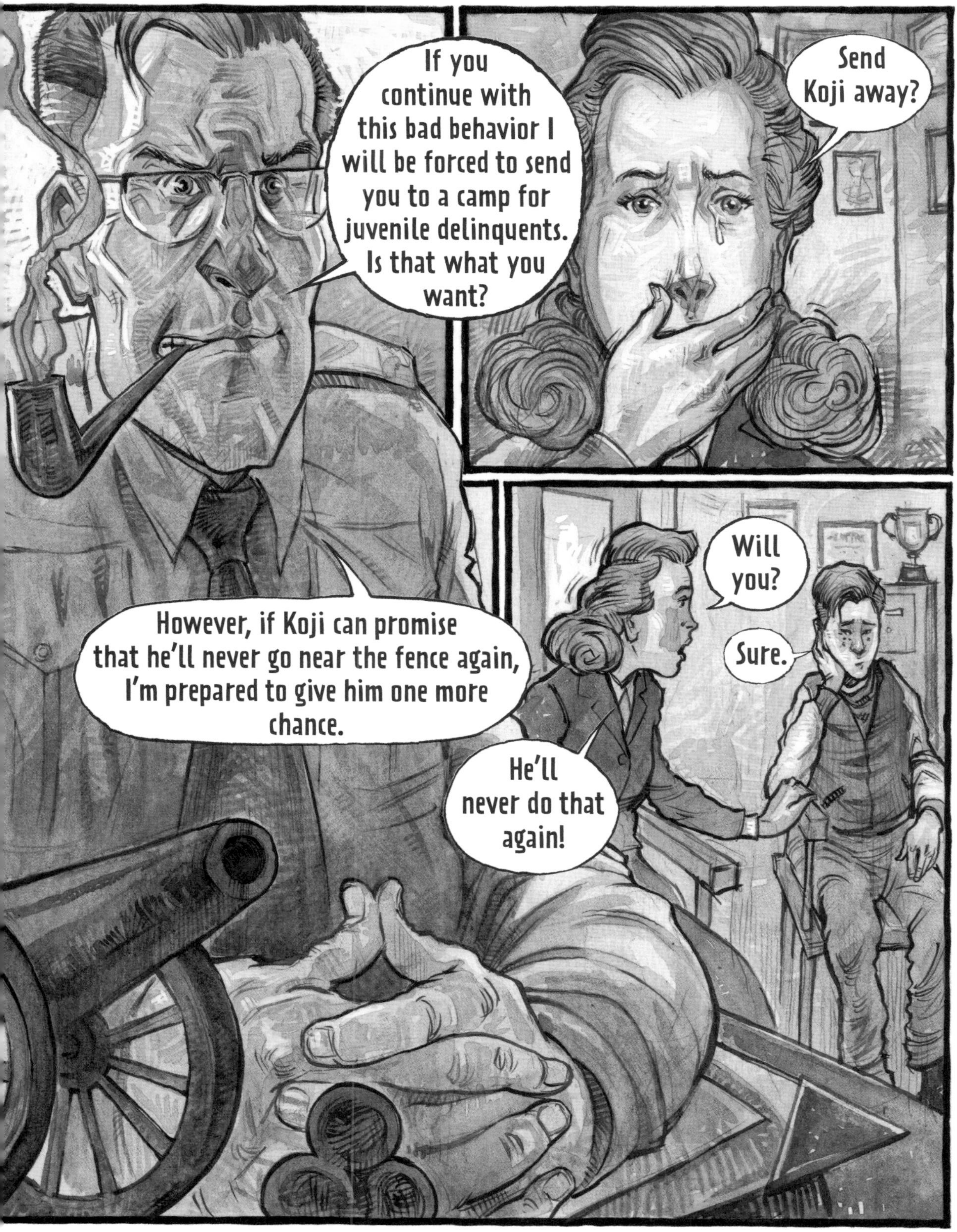
If you continue with this bad behavior I will be forced to send you to a camp for juvenile delinquents. Is that what you want?
Send Koji away?
However, if Koji can promise that he'll never go near the fence again, I'm prepared to give him one more chance.
Will you?
Sure.
He'll never do that again!

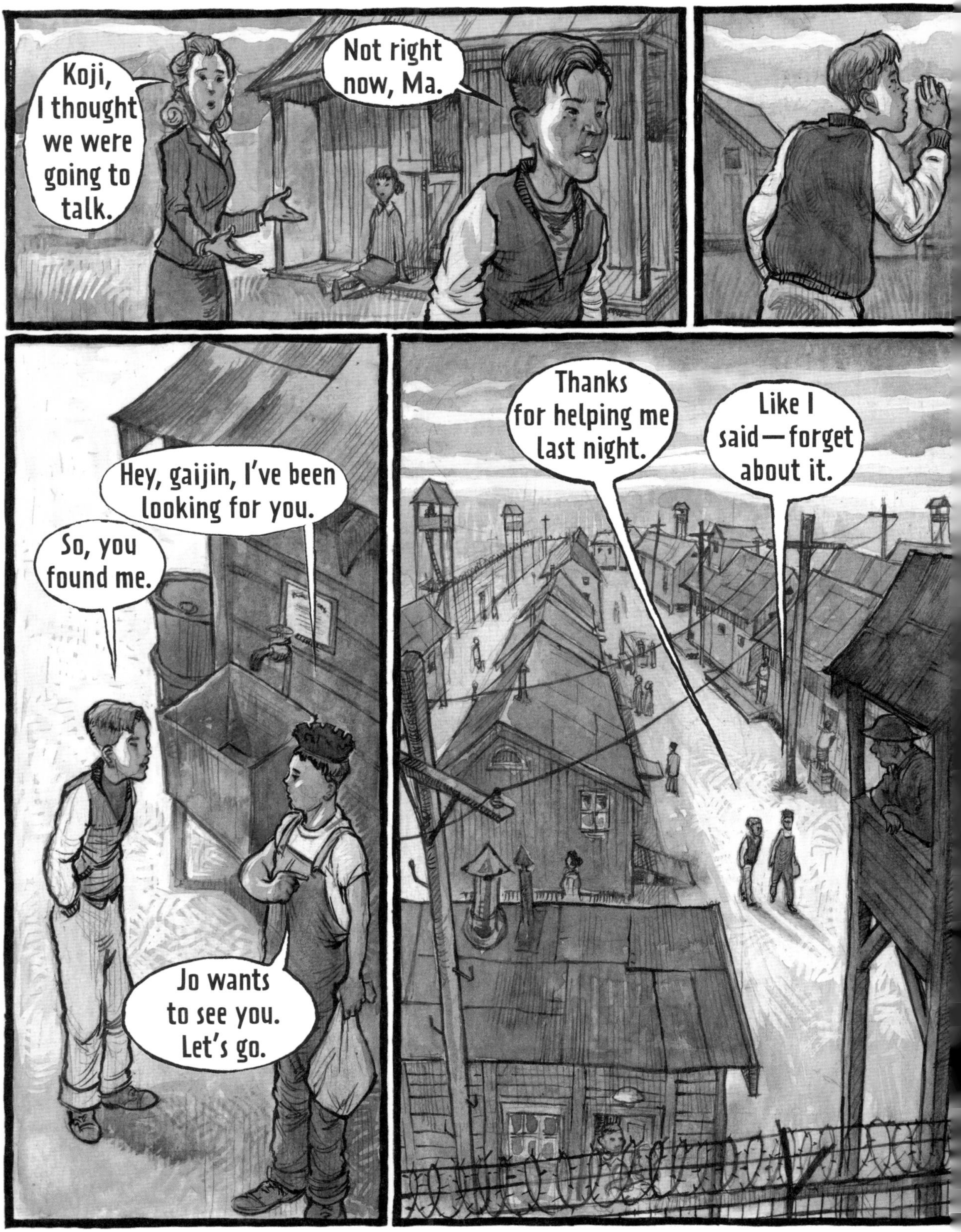
Koji, I thought we were going to talk.
Not right now, Ma.
Hey, gaijin, I've been looking for you.
So, you found me.
Jo wants to see you. Let's go.
Thanks for helping me last night.
Like I said—forget about it.

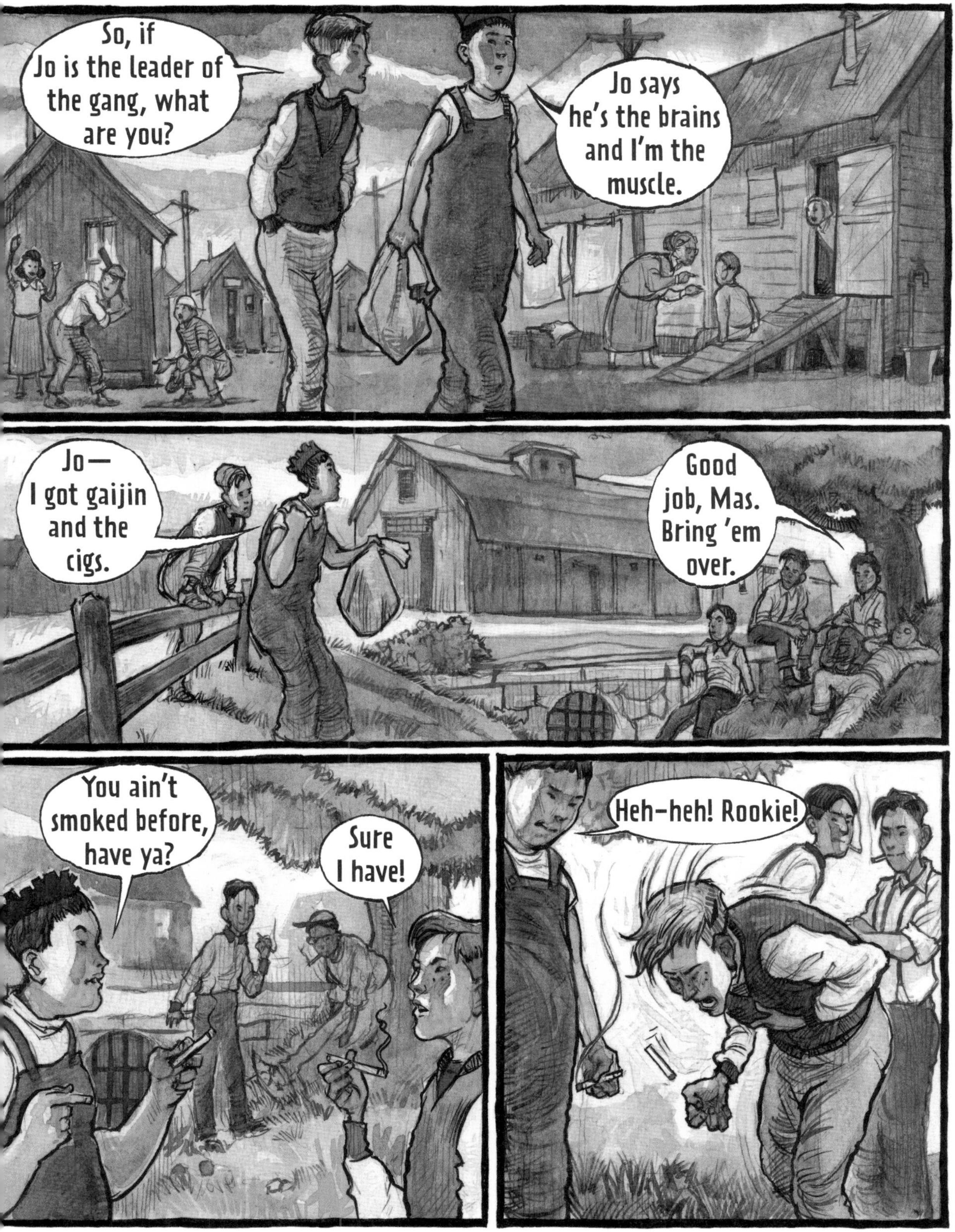
So, if Jo is the leader of the gang, what are you?
Jo says he's the brains and I'm the muscle.
Jo— I got gaijin and the cigs.
Good job, Mas. Bring 'em over.
You ain't smoked before, have ya?
Sure I have!
Heh-heh! Rookie!

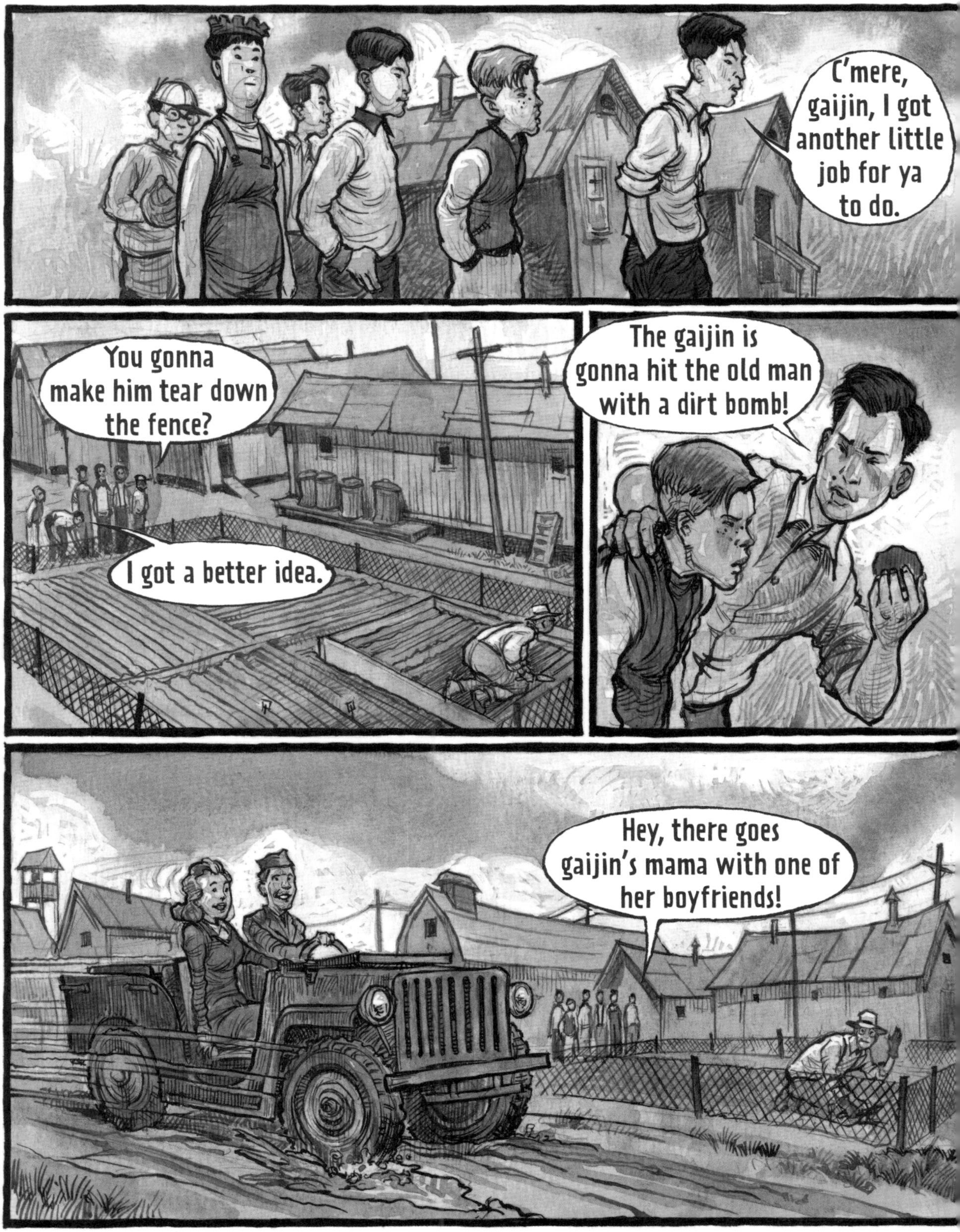
C'mere, gaijin, I got another little job for ya to do.
You gonna make him tear down the fence?
I got a better idea.
The gaijin is gonna hit the old man with a dirt bomb!
Hey, there goes gaijin's mama with one of her boyfriends!

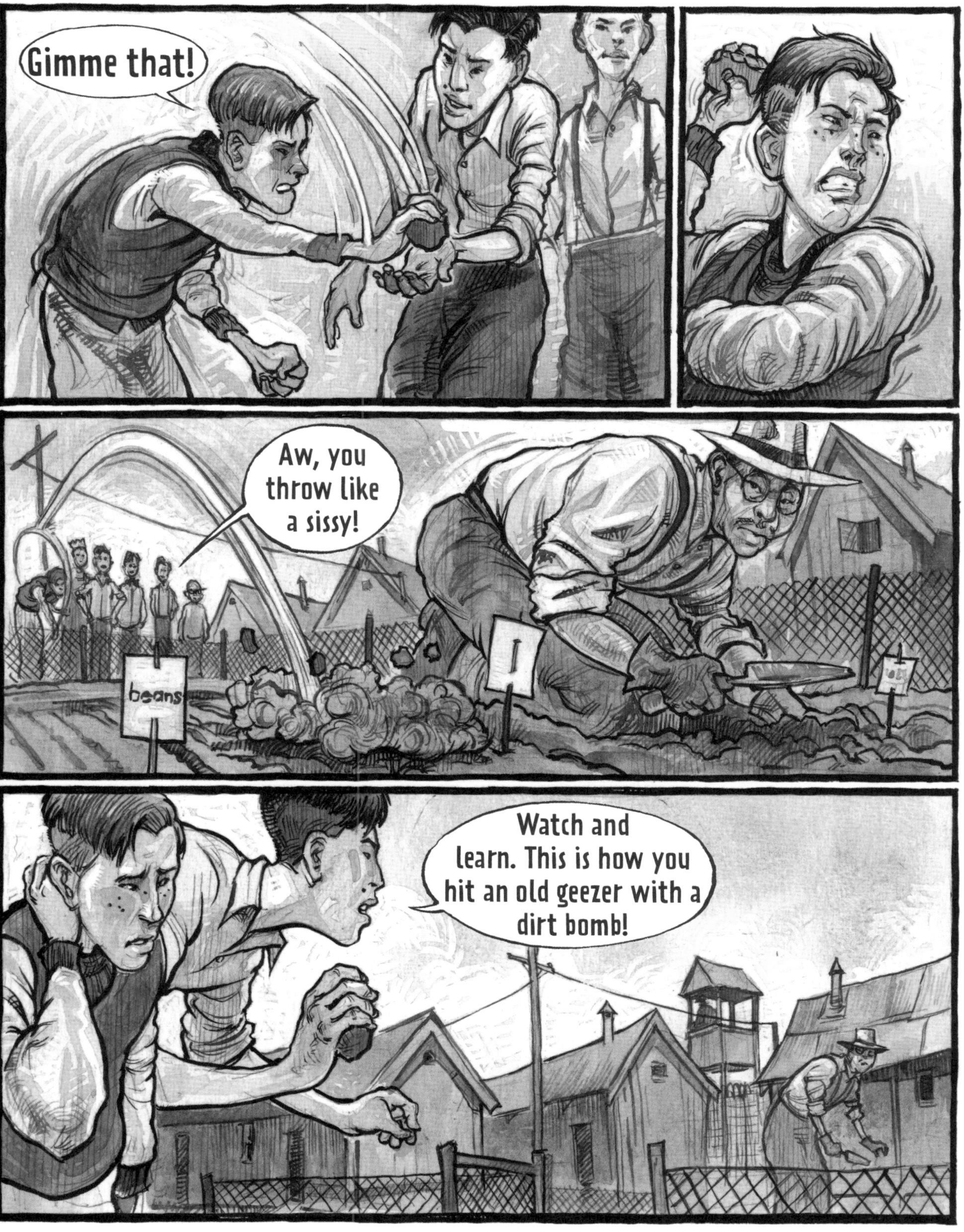
Gimme that!
Aw, you throw like a sissy!
beans
Watch and learn. This is how you hit an old geezer with a dirt bomb!

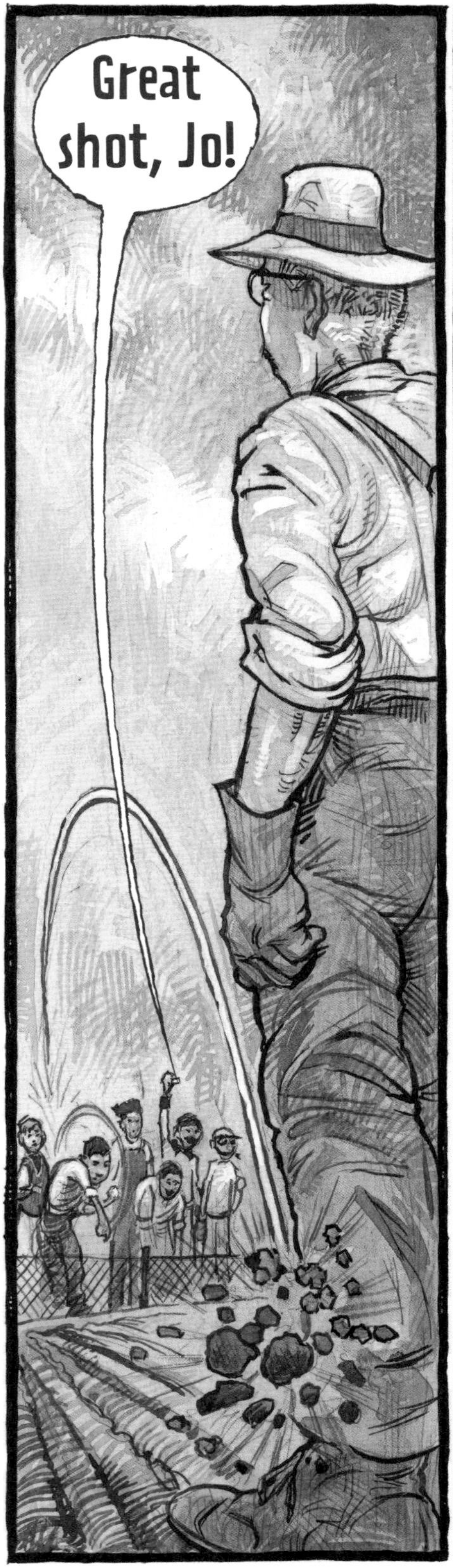
Great shot, Jo!

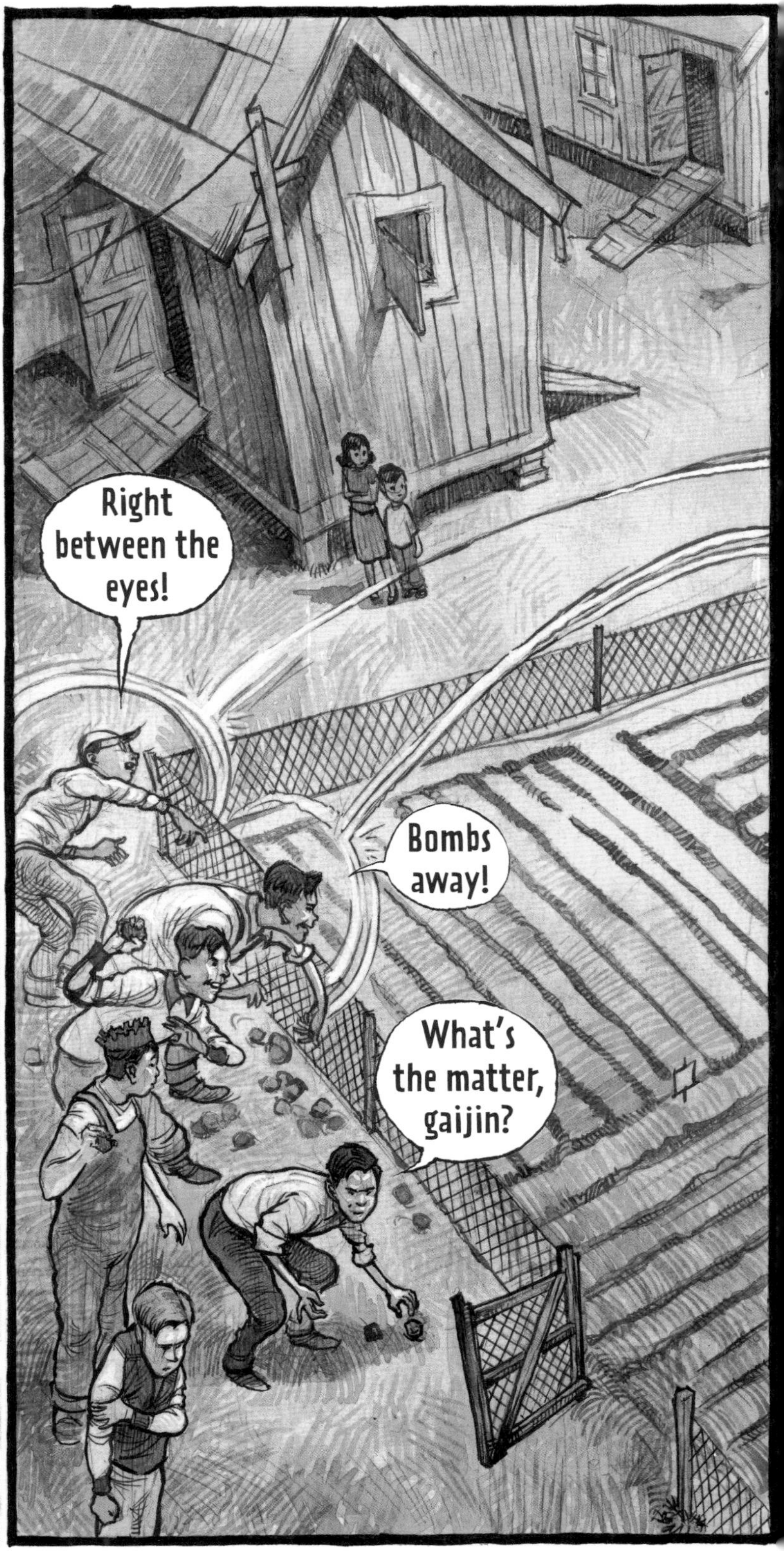
Right between the eyes!
Bombs away!
What's the matter, gaijin?

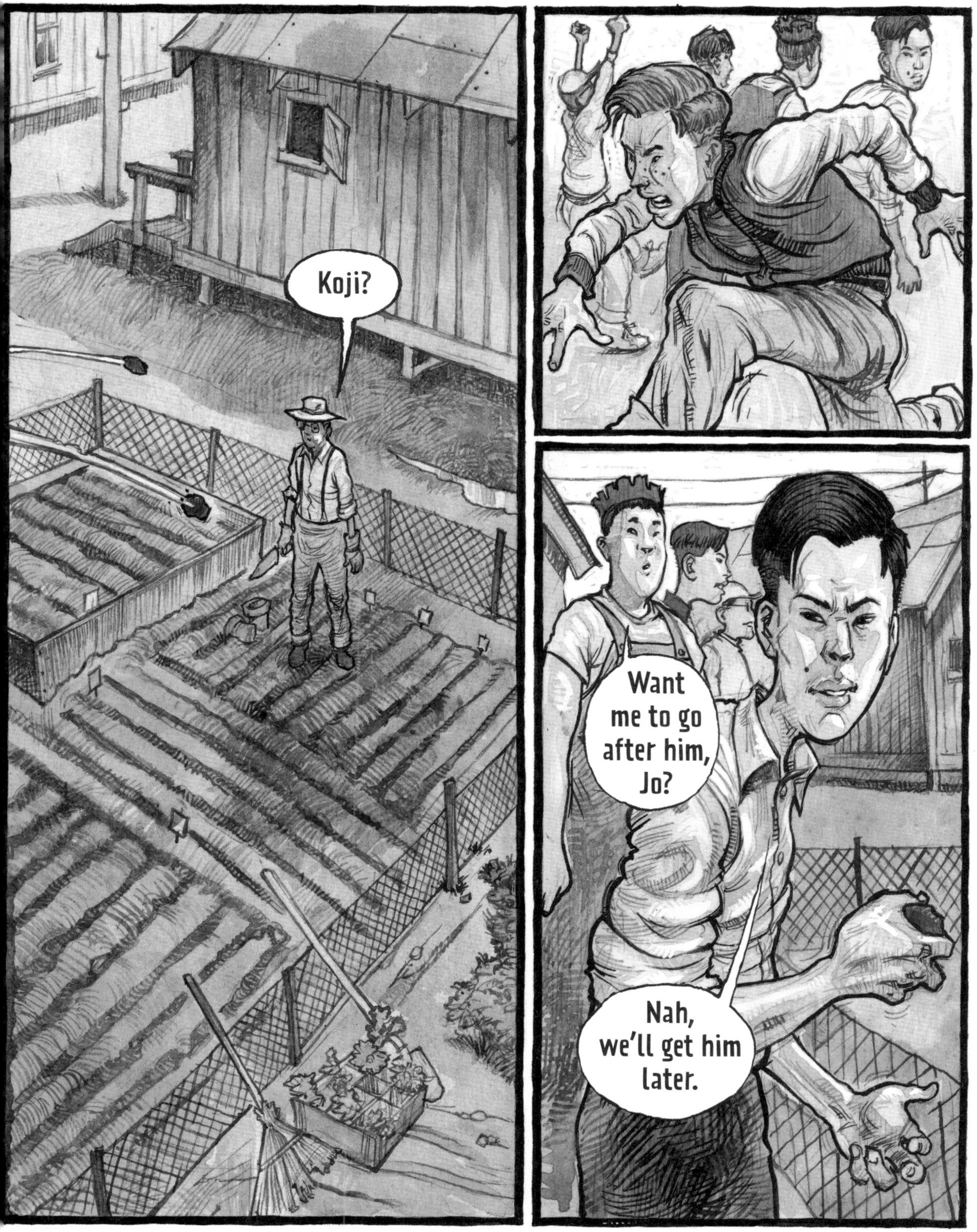
Koji?
Want me to go after him, Jo?
Nah, we'll get him later.

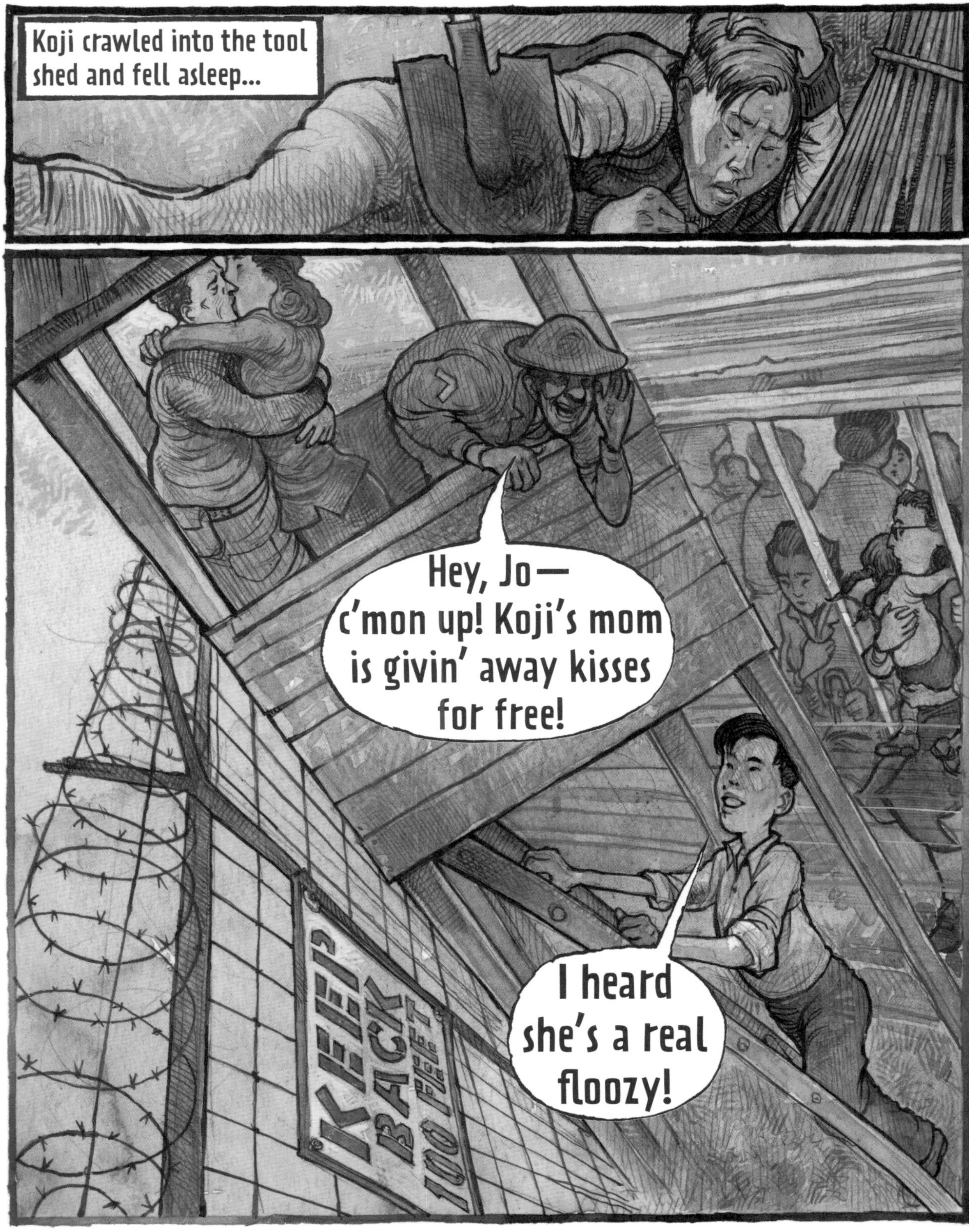
Koji crawled into the tool shed and fell asleep...
Hey, Jo— c'mon up! Koji's mom is givin' away kisses for free!
I heard she's a real floozy!
KEEP
BACK

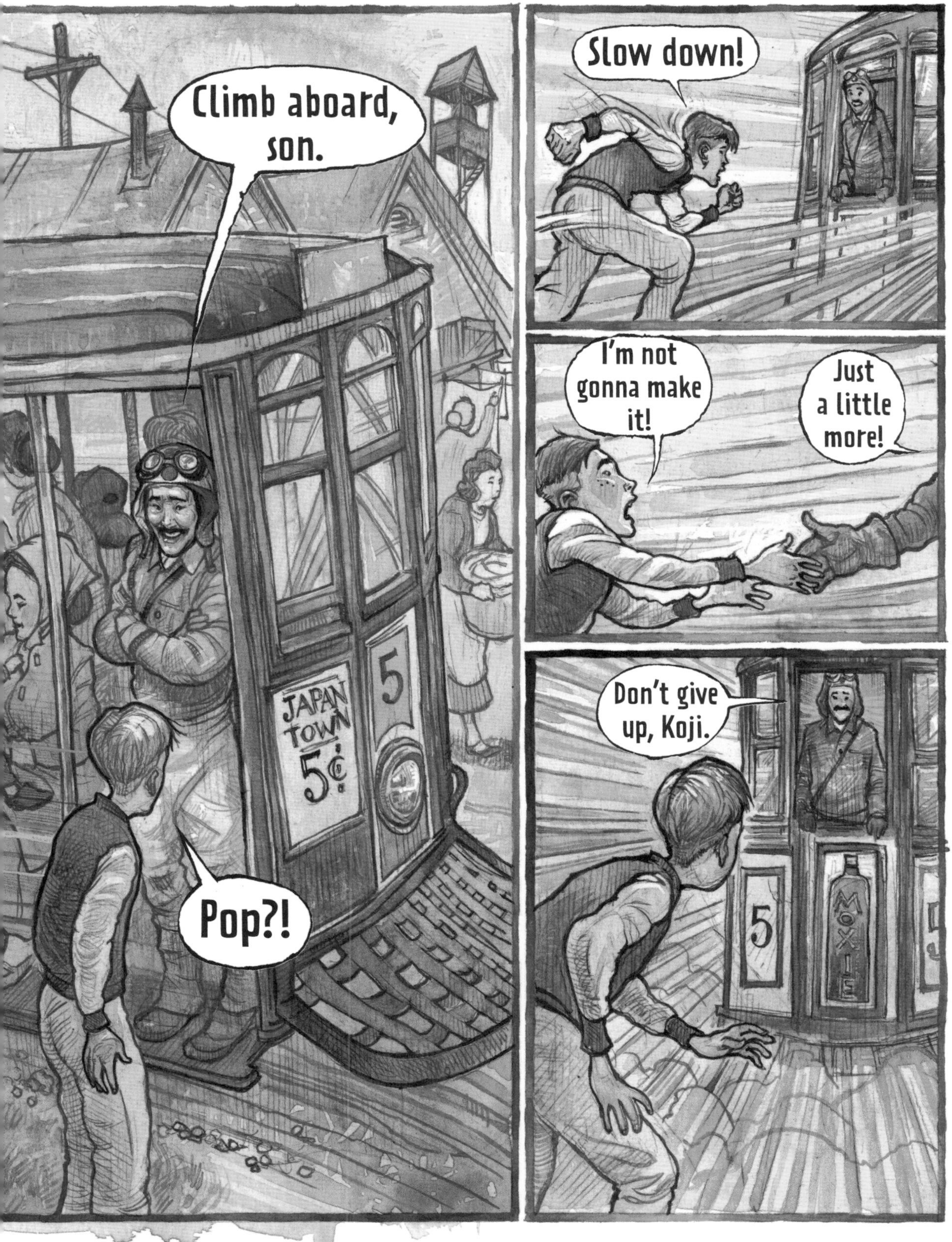
Climb aboard, son.
JAPAN TOWN 5¢
5
Pop?!
Slow down!
I'm not gonna make it!
Just a little more!
Don't give up, Koji.
5
MOXIE

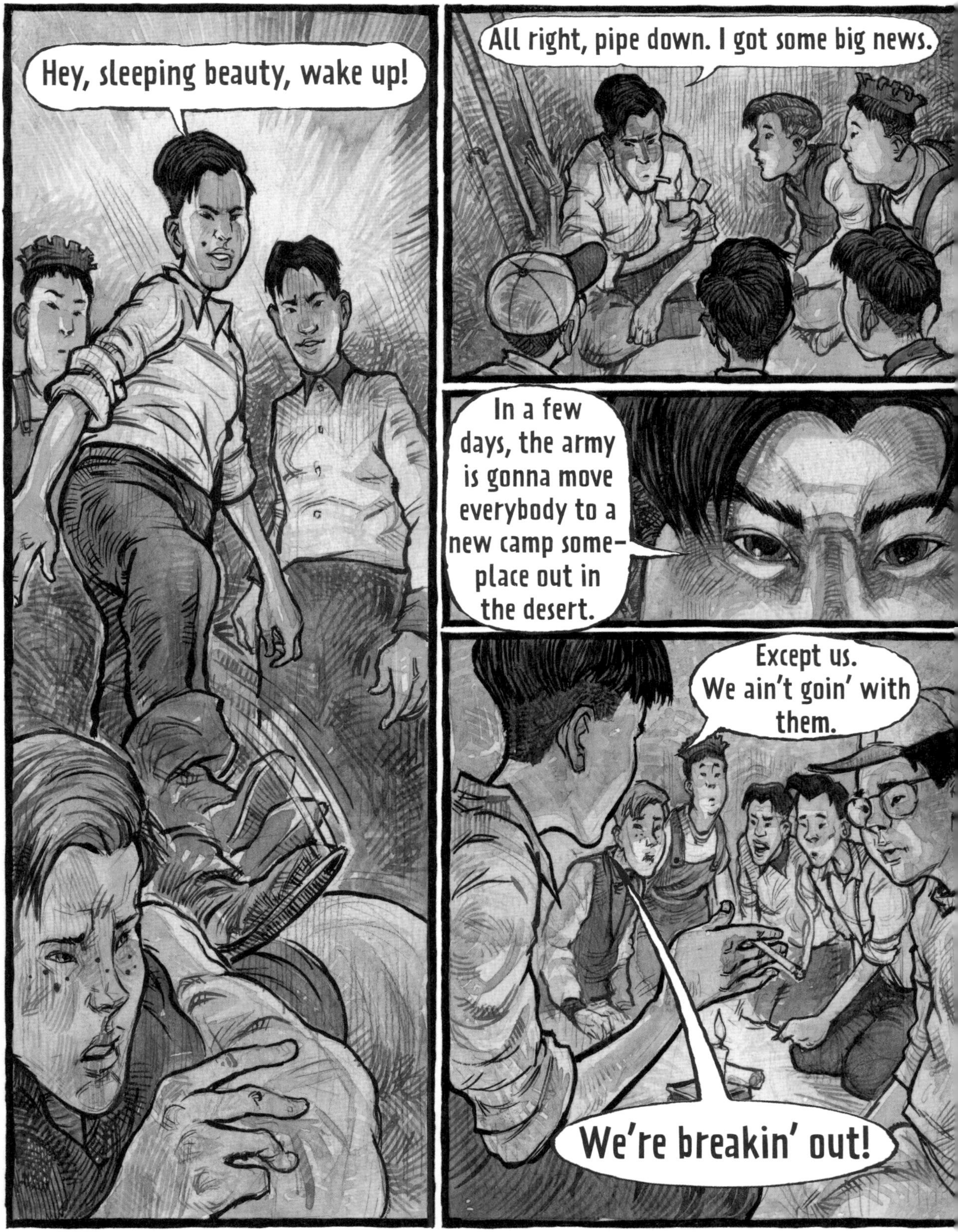
Hey, sleeping beauty, wake up!
All right, pipe down. I got some big news.
In a few days, the army is gonna move everybody to a new camp some-place out in the desert.
Except us. We ain't goin' with them.
We're breakin' out!

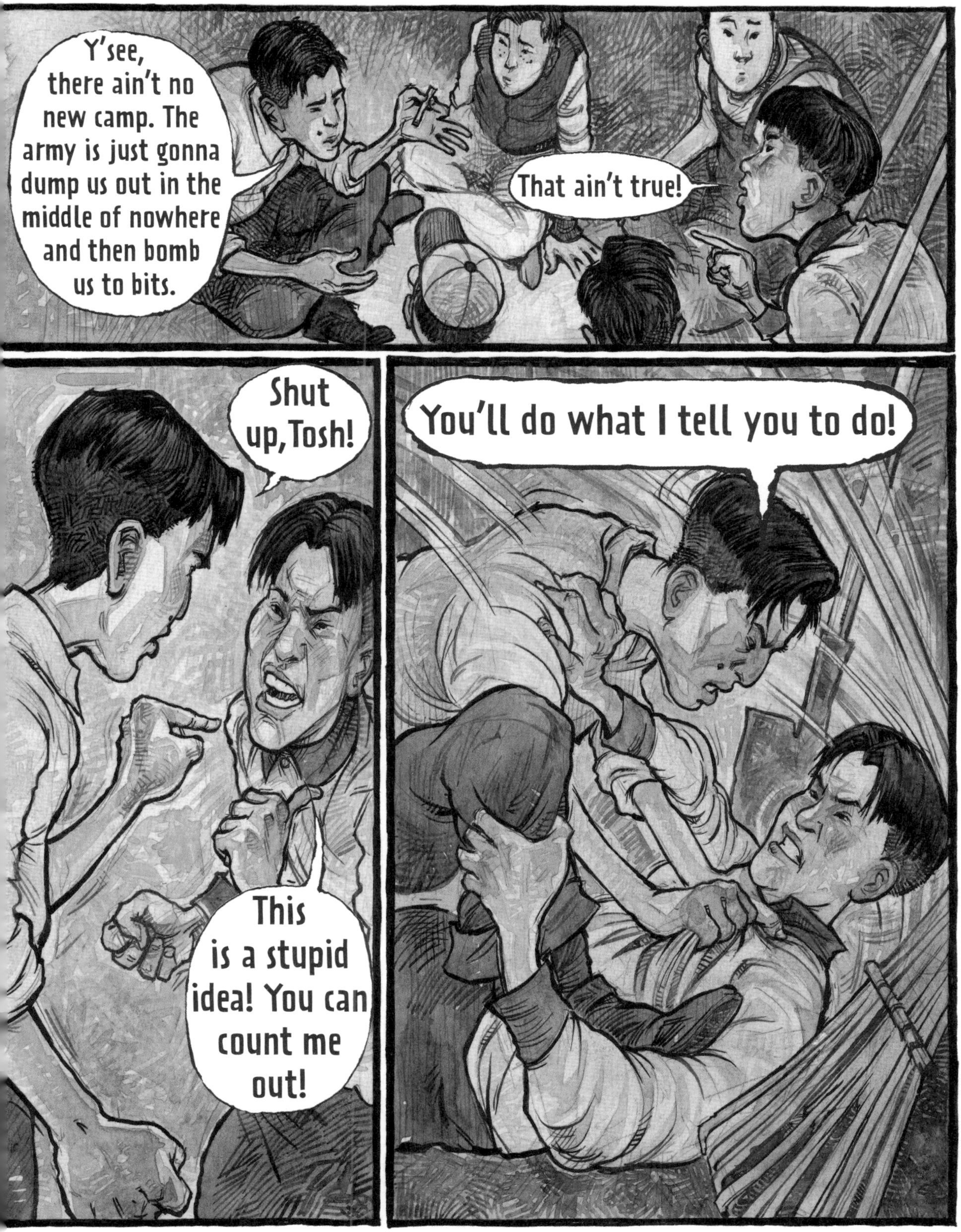
Y'see, there ain't no new camp. The army is just gonna dump us out in the middle of nowhere and then bomb us to bits.
That ain't true!
Shut up, Tosh!
This is a stupid idea! You can count me out!
You'll do what I tell you to do!

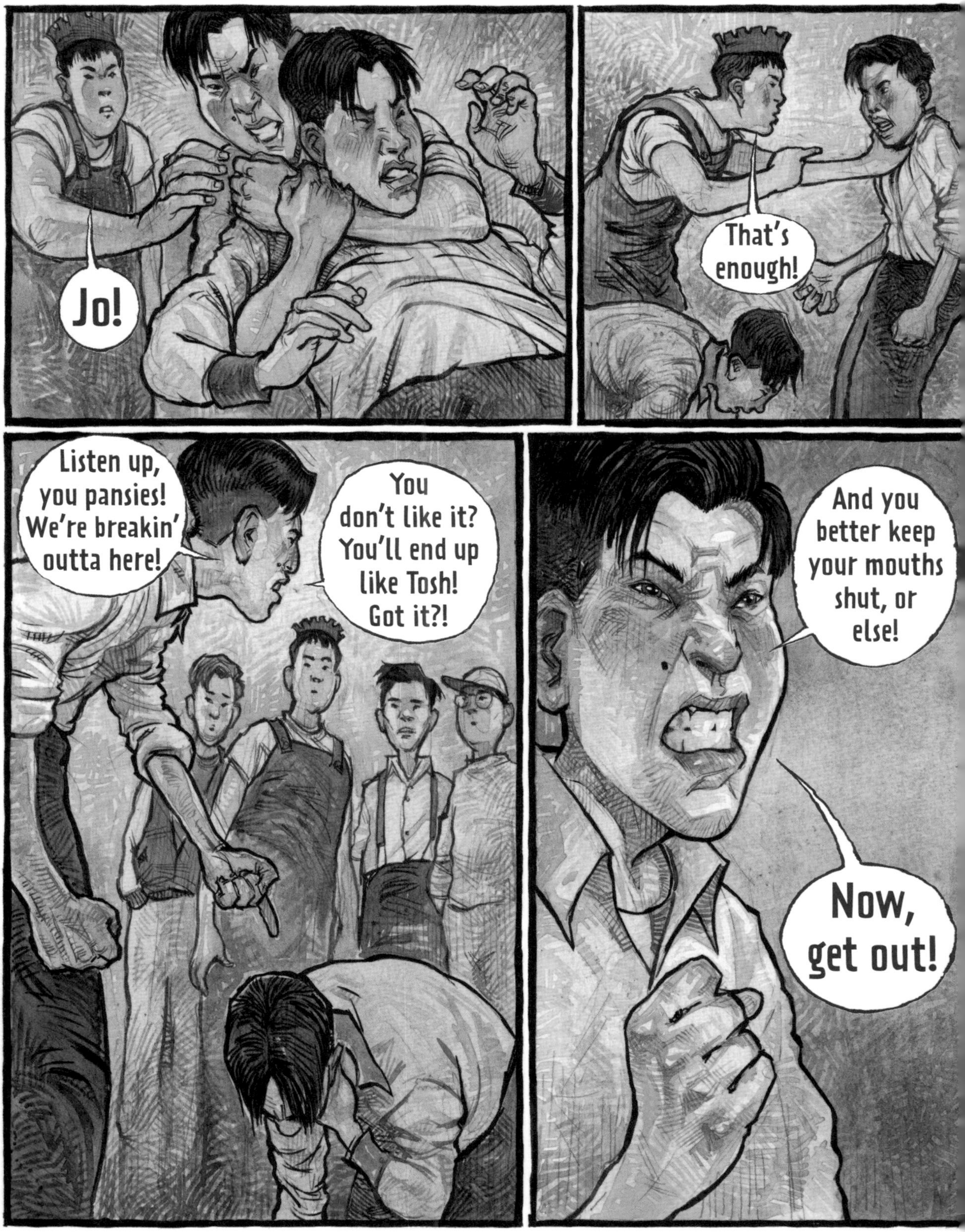
Jo!
That's enough!
Listen up, you pansies! We're breakin' outta here!
You don't like it? You'll end up like Tosh! Got it?!
And you better keep your mouths shut, or else!
Now, get out!

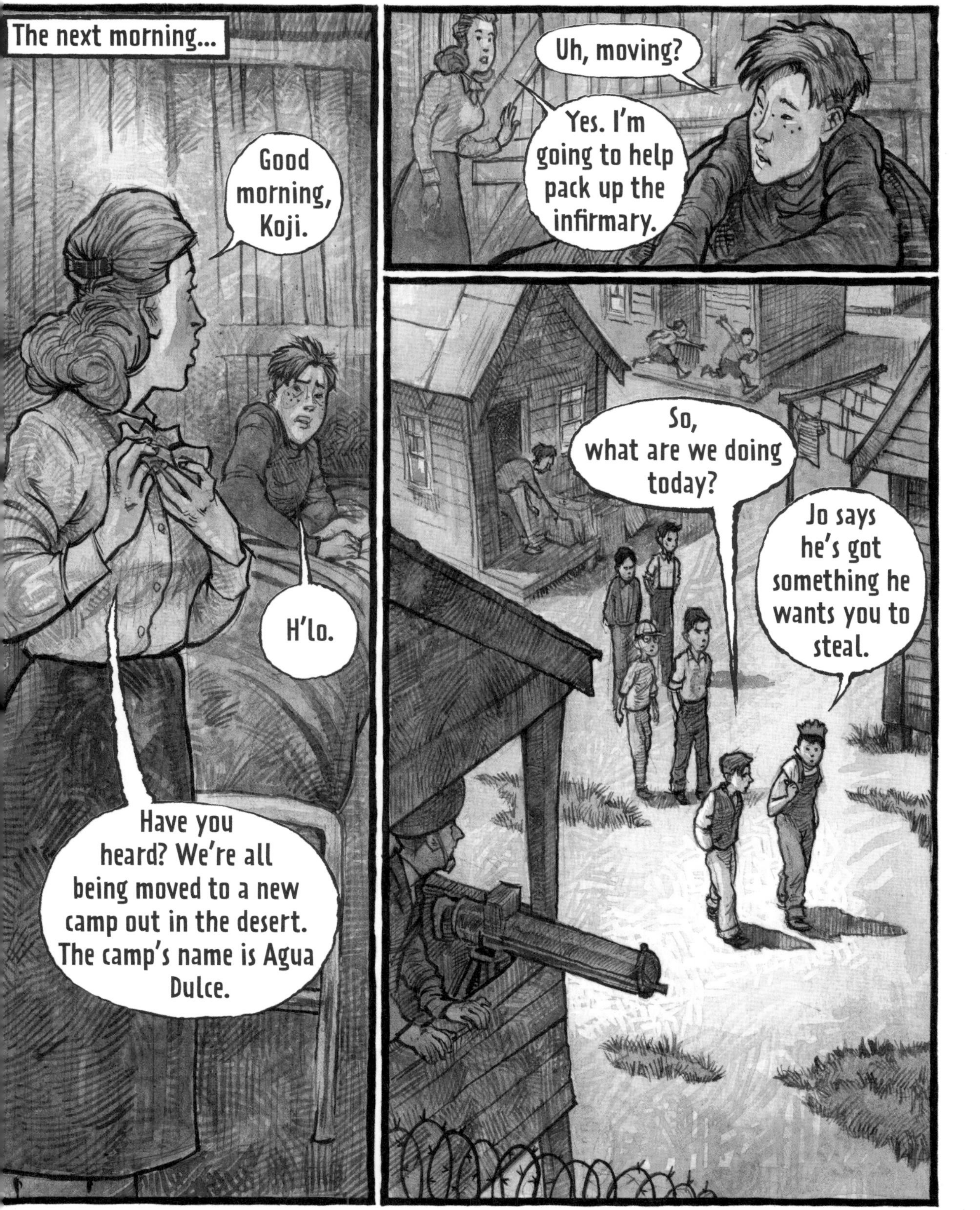
The next morning...
Good morning, Koji.
H'lo.
Have you heard? We're all being moved to a new camp out in the desert. The camp's name is Agua Dulce.
Uh, moving?
Yes. I'm going to help pack up the infirmary.
So, what are we doing today?
Jo says he's got something he wants you to steal.

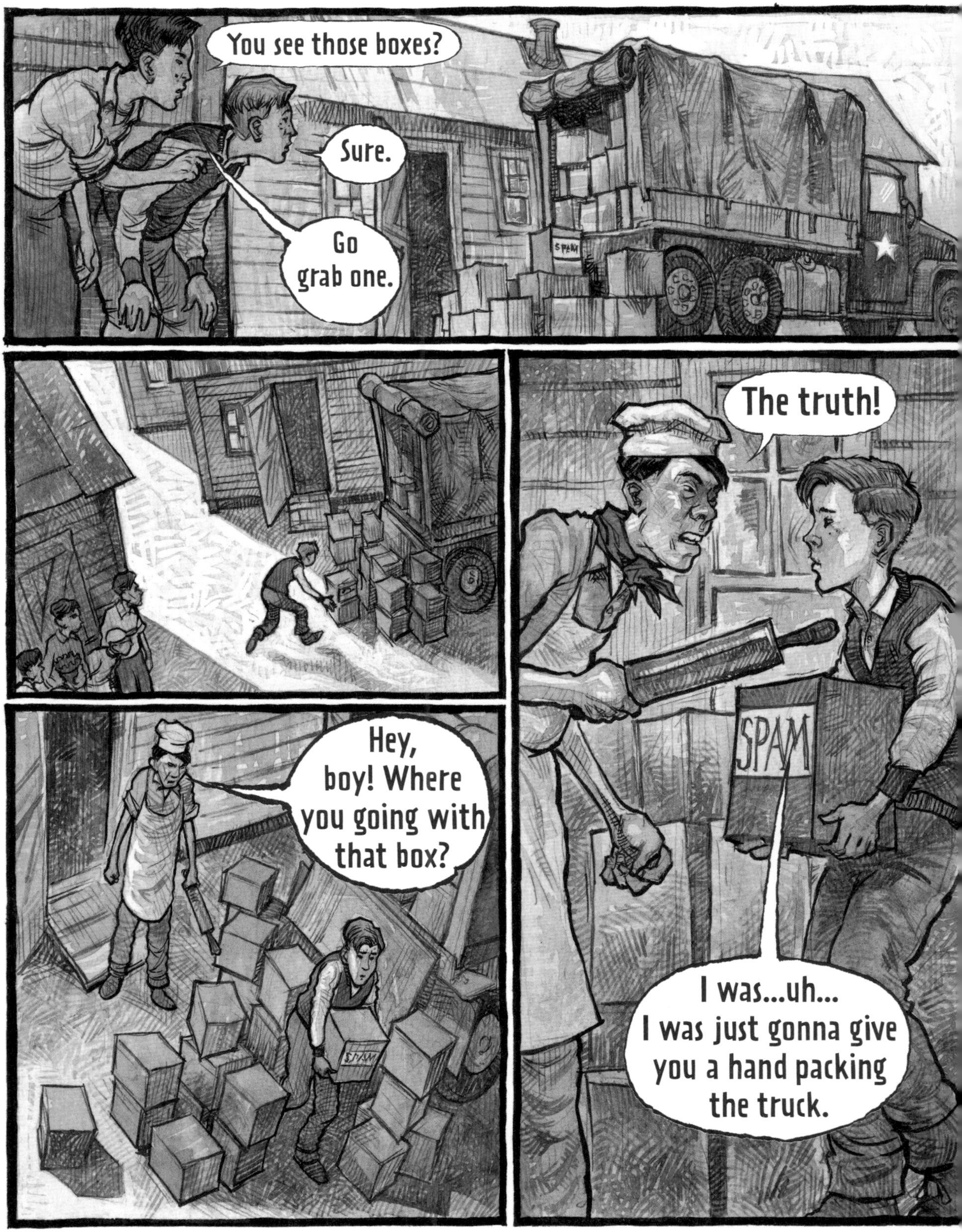
You see those boxes?
Sure.
Go grab one.
SPAM
Hey, boy! Where you going with that box?
SPAM
The truth!
SPAM
I was...uh... I was just gonna give you a hand packing the truck.

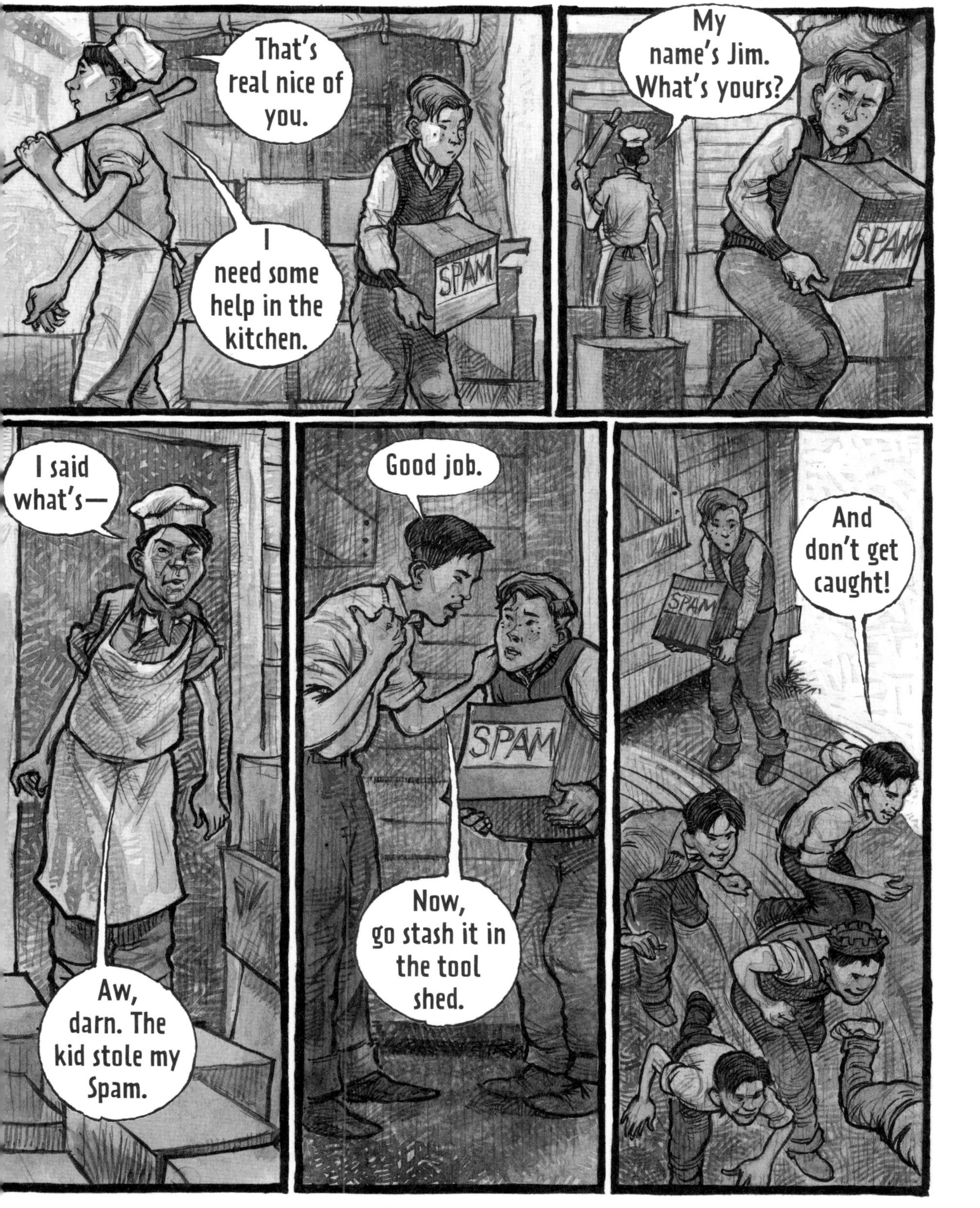
That's real nice of you.
I need some help in the kitchen.
My name's Jim. What's yours?
I said what's—
Aw, darn. The kid stole my Spam.
Good job.
Now, go stash it in the tool shed.
And don't get caught!
SPAM
SPAM
SPAM
SPAM

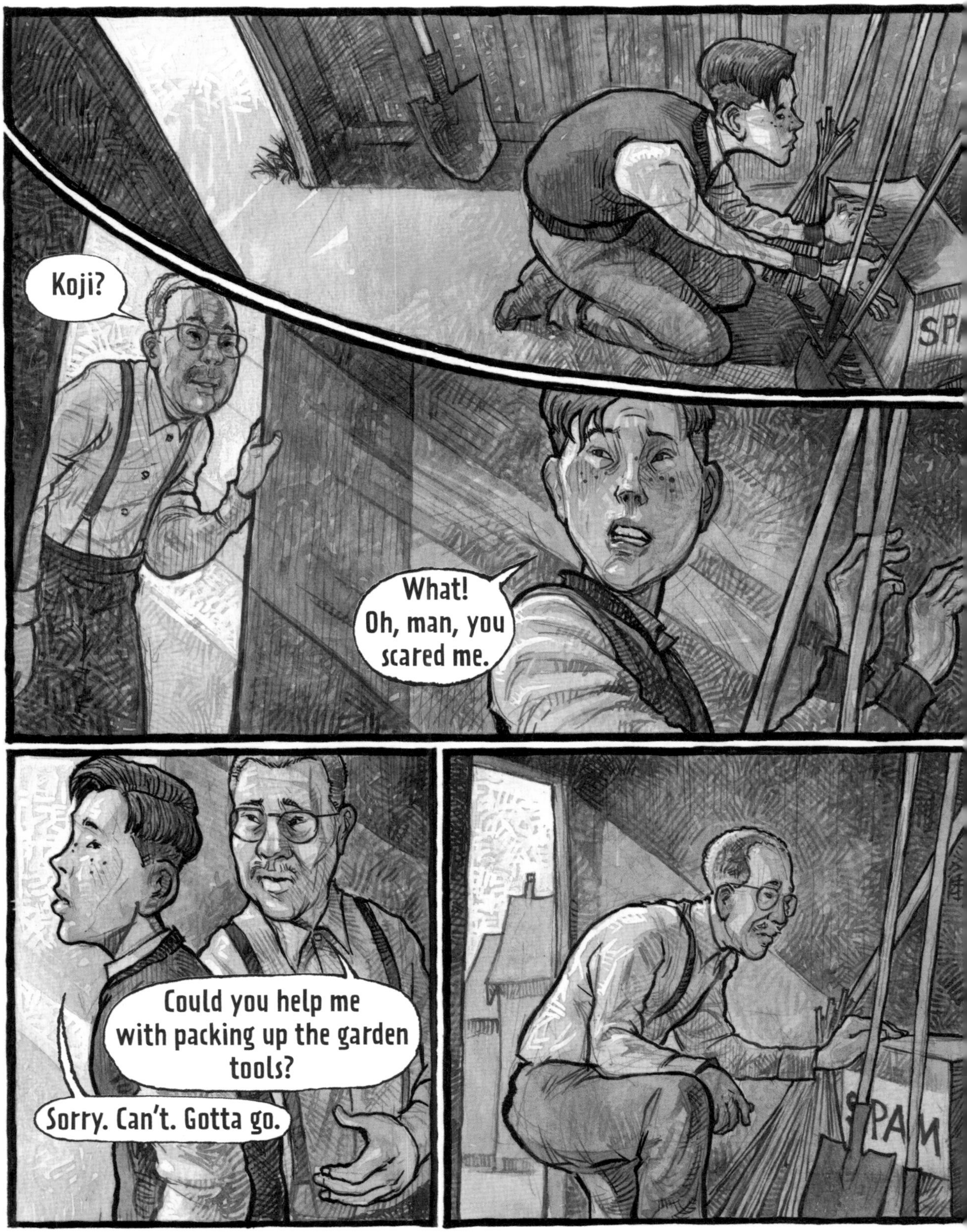
Koji?
What!
Oh, man, you
scared me.
Could you help me
with packing up the garden
tools?
Sorry. Can't. Gotta go.
SPAM

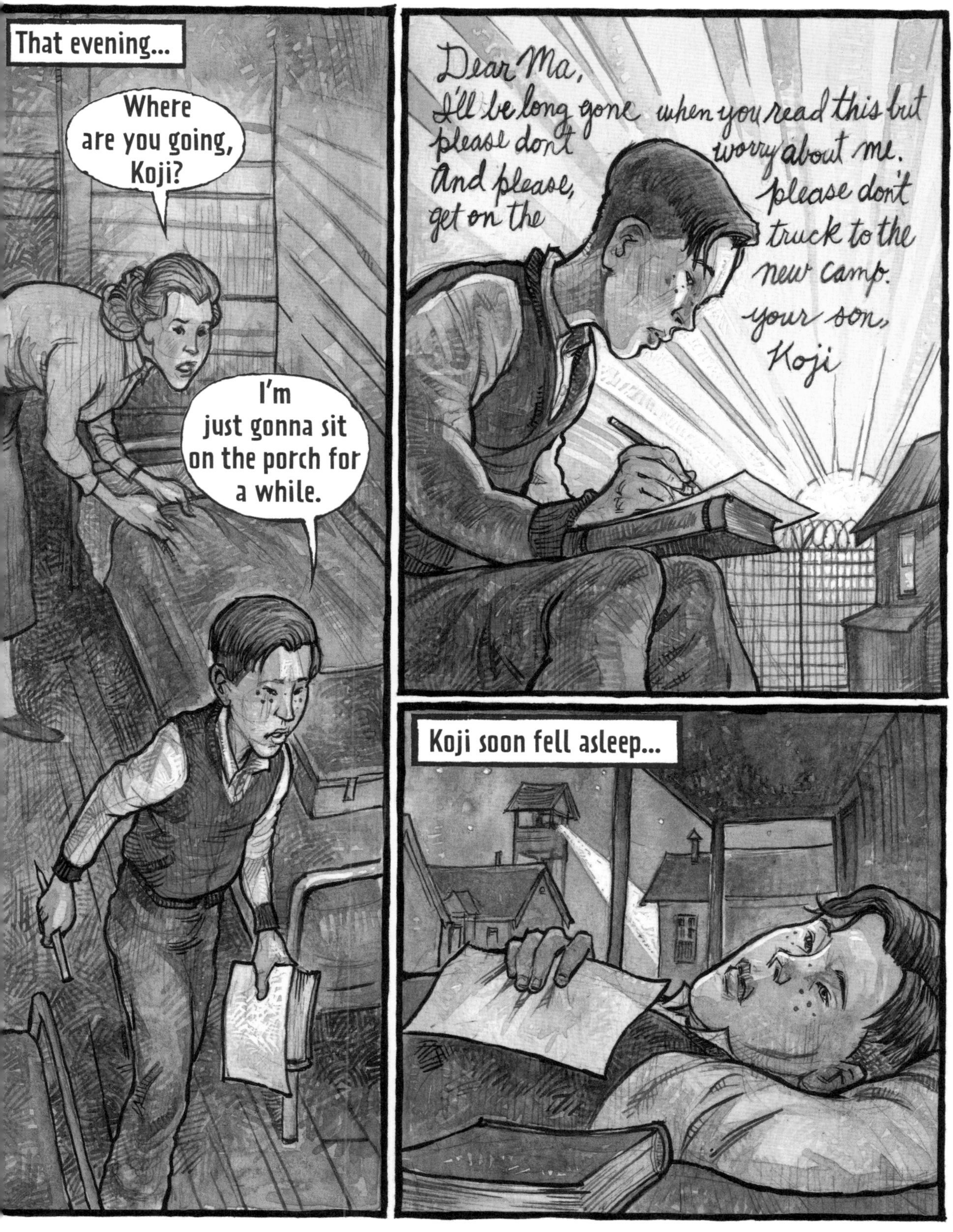
That evening...
Where are you going, Koji?
I'm just gonna sit on the porch for a while.
Dear Ma,
I'll be long gone when you read this but please don't worry about me.
And please, please don't get on the truck to the new camp.
your son,
Koji
Koji soon fell asleep...

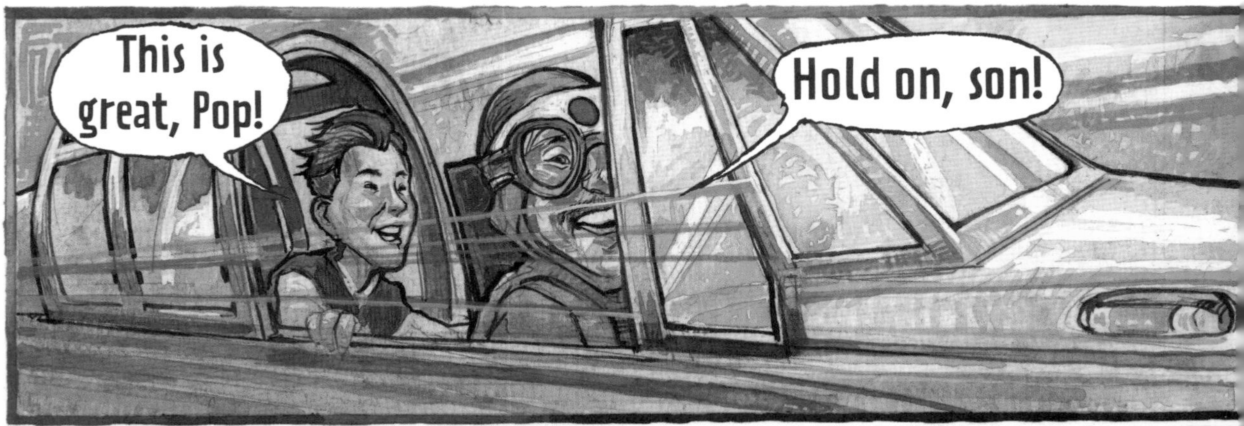
This is great, Pop!
Hold on, son!
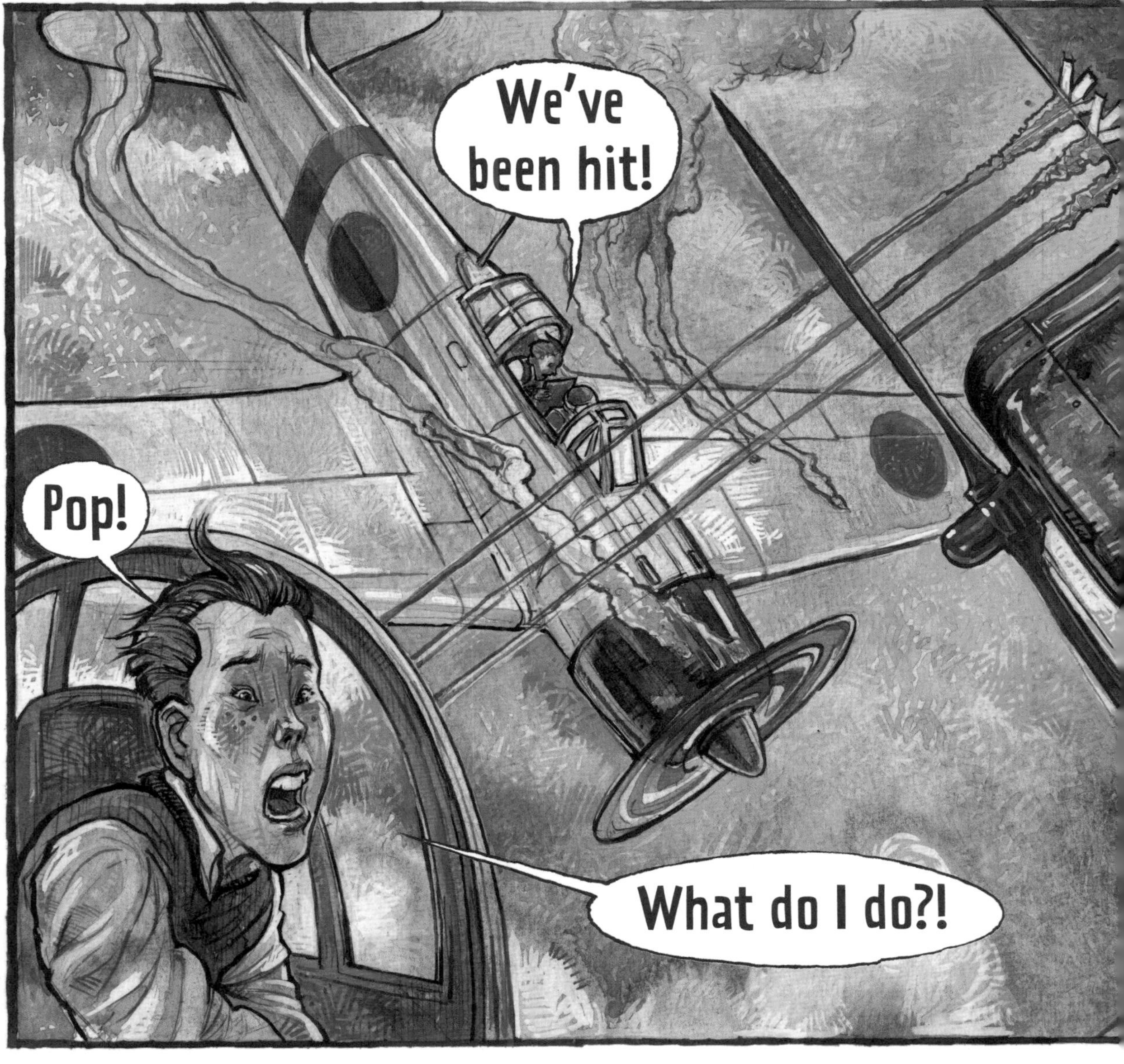
We've been hit!
Pop!
What do I do?!

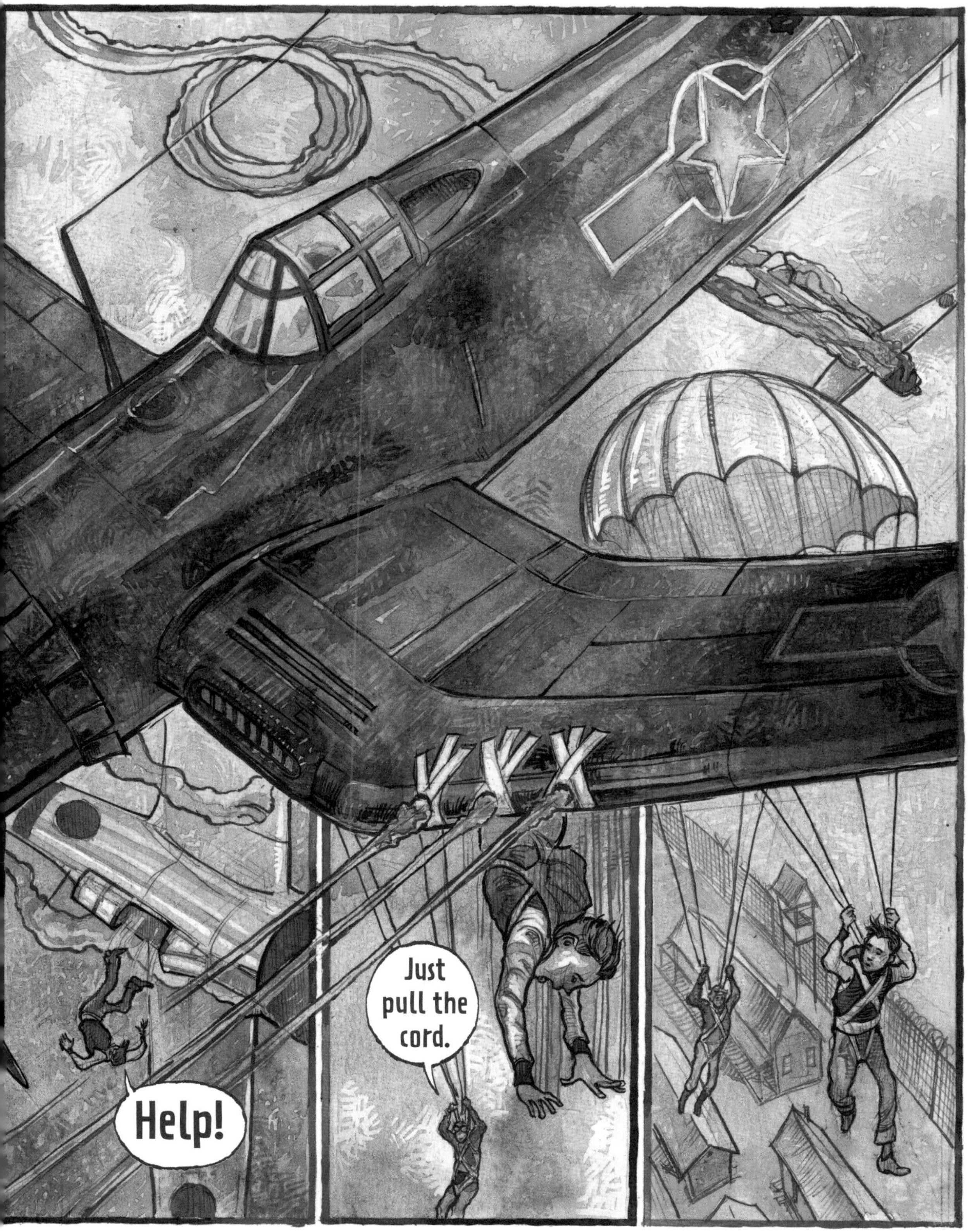
Help!
Just pull the cord.

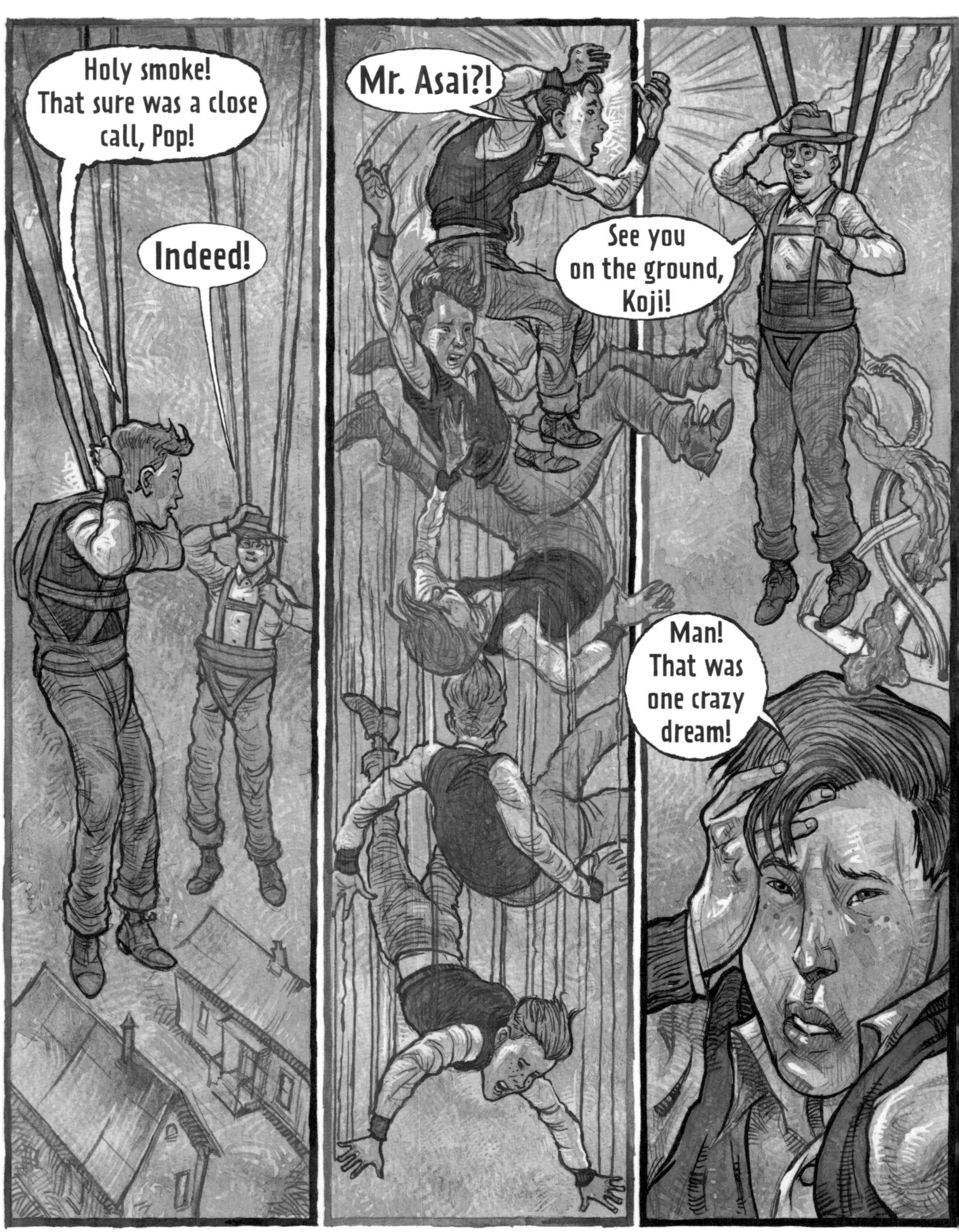
Holy smoke! That sure was a close call, Pop!
Indeed!
Mr. Asai?!
See you on the ground, Koji!
Man! That was one crazy dream!

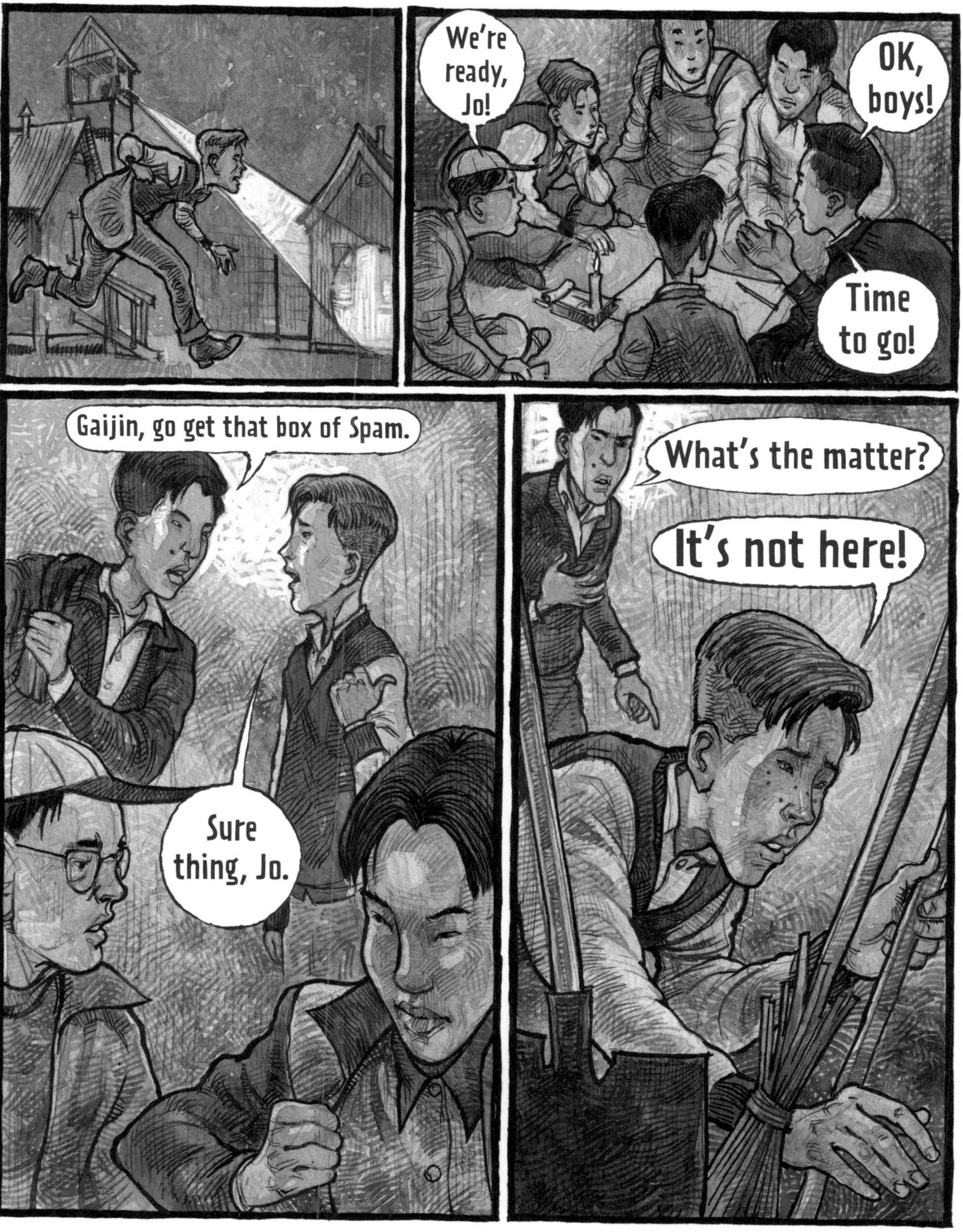
We're ready, Jo!
OK, boys!
Time to go!
Gaijin, go get that box of Spam.
Sure thing, Jo.
What's the matter?
It's not here!

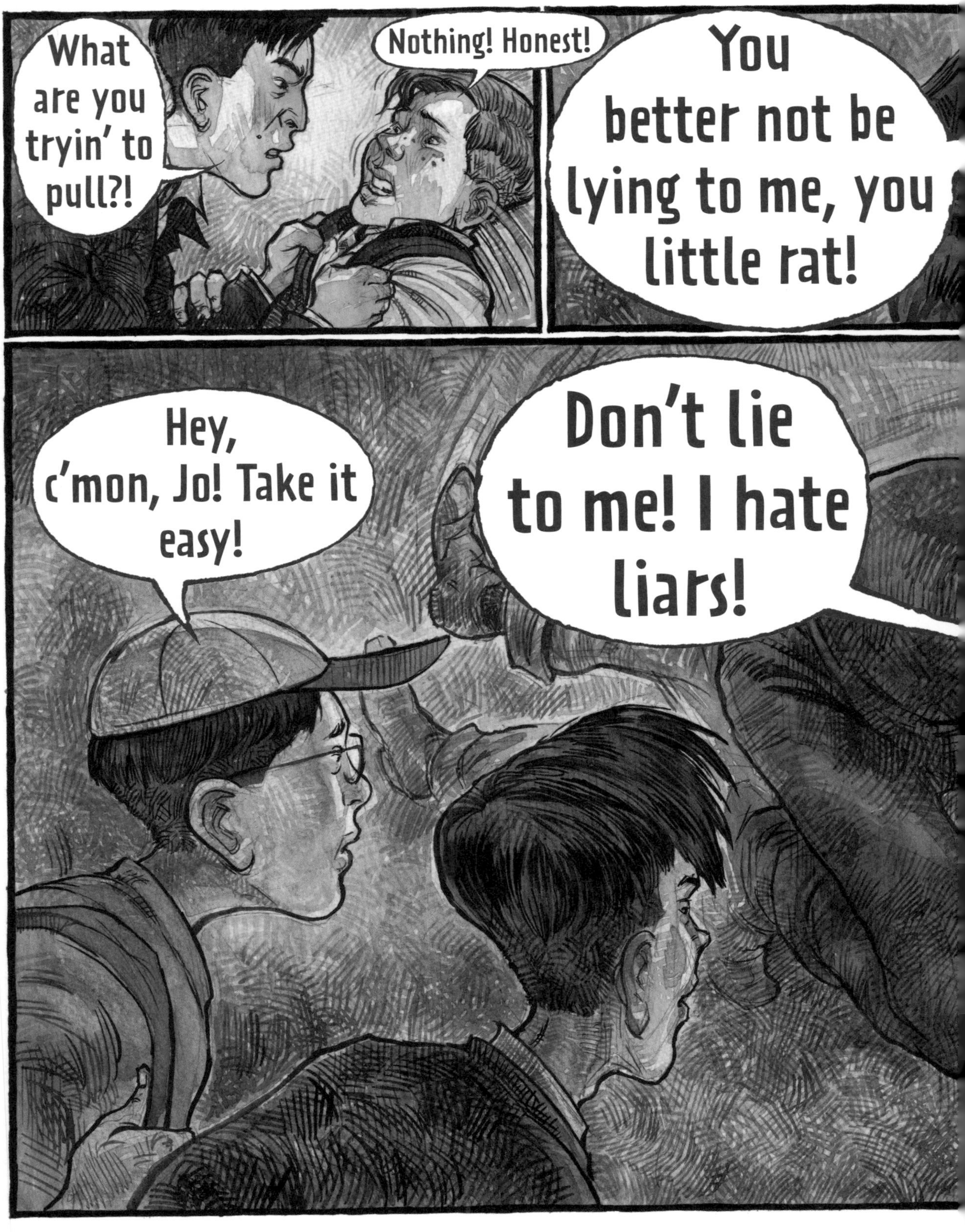
What are you tryin' to pull?!
Nothing! Honest!
You better not be lying to me, you little rat!
Hey, c'mon, Jo! Take it easy!
Don't lie to me! I hate liars!

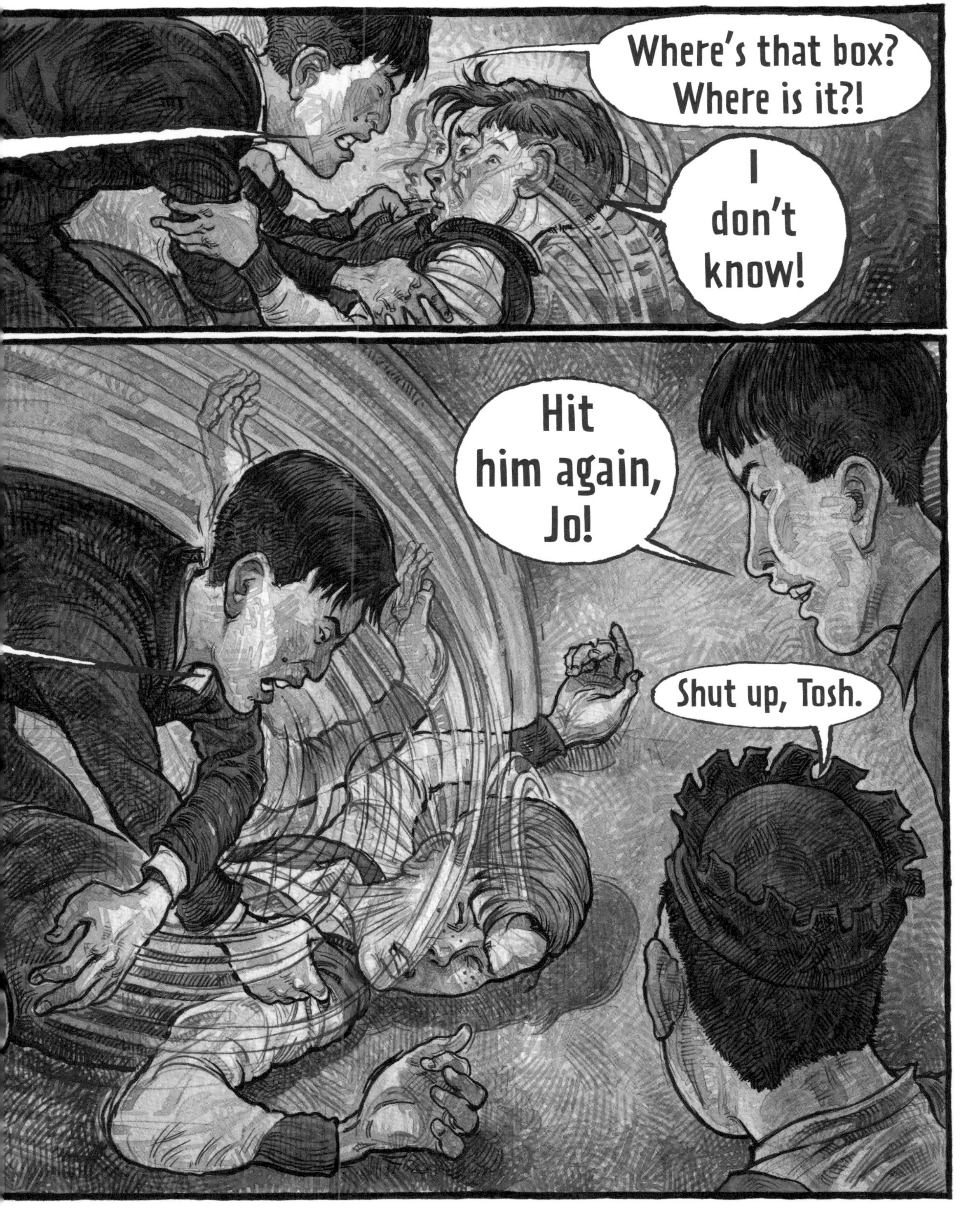
Where's that box? Where is it?!
I don't know!
Hit him again, Jo!
Shut up, Tosh.

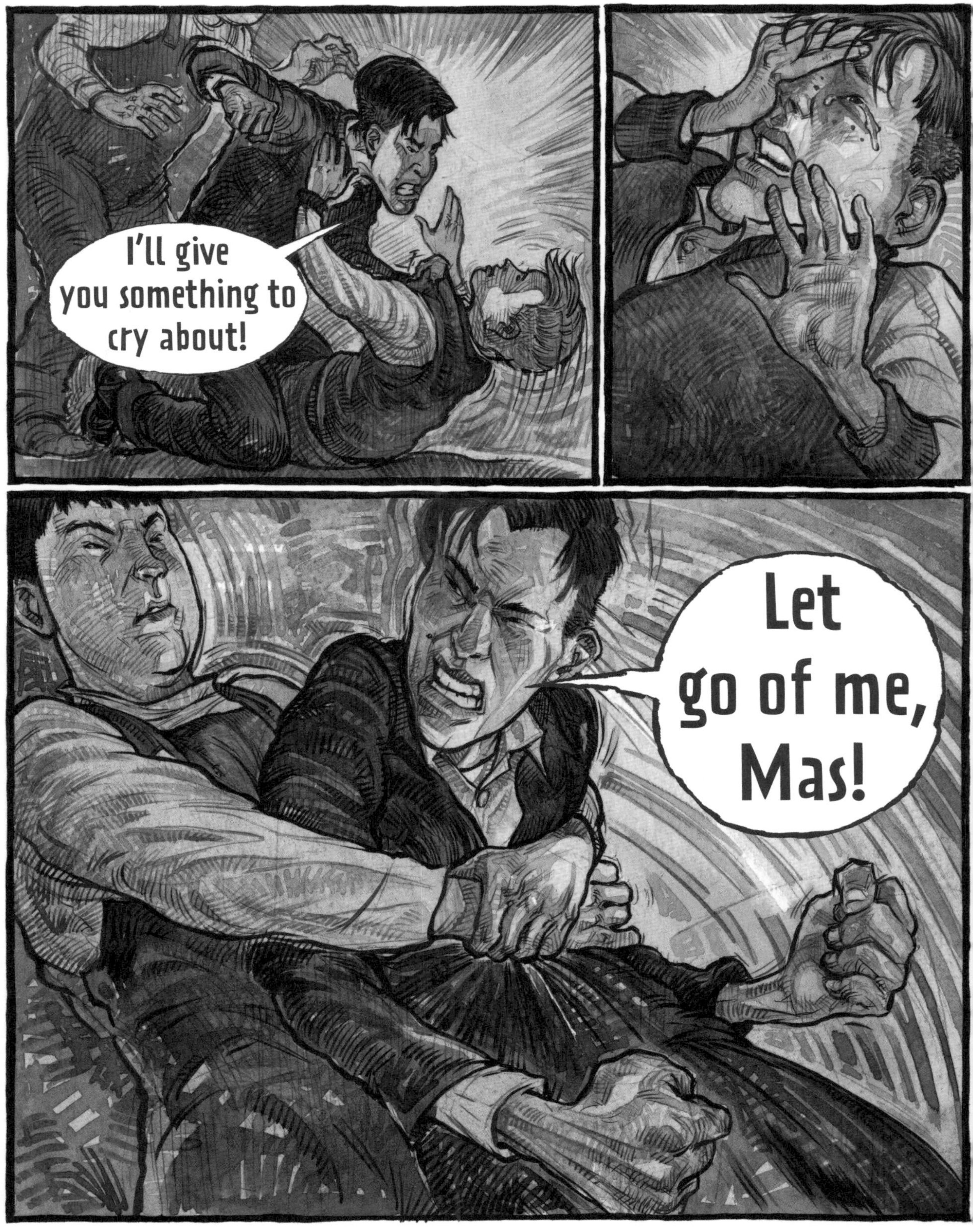
I'll give you something to cry about!
Let go of me, Mas!

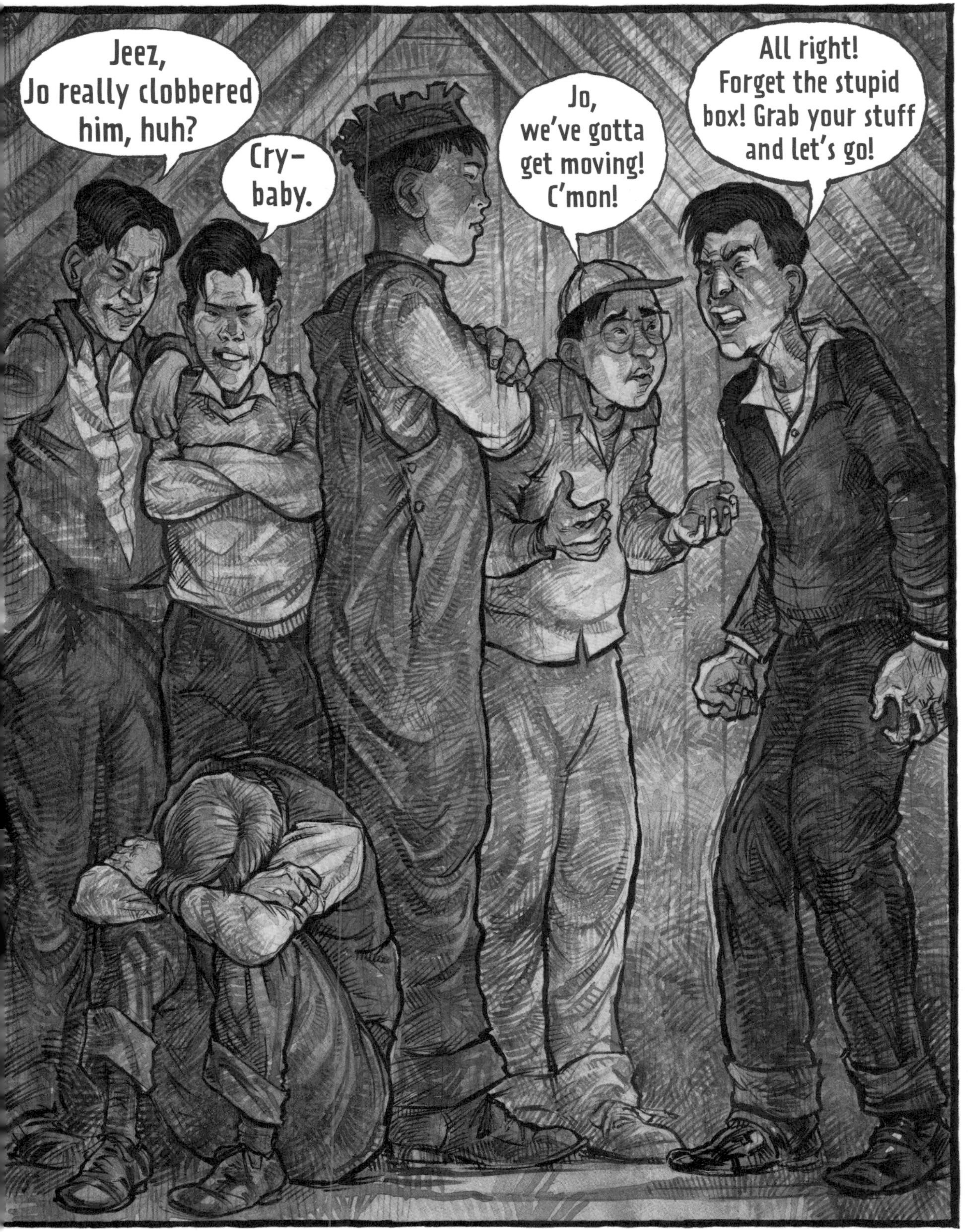
Jeez, Jo really clobbered him, huh?
Cry-baby.
Jo, we've gotta get moving! C'mon!
All right! Forget the stupid box! Grab your stuff and let's go!

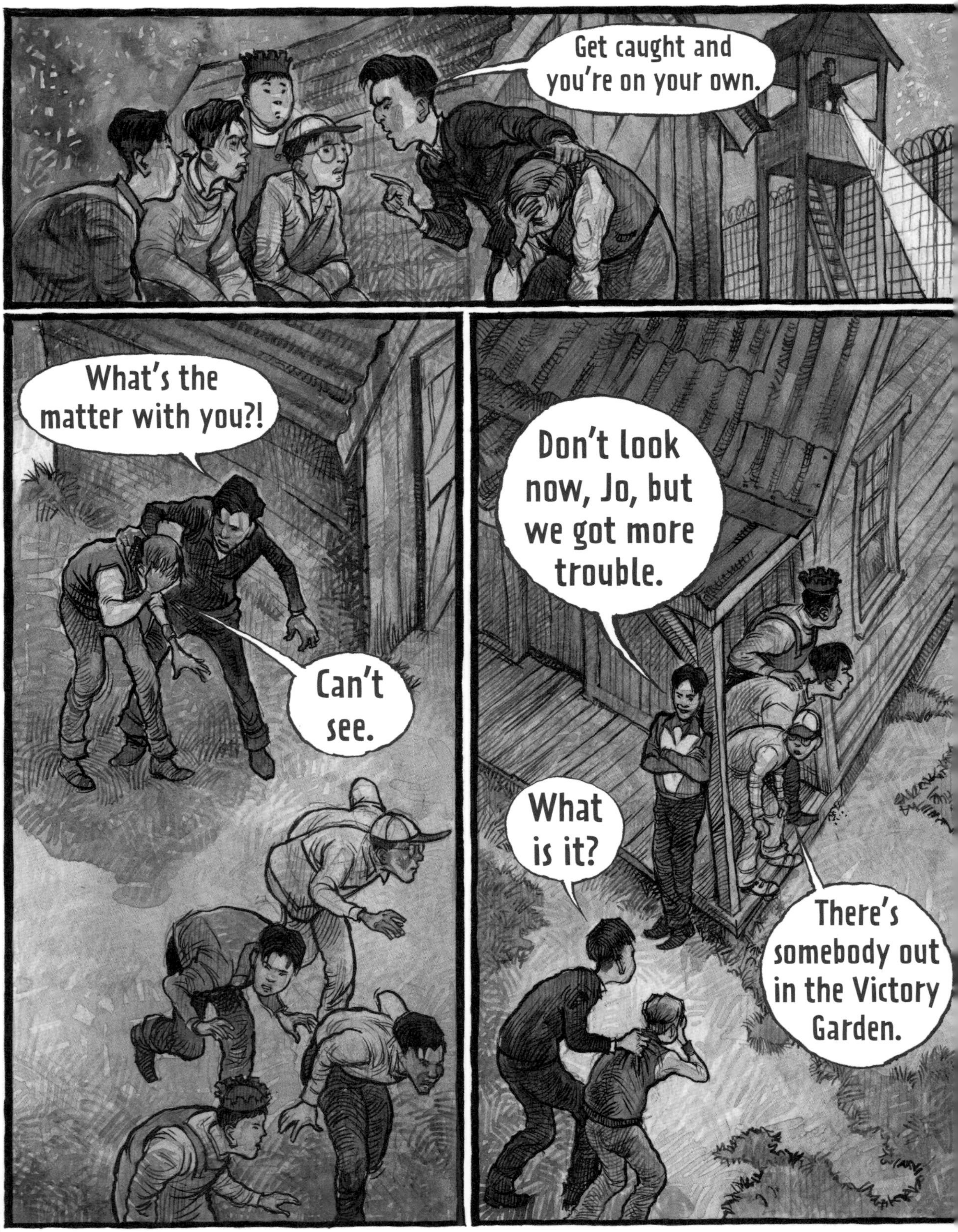
Get caught and you're on your own.
What's the matter with you?!
Can't see.
Don't look now, Jo, but we got more trouble.
What is it?
There's somebody out in the Victory Garden.

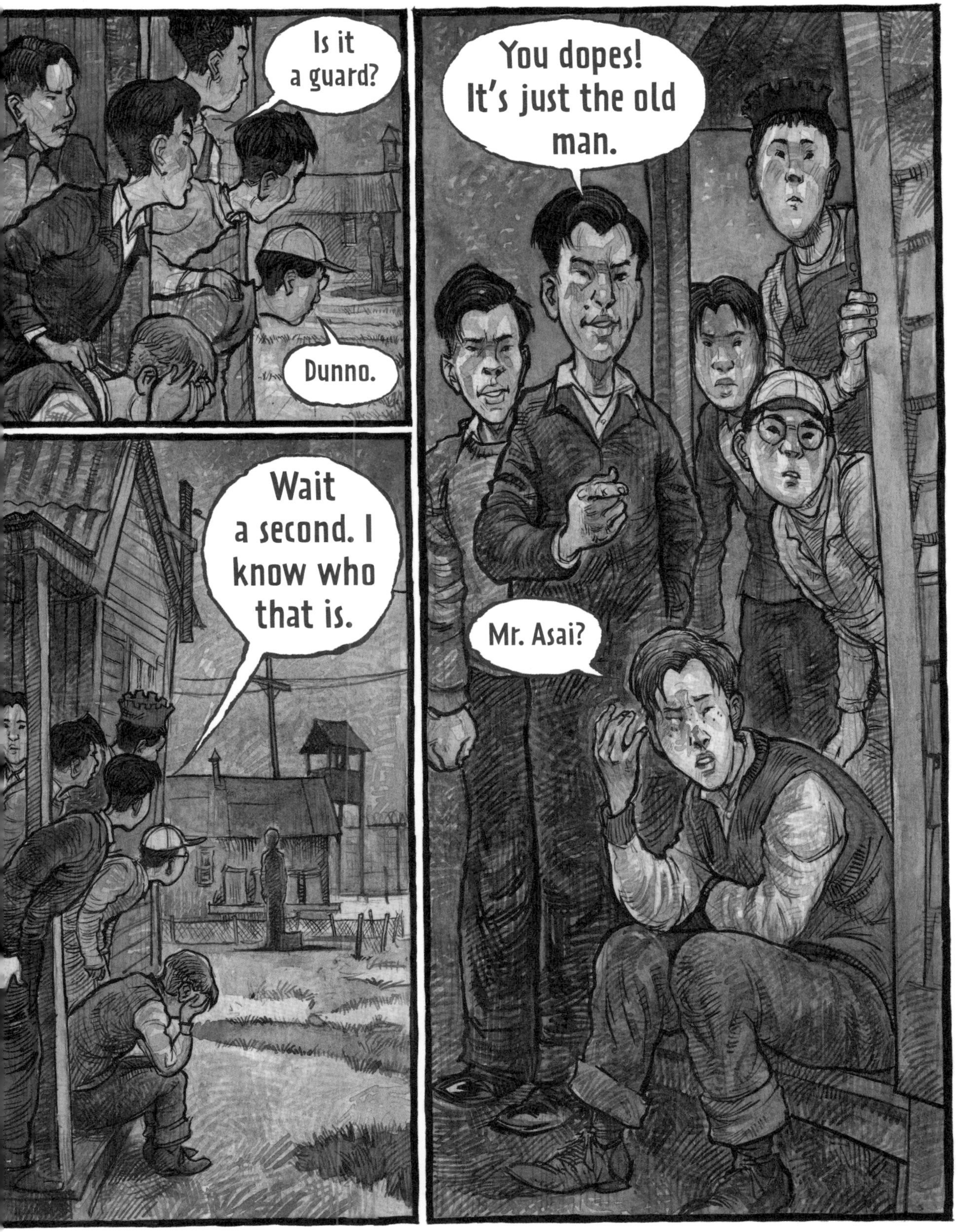
Is it a guard?
Dunno.
Wait a second. I know who that is.
You dopes! It's just the old man.
Mr. Asai?

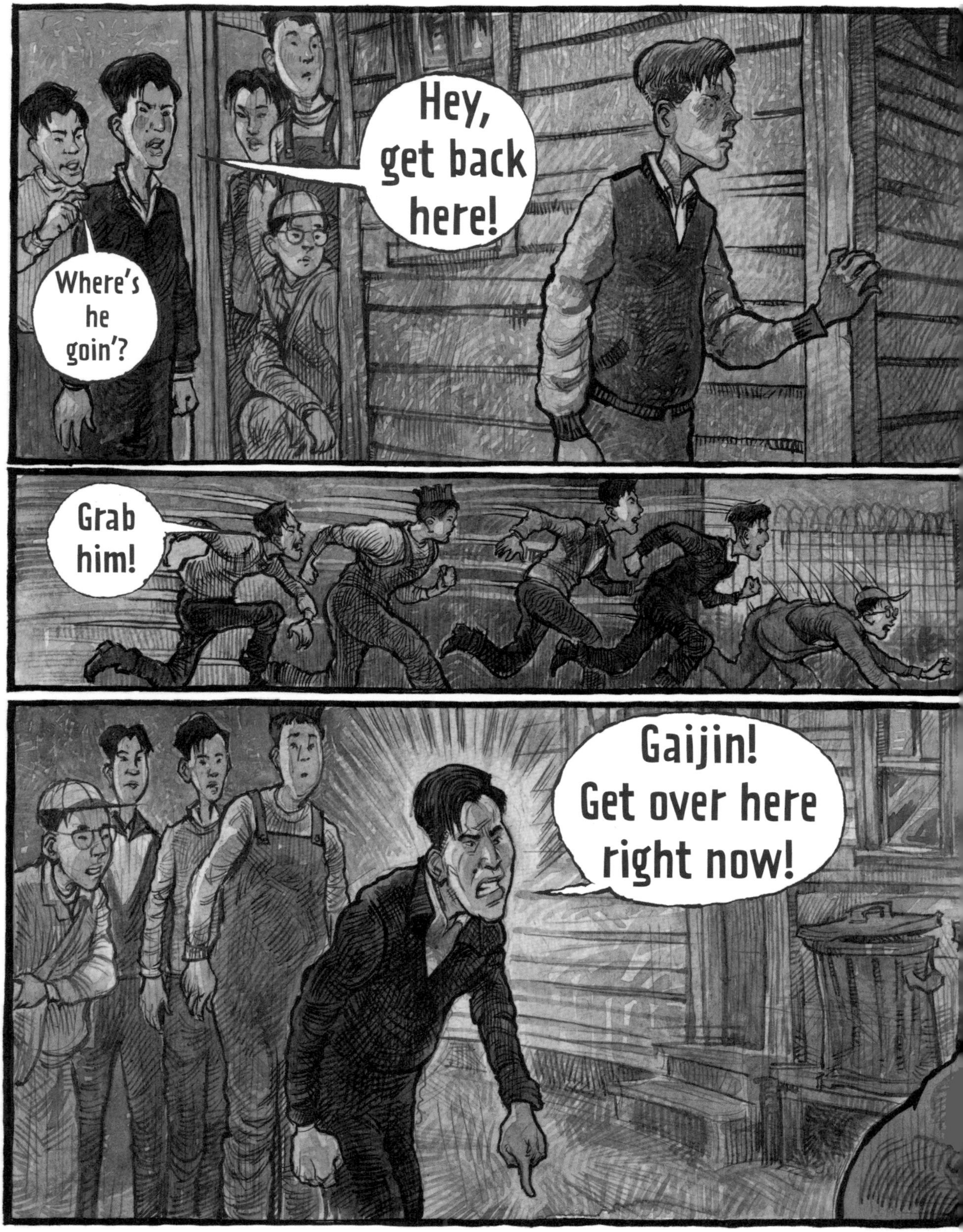
Hey, get back here!
Where's he goin'?
Grab him!
Gaijin! Get over here right now!

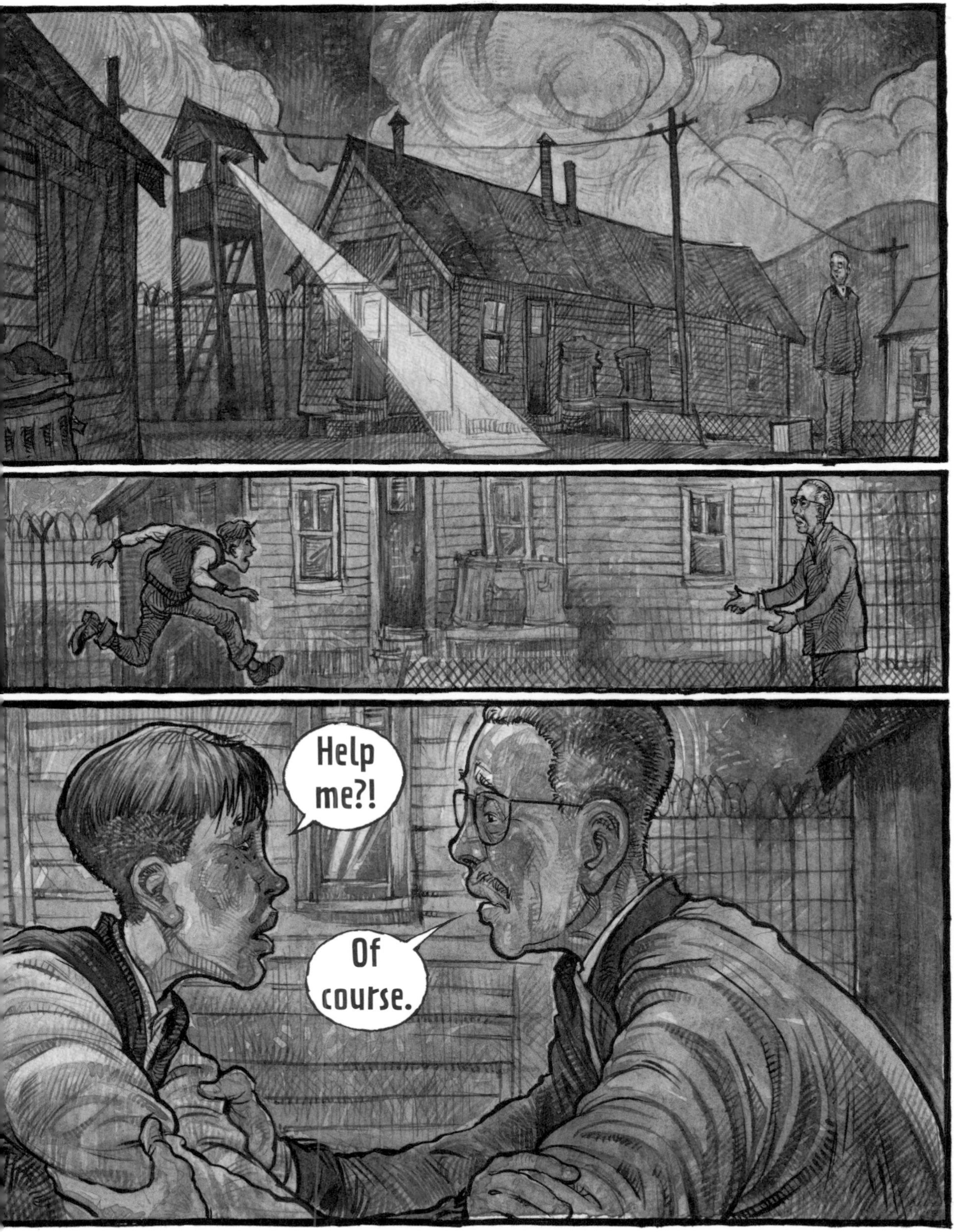
Help me?!
Of course.

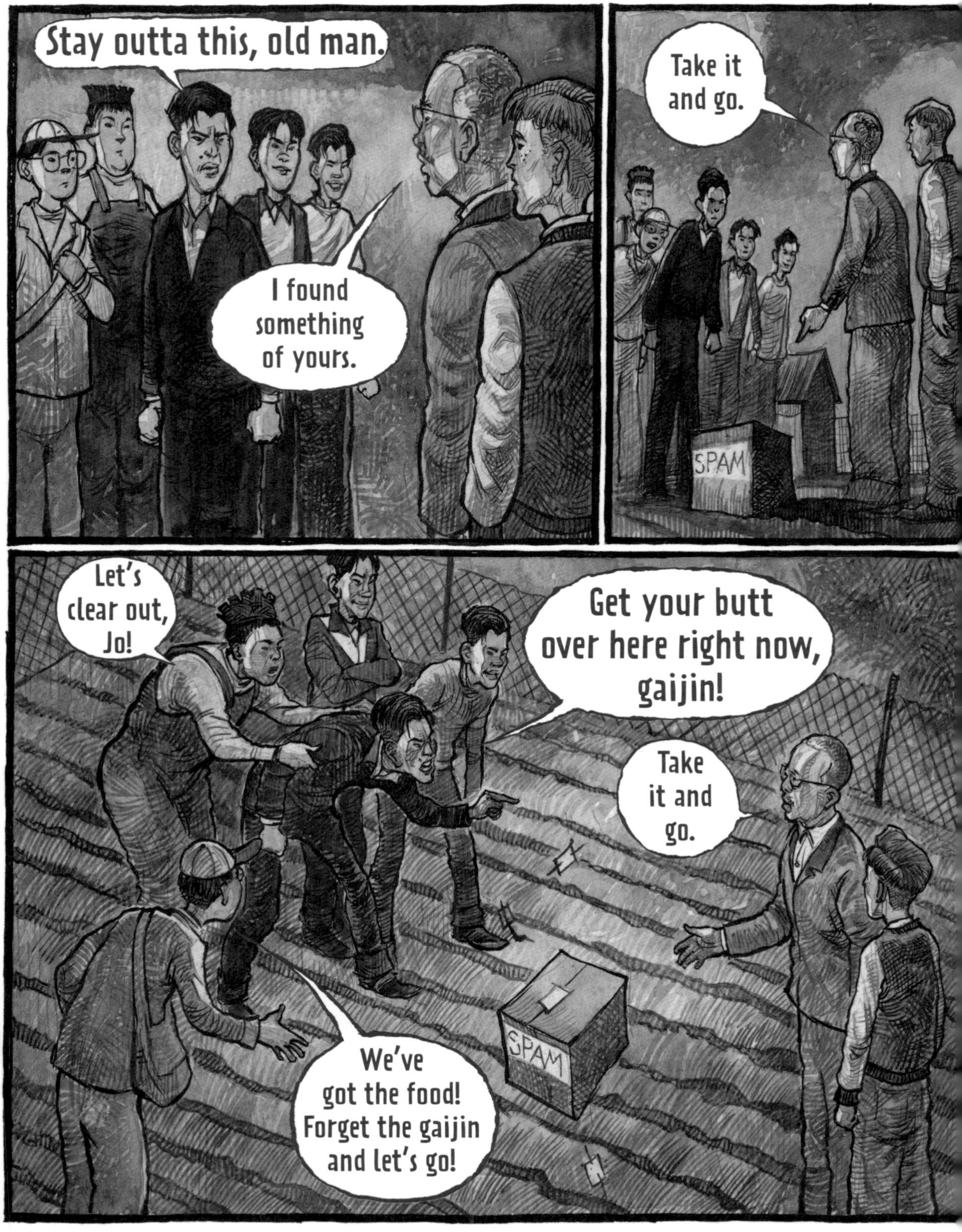
Stay outta this, old man.
I found something of yours.
Take it and go.
SPAM
Let's clear out, Jo!
Get your butt over here right now, gaijin!
Take it and go.
We've got the food! Forget the gaijin and let's go!
SPAM

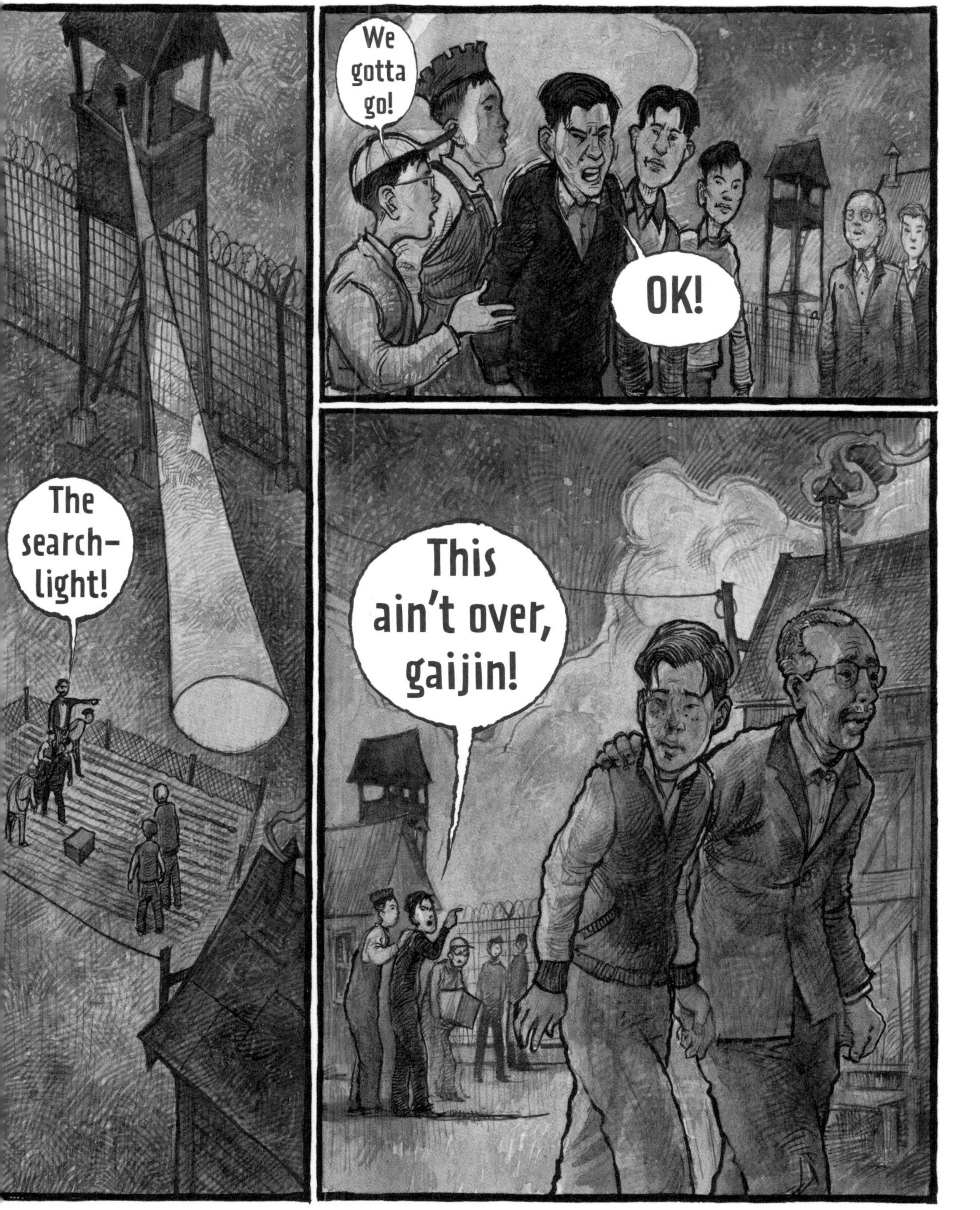
The search-light!
We gotta go!
OK!
This ain't over, gaijin!

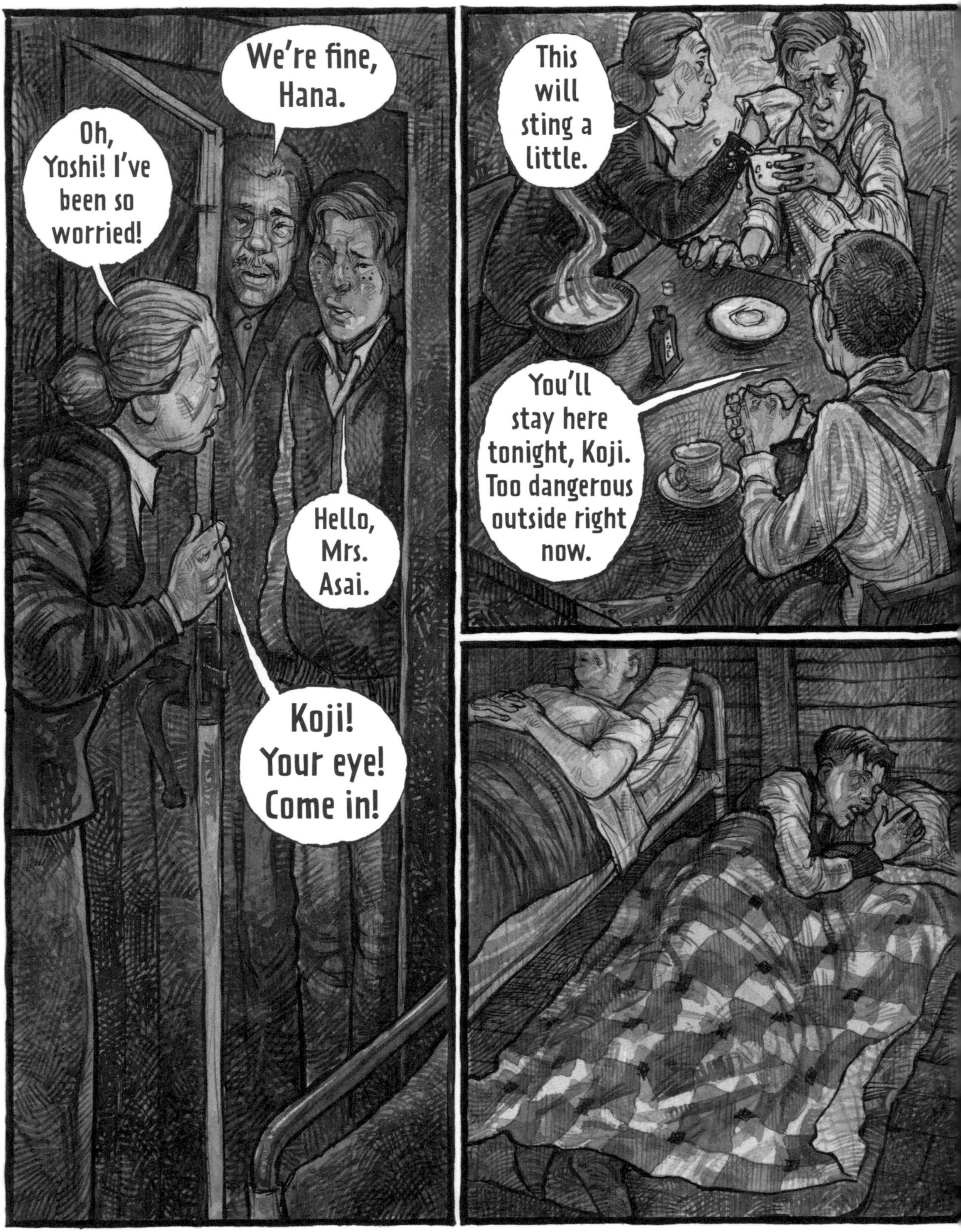
Oh, Yoshi! I've been so worried!
We're fine, Hana.
Hello, Mrs. Asai.
Koji! Your eye! Come in!
This will sting a little.
You'll stay here tonight, Koji. Too dangerous outside right now.

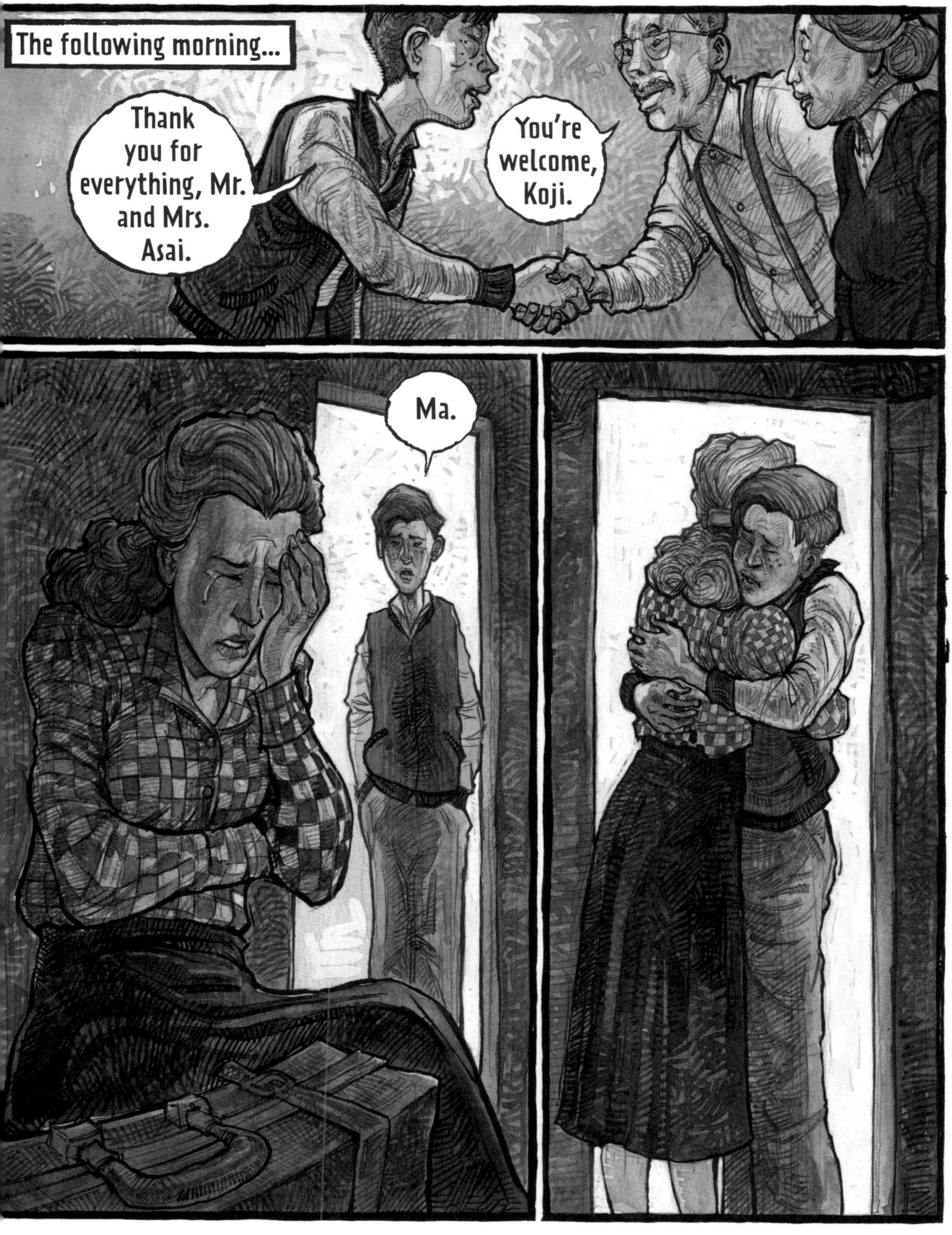
The following morning...
Thank you for everything, Mr. and Mrs. Asai.
You're welcome, Koji.
Ma.

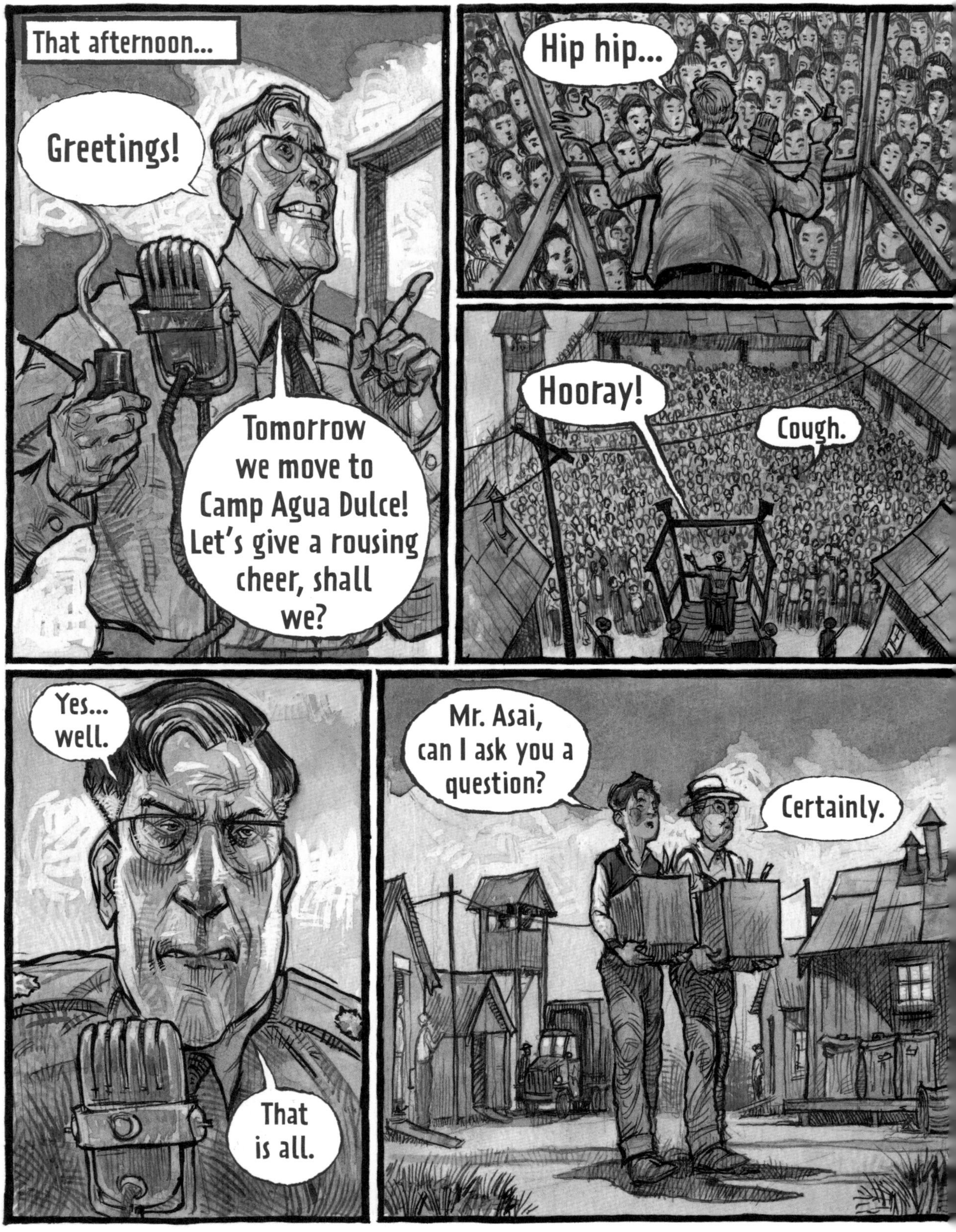
That afternoon...
Greetings!
Tomorrow we move to Camp Agua Dulce! Let's give a rousing cheer, shall we?
Hip hip...
Hooray!
Cough.
Yes... well.
That is all.
Mr. Asai, can I ask you a question?
Certainly.

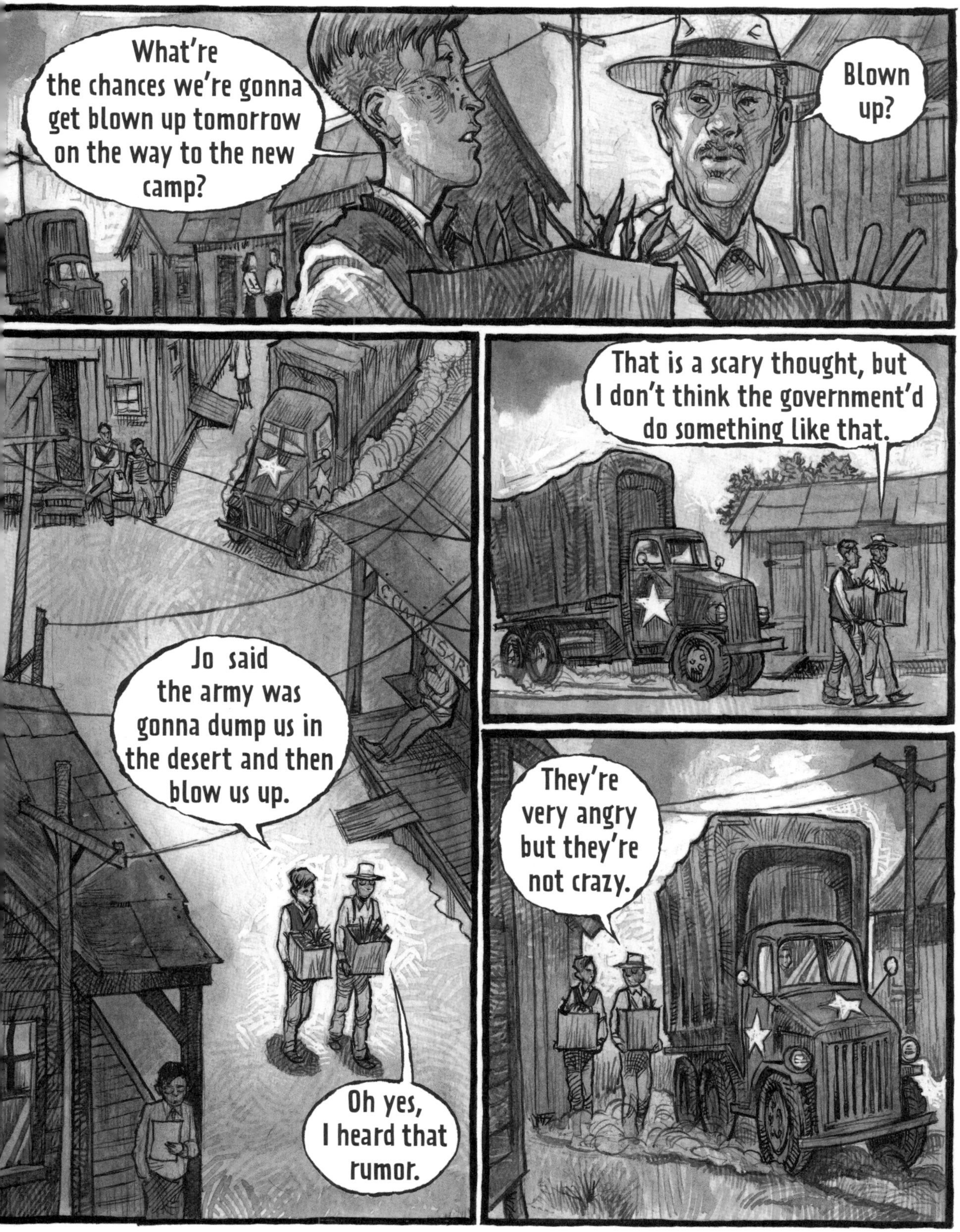
What're the chances we're gonna get blown up tomorrow on the way to the new camp?
Blown up?
Jo said the army was gonna dump us in the desert and then blow us up.
Oh yes, I heard that rumor.
That is a scary thought, but I don't think the government'd do something like that.
They're very angry but they're not crazy.

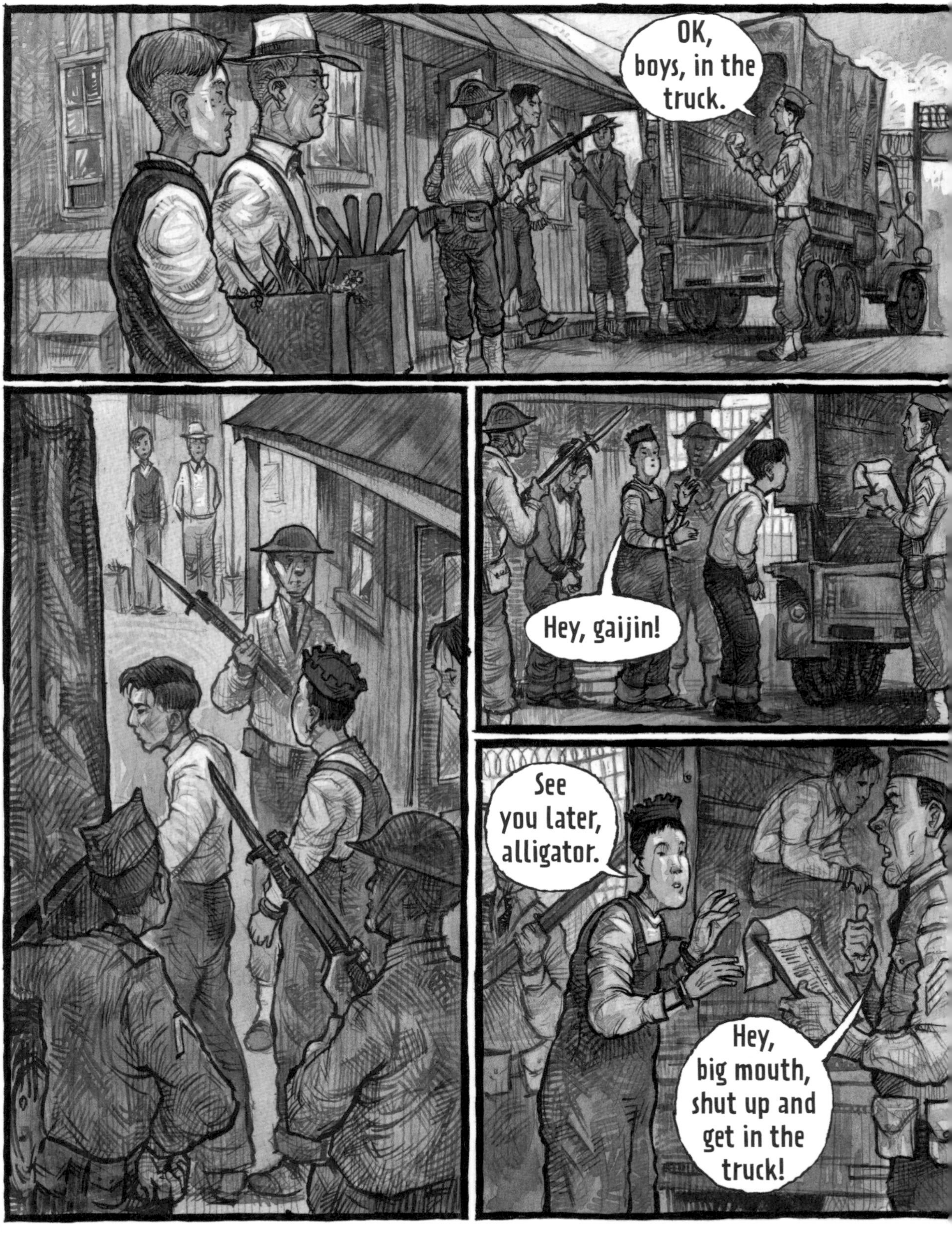
OK, boys, in the truck.
Hey, gaijin!
See you later, alligator.
Hey, big mouth, shut up and get in the truck!

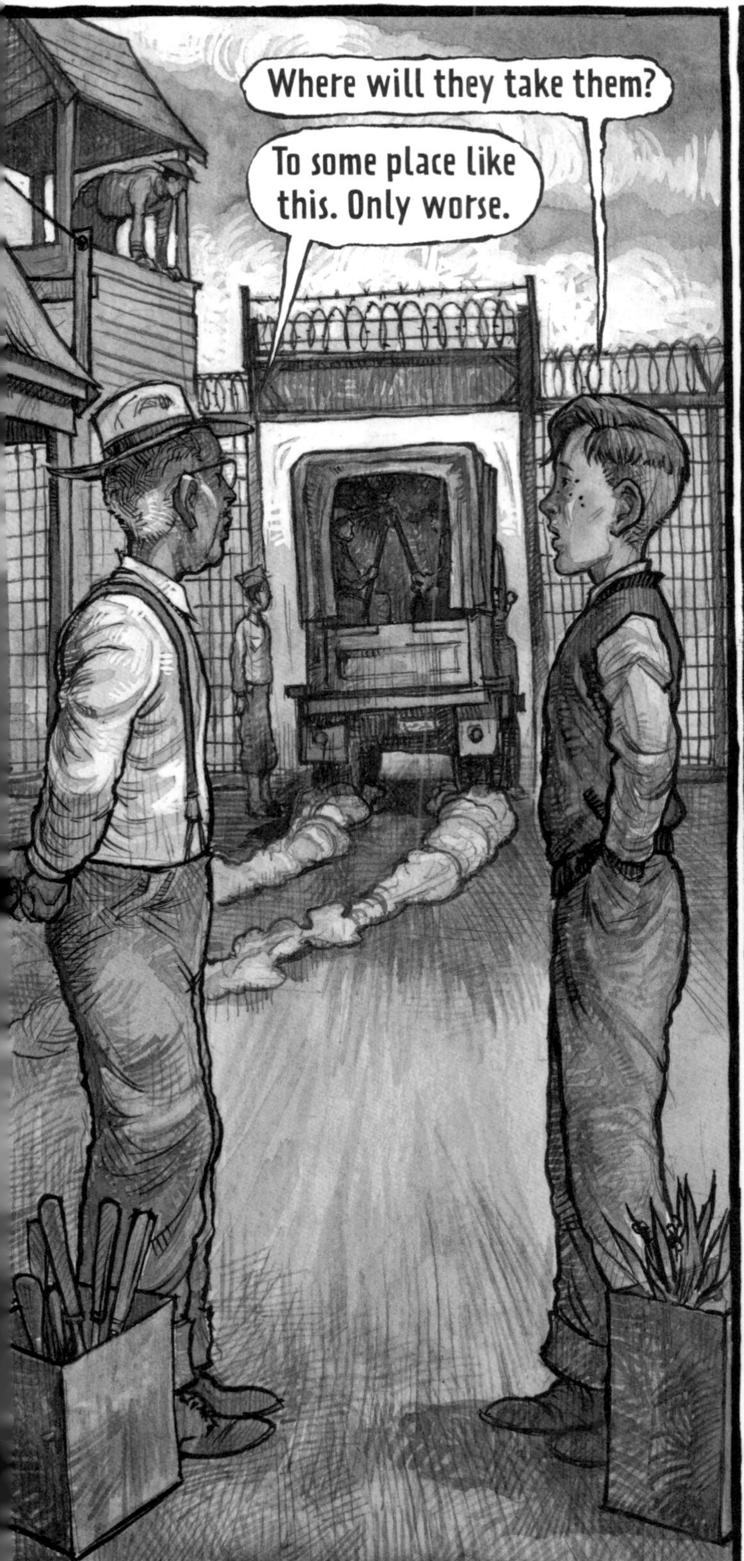
Where will they take them?
To some place like this. Only worse.

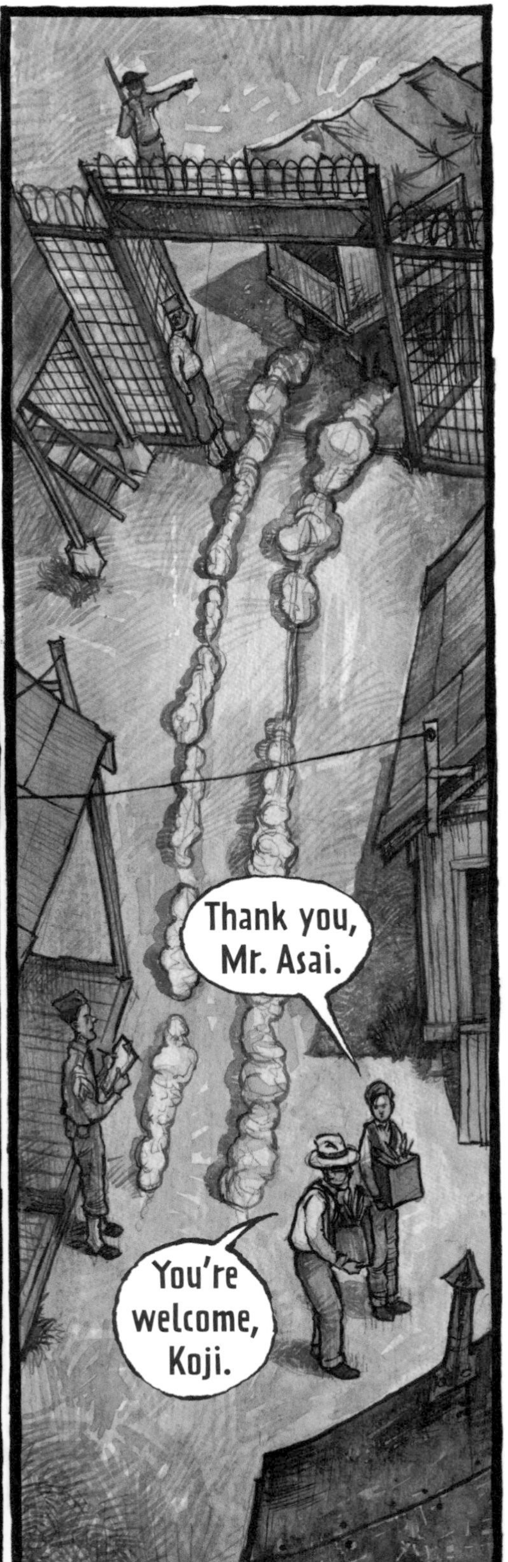
Thank you, Mr. Asai.
You're welcome, Koji.

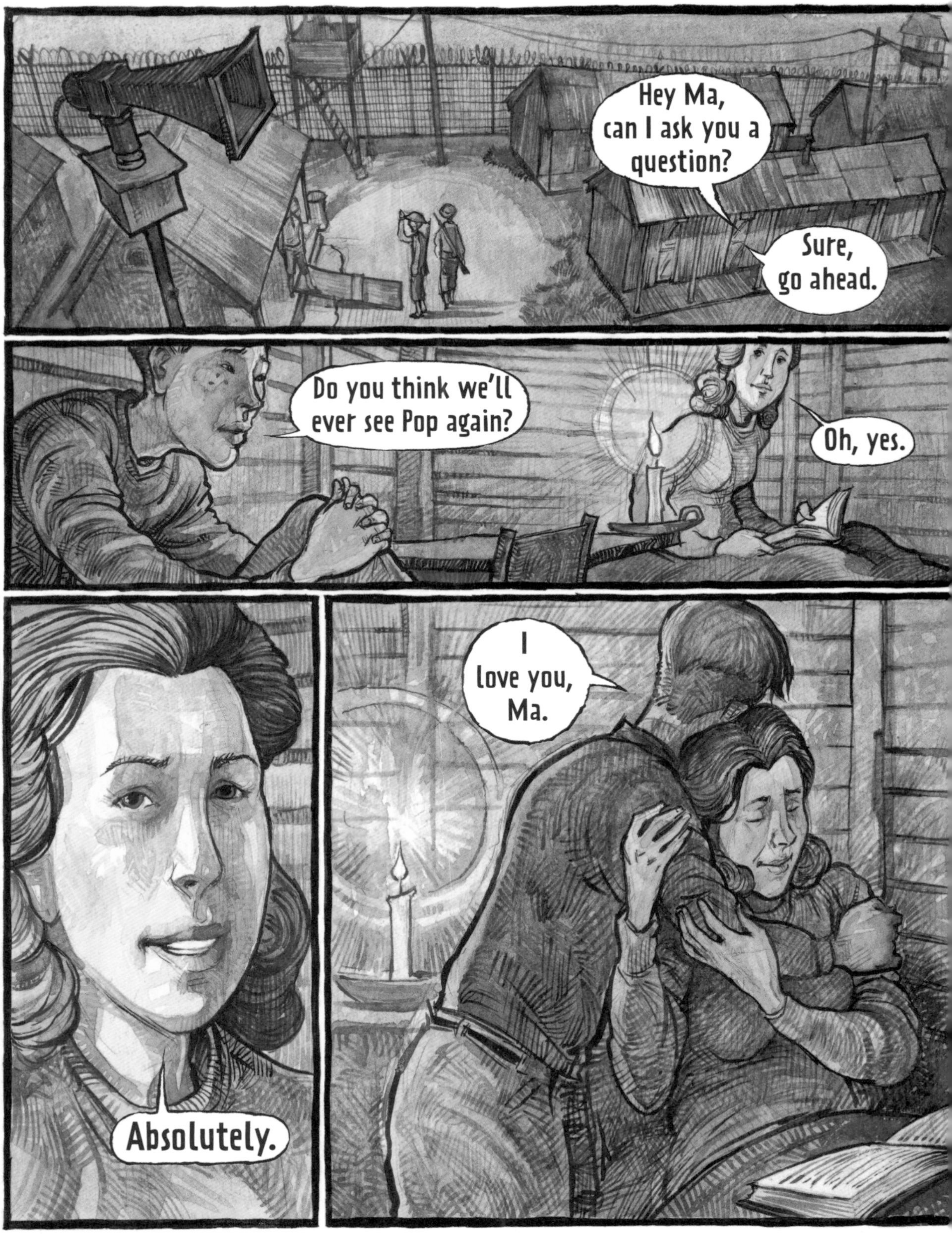
Hey Ma, can I ask you a question?
Sure, go ahead.
Do you think we'll ever see Pop again?
Oh, yes.
Absolutely.
I love you, Ma.

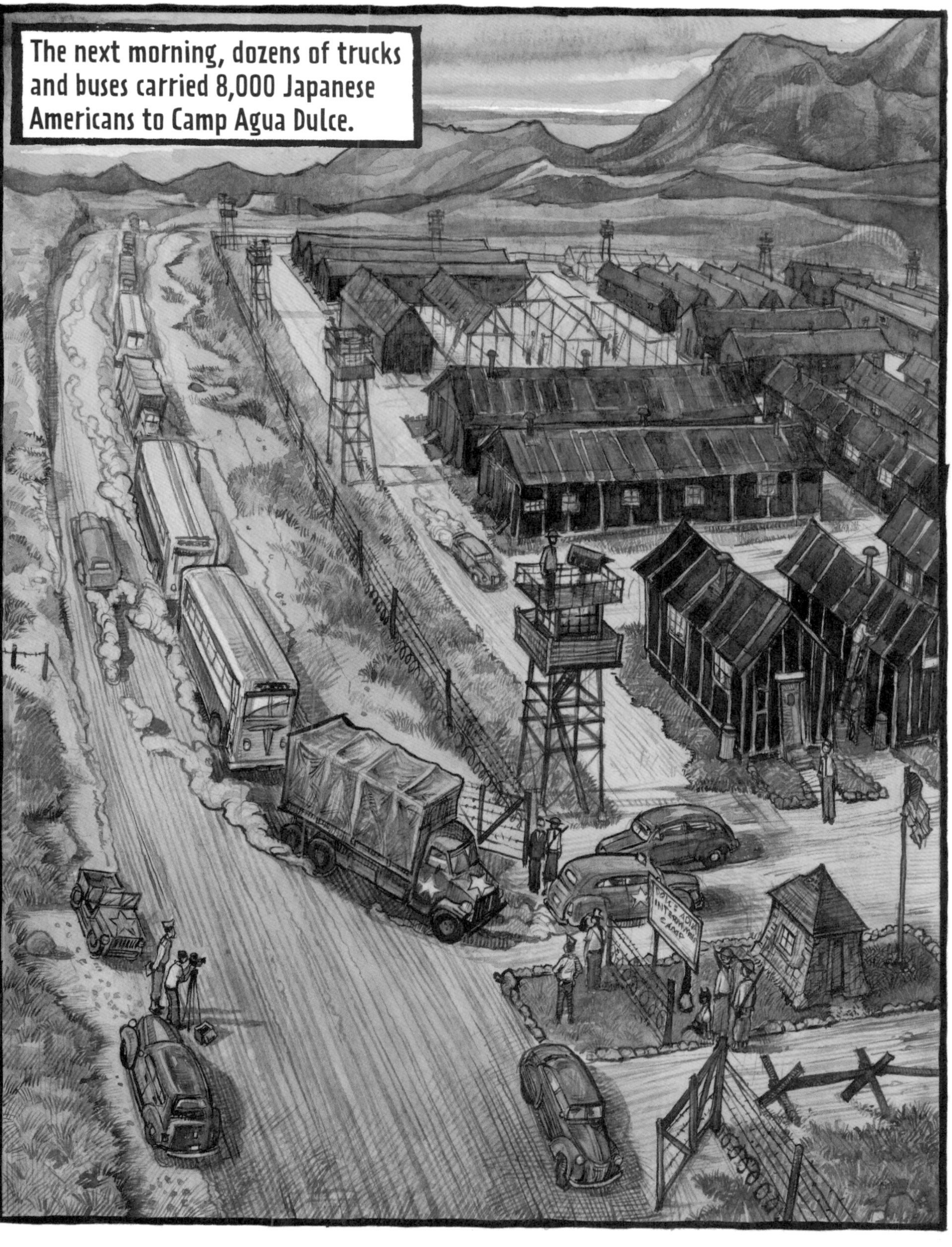
The next morning, dozens of trucks and buses carried 8,000 Japanese Americans to Camp Agua Dulce.

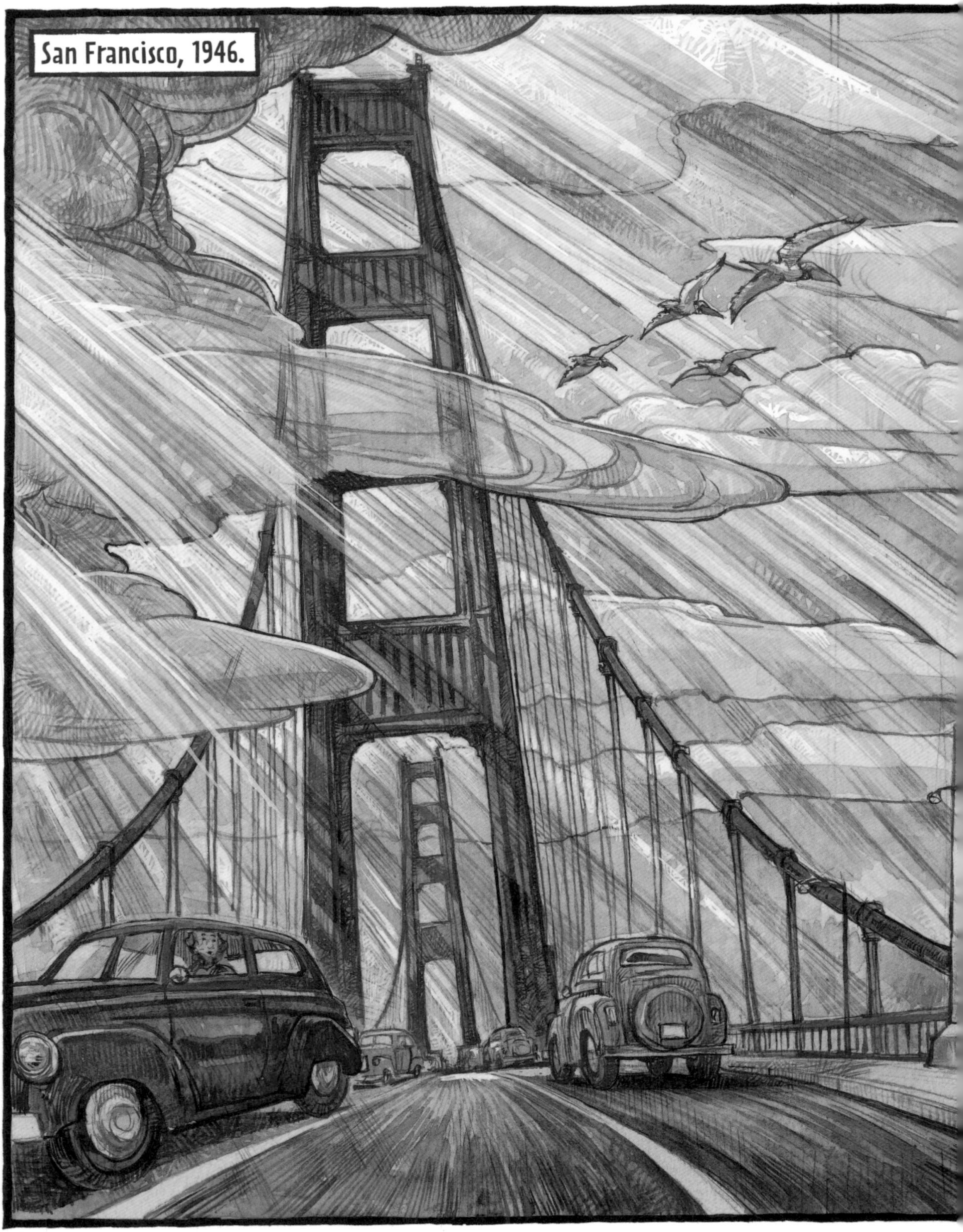
San Francisco, 1946.

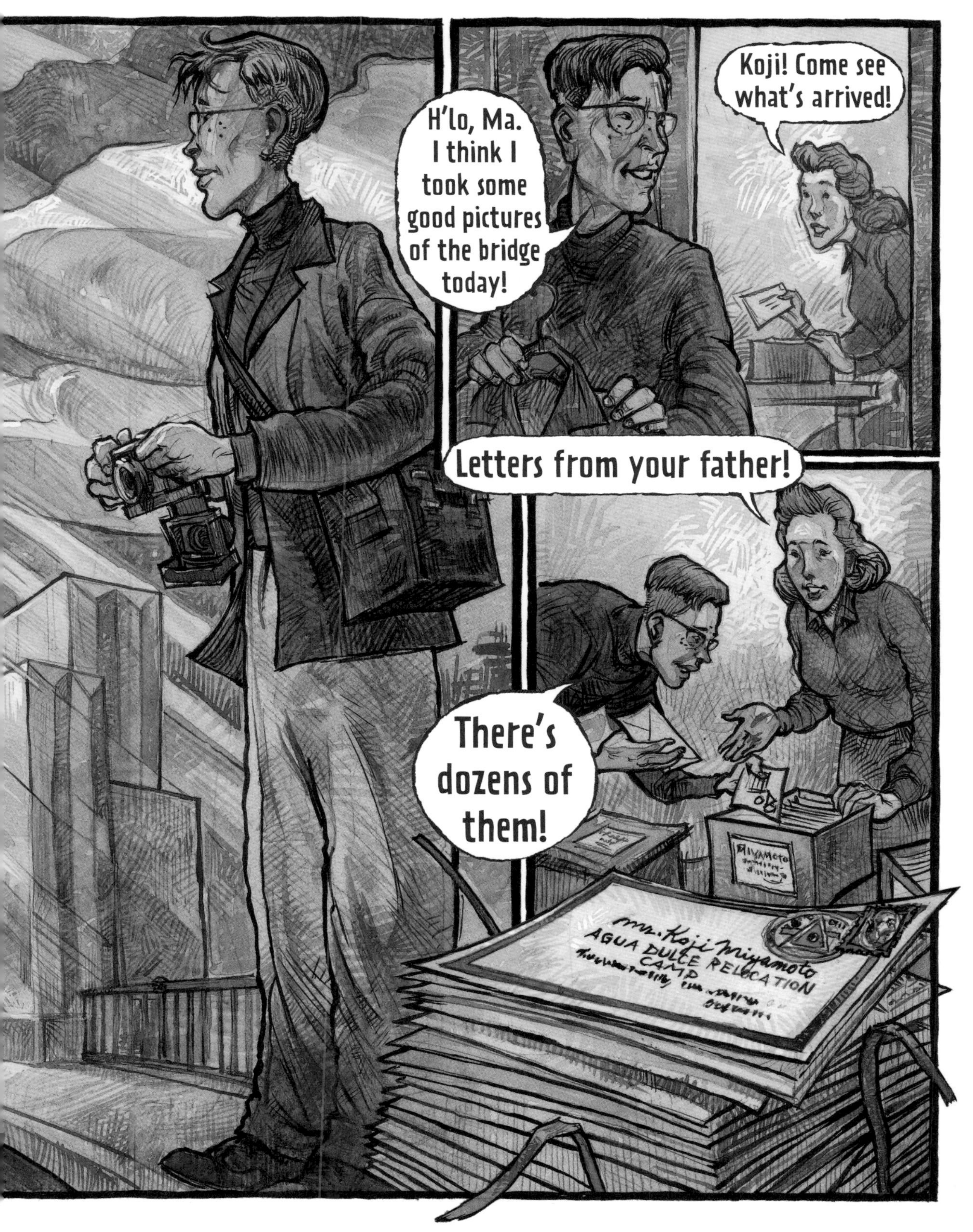
H'lo, Ma. I think I took some good pictures of the bridge today!
Koji! Come see what's arrived!
Letters from your father!
There's dozens of them!
mr. Koji Miyamoto
AGUA DULCE RELOCATION
CAMP

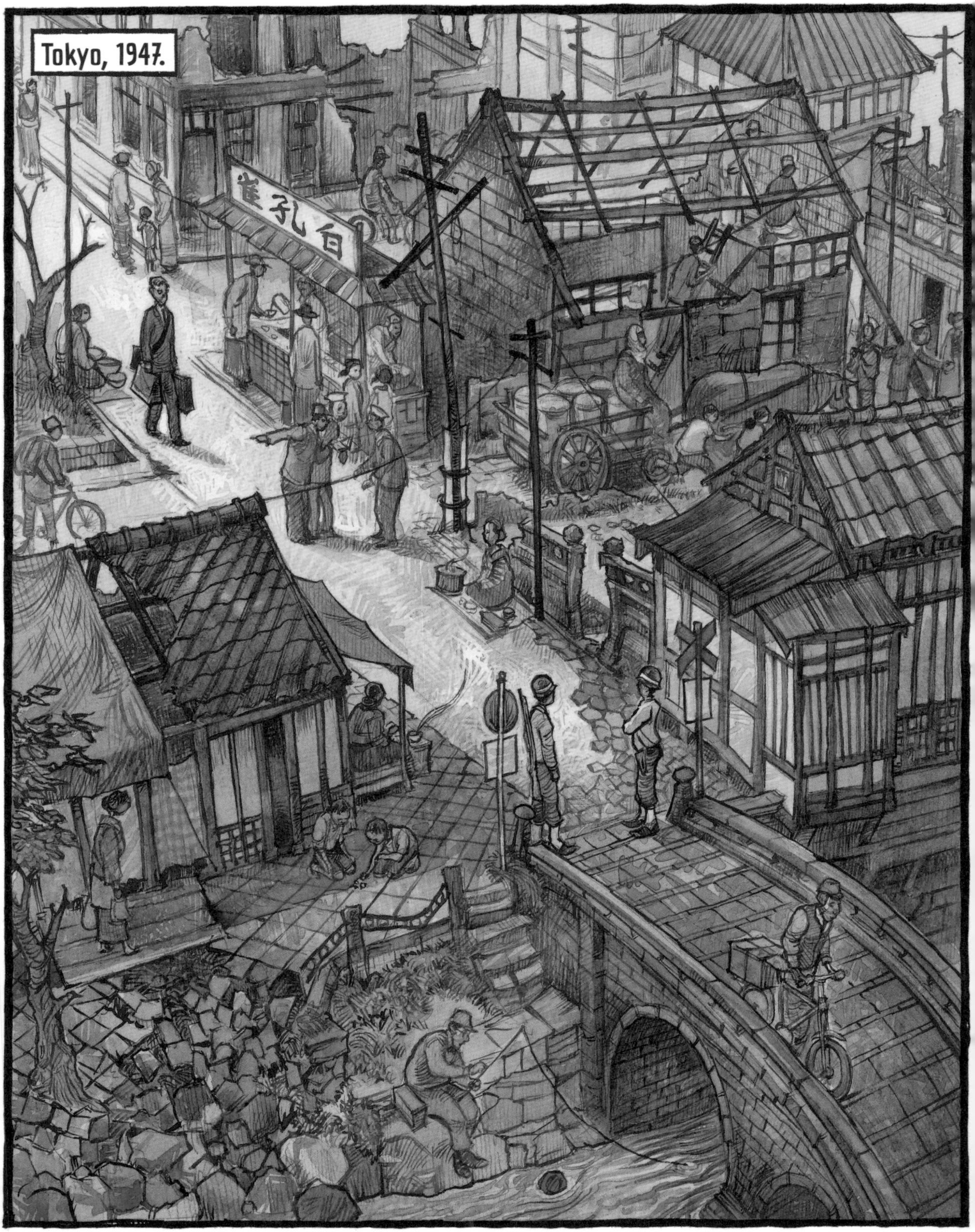
Tokyo, 1947.
白孔雀

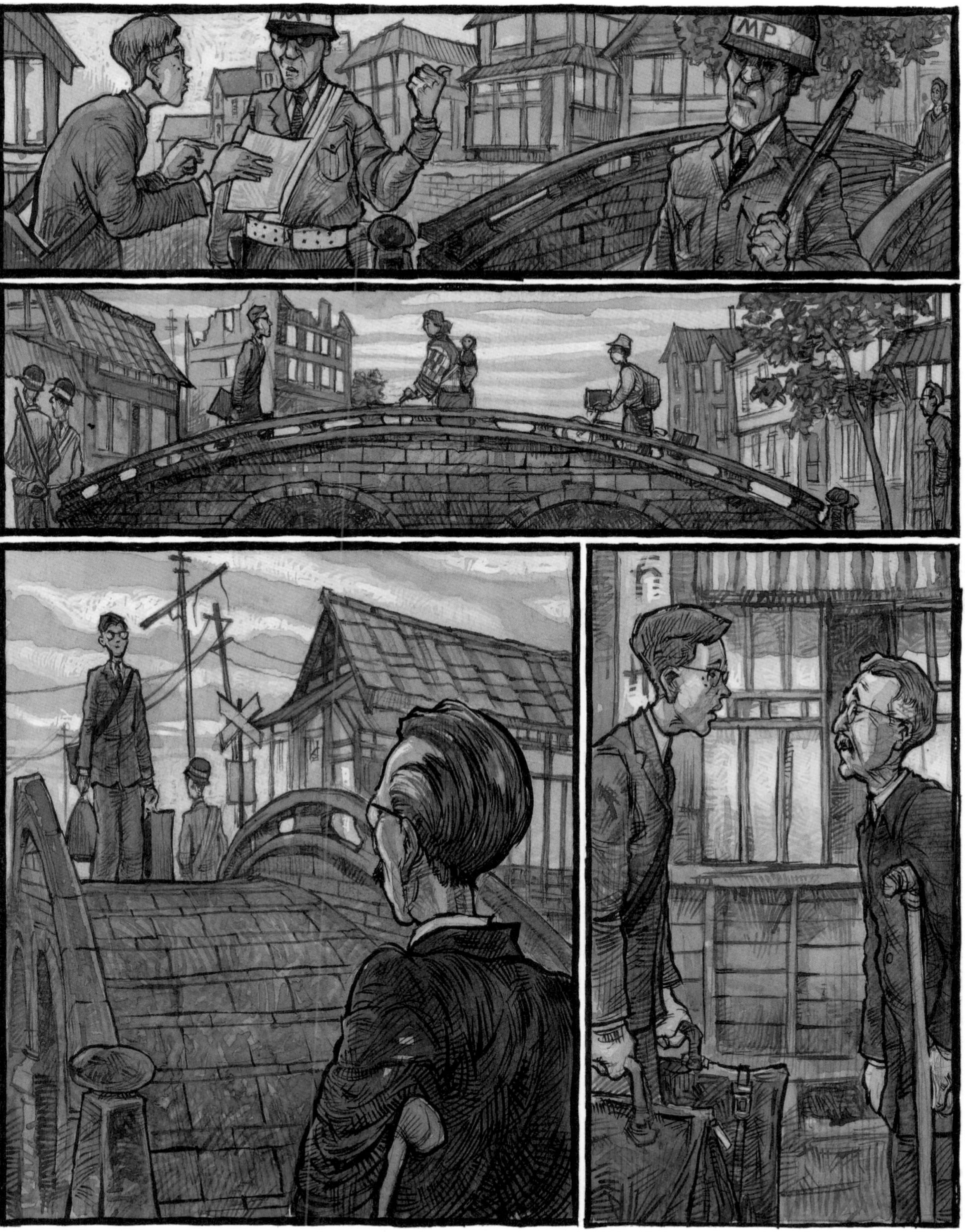
MP

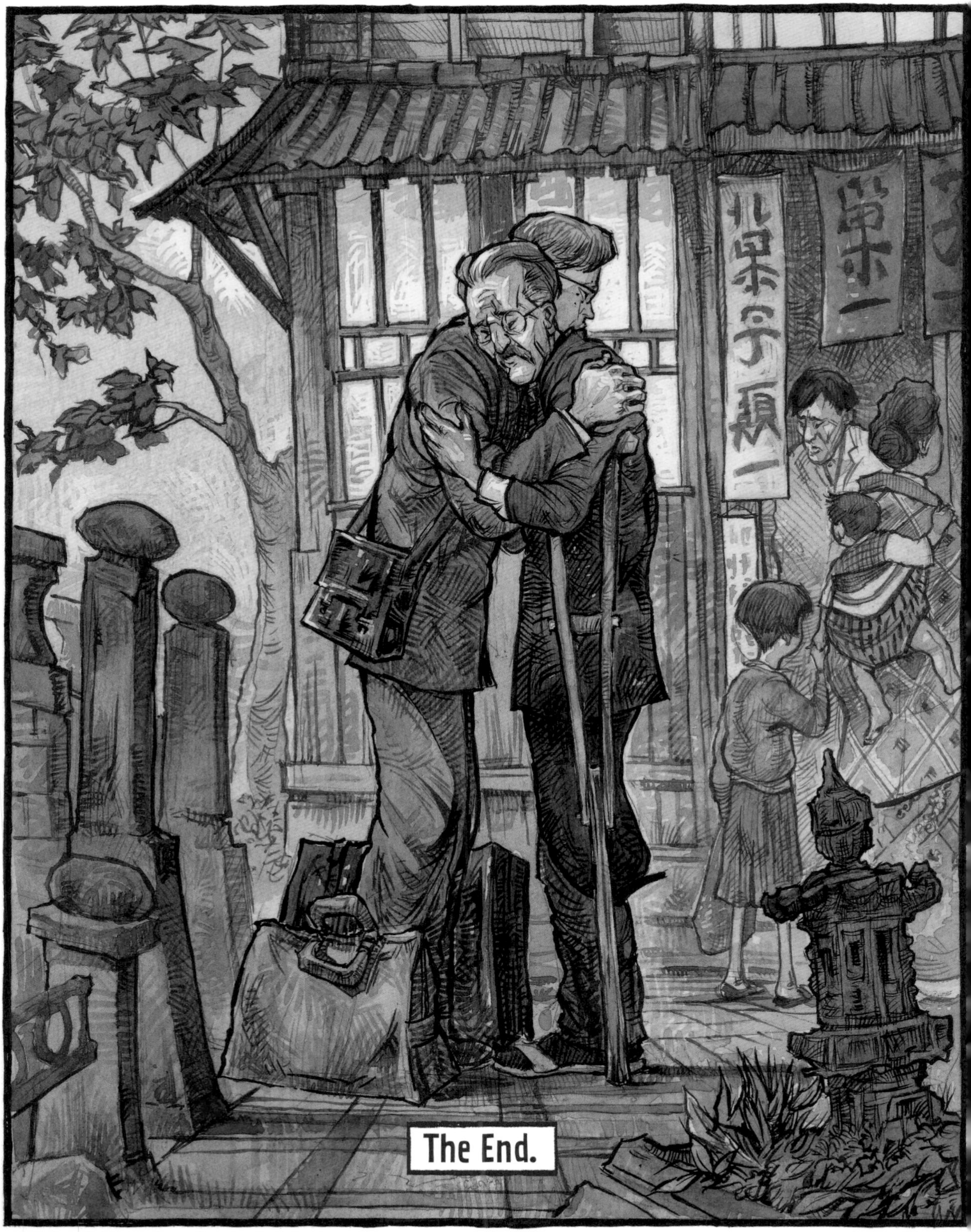
The End.

Acknowledgments

The author would like to say thank you to:

My wife, Kris. Your love, support, and humor made this book possible. Thank you so.

My agent, Jennifer Laughran.

My editor, Rotem Moscovich, and designer, Tanya Ross-Hughes.

All the many friends, too many to name here, who shared articles, books, personal history, and support for this project.

My mother, Ruth, for keeping Adeline's story alive all these years.

My cousin Anita and all the "Adeline Cousins." Obachan Adeline would be so happy that we found each other!

Finding Adeline

Adeline Conlan, my great-aunt, was a celebrated Irish American singer in 1920. Against her parents' wishes, a teenaged Adeline joined a renowned vaudeville troupe and traveled the world. On a tour of Japan, she fell in love with and married Ichiro. Not long after, they had a baby girl named Mary.

During the late 1920s and early 1930s, attitudes toward Westerners and gaijin (outsiders) made life difficult for Adeline and Mary; tensions rose between Adeline and Ichiro. When an enormous earthquake shook Tokyo in 1923, killing thousands, a terrified Adeline decided that she and Mary would travel back to Boston, her hometown. They planned to return to Japan when things calmed down.

Unfortunately, they made the long journey from Japan to Boston only to find they weren't accepted there, either. Mary was ridiculed for being "half-caste." Adeline was ostracized for marrying outside her race and religion. Once again, they packed their things and moved, this time across the country to California, where they made a home in the Los Angeles area.

When she grew up, Mary became a wife and mother of two children. After the attack on Pearl Harbor by the Japanese navy, Mary and her babies received a letter from the United States War Office informing them that, because they were part Japanese and lived in the exclusion zone on the West Coast, they would be "interned" for an undetermined length of time. Irish American Adeline was not required to go to the internment camp, but she was not about to let her child and grandchildren be taken away from her.

On the first day of June 1942, Adeline and her family joined over 10,000 Japanese Americans from California and Washington and traveled the hot, dusty road to Owens Valley, California, where they were interned in the Manzanar War Relocation Center. Over two thirds of those interned at Manzanar were American citizens by birth. More than half of the 120,000 who were interned in the ten main camps during the war were children.

Adeline and her family lived in the camp for over a year. In the autumn of 1943, they found a sponsor and were allowed to move to Chicago. During the war, internees were encouraged to move eastward, away from the exclusion zone, if they had a good record and an established sponsor to speak for them. After the war's end, they were allowed to move back to California. Neither

Adeline nor Mary ever went back to Japan. And, sadly, although she and Ichiro exchanged letters, Adeline never saw her husband again.

In the late 1990s, I began to consider making a graphic novel based on the history of my great-aunt. All I had to go on was the return address on a corner of an old envelope shown to me by my mom when I was a kid. I did some searching on the internet; but for many years, I couldn't find Adeline or her family.

The Friday on which I turned in my first set of sketches to my editor, I found a post on the National Park Service–Manzanar website asking for anyone who might be related to Adeline Conlan to contact Anita, her great-granddaughter. I literally jumped when I read this.

I e-mailed Anita right away. Not long after, my son, Gabriel, and I drove to southern California to see a side of our family with whom we'd lost contact nearly forty years before. On the way there, we stopped for a day at the remains of the Manzanar War Relocation Center, now a National Historic Site. It was hot, maybe 100 degrees. As we stood in the shade of a withered tree, the wind howled and whipped dust into our eyes, and I marveled at the fortitude of those who had been interned there, prisoners in their own country.

Matt Faulkner
Southeastern Michigan
2014

Adeline Conlan and her family, Japan, mid-1920s

Selected Resources

BOOKS AND PERIODICALS

Fugita, Stephen S., and Marilyn Fernandez. *Altered Lives, Enduring Community: Japanese Americans Remember Their World War II Incarceration.* Seattle: University of Washington Press, 2004.

Ishizuka, Karen L. *Lost & Found: Reclaiming the Japanese American Incarceration.* Champaign: University of Illinois Press, 2006.

Japantown Task Force. *San Francisco's Japantown.* Mount Pleasant, S.C.: Arcadia Publishing, 2005.

Manbo, Bill, photographer. *Colors of Confinement: Rare Kodachrome Photographs of Japanese American Incarceration in World War II.* Edited by Eric L. Muller. Chapel Hill: University of North Carolina Press, 2012.

Price, Willard. "Unknown Japan," *National Geographic Magazine,* August 1942.

Styling, Mark. *Corsair Aces of World War 2.* Oxford: Osprey Publishing, 1995.

Time/Life Publications. *Our Finest Hour: The Triumphant Spirit of America's World War II Generation.* New York: Time/Life Publications, 2000.

DOCUMENTARY FILMS

Burns, Ken, producer. *The War.* PBS Broadcasting: New York, 2007.

Satsuki, Ina, PhD, producer/project director. *Children of the Camps—The Documentary.* PBS Broadcasting: New York, 1999.

WEB SITES

Manzanar National Historic Site:
http://www.nps.gov/manz/historyculture/japanese-americans-at-manzanar.htm

Manzanar, Virtual Museum Exhibit:
http://www.nps.gov/history/museum/exhibits/manz/imgGal.html

Children of the Camps, Internment History:
http://www.pbs.org/childofcamp/history/index.html

Smithsonian Education, Letters from the Japanese American Internment:
http://www.smithsonianeducation.org/educators/lesson_plans/japanese_internment/index.html